single mom's guide to love

Guide to Love
Book Two

chelle sloan

Cover Design: Chelsea Kemp Art

Editing: Kiezha Smith Ferrell, Librum Artis Editorial Services

Proofreading: Michele Ficht

*To the oldest daughters who grew up with a constant need to take care
of everyone around them, who always put themselves last, will never
ask for help and have a life long perfectionist complex because teachers
left you in charge...*

I see you.

I am you.

Now go enjoy this smutty little romance book like the good girl you are.

guide to love rule #3

Picking up a man at the bar is never a good idea. But a bar at the airport doesn't count because airports are lawless societies.

1
maeve

"Jack and Diet Coke, please. Actually, make it a double."

The bartender listens and, most importantly, doesn't judge as he sets the cocktail napkin in front of me and goes off to make my drink.

Now, I'll usually have a drink before a flight—especially when I plan to take an in-flight nap—but a double is a lot even for me.

Then again, this week was a lot, so I think I'm justified. One would think the glamorous world of interior design is easy and wouldn't require double pours. It's just picking pillows and buying pieces of art, right?

Wrong.

This business trip started with four days in Miami, executing a job for a man who probably knows intimate details about how cartels work. That was followed by a quick pit stop in Charlotte for a consultation with a former client who just made partner at his law firm and wanted to spruce up his condo. This normally wouldn't be stressful—he was easy enough to work with back in the day—but his new girlfriend was very opinionated.

And very wrong. Needless to say I politely declined that commission when she was unwilling to admit that teal blue and yellow floral wallpaper with pineapples mixed in was not a good idea for the living room.

After that debacle I headed to Atlanta for a three-day interior design and architecture conference where I was not only attending but also a panelist. I normally don't go to things like that, but I've been wanting to branch out my connections in the industry and thought this would be a good way to do it. The only problem was that I've become very well known for what I do—and do well—so every conversation turned into them picking my brain about how to expand their services to men.

I guess that's what I get for being Maeve Banks, Designer for the Rich and Douchey. And no, that's not my title, just the one my sister Quinn wants me to use for the reality show she insists I pitch to a network. I'd call it more like "Maeve Banks comes up with another version of gray walls and black leather couches for pompous assholes with too much money." I'll admit that doesn't have the same ring to it.

I smile at the bartender and take a sip of the drink he delivered as I let hysterical thoughts of a reality show pass through my mind. I'd be the worst reality star in the world. Unless there's a market for cynical, Type-A women who roll their eyes when clients hit on her while also telling them they aren't unique for wanting a wet bar to show off their scotch collection.

You're not original, Carl. You're just going through a midlife crisis.

As I look around the first-class airport lounge while I wait for my flight back to Nashville, all I see are the men who are my ideal clients, wearing custom suits and sipping on expensive whiskey. Some reading the financial section of newspapers because they want to show how intelligent they are, others scrolling on their phones to make sure their favorite stocks aren't plummeting. Men who go out of their way to make sure the women they hit on see their expensive watches.

They're all around me, but even if they weren't, I could spot them a mile away. I've worked with enough to know the type. These men don't balk at my consultant rates, because they want a stylish place to live and don't know the difference between an ottoman and a duvet.

Then again, if these kinds of men didn't exist, I wouldn't have a job, which is why I might vent, but I'll never be ungrateful. Would I love a change of pace? Absolutely. One can only design so many man caves before her head explodes. But on the other side of that coin, I've found a niche in a market that pays me well and keeps me busy. They have the means, I have the ability, and my son is going to one day go to college without a dime of financial aid.

That's what I call wins all around.

"Whiskey. Neat please."

I normally wouldn't pay attention to a stranger's drink order while sitting at a bar, but this is going to be the exception. And not just because we're at an airport bar where rules don't exist, but because the accent that I just overheard sent a tingle through me. I don't know what it is about a British accent, but it'll make me go from a put-together single mother to a thirsty, horny woman in two seconds flat.

I do my best to catch a glimpse of the man next to me, and thank God I wasn't drinking at that moment because good Lord...I don't know if I've ever seen a more attractive man in my life. With his looks and his accent he could be the next James Bond.

He can shake me, stir me, do whatever he wants to me...

I do my best to avert my eyes, but it's no use. In my defense, he's unbuttoning his navy-blue suit jacket, so it's like he's begging me to keep watching him. At least, that's what I'm telling myself so I don't feel like a gawker.

Even though I totally am.

He pulls back his arms to stretch, showcasing his muscled chest. I do a quick up and down on him, and even though he's sitting, I can tell he's well over six-foot. His dark hair is full, and if I was a woman who still had sex—I don't because men are trash and I don't have the time—I'd want to run my hands through it while he was sliding into me.

His jawline could cut glass and is clean shaven. The black-rimmed glasses he's wearing fit his face perfectly, and it makes me wonder if he wears them all the time or if this is a special occasion. I have this instant image of him lying in bed, shirtless of course, wearing pajama pants and reading something serious like *The Rise and Fall of the Roman Empire.* And yes, I might be next to him with my latest thriller.

"Ma'am, would you like another?"

The bartender's words snap me out of the delusion of reading in bed with this stranger. Because apparently *that's* what I fantasize about these days. "Yes, please."

"Put it on my tab?"

Shit. Did he notice me watching? Is he buying me a drink so I stop ogling him? I guess there's only one way to find out…

When I turn back to James Bond, I wasn't prepared for his emerald green eyes to be staring at me. There are a few seats between us, but that doesn't lessen their impact.

"Thanks, but you didn't have to do that," I say.

"I know."

I was expecting some sort of pickup line, so his direct answer throws me. "Then why did you?"

He shrugs and takes another sip of his drink. "A beautiful woman at a bar should never pay for drinks."

And there it is. The line. I knew it was coming sooner or later. Doesn't matter if they're broke boys trying to get you with a Smirnoff Ice and the promise of a fun night, or a gorgeous man with a panty-melting accent buying you overpriced airport cocktails in a custom suit, they all are made the same.

Smooth lines. Good smiles. A few drinks.

Next thing you know you're marrying the wrong man for the wrong reasons, and you're divorced before the ink is dry on the marriage license.

Okay, maybe that last part is just me, but I'll shout from the rooftops about the first part.

"Thank you," I say, not wanting to come off rude. "But I can afford my own drinks."

"I know you can, Love," he says, turning toward me. "Just because you can doesn't mean you should."

Wait…did he just call me…

"Love?"

Yes, I could have dissected the last part of his pickup line, but for some reason I'm choosing to fixate on that one word. For one, I don't do pet names. I think they're stupid and juvenile. Second, I need to react angrily because him saying that one little word made me feel a very inconvenient way. Especially coming from a stranger.

"My apologies," he says, almost bashfully. "What would you prefer I call you? Ma'am? Mrs.?"

I feel my face turn red. And also give him credit for sneakily asking if I was married. "Do *not* call me ma'am. And I'm not a Mrs. Not anymore."

I watch as the grin grows on his annoyingly handsome face. "Then 'Love' it is."

I start to protest—my mouth is open and everything—but for some reason I don't. Why don't I? No man calls Maeve Banks "Love." Or any other name, for that matter.

I shouldn't like it.

I don't like it.

Except I kind of do.

No! I don't! What the hell is wrong with me? I don't get butterflies in my stomach over a pet name. Even if it does come with a sexy accent. Maybe it's that accompanied by his bright, yet soft smile and broad shoulders that could pass as a brick wall. Or the leathery, smooth cologne that I'm starting to get a hint of.

I blame the Jack Daniels. I just had to have a double…

"Or," he continues, sliding over a seat so there is only one between us. "I could call you by your actual name."

The second not-awful pickup line snaps me back to my senses.

"You seem very nice, and thank you for the drink," I begin. "But I'm going to be heading to my gate soon. We don't need to go through that."

He shakes his head as he takes a sip of his whiskey. "All flights are about to be grounded. Huge storm is about to pass through."

I lift an eyebrow. "And how do you know that? Do you moonlight as a meteorologist?"

God, I need him to quit smiling like that. It's a grin that's filled with mischief and flirtation and charm.

It's unsettling.

And panty melting.

"I don't, but there's a storm about to pass through in the next thirty minutes that's going to last until morning. We aren't going anywhere."

Storm? I didn't hear about any storm. I would have heard about a storm that could've grounded a plane, right?

"Don't believe me?" he says, almost as if he can read my mind, which on its surface is alarming. "Check your mobile to see if I'm right."

I give him one more glare to see if he's fucking with me before I do just that.

And holy shit, he's right.

Huge weather alerts. Email, text, and app notifications of my now-canceled flight. And just as I look up at him, still a bit confused, an announcement blares through the lounge.

"All passengers. Until further notice, all flights have been grounded. We're sorry for the inconvenience."

Fuck, inconvenient is right. Not only have I been away from home for too long, but it's a Tuesday. It's a school night. My sister Ainsley was staying with my son Jayce until I got home so he could be in his routine for school tomorrow. Now I'll have to ask her to stay or hope that his dad can take him on short notice.

Fuck my life…

I start to grab my things while also firing off text messages to my sister, when I feel a hand on my arm.

"Don't go."

His smooth voice and that damn accent stop me in my tracks.

"What do you mean 'don't go'? I need to rebook my flight. See about my checked luggage. Change plans at home. Figure out a hotel."

He shakes his head and signals for me to take back my seat. "Have another drink with me. We'll figure everything out."

I don't sit back down, but I also don't continue to walk as I intended. How is his stare freezing me in place? How can eyes be that green? It's disarming.

So much so that I'm considering doing what he's asking.

"Look at it out there," he continues, clearly seeing that I'm wrestling with the decision. I look toward the terminal and see droves of travelers speed-walking past. "It's a madhouse. We don't need to be part of that. Book a flight from your mobile. Call the airline next week for a refund. Sit here and figure out any sort of plans at home. But do it from here, in the calm."

He's right about that. It is calm here, at least comparatively. "But what about a hotel? If no one is flying out tonight, the nearby hotels are going to be swamped."

Like my words spring him into action, James Bond pops up from his barstool, takes out his wallet and drops a hundred-dollar bill on the bar and buttons his jacket.

"You're right. Let's go."

"Excuse me, stranger danger. I don't think so." He might be hot, but I remember what they taught me in elementary school.

"All I'm suggesting is that we get a jump on a hotel. After everyone is done panicking about flights, they'll realize they need a place to stay for the night. In the meantime, we'll already be checked in and enjoying a drink at the hotel bar. And I just happen to know of one not far from here that makes a damn good gin martini."

I wonder if he likes them dirty...

No! Stranger danger! Why do I keep forgetting that?

He holds out his hand, and I still haven't moved because I have no idea what's happening. I feel out of control, and that's not a typical feeling for me.

Who is this man?

Why does his presence shake me?

And why am I considering going with him?

"I'm not sharing a room with you," I say, needing to make sure he knows that this isn't a gateway to a hookup.

"I never thought you were." He leans down to grab his laptop bag then takes a few steps toward me and takes my carryon. "What do you say? Care to join me?"

Why am I considering this? He's as stereotypical as any other man in here. Is it just the accent? Am I that weak of a woman? There's something different about him that I can't put my finger on.

"I don't even know your name," I say. "You're a stranger at an airport bar. This is how true crime podcasts start. And I'm sorry, but no one will say I was a wonderful person who lit up a room when they're asked about me for the reboot of *Unsolved Mysteries*."

That should've scared him off. Between the ramble and the fact that my mind jumps to him making me disappear, he should be saying goodbye.

But he isn't. He looks oddly shocked, though I'm not sure by what. It wasn't the reaction I was expecting.

"You're right. Not about the killing thing, but about the name." He slings the bag over his shoulder and extends his hand. "I'm Logan. And, since I know that your name isn't Love, what do you suggest I call you?"

It's an easy question. Introducing myself to a man, or anyone really, shouldn't be a big deal.

But for me it is.

I don't date. I don't flirt at bars. I barely make friends. I certainly don't go with men I've just met to bars at hotels when it hasn't been ruled out yet that they're a serial killer.

Except the entire time we've been sitting here, my body and my reactions have betrayed my always logical brain.

And it's about to do it again…because apparently I have zero self-control tonight. Or I just have that much of a James Bond kink.

"Maeve."

The smile that forms on his face is slow and sends a tingle down my spine. "Maeve. That's a beautiful name."

Am I blushing? I don't fucking blush. Sure, I might turn red from time to time when I'm trying to keep a secret, or I've been called out on something, but I don't blush because of some flowery words from a man.

"Thank you."

"Okay then, Maeve…" he cocks his head toward the exit of the bar. "What do you say? Join me away from the chaos?"

2
logan

She doesn't know who I am...

I know I should be worried about ten other things. Like actually rebooking my flight so I can get back to Nashville after the hellish week I just spent at pointless parties, in board meetings, and talking with developers. Or alerting my assistant that my flight is delayed so she can move meetings around.

But no, all my brain can focus on is the brunette sitting next to me at the bar who doesn't know me from Adam.

It's been four years since I could just be Logan, a man in a bar wanting to strike up a conversation with a beautiful woman. Four years since I started to lose my cloak of anonymity. These days it seems wherever I go it's people wanting to shake my hand for hopes of a possible business connection or women who checked out a popular magazine's most eligible bachelors issue and saw my face.

But not Maeve. She didn't have a clue who I was the entire time we spoke at the bar. I was already drawn in by her beauty. Her poise and directness intrigued me.

Then she said she didn't know who I was, and somehow that passed any other test there could be.

Because now, tonight, whatever this night turns into, I can

just be Logan. Not Logan Matthews, video game developer of SpaceCraft, the hottest game to come out in decades. Not Logan Matthews who went from eating ramen to having ten figures in his bank account seemingly overnight. Not the man who was in a sexiest man alive magazine issue this past year.

No, tonight I'm just a man at a bar talking to a beautiful woman.

A woman who looks like she wants to be anywhere but here.

"Relax," I say, trying to calm her nerves as she checks the hotel check-in counter for the thirtieth time. "They said they'd call us when our rooms are ready."

She turns back to me, but her shoulders are still tense. "I thought you said we were going to somewhere calm. This is *not* calm."

She's right. I did promise that.

"Sorry," I say as I look back at the bar bustling with customers. "Maybe we weren't as smart or ahead of the game as I thought."

My attempt to lighten the situation doesn't work. She turns back to look at the check-in counter, as if anything changed in ten seconds.

"I'm going out on a limb to say that you're not good at being patient or not being able to control situations."

Her eyebrow is raised as she turns back toward me. "Am I that transparent?"

I don't know if she's any more relaxed, but at least she's distracted from the growing bustle of angry travelers. "Yes. But also, my best mate Kat is like that. I think there's a picture of her in the dictionary next to 'control freak.'"

"Sounds like my kind of woman," Maeve says as she sips on her martini. "My siblings call me 'Mama Maeve' because of my need to not only plan everything, but also to try and fix their problems."

"Oh, you really need to meet Kat," I say with a laugh. "I

swear she derives far too much pleasure from controlling my life."

"Well, I don't know about pleasure. I think the only pleasure I'd get is that of relief if my siblings figured out, say, the holiday schedule without me."

I quirk a brow. "Really? You'd be fine giving up control and letting others figure it out for themselves? No one knows who's bringing the Christmas crackers...the Secret Santa wasn't perfectly arranged so three people got themselves and never said anything...Or! Maybe they didn't plan an itinerary. Or worse... they would say things like 'come over whenever.' Put that together with Grandma putting too much booze in the Christmas pudding and you have a day of disaster."

She starts to speak, but stops herself as she visibly shudders. "No. You're right. It would give me hives."

I pick up my drink and tip it to her. "That's what I thought."

We share a smile and take sips of our drinks when her mobile vibrates on the bar.

"The hotel?" I ask as she looks at it then shakes her head.

And I let out a breath of relief. If it's the hotel she's gone. And I'm not ready for this night to be over yet.

"No. My sister," she says, starting to type something back. "With the delay, I needed to mobilize the team to watch my son for the night and get him on the school bus tomorrow morning."

"You have a son?"

"Yes. In first grade."

I start to ask her if he's a video game fan, but I don't. I want to remain invisible as long as I can. "Is everything straightened out?"

She nods and puts her phone down. "Yes. My sister is going to spend the night at my house. Just so his routine can be some-what normal in the morning."

"Does your son also like things nice and organized?"

She shrugs. "I mean, he's six. He understands the concepts of bedtime, school time, play time, and screen time. And he's pretty good about staying on it when he's with me. But I think that's also because he knows when he's with his dad that it's a free-for-all. I swear, when he's with him, it's just a video game binge session."

I fight the smile that's threatening to pop. I wonder if he's a SpaceCraft fan. He's the perfect age range for it.

"Mom is the strict parent?"

I meant the question to be so we didn't accidentally fall down talk of video games where I'd say something revealing, but the sigh she releases signals that I hit a nerve.

"My ex-husband is many things. Strict is not one of them."

The way she clips the end of that sentence, I can tell she's done with this line of questioning. Which is fine by me. I have a feeling if I hear any more about her ex I'll want to do something like track him down, hack into his computers, and make his digital life very uncomfortable.

You don't become a video game developer and not learn some hacking skills along the way.

Plus, the silence in conversation lets me take her in. Not that I haven't done it a dozen times tonight, but every time I look at her, I swear she gets more lovely.

Her slender face has sharp features, but somehow she's still soft despite the edges. Her hardness is only doubled down with her brown hair being slicked back into a tight bun. Her blue eyes are a sapphire that radiate against her ivory complexion.

The woman screams in control and in charge, both in conversation and appearance.

And as a man who thrives on a challenge, it only makes me want to crack that exterior even more. Call me crazy, but I'd wager my first-edition Pac-Man arcade game that somewhere in there is a softness she doesn't let out often.

Because the conversation has paused, Maeve takes the opportunity to look back to the lobby desk. The line might be longer than it was before.

"Can I ask you a question, Love?"

She turns to me, a little bit of fire in her eye. "Can we be done with the 'Love' stuff? I'm not a nicknames kinda gal."

Now I'm all for consent. No means no, and the women always call the shots. But pushing her buttons a little is getting a bit of a rise in me. Just that one little word, which until tonight was as generic a word as anything, is making this pretty terrible travel day a most enjoyable one.

"Would it feel better if you had a nickname to call me?" I ask. "I feel it's only fair, since I have a habit of calling you that."

I see the wheels start to turn in that beautiful head of hers. She bites her lip slightly, clearly thinking. Is she doing that on purpose? Can she tell that with that little action my pants are tightening in a way that is not conducive to sitting on a bar stool in a suit? I try to subtly adjust, but to no avail.

"I'll admit, I did call you James Bond in my head when we first met."

"I like that," I say, sitting up a little taller at the mention of one of my favorite action heroes of all time. "The martini feels even more fitting."

She nods, but the glint in her eye tells me she's not done.

"You are. But I don't know… I don't know if James Bond is fitting."

"What do you mean?" I gesture to the custom suit I'm wearing. "This is one step away from a tuxedo. I have the accent. Not to brag, but I'm no stranger to a gym. And I have a definitive order of who was the best actor to ever play Bond. I feel I've earned the name."

She shrugs coyly. "I don't know. If you're not going to use the name I'd like, which is Maeve, because that's my name, I shouldn't use the one you want either."

I know she's about to fry me, but seeing the sparkle in her eye, I'm ready to get burned.

"What are you thinking?"

"I think asshole has quite the ring to it."

I throw my hand over my heart and let out a dramatic gasp. "You wouldn't. That's just cruel."

She gives me a wicked smile before signaling to the bartender for another martini. "That's what you get."

Any other man would be insulted. And it might say something about me that I'm not. But more than anything right now, I not only want to crack that shield she has firmly in place, but I want to hear her scream my name while I do it.

Hell, she can scream asshole for all I care, as long as I'm feeling her against me.

"Okay, if that's how it's going to be, how about we make a little wager?"

She slowly turns her head toward me, that sparkle still in her eye. Is she competitive? Oh that could be fun…

"What kind of wager?"

I signal to the front desk. "If your room is ready first, I'll quit calling you Love and you can forever call me an asshole. But if my room is ready first, it's Love and Bond."

She thinks about it for just a second before extending her hand. "Bet."

I return the gesture, and it's probably the alcohol talking, but I swear a dash of heat just crossed between us.

Maeve looks back to the lobby, which is now packed to the gills with people trying to get rooms, before looking back to me. "So what do we do until then?"

The bartender sets two martinis down in front of us. "We drink."

———

"What do you think about them?"

I point to a couple sitting across the bar from us who are our next contestants in the game we've dubbed, "Hooker, Home-wrecker, or Housewife."

We tried to be politically correct first, but Sex Worker, Mistress, or Wife didn't have the same ring.

And we're quite drunk.

So far we've decided that we've spotted one woman working hard for her money, two housewives who look like they'd rather be anywhere but in a hotel bar, and three couples likely having an affair.

I know I am one, but men are truly horrible beings.

"Oh for sure home wrecker," Maeve says, tilting her head to the side for better examination. "He didn't even bother taking off his wedding ring. And no way she bought that dress herself."

I look again, and damn if she isn't right. "Good eye, Love."

She tips her drink to me, and she must be getting drunk, because she didn't chastise me or call me an ass for using the nickname. "I'm undefeated in this game. I can spot a cheating man a mile away."

"Is that what happened with your ex?"

I probably shouldn't have asked it, but I'm dying to know what kind of man would let a woman like this go. Much to my surprise, she shakes her head.

"No. To my knowledge, he never cheated." She pauses to take a sip of her martini, and at this point, I've lost count of how many drinks we've consumed. "My job unfortunately deals with men who have no qualms about cheating. And while I think they are scum and should never get hard again, their money is green, and I have a kid to feed."

"And what is it you do?" I ask as I polish off my martini.

"I'm an interior designer, specializing in home design and decor for men."

"Fascinating," I say.

"It's not, but thanks for the enthusiasm."

I shake my head. If she only knew the battle I was having about decorating my new home with Kat, my publicist/fill-in assistant/best friend, she'd know how serious I am. "I'm not mocking. I've never had an eye for anything that includes colors, patterns, or furniture."

She laughs and shakes her head. "You and most straight men in the world."

"Are you calling me a cliché?"

She turns more toward me, crossing her long leg through the slit of her skirt. God, I bloody love a pencil skirt…

"Let's see," she says as she makes a show of eyeing me up. "Your Rolex isn't fake. You don't exactly have the frame of a guy who can buy a suit off the rack, so I'm going to guess this is custom made."

She takes a second to gently feel the material of my suit, which she is right about—It most certainly is not off the rack.

I also can't help but notice her fingers linger a little longer than they likely need to.

"Good quality material. Feels expensive, and I'd actually say it is. It goes well with the cologne, which *is* a cliché scent for a man of your caliber, but that doesn't mean I don't like it."

Maeve gives me one more long look—of course while taking another sip.

I also make note to buy the cologne in bulk. You know, just in case I ever see her again.

"You're cliché in the fact that you're likely a high six-figure businessman. Finance, of course. No. Correction. A vice president of something or other at a company that makes the parts for the parts of clock radios."

"Clock radios?"

She shrugs. "Sure. Why not? Doesn't matter. You're so high up you couldn't even tell me what your company produces. You probably just collect checks, send out meeting invitations for things that could be emails, because you need to seem like you're working, and pretend you know what you're doing while your assistant actually runs everything. Oh, and I need not forget about your likely standing tee time and auto-renew membership at some swanky men's club where you sip disgusting scotch and talk about the stocks."

I laugh. Little does she know how wrong she is. "Anything else to add to my apparent mediocre resumé? Or would you like to fast-forward to the part where I tell you how off base you are?"

Her eyes double in size. Apparently she wasn't prepared for me to push back. And frankly, neither was I.

Because yes, I've quite enjoyed being just a guy in a bar having drinks and conversation with a stunning woman. But I can't let her think I'm someone I'm not. I've always been unapologetically me, so it's time to come out from behind the curtain.

So as much as I've enjoyed just being Logan from Birmingham, it's time she knows who I am.

"Have you heard of the video game SpaceCraft?"

It takes her a second to acknowledge what I'm saying, though I think the bottle of gin she's consumed tonight has something to do with that. "My son plays that. And when I say play, I mean is obsessed."

I smile and hold out my hand. "Logan Matthews, developer of SpaceCraft and CEO of GameTech, also known as the company that developed it. So actually, I'm worth ten figures, and it's not for clock radios. Though we do have consoles with an alarm and clock in them, if you're in need of one."

She's too stunned to laugh at my clearly hilarious joke. "And as for being in finance, I stay as far away from the books as possible. I only do enough math to code a game."

It's entertaining to watch her jaw drop as I lay out my confession. I've never told anyone about me like this, and it's quite fun to watch the realization play over her face.

"Also, I never schedule a meeting that could be an email. Actually, I prefer to never have any meetings, if at all possible. Oh, and yes, while my assistant does handle many things for me, she's compensated handsomely, as are my other employees."

She thinks I'm done, but I curl my finger, asking her to come closer. When she does, I breathe her in, wanting to memorize the hints of vanilla and amber. "The only cliché thing about me is that from the second I saw you in the bar, I couldn't stop wondering what it would be like to make you scream and come apart underneath me. Which makes me no different from every man you've ever met."

She shakes her head, but doesn't pull back. "Men don't think of me like that."

"Then they are all bloody fucking fools."

guide to love rule #92

One-night stands don't count when they're in different zip codes from where you live.

3

maeve

His lips are right there.

Inches away from me.

If I moved ever so slightly, they'd be on me, touching me in a way I haven't been in such a long time.

Can I do it? Should I do it? I told myself years ago, after my divorce, that men weren't worth it and I needed to focus on my son. So I did what any single mom would do—I swore off the opposite sex and everything to do with them.

That means sex. Dates. Anything. They were out of my life until an unknown future date and time.

Is that time now?

No…can't be. When I made that rule for myself, I figured it would be when Jayce was at least a teenager, not the first grade. And until this night, I've never even considered ending my self-made sexual hiatus.

But I'd be a fucking liar if I said I wasn't attracted to Logan. Or how I want nothing more than to feel his lips on mine.

Or on other places…

But just as I'm about to move in ever so slightly, hoping he comes in the rest of the way, my phone vibrates loudly on the bar next to me.

The buzzing snaps us both out of the spell and I quickly grab it, hoping it's the hotel telling me my room is ready so I can leave this situation before I get myself into a lot of trouble.

Except when I look at the phone, it's not the hotel. It's a Face-Time from Jayce.

"Hey, buddy," I say, looking around to see if there's somewhere quiet. "Hold on one second, okay?"

I lower the phone and signal to Logan that I'm going to step outside to take the call. It's still raining pretty hard, but luckily I see an awning that appears to be keeping the rain out. I take a deep breath as I hurry to it, allowing the air of the storm to cool me off from the stuffy bar and hotel.

And the presence of Logan.

"Okay, I'm here," I say as I lean against the building. "Getting ready for bed?"

Jayce nods as he holds the phone with one hand, but cuddles the blanket that he's slept with every night since he was born in the other.

"Yeah. Aunt A-Mae just tucked me in."

He switches over the angle of the call so I can see my younger sister, who he calls A-Mae since her name is Ainsley Mae and that's what he grew up hearing us call her. He calls my other sister Tella, but that was because he couldn't say his "s" sounds. "How are you? How bad is the storm?"

"It's a madhouse," I say. "Every flight is canceled. I'm supposedly waiting on a room, but it's so insane I wouldn't be surprised if they gave it away or never had one to begin with."

"That stinks," Ainsley says. "But don't worry about us. We got pizza for dinner, did bath time, and Jayce even taught me how to play SpaceCraft. I must say, for a first timer, I'm pretty good."

"She made it through five levels, Mommy! She's better than you!"

I laugh as I look back into the bar at the inventor of said game. I smile as I watch him casually sit at the bar, phone in hand. I wonder if he'd be impressed with Ainsley's accomplishment? Or that Jayce is probably his number one fan in the world? And what would Jayce say if I told him who I'm sitting next to? More importantly, what would my sister say if I admitted that I met a man who is tempting enough to make me consider ending my self-imposed dry spell?

"Why are you smiling, Mommy?"

I jump slightly at Jayce's voice. "I'm just happy you called."

That was a shitty recovery, and judging by the look from my kid and sister, neither are buying it.

"I call every night you aren't home," he says, clearly wondering why he has to explain this to me. "It's story time."

"You're right." I let out a breath and square my shoulders. "You ready?"

He nods and cuddles himself into bed, Ainsley holding the book that we read together every night.

I've read this book to him since he was a baby. I memorized it a long time ago. He probably has, too. Age wise, he should've outgrown the book years ago. But it's our thing, and I'm grateful my baby still wants this time with me. I know one day he won't, so I'm not going to miss a minute while I still have the chance.

We say goodnight to all the things in the book—the socks, the balloons, and the people. We go on for the six minutes and thirty seconds it takes to read the book. We go back and forth on the parts we perform—my very particular son is insistent I only voice certain pages and he does the others.

Then when we say "the end," it doesn't stop there, because Jayce has to say goodnight to everyone in his life that he loves.

"Goodnight Mommy, Goodnight Daddy," he says. "Goodnight Aunt A-Mae and Tella and Quinn. Goodnight Emmett and Winnie the dog. Goodnight Uncle Simon, Aunt Charlie, and baby Lainey. Goodnight Didi and Pappy. And goodnight Rosie."

I was ready to tell him what I normally do after his goodnights, but his last one throws me for a loop. "Who's Rosie?"

"My girlfriend," he says, a big yawn coming from his tiny mouth. "Goodnight, Mommy."

I stutter a bit, wondering how my son could drop this bomb on me then just go to sleep. "Sweet dreams, buddy."

Ainsley gives him one more kiss on the cheek and promises to do some recon at drop-off in the morning, so I hang up the phone and I make my way back into the bar.

"Everything okay?" Logan asks, standing up and giving me his hand as I climb back onto the bar stool.

I grab my martini and finish it in one go. "I think my son has a girlfriend."

This makes Logan laugh. "How old is he again?"

"Six," I say, setting it down and ordering another drink. "I wasn't ready for this yet."

"Oh, the days of primary school," Logan says with a touch of nostalgia in voice.

"Let me guess, you were the cute boy with dozens of girl-friends?"

He lets out a loud, singular, laugh. "You're hilarious. Quite the contrary. A girl didn't give me the time of day until Year Twelve, and that's only because I was doing her homework for her."

I find that hard to believe. "Really? You weren't the flirt of the school? The cute boy everyone wanted to take to the dances?"

"The complete opposite," he says. "I was a shy, nerdy boy who'd rather play with his video games and build Lego sets than play outside. My glasses were thick and my know-it-all was thicker."

"That I can see," I say, though I do wonder when the shy nerdy boy found his way to a gym. "When did you move to the States? Or are you only visiting?"

Was that me prying a little? Yes. But did I do it cleverly? Also yes. I guess I haven't entirely lost my game.

"I actually came here from Birmingham for university," he says. "That was eleven years ago and I've been here ever since."

I know I'm drunk. And math has never been my strong suit. But I'm staring at him, and if he came here for university at eighteen…and that was eleven years ago…

Carry the one…subtract the smolder…

"How old are you, Logan?"

A blush creeps on his cheeks. "I actually just celebrated my twenty-ninth birthday."

"Jesus fucking Christ," I whisper, all but snatching the fresh martini from the bartender's hands and take a big gulp, nearly finishing it in one go.

"What's the problem?"

I shake my head so much it might spin off. "Now you *really* can't call me that. I'm a creepy old lady."

I've been fantasizing about this man all night. I wanted him to kiss me. Dare I say I've even been flirting with him in my own way.

And for what? For me to find out that I technically could have babysat for him, if I would've been in England?

"Not creepy at all," he says. "I like to say I'm a good judge of character."

I shoot him a glare. "I'm a thirty-six-year-old single mom, Logan. There should be no world where I'm talking to, or being called Love, by a man in his twenties."

"Late twenties."

Did he just make a joke? This isn't the time for jokes.

"Logan, I'm closer to forty than thirty. No way should I be drinking with a man who still has a two as the first number of his age."

"It's just a number."

I give him the same look that I give to my son when he's being ridiculous. "Are you going to tell me next that 'you're only as young as you feel?' Oh wait, I know. You're going to tell me how mature you are for your age. And you said you weren't cliché…"

I check my phone again, really wanting there to be a message from the hotel about my room, when I feel Logan's hands on my legs, turning me toward him. As soon as I'm stopped and facing his direction, he stands and holds out his hand for me.

"Dance with me."

"What?" I look to the pseudo dance floor, where no one is dancing. And you can barely hear the piano over the crowds of the guests at the bar.

"Come on," he says, jerking his head toward the piano. "I need to stretch my legs and you need to get out of your head. Plus, asking you to randomly dance in the middle of a hotel bar is the least cliché thing I could've done."

I look to the makeshift dance floor then back to the man who is apparently not only young, but slightly delusional. "I'm not dancing with you."

"May I ask why not?"

"Oh, let me count the ways!" I hold out my hand for extra emphasis. "One, no one is dancing, and we'll look ridiculous. Two, we'll lose our spots at the bar, and this is prime seating. Three, it's one thing for me to mildly flirt with you. It's a whole other for me to dance with you. That's a step toward Cougarville I'd rather not take. So you can stand and stretch your tree-trunk legs and I'll sit here and finish this martini."

The sexy smirk that forms is not the reaction I was going for or expecting. "You're flirting with me?"

"Not the point."

"Oh, but it is," he says. "Now we really have to dance."

He doesn't say anything else as he flags down one of the bartenders. "Mate, will you make sure our seats are safe so I can take this lovely woman for a dance?"

"Absolutely, Mr. Matthews," he says, pulling out reserved signs and setting them at our places.

"Good man." Logan holds out his hand for me again. "As for your first point, who cares if no one is dancing? We'll be trend-setters."

"Or people will laugh at us."

"I doubt that. If anything, people will wonder how I got so lucky as to dance with the most beautiful woman here."

"Your lines aren't working."

My snark doesn't seem to scare him off. If anything, it seems to turn him on.

"As to your last, and most important point—if you were mildly flirting with me, then I should be clear that I was majorly flirting with you. I think you're the most beautiful woman I've ever met, and this is probably the only night I'm ever going to spend with you. So, will you do me the honor of a dance?"

I have to blink a few times at his monologue. Who just comes out and says things like that?

And why is my body reacting to it?

Why am I giving him my hand? Why am I walking behind him to the dance floor?

I should be at home tucking in my son and preparing for a busy week. In fact, I have a huge meeting with a mystery client who has promised a large commission. That is, if they don't cancel on me again. That's what I should be focusing on right now—not talking with a younger man, getting drunk on dirty martinis, and about to dance when no one else is.

None of this makes sense.

Yet, I can't seem to stop myself.

The only night I'm ever going to spend with you…

He's right. This is only one night. I'm never going to see him again.

So you know what? Fuck it. Maybe this is the gin talking, but I'm going to enjoy this night. I'm not going to be Jayce's mom. Or Mama Maeve to my siblings. Or someone who has to check my phone every five seconds. I'm even going to forget who Logan Matthews *actually* is. Instead, I'm just going to focus on how his hand feels on my back, his scent surrounding me, and how for the first time in a long time, I'm just a woman enjoying the company of a man.

"There we go," Logan says as he pulls me in, our clasped

hands resting between our chests. "Now just follow me. Find the calm."

I try and ignore the crowd around us, but it's easier said than done. I want to relax, but all I keep thinking about are people staring at the cougar and her younger date.

Oh my God! Are people playing Hooker, Home wrecker, or Housewife with us?

"Relax," he whispers.

"I am."

"Liar."

I don't bother arguing with him. We both know he's right.

"Do me this favor," he says as he brings me in a little closer. "Lay your head on my shoulder."

I don't want to, but between the liquor, his voice, and his overall demeanor, I can't fight it.

Plus I think his cologne has magical calming properties.

"There we go." He doesn't say anything for more than a few seconds, and somehow, even though I know the bar and hotel are still packed, the noise dies down. Soon all I can hear is the ballad from the piano and the sound of his beating heart.

"That's it. Now just sway. Block out the chaos and just breathe. Even if just for a few minutes."

It takes me a second to truly relax, but when I do, it's a peaceful bliss that feels foreign. The song has changed to a popular ballad I've heard a few times but never really listened to just the music behind it.

It's gorgeous. Melodic. And the way the man is playing it on the piano is almost lulling me to sleep. I don't remember the last time I've not thought about eighty-thousand things at once and just sat back and enjoyed the moment.

Yet here I am. In a hotel bar. Dancing with a stranger. Finding the calm.

"That's it," Logan whispers, pulling me in even closer. "You're doing so good, Love."

His praise of something so simple sends an unexpected zing

through me. When is the last time anyone told me I was doing good at anything? Usually it's clients demanding more from me without saying thank you, or my family asking me to do things that they thank me for on the surface, but also know I'd do even if they didn't.

"How do you do that?" I ask.

"Do what?"

"Get me to relax."

I don't know how, but without looking at him, I can feel him smile.

"I want to say 'there must just be something about me,' but I know you hate clichés."

My smile is instant. "So what would you say, you know, that's not typical?"

He stops our movement. I pull away slightly, but just enough so I can look up into his warm eyes.

"That in some strange way, we were meant to meet tonight. And if it's just one night, then we've changed each other for the better."

"How do you mean?"

He removes the hand from my back and lets it slowly stroke down the side of my cheek. The goosebumps are instant as he slowly traces my jawline.

"Well, for me, I've recently been set up with women who I grinned and bared it for the cameras. But they weren't my type. And even before that, it had been years since I could spend my time with an absolutely breathtaking woman and just be myself. And so, from now on, when I'm out on a mind-numbing date, or being set up with a woman my publicist thinks is good for my image, I'm going to remember that there was at least one woman I could spend an evening with who could make me feel alive."

My body flushes with his words. This man, if my memory serves me correct, has been out with legitimate runway models. And he's calling me breathtaking? I've never had self-confidence issues, but holy shit…

Logan is making me feel...I don't know what these feelings are. They're foreign and exciting, and I'm on pins and needles to hear why he thinks he's changed me.

Because he has, even if our night ends right here. I know this night will live in my memory forever.

"And what do you mean for me?"

He leans down ever so slowly, placing the softest and warmest, kiss on my cheek that I've ever felt. But he barely moves away, leaving his lips right next to my ear.

"That whenever you're starting to get into that beautiful head of yours, or your control freak is coming out a little too much, I want you to remember this night. This moment. How you were able to take a step back and find the calm in the chaos. To dance with a man who wants nothing more than to kiss you right now and make you forget even more."

Find the calm in the chaos...I like that.

And I like him.

Fuck do I like him.

As for the kiss? I want that too.

And not just the kiss.

I want more. More from him.

I want tonight...

That's the only reason I can think of as to why I'm pulling him into me, kissing him like I've never kissed anyone before. His body immediately responds, pulling me in tight against him as our lips become acquainted.

First kisses aren't supposed to be smooth or perfect. But this? I don't know how it can get much more perfect.

Just as the kiss starts to deepen, I pull myself away. And it's not because I want it to stop.

It's because I want even more.

Five years ago, I declared that I was done with men, dating, and anything along that avenue. I was going to be a business woman, a daughter, a sister, and a mother. Therefore, I couldn't fit in another thing.

Figuratively and literally.

Until now, I've never wavered in that decision. I've never thought that there was something missing.

But as Logan holds me, our bodies swaying together with the music, his heartbeat thumping against my chest as his strong hand holds me against him, and liquid courage in the form of gin martinis rushes through me, I realize I want this. And him. Frankly, I probably want this too much from a man I just met and am never going to see again.

I'm never going to see again...

"Logan?"

"Yes, Love?"

"Is that room ready?"

4

logan

I'VE ALWAYS PRIDED MYSELF ON BEING A GENTLEMAN.

I open doors and help women into seats. I carry their bags and hold their hands as they step out of cars.

I wasn't gentlemanly earlier tonight when I made a bet with Maeve about who would get a room first. I didn't have the heart to tell her that I got mine when we arrived and already had the keycard in my wallet.

Now all I can think about is getting her into that room and tasting her lips again.

Except now I must wait for a bloody lift that I apparently have to share with six other people.

"Patience," she whispers, sensing my eagerness.

"Not one of my virtues."

"You'll be fine," she says. "It's just a few floors."

"Try twenty-three," I groan as I pull us to the back, placing her in front of me as the other people get situated. Everyone else calls out their floor numbers, but I keep quiet. I don't need to bring attention that we're going to the penthouse. I don't want any attention on us at all. Not for what just came through my mind.

"Stand still," I order through a whisper, my lips against her ear. Her body goes still at my command, which makes my cock harder than it already is.

Oh…does Maeve like being told what to do? That makes sense. Because Maeve is the kind of woman who wants control. Needs it. Dare I say *craves* it. Has she ever let go? Does she want to? Judging by how her body is reacting to my simple order, I think she does.

And luckily for her, I'm just the man who can give that to her.

Not because I'm some sort of dominant in the bedroom, but I can take the lead. I can be whatever she wants me to be, because all I want is to see her come apart at my touch. I want to hear her scream my name. Knowing that I made a woman find that release? There's no better high. So however I need to be, and whatever I need to do, to get them there—sign me up.

But I have a feeling Maeve isn't going to be as easy as asking if she wants top or bottom. I'm going to guess that she's always been in charge, but until right now, she didn't know she wanted to just let go. To feel pleasure so deeply that her brain shuts off. To take every decision out of her hands so she can truly experience what it's like to be cared for.

And because I have only this one night, I'm going to make damn sure that's what I do.

Doing my best not to make a sound, I kneel down behind her, pretending that I'm tying my shoe. When I'm sure no one is looking, I slowly start moving my hand up her leg.

"Oh!" she yelps, causing a few people to turn and look. They apparently don't notice me on the ground, or where my hand is, because they just go back to staring ahead after Maeve mouths an apology.

I look to catch her biting her lip as she subtly widens her stance as my hand travels up her leg. I swallow a groan as I keep going, her pose now perfect as I slide my hand over the wet lace at her pussy.

I hear a slight sound from her just as the bell alerts us to a floor stop. Two couples exit and I stand up, realizing I can't keep kneeling without drawing attention.

When the door closes, I let my fingers play a little more, sliding her panties to the side so I can insert a finger into her wet pussy. I look up at the beautiful sight that's Maeve's face growing redder, her head tilting back as she lets me finger her in front of an audience.

I push thoughts away of my apparent newfound fondness of public displays of sexual affection as the lift stops on the eighteenth floor, letting out the last couple. I slowly lower my hand, and hear a whimper from Maeve, as the doors close.

"Holy shit," she breathes out as I take the few steps needed to scan my keycard for the penthouse level. "Wait! When did you get a key?"

Ah…yes. Our bet.

The bet I knew I won the second she proposed it.

"I've had it all night. Got it at check-in and didn't tell you since you didn't have yours yet. Perks of being Logan Matthews."

She looks almost shocked that she was duped. "So when we made that bet earlier?"

I shrug and walk back to her, pressing her body against the wall of the elevator. "Guess you'll just have to get used to me calling you Love…Love."

She narrows her eyes at me, which somehow turns me on even more. Wait, do I also like my women a little angry? I'm learning so much about myself tonight…

"New bet," she says confidently. "Double or nothing."

I didn't expect her to say that, but I'm here for it. The competitor in me loves a challenge. And maybe if I press into her a little more so she feels how hard I am, the bet stipulations will fall under the orgasm category.

"If you can make me come twice tonight, but in different ways, you can continue calling me Love," she says.

If I had the room, I'd run a victory lap. Hell, another minute in here and I would've had her screaming.

"Deal," I say as the lift door opens and I take her hand to lead her out.

"Aren't you going to propose a return wager?" she asks.

"No need." I tap the keycard against the lock, the green light flashing, signaling for me to open the door.

"It's okay to admit your shortcomings," she says with a teasing tone. "That's very gentlemanly of you to lose with grace."

Oh Love…you have no idea what you're getting into…

The door is barely shut before I take her hand and pull her back toward me, swiftly pinning her against the door.

"You seem to forget I've played video games my whole life. Which means I'm very, very, good with my fingers."

Her eyes go wide and she opens her mouth like she's going to fire off a witty comeback, but I plant mine on hers before she can say anything else, bringing up her skirt in the process.

Fuck…her lips are perfect, just like I knew they'd be. They're soft, yet somehow also demanding. I can tell this is a woman who's used to being in charge in the bedroom just by how her hand wraps around my head, holding me in like she's calling the shots.

I love it when I'm right…

Without breaking our lips, I take her hands in mine, bringing them over her head and holding them in place with just one of mine. I use my free hand to trace down the side of her face, her breast, and waist, before trailing over to cup her throbbing pussy.

"You got so wet for me," I moan into her lips as my fingers resume where they left off.

Maeve seems to like this, deepening the kiss while also begging me with her hips to give her more.

"I thought you were patient?" I whisper as I allow my lips to start kissing their way down her chin and onto her neck.

"That was before I knew you were a tease."

I chuckle against her pulse. "You haven't seen anything yet."

I press one more kiss against her neck as I drop to my knees. I wasn't lying to her about my agile fingers, which are coming in quite handy as I quickly undo the clasp of her skirt and lower the zipper in record time. I push it down, leaving her standing in nothing but a blouse that's fighting to stay closed, and a pair of red lace panties calling to me like a matador.

"So sexy," I say, sliding my fingers through her soaked thong before I rip it off her body.

She gasps at the sound of the thread tearing. Or maybe it's the feeling of me inserting two fingers inside her. Either way, I have Maeve panting, begging, and right where I want her.

"Since I'm going to win, I'm going to let you choose how you want to lose."

"What?" Her voice sounds like she's not in her body, which balloons me with a swell of pride. "What do you mean choose?"

I take one of her legs and throw it over my shoulder. Her hands press against the door for balance, which is a good thing. She'll need it.

"I'm going to make you come on my cock. That's a given. But for the other…do you want my tongue?" I pause to show her, giving her a slow, long, lick.

"Holy shit…" she moans as her other leg wobbles.

"Or do you want my fingers? Your choice."

I slowly take the two fingers I was teasing her with earlier and mimic the motion I just made with my tongue, slowly grazing over her, inserting them just enough so she can feel it, before continuing the motion.

"Fuck!" she screams. Luckily we're the only ones on this floor. Though, if she keeps this up we might wake the hotel. "Both. Fingers. Mouth. I don't care. Please, Logan."

"Oh Love…was that begging I heard?"

She nods her head as she does her best to try and ride my

fingers, begging with her body for more pressure. "Yes. Please. Just make me come."

I have a feeling this is the first time ever in her life Maeve has begged for anything. And who am I to deny her?

I don't say anything else as I push my two fingers further inside her, giving her what her body had been asking for. I don't think she was ready for them, as I hear her hands smack the door. It only takes a few curls and swipes before her hands fall to my shoulders, needing me to keep her balance. When I fully insert them she lets out a feral scream and falls onto me, her hands holding onto my shoulders for dear life.

"Jesus Christ, Logan," she whimpers, her nails now digging into me. "How are you…shit I'm…"

I slowly put her foot down on the floor so I can stand up. I want to watch her face as I make her come all over my hand.

"Now, Love. Come for me now."

Our eyes lock as I watch in awe as I feel her start to come apart on me. She throws her head back, and I quickly catch it with my free hand so she doesn't bash it against the door. And… holy shit, did her eyes roll back in her head? Bloody hell, that was fucking amazing.

And this is why I say I get off by watching others. Tell me something fucking hotter than what I just witnessed. Go ahead. I'll wait.

I know I should be a gentleman and bring her down. A little after care. But no. Instead of letting Maeve catch her breath, I'm picking her up and carrying her into the suite.

"What are you doing?"

I make quick work of the distance between the entrance of the room and the bedroom, our breathing the only sounds in the air as I place her on the mattress. She still looks slightly dazed as she gets her bearings. Her brown hair is tousled, and her shirt is disheveled. I don't think I've ever been turned on more in my life.

"I'm going to fuck you. Any objections?"

I know my in-charge tone is a risk. I might have her a little off guard from the orgasm, but this is still a control-freak woman who has likely never been ordered around in the bedroom before. But just as I'm questioning my tactics, I see her bite her bottom lip. Her eyes look me up and down. And when they lock on mine again? I knew I was right.

This woman wants to lose control.

"Rest of your clothes—take them off," I demand as I take off my jacket and start unbuttoning my dress shirt. I'm in such a rush I don't fully appreciate the show in front of me with Maeve, though I do catch the finale as she unclasps, then tosses aside, her lace bra.

Holy fuck, I knew this woman was gorgeous. But the vision before me now? There are no words to describe her. She's now kneeling on the bed, her perfect tits on display. A trim waist, but it also doesn't look like she's starving herself. Hips that I can see myself grabbing onto.

God, where should I start…

I push down my trousers and snug briefs in one motion before closing the distance between us. I reach down for her, bringing our lips together again. Her soft lips and begging tongue are doing something to me that I haven't felt maybe ever. I wish I could kiss her all night, and maybe after this I will, but there are some things I need to check off the list before this woman vanishes from my life.

A grunt escapes my mouth as her hand snakes between us and she starts stroking my cock. Christ, she feels so good. Her strokes are firm and long, and I can't get the image out of my mind of her mouth working me in tandem with it.

Which is why it nearly kills me to say what I'm about to.

"Stop."

She jerks away with a panicked look in her eye. "Stop?"

I lean in for a reassuring, yet hard, kiss. "Only because I can't wait any longer to fuck you."

Her eyes flicker a shade darker. "You trying to win the bet?"

"Something like that." I grab her hips and start turning her around. "On all fours. Let me see that perfect ass in the air."

She bites her lip again as she does what I say. I don't take my eyes off her as I fumble for my wallet, quickly grabbing a condom.

"You ready?" I ask, stepping closer as I sheath myself.

She looks over her shoulder, her eyes burning in anticipation. "Win that bet, Logan."

"Gladly," I groan, stepping up to her and kneeling on the bed, perfectly positioning myself to enter her.

"Ah!" she yells, falling to her elbows as I slide in. She's still wet from earlier, but holy fuck is she tight. And I'm not just saying that to make me feel better about the size of my dick. The woman's pussy is gripping me like a fucking vise, and I've barely entered her.

"So fucking tight." I grit out, slowly starting to move in her.

She whimpers something unintelligible as I slowly work her up. She doesn't move from how she's fallen on the bed, which, if I do say so myself, gives me such a better angle and picture of her ass that I do appreciate. I give it a slap for good measure, which seems to perk her up as I continue slowly thrusting into her.

"Harder." Her word comes out as a muffled whisper.

Did she just ask me to go harder?

"Say it again. Tell me what you want."

She pushes back up to all fours and turns her head around. Her eyes are determined, and her cheeks are flushed. At this moment, she's a siren. I know I said I'd be in charge tonight, but this woman could tell me anything right now and I'd do it.

"Fuck me harder, Logan. Please."

I feel a roguish smile form on my lips. "Gladly."

And I do. I fuck her with reckless abandon. I squeeze her hip and smack her ass. I pound into her as if I'm trying to imprint myself onto her.

Needing more, and wanting to see her come apart again, I

quickly pull out and flip her over, throwing one leg on my shoulder as I ram back into her. The position makes her back arch, and the scream she gives out as I rub her clit with my finger was worth not seeing her ass bounce against my hips.

"Logan…" She doesn't say anymore as my name trails off on her tongue. But I know what she was about to say. I can feel it. Her cunt is squeezing me again, and if I'm being honest, I'm not too far behind. Watching her fall apart underneath me is going to be my undoing.

"Just let go, Maeve. Just let go…"

And she does. With one more hard thrust, combined with a perfectly timed rub of her clit, I watch as this beautiful woman has an orgasm that goes through her entire body. Her body is shaking as it hits her, which is plenty to send me over the edge with her.

That feeling of pure bliss shoots up my spine and I fall down on top of her, feeling my cum spill into the condom, but I refuse to pull out. No, not yet. Not as I feel Maeve's body under me, both of us recovering from an experience I don't think either of us are going to forget.

At least I know I won't.

guide to love rule #65

Fall asleep on a plane at your own risk. You might wake up with drool on your face and a man who's seen you naked sitting next to you.

5

maeve

I'M A DIRTY, FILTHY WHORE.

That's the only words I can think of as I board the airplane and take my seat in first class. The second I hit the leather, I feel the tidal wave of the last day wash over me. And none of it is good.

That's a lie. My body feels more relaxed and sated than maybe ever in my life. I'm also thoroughly exhausted because the sex was nothing short of earth shattering. And the orgasms? Out of body experiences. Apparently when you don't have sex for five years, your orgasms are triggered a little more easily than you remember.

I've also never had two in one night. I didn't think my body could do it, hence why I dared Logan that task. I figured it was an easy win. But apparently even my own orgasms stood no chance against Logan Matthews. That was further proved sometime in the middle of the night when I was woken up by Logan's face between my legs. I think I came in thirty seconds.

Who was that woman? It's like I was me—I mean, I felt every single thing he did to my body—but I was an alternate version of me. A version who begged a man to fuck me. Who got fingered in an elevator. Who enjoyed getting spanked while getting fucked from behind. All by a man seven years younger than me who I saw on a magazine cover at the airport with a model as they were entering a club in New York.

Seeing that cover made me feel more at ease about my decision to sneak out this morning. I knew I couldn't face him sober in the harsh light of day. What would I have said? "Thanks for the orgasms! You win!"

I was already humiliated by my actions enough, so I did the smartest thing I could do—I crept around in the dark looking for my clothes, realized I didn't have any underwear, got haphazardly dressed, went to the front desk to ask for my bags that they were still holding and got changed in the lobby bathroom. I then did the walk of shame to the airport and got here way too early, all because I didn't want to make eye contact with the man who made me see literal stars.

"Can I get you anything, ma'am?"

I slowly nod at the flight attendant. "A Diet Coke. Please."

Seconds later it's in my hand and I'm nearly chugging it. I already had my hangover cure this morning of bacon, egg, and cheese on a bagel, but the familiar fizz is hitting the spot.

My eyes are heavy, and I let them close as the rest of the passengers filter onto the plane. Luckily, this is a direct flight back to Nashville, so the goal is to let the exhaustion take over so I can be alert when I get home tonight. I haven't seen my son in more than a week, and I need to relieve my sisters, who've been pulling shifts to cover me during my custody time.

My guess is that Jayce will want to stay up tonight, and because I'm a guilty mother who's been away, I'll let him. The problem with that is the morning will still come at its normal time—promptly at 7:14 a.m., when Jayce will wake me up to pour him his juice and cereal so he can eat while cramming in an episode of Paw Patrol before school. I could go back to sleep after I drop him off. But will I? Absolutely not.

Which is why I need to catch as many Zs as I can now. Between the tiredness from travel, and my body being exhausted from last night, I should be able to sleep just fine on the flight. If I were currently in my bed, I might actually sleep for more than five hours. That would be a new record.

I've never been a great sleeper, but as I've gotten older, and the stress of being a single mom and running my own business has grown, there isn't a pillowcase, blackout curtain, or melatonin dosage in the world strong enough to get Maeve Banks into a REM cycle. But judging how I'm already feeling like I'm dozing off, and I won't be self-conscious as there's no one sitting next to me, maybe the trick all along was a healthy dose of dick —specifically of the tall, handsome, and British variety.

No brain! Stop it! You're a dirty whore, and you need to stop thinking about him!

I turn my head toward the window as I try to shake the thoughts from last night. My brain has always gone a mile a minute, but it's usually with things about work, or Jayce's schedule, or what is going on with my family. That's another reason why I swore off sex. I didn't have the capacity to deal with dating. And my days of hooking up were over, both because I was a grown-up and they just weren't good enough to bother.

Then again, if I'd had sex with Logan before I made this declaration, I might have been singing a different tune.

"Passengers, if we could have you all find your seats as we begin the in-flight announcements..."

That's the last thing I remember hearing before I'm in a full slumber. I somehow block out the takeoff. If there's a baby crying in economy, I wouldn't know. Because somehow, I'm currently falling into the best sleep I've had in ages while I guiltily think about Logan's tongue between my legs...

———

Ding! Ding! Ding!

The sound of the airplane call, combined with a shake of turbulence, snaps me awake. Which is a fucking shame, because I was in the middle of a dream where Logan was fucking me on the glass dining table of the penthouse.

I'm thrown by a huge bit of turbulence that sends my head into the window, which also causes me to drop the glass of now-melted ice and Diet Coke that somehow I've been holding the whole time.

"Shit-mother-fucker-bitch!"

I try to look around for a napkin or something to wipe the cold liquid off my lap when a familiar chuckle turns my blood cold.

No…it can't be.

"Here, Love. Let me help you."

What in the literal, actual, and metaphorical fuck is happening?

I freeze at the sound of the voice that's coming from next to me. I know it's him. There's no other voice like that in the world. But I refuse to look to make sure. Between the spill, the dream I was just having where I'm not sure if I was talking in my sleep and called out his name, and the unknown of whether I have drool on my chin, it's best I stay facing forward.

"Oh, come on, Maeve. Aren't you happy to see me?"

I reluctantly turn my head and if I had another drink to drop, I would.

Yup. There he is, in all his sexy, British glory. The man who made me beg. The man who made me scream. The man I can still feel inside me.

The man I was banking on never seeing again.

"What the fuck are you doing here?"

I don't know what about my tone just now made him smile, but I want to wipe the smug grin off his face. "Flying to Nashville."

I shake my head a little, because obviously this has to be some sort of dream.

"Aren't you a billionaire or something? Why are you flying commercial?"

He shrugs as the flight attendant comes over to hand me a napkin. I should thank her—or at least make eye contact with her—but I'm too confused and a little angry by my current situation.

"A private jet just seems wasteful," he says. "Plus, you never know who you'll sit next to on a plane. It's an experience you can't replicate."

I feel ridiculous thinking about this, but I need to ask it to ease my mind. "Did you get on this flight to see me? I didn't tell you where I was going."

This gets a laugh out of him. "I wish that was the case. But sadly no. This is pure serendipity."

"Really? This is coincidence?"

"It is. And a pleasant one. Since we didn't get to see each other this morning, this can serve as our goodbye."

I feel my cheeks turn beet red. How dare he call me out with the truth. Rude.

"I wanted to get to the airport early," I reply, my defensive tone telling him exactly how much a liar I am.

"I didn't know it was open at five in the morning."

Shit, he knew when I left? I thought he was asleep.

"But no matter," he continues, since I'm still too stunned to speak. "I still got the experience of sleeping next to you, even if only for a little bit. Your snores are adorable, by the way."

I audibly gasp. He did not! I mean, I probably was, but you don't say things like that out loud to strangers. Shit, you're probably not strangers with someone who you've seen naked.

"I was not."

I try to ignore the flirty smile and his dazzling green eyes behind his black-rimmed glasses. The whole look is sexily unsettling, especially when I can still see that face buried in my pussy.

"You tell yourself whatever you need to, Love."

Ugh! That fucking name!

"I wasn't snoring. And quit calling me Love."

He shakes his head as a small laugh escapes. "Can't. We made a bet. And I believe I won. Twice. Or was it three times?"

The audacity of this man…how dare he use things I said and did against me?

I could blame the booze. Say the gin was talking, and I wasn't aware of what my body was doing under the influence. But that would be a damn lie. I knew every second of what I was doing. I felt every delicious thing he did to my body. And now I have to pay the consequences.

Which apparently is him sitting next to me for the final forty-five minutes of our flight.

In maybe a more frustrating move than him calling me out on the bet, or the snoring, or calling me Love, instead of waiting for me to respond, the bastard turns away, focusing on something on his phone while I'm left slack-jawed and still wet.

From the ice.

Not for any other reason.

I try not to make it obvious, but I glance over to him. Maybe in the daylight, and him not teasing me, I can realize that he's not as sexy as he was last night.

Much to my disappointment, he's even better looking now. Because of course he is.

Gone is the suit and tie. Instead we have a fitted henley and a pair of blue jeans. I'm sure they're designer, but just the look of jeans and a shirt makes him seem so…normal. Combine that with him wearing his glasses and his messy brown hair, and no one would guess that the man is worth billions.

Don't get me wrong, I love a man in a suit. Especially a custom, tailored one like he had on last night. But this look? The one of relaxation and a guy who you could picture sitting at a sports bar with his buddies? That also scratches an itch for me.

And a man who can be both? Let's just say it's a good thing I'm never going to see him again.

Needing something to distract me, I take my cell phone out of the seatback pocket. I didn't want to check my phone on this flight, wanting a few hours of being off-line, but when I decided that, I didn't realize my one-night-stand was going to be sitting next to me.

At first I don't see anything alarming when I connect to the airplane WiFi. A few back and forths on the family group chat, as we begin preparations and planning for the holidays. Thanksgiving is in two weeks and Christmas is right around the corner, which means not only coordinating my family's schedules, including when Jayce will be with his dad and when my sister Quinn will be coming home from Arizona over her winter break.

I ignore the texts and head over to my emails. I doubt there's anything urgent, but the little red number at the corner of the icon says I have thirty-four emails, and that's just unacceptable.

Zero notifications is where I like to live.

I scroll through, reading, replying, or deleting what I need to. Nothing major. Clients wanting follow-ups or additions, now that their spaces are done. A few past clients wanting to know if they can hire me for holiday parties.

Just as I'm getting down to the final emails, I read the name that makes my blood boil every time it pops up in my inbox.

To: Maeve Banks, Banks Interiors
From: Katherine Smith
Subject: Reschedule?

"Fuck my life, not again," I groan as I read the email. I mean to keep it to myself, but I know I said it louder than I should've.

Though in my defense, if they knew I've now received six of these emails from Miss Katherine Smith—who I am starting to think is a fake person—you'd let out audible obscenities too.

Ms. Banks,

We're sorry to have to cancel our consultation. The client's schedule has changed and won't be able to meet with you tomorrow at the agreed upon time. Please let me know what your availability is next week so we can try and make this happen.
Regards,
Katherine Smith

6
logan

"Un-fucking-believable!"

I nearly jump at the hissed outburst from Maeve. I had turned away from her, knowing I needed to because the amount of staring I was doing when she wasn't looking at me was borderline harassment. But now that I'm looking at her again, her face getting red as she throws her phone into the seat pocket in front of her, only for it to bounce back into her lap, I can't help but think back to last night when I made her cheeks red for a whole other reason.

Both sets of cheeks.

"Is everything okay, Love?"

She snaps her narrowed eyes my way and I flinch. "I know there was a bet and I lost and blah-blah-blah. But that was past me. I was a very different person last night. So I'd appreciate it if you quit calling me that."

"A different person?" I say it in a teasing way, because I have a feeling she doesn't mean that. No, clearly whatever has her tossing her phone is making her say such things. "So what kind of person are you today? You know, since I didn't get to ask you that this morning."

I wasn't surprised when I felt Maeve slip out of bed before the sun came up. Frankly, I was surprised she didn't do it sooner. I knew last night was out of her comfort zone. I'd be a liar if I said I'd never snuck away in the middle of the night from an encounter. Then again, mine was to avoid the paparazzi. Maeve's was to avoid me.

But I'm not focusing on that. Instead I'm choosing to focus on the positive, which is that the Gods of Airline Travel were looking out for me when they rebooked us on the same flight. And that she likely lives in Nashville. And since I'm now a Nashville resident, this very much delights me.

All night I kept going back and forth between feeling grateful for the time I had with her and wishing for more. I didn't get to explore her body how I wanted. I wanted to fuck her across every inch of that hotel room. But I knew my time was limited.

Now it's not. Now maybe there's more time.

That is, if she quits shooting daggers at me with her blue eyes.

"I told you, I wanted to get to the airport early," she huffs. "And speaking of last night, I'd really appreciate it if we could just forget it ever happened."

I snort out a laugh. "No can do. You don't forget a night like that, especially when it's the bloody best sex of your life. Wouldn't you agree?"

Is it presumptuous of me to assume that I'm the best she's ever had? Yes. Do I still have nail marks in my arms from when she clung onto me? I do.

"You're unbelievable."

"Why, thank you," I say, knowing full well she meant it in a negative way. But I'm coming to find that getting under Maeve's skin is my new favorite hobby. Her cheeks are red and her eyes are narrow, and I know she's trying to come off as intimidating, but I just find it sexy.

I don't know what that says about me, and I can talk to my

therapist about it later. Now, I'm just going to bask in the fact that I'm enjoying spending time with this woman, even if she's pretending she doesn't like me. It's been too long since I've been able to flirt with a woman who didn't seem to care about my bank account. And Maeve has proven she doesn't give two shits about my money or my celebrity.

"Are you always this full of yourself?" she asks.

I shake my head. "Only when I know I'm right."

We stare at each other for more than a few seconds. The second I lock in with her beautiful blue eyes I'm immediately transported back to last night. It feels like a dream, almost. I lick my lips, and I swear I can still taste her.

"I can't with you," she says, turning her attention back to her phone. Her cheeks start to redden again as she furiously types on her phone. I know it's none of my business, but I have to know what's making them turn that color, because this time I know it isn't me.

"Is everything okay? It looks like you want to throw that mobile out the emergency exit."

She eyes me for a second before letting out a frustrated breath. "A client. Well, not a client. A potential client? I'm not even sure."

"How can you not be sure?"

She quickly glances to me, then to her mobile, then back to me. "Because they keep canceling on me. Multiple times. It's just frustrating. Not as frustrating as you, but close."

I want to come back with a zinger, but a twinge of guilt passes through me. I'm the worst when it comes to canceling meetings. I hate them. They're pointless. Can't it be covered in an email? Most of them can. Or even on a blasted Teams Call. I mean, if I'm going to be scarred for life by the sound of that incoming video call ring, let's at least use it for the meetings function.

"I mean, they reached out to me," she continues without

prompting. "And I don't even know who 'they' are, which is why I keep saying 'they.' It's a random email from an assistant with a name that is so generic it sounds made up. The company isn't even on it, so for all I know this could be fake as hell. But if it was fake, that's just dumb, and the worst prank in history. I mean, why would someone contact me for my services and then just cancel on me?"

Her words have me sitting up a little straighter.

She's an interior designer.

Specializing in men's homes.

When I woke up, I messaged Kat to cancel all my meetings today and push everything back this week.

Which I'd bet includes a meeting with an interior designer.

Because I've canceled that meeting multiple times.

Bloody hell…Is she—No. What would be the odds?

"Do you know anything about the job?"

She shakes her head. "No. Well, the bare minimum. I know it's in Nashville. I know it's for a multi-million-dollar home, though I don't have the address for it, and that it was promised to be a five-figure commission. That's the only reason I've put up with this nonsense."

The more Maeve talks, the more I think that the mystery home is none other than mine.

It would make sense. I've kept the move quiet because it's not yet announced publicly that I'm moving from California to Nashville. I was starting to feel stifled out west, and Kat thought it would be a good idea to move part of the operations to the southern part of the country, to hedge bets against environmental catastrophes and bad weather. But we didn't want to make a big scene out of it. Building permits were filed under Kat's name. My board of directors hasn't leaked it. And no one who has worked on the house has violated their NDAs.

I didn't know how Kat was communicating with contractors that needed to come in for jobs, but I'm guessing she was going with the premise that the least amount of information the better.

And no, it's not Kat's job as my publicist—or as my temporary assistant until I can find one in Tennessee—to be my liaison in home building, but as my best friend, she's taken it as her mission to make sure that I'm living in a space that reflects my status in the business and tech world.

Actually, I believe her exact words were "you're not a gamer nerd in the dorms anymore. You need to fucking act like it."

But since I couldn't give two shits how my new home was decorated, I relented and told Kat to find someone to handle it, but that I didn't want to be a part of it. She insisted that I needed to make some decisions personally. I then told her to please handle it herself if she was so insistent on it. She again said it was my house and I needed to pick out the flooring.

So she scheduled the appointment.

I made her cancel it.

She scheduled it again.

Rinse and repeat.

All of this happening, I'm guessing, under her legal and professional name, Katherine Smith.

A very generic sounding name.

Selfishly, I didn't think about how this would affect the designer. Or, if my guess is right, the woman sitting next to me who I experimented in exhibitionism with.

"Fascinating," I say as I swallow the lump in my throat. "And you said they keep canceling?"

This is the only line of questioning I can think of to make sure I'm not jumping to conclusions.

She nods. "Six times. Today's email is the sixth cancellation."

Fuck, it's up to six? I've canceled on this woman six times? I'd throw a lot more than a phone if I were on the other side of my actions.

Also, I could have met her months ago. Damnit. But you know what? That's my punishment. I canceled, therefore I was denied meeting the woman I'm becoming more and more transfixed with by the second.

"Did they say why?"

She shakes her head. "Never. Just some bullshit about a scheduling conflict."

"I'm sure they feel bad about it."

Since I've known Maeve, which is now a total of twenty-four hours, I've seen her in varying degrees of anger. There's been annoyed anger, mock anger, and frustrated anger. But now? I don't know if it was the words I just said or the actions she didn't know I've done, this is downright pissed off.

"I don't want to fucking hear it," she snaps. "My time is just as valuable as this phantom person's. And you know what? I've been nice and not charging them missed appointment fees, but I'm about to. Do you know how many clients I might have missed out on because they can't be bothered to keep a fucking meeting?"

She stops like I'm supposed to answer the question, so I do, guilt prickling my skin. "A lot?"

Her eyes crinkle at my attempt at a genuine, albeit hypothetical, answer. "Yes, a lot. I have about half a mind to email this Katherine Smith back and tell her that her client can pay me a stupid amount of money for the cancellations and that I'm done."

Yup. There it is. Katherine Smith.

No need for an internet forum to tell me what I already know…I am, indeed, the asshole.

And an even bigger one because I'm not going to tell her.

Not yet, at least.

"Done? You're really going to put your foot down?"

"Yup," she says confidently. "They can find someone else to decorate this unknown home."

Well, that's not going to happen.

"Passengers, we ask you to put your tray tables up and to have everyone return to their seats as we prepare to land in Nashville."

With the interruption of the announcement, Maeve turns her

attention back to her phone, typing something as I just watch her. The way her fingers are flying and her nose is crunching, she's emailing Kat.

I need to stop her from sending that email, but what do I say?

"Oh, hey, funny story. It turns out I'm the client who keeps canceling on you. Yeah, that vague assistant who goes incognito until NDAs are signed? She's mine. Sorry about that. Care to still decorate my home? And while we're at it, would you like to go on a proper date with me?"

Yeah, I'm sure that would go over well…

"You firing back that response?"

She shakes her head and puts her phone on her lap. "No. I was. I typed it. It's saved in my drafts. But I know better than to react while angry. I watched my brother for years act before he thought, and while I love my brother, that is one of many ways I strive to be the opposite of him."

I laugh, and also inwardly let out a sigh of relief. "But acting on impulse can be fun." I give her a wink.

She fixes her eyes on me, making sure I hear whatever is about to come out of her perfect mouth. "Not in the least."

The double meaning is clear as day, and while I might love pushing her buttons, I also know when to give an angry woman room to simmer down.

Neither of us say another word as the flight starts to descend. I still can't believe the odds of all this. I had only entered the first-class lounge where we met because I finished my business in Atlanta early, so I arrived at the airport ahead of schedule. When I saw her sitting there alone, I knew I had to say hello. The rest of the night was gloriously unplanned.

We're not the only two flying first class today, though I couldn't tell you who else was around me. Once I realized I was sitting next to Maeve, I couldn't take my eyes off her.

Or replaying the events of last night.

Before I know it, the wheels of the plane hit the runway at the airport. The second our plane comes to a stop and the seatbelt light flashes off, Maeve has jumped from her seat, grabbing her overhead suitcase and tossing her mobile in her oversized purse.

"In a hurry?"

She doesn't even look back to me. "I just want to go home. Return to real life."

"I get that," I say, standing to grab my bag from the overhead bin as well. "Good luck with your client. Maybe I'll see you around sometime?"

A cocky thing to say? Yes. Especially because I'm choosing not to tell her who I am.

She finally turns to me, eyes tired and a drained look on her face. "Logan. Last night was fun. But that's all it was. One night of forgetting responsibilities and letting go a bit. Can we call that for what it is?"

"I get it," I say, but not before leaning in toward her. "Can I ask you to do one thing for me though?"

She swallows a lump in her throat. "What's that?"

"Don't forget me, Love," I whisper. "When you need to find the calm, remember last night."

I turn my head just enough to place the smallest kiss on her cheek. I see her shiver when I do, but we're quickly snapped out of it by the loud rush of air coming in as they open the exit door.

Maeve quickly steps away, her cheeks flushed as she hurries out of the plane. I should follow her, but I think she needs a minute.

Which is fine. I have a very important email to send.

To: Katherine Smith
From: Logan Matthews
Subject: Interior Designer Appointment

Kat,

Put the meeting with the interior decorator back on the schedule for tomorrow. If she can't do it then, ask when she can. Whatever her answer is, cancel any meetings I have. My appointment with her is *now top priority. Also, issue a check to her for $25,000 for the canceled meetings. Scratch that. Make it $50,000.*

And make sure there's cold Diet Coke at the house for whenever the meeting is scheduled.

Talk soon,

Logan

guide to love rule #29

You can never have a private moment when you're a single mom. So it's best to keep your mind out of the gutter when possible.

7

maeve

I KNOW I'M NOT THE ONLY MOM IN THE WORLD WHO WONDERS THIS, but I often think to myself if I'm in the higher or lower percentage who ask themselves, "Am I a bad mom?"

We all think it. I know we do, even if the Taylor Anns and Becky Lynns in the pickup line want to deny it. I have to assume I'm on the higher end of the median line. Mine is at least three times a day with an added one at the end of the night when I remember that he didn't eat a single vegetable.

Tonight's bad mom question comes from the front seat of my SUV as I sit in my garage as I suck up the will to exit the car and head back into real life. Don't get me wrong, I'm tired of traveling and want to snuggle with Jayce and sleep in my own bed. But the second I step out of this vehicle, I know real life is going to smack me on the face. Packing lunches. Holiday shopping and organizing. Basketball practice for six-year-olds, which is pointless but also adorable because they just run around in a pack chasing a ball. Remembering what day of the week it is. And oh yeah, running my own business.

And actively pushing aside thoughts of a certain Brit.

Real life fucking blows.

So in the name of avoidance and procrastination, I'm going to sit here for a few more minutes, clear my head of all thoughts Logan Matthews, and get ready to get back to my life as Maeve Banks, do-it-all extraordinaire.

"Just let go, Maeve. Just let go…"

Why did my brain go back to that moment? Is it because those were the last words he said to me before I came harder than I ever have in my life? Was it because he used my name instead of that damnable nickname? He didn't do it much, but I feel like when he did, somehow that was more intimate than the pet name.

Or am I now just forever screwed because I screwed Logan Matthews?

"Mommy!"

Jayce's voice cuts through the quiet as he barrels into the garage. I open my eyes to see him running around to the driver's side in his Batman footy pajamas.

"Back to reality," I whisper to myself as I open the door. I barely have a foot out before Jayce is hugging my leg.

"Hey, buddy," I say as I lean down to hug him. "Did you miss me?"

"So much!"

God, I really am a bad mom. How could I choose a moment for myself over this greeting? I lean down and hug him, which is more like me wrapping my arms around his neck, but it will do.

I'm home. Where I'm supposed to be.

"Jayce, what did I say about letting your mom come into the house before you tackled her?"

Hearing my sister Stella's words only makes him squeeze my leg harder. "I was waiting forever!"

His response makes me chuckle. "Okay, buddy, how about you loosen the grip just a little so we can go inside? That way I can hug you properly."

He does the bare minimum of my request as we start walking into my house in Brentwood, a southern suburb of Nashville. I realize I still need to get my bags out of the SUV, but that's clearly going to be an after-Jayce-goes-to-bed task. Or in reality, a tomorrow morning task, when I realize I need my makeup.

"Thanks again," I say to Stella as Jayce finally lets go of my leg to run back into the living room. He might be excited to see me, but not excited enough to stay away from his favorite movie of all time, *Lego Batman*. "This really helped me out."

Stella waves me off as she starts gathering her things into her white and pink monogrammed tote. "It was no problem. Emmett's working on a design anyway, and he says I distract him. Which is not my fault."

I lift an eyebrow at my baby sister. "Really? You don't do *anything* that your boyfriend would find distracting? It's all him and his fragile male willpower?"

She pretends to think about it before her smirk gives her away. "Fine. Maybe sometimes I *happen* to walk by in just one of his T-shirts. And I might accidentally drop my phone. And sometimes it slides under the table so I have to crawl under. And—"

"That's enough!" I yell, holding up my hands in surrender. I might love that my sister is finally in a loving and healthy—and apparently very active—relationship, but I don't always need to hear the details. Especially with my six-year-old in listening range.

"Sorry," Stella singsongs, though judging by the smirk on her face, she really isn't. "So, how was your trip?"

I feel my cheeks flush the second she brings it up. Shit. My face needs to quit giving me away. I feel like I've blushed more in the past forty-eight hours than in my entire life.

"Fine," I choke out, striving for casual but sounding like I'm strangling.

Judging by Stella's arched eyebrow and head tilt, she doesn't believe me. "Fine? Really? That's it?"

"Yup."

I move to start putting things away in kitchen cabinets that don't need to be put away, all in the name of turning my back to my youngest sister so she can't see my traitorous face.

"Nothing happened? At all? Your cheeks are just getting red because you're warm in here?"

Why is she pressing so hard?

"Nope," I say, feeling more confident to turn back to Stella. "Nothing exciting. Speaking, decorating, black leather sectionals. Same ol', same ol'."

Stella's face grows a little sad. "That's really it?"

"Sorry to disappoint," I reply as I pour myself a glass of water. "Were you expecting more?"

I do feel bad lying to my sister, but I'm barely able to admit to myself what I did, let alone voice it out loud. Also, telling one sister means I'm telling the other two, and I'm not ready for that conversation. Maybe ever.

"I don't know," she says. "I mean, you were gone for ten days. Well, eleven with the delay. I was maybe hoping there'd be some report of a drink with a guy at a bar. Or maybe an impromptu dinner with a fellow designer at a five-star restaurant that just happened to be on a patio looking out over the ocean."

"It's November," I deadpan. "And I went to Atlanta. There is no ocean."

"You know what I mean."

"No, my dear sister, I don't."

She looks into the living room, I'm assuming to make sure Jayce isn't coming in. "Maeve, I know I'm not the sister to give advice, or to tell you how to live your life."

"No, because I'm that sister."

And that's not tooting my horn, that's the truth. Out of the four Banks sisters, we all have our roles in the family. I equate them to the duties we'd have if we ever needed to dispose of a body.

Stella is the one who will dig the hole and ask questions later.

Quinn is likely the reason the body needs buried in the first place.

Ainsley is the eternal optimist who, while driving to bury said body, is spouting off all the reasons why this is a good thing and we aren't bad people.

And me? I plan the disposal and call the lawyer and make sure we have alibis set up. Oh, I also called our brother Simon to make sure he paid off whoever needs to be bribed.

That's how it goes. So Stella here, trying to give me advice, is really throwing my world off its axis.

"I know you are. And you always will be. I'm just saying that maybe it's time you start living a little. Using your work trips to have some no-strings-attached fun? Might not be the worst idea…"

She had to say it like that, didn't she? Just that slight mention of no-strings fun immediately transports me back to the penthouse suite where I had exactly that. Where I forgot my responsibilities. Where I was selfish for one night.

"There!"

Goddamn it, is there some medication that will stop my chronic blushing?

"There what?" I try to play stupid, which doesn't work.

"Why are your cheeks on fire? Maeve Banks, what are you not telling me?"

I've never been a good bullshitter. In fact, I've been told my bluntness is both a gift and a curse. But I'm not ready to tell Stella yet. For now I want to keep this just for me.

Even if just for a little while longer…

"Okay, something did happen." I barely have the words out before Stella squeals so loud the neighbor's dogs start barking. "But! I'm not ready to talk about it yet."

I nod toward the living room where Jayce is still content watching television, feeling only slightly bad that I used my kid to get out of this conversation. Chalk it up to my bad mom score of the day. Though I argue that if you don't use your kids to get out of stuff, what are you even doing with your life?

"Ugh, fine," Stella groans. "I'll drop this for now."

"And please, don't tell Quinn and Ainsley. I'll tell...eventually. Just not yet."

She nods in understanding, like only a sister can.

"I get it," she says. "Oh the days of secrecy…"

I laugh as Stella talks about the days of her secret relationship like it was some huge saga. It was a month, tops.

"Thanks," I say. "And not just for keeping this secret, but for watching Jayce. I don't know what I would've done without all of you."

I've been traveling more for work over the past six months, and each time I go out of town, it takes every person in my arsenal to make it happen. And then when you add on a night like last night, it's a scramble. Josh had had him for his normal Sunday and Monday schedule when I first left. Since he owns a bar—and it's pretty successful since he opened it with country mega star Walker Boone—Fridays and Saturdays are tough, which I understand. After that, my parents took over, staying at my house for the week so he could be on his school routine. Stella and Ainsley took over on rotation for the weekend and the beginning of this week, because it was easier for them than for Josh to change his work schedule.

Or so he said.

"It was my pleasure," Stella says. "Bye, Jayce!"

My son comes running back in the room, wrapping his tiny arms around Stella's waist as she bends over to return the hug. "Bye, Aunt Tella."

"Love you," she says, kissing his forehead before looking back at me. "Love you too."

I nod. "Right back at ya."

As Stella exits my house I look over to the clock and see that it's now close to seven. I'm guessing Jayce already ate dinner, and I'm trying to remember if I've had anything since this morning when I got to the airport before the coffee shops even opened. My stomach takes that cue to let out a loud groan, which I ignore. It's almost time for Jayce to wind down for bed, and I need a few minutes with my boy before I tuck him in.

"So, *Lego Batman*, again?" I ask as I sit on the couch, making sure to grab my phone so I don't have to get up if it goes off. And because we've done this a thousand times, Jayce climbs up and snuggles into my side.

"It's the best."

Neither of us say anything as the movie plays, which is on par for us. Jayce is one of those kids who doesn't need to talk all the time.

He gets that from me.

The fact that he's super hero and video game obsessed? That's from his dad.

I hear a tiny snore from Jayce. I look down, and yup, my boy is out. He's somehow slid down my side so he's now lying on my lap, his thumb by his mouth, which he still does from time to time. It's adorable—a little signal that, yes, he's growing up, but he's still my baby.

My eyes were starting to get heavy as well when my phone dings, startling me so much I nearly wake Jayce as I scramble to grab it. As soon as my eyes focus on the device I see a notification of an email from my favorite maybe-not-so-real assistant, Katherine Smith.

"What does she want now?" I mumble as I click open the alert.

To: Maeve Banks, Banks Interiors
From: Katherine Smith
Subject: Re: Reschedule?

Ms. Banks,
Sorry about the confusion, but it turns out the client will be available to meet tomorrow afternoon at the designated time. Directions and an

address are attached to this correspondence. If for some reason you have already booked another appointment, please let us know your next availability, and we will move all of our meetings to make it happen. We look forward to meeting with you and thank you again for your cooperation.

Best,

Katherine Smith

I roll my eyes, wondering if this is finally going to happen. The cancellations and the reschedulings have been going on for months now. And while this might be the closest we've ever gotten to it happening, I'm still not holding my breath.

No, we'll wait and see.

And until then, I'm going to sleep on my very expensive, comfortable couch with my son resting peacefully on my lap. And for just these few moments, I'll relish in the fact that I'm not a bad mom.

Just a very tired one.

guide to love rule #77

If men have one thing in common, it's that they all have the audacity. It just manifests itself differently.

8

maeve

I'M NOT ONE TO WASTE HOURS IN THE DAY. THE SECOND MY ALARM goes off, I'm up and my day is starting. No rest for the wicked. Or Maeve Banks.

But this morning I decided to take my time. I had no faith that the lunchtime meeting with Katherine Smith's boss was actually going to happen, so I was in no rush. I took Jayce to school in a pair of stylish pajamas. I treated myself to coffee and a breakfast wrap. I even took the time to throw in a load of laundry before settling in for my workday, which I was going to do from home. But even then it was just checking emails and making sure nothing was pressing. I put on a comfy lounge set, made myself some tea, and sat back waiting for the email to come that was going to inevitably say "we need to cancel."

And I kept waiting.

And waiting.

I'd still be waiting if I didn't look at a clock. And because I tried to be a go-with-the-flow woman today, everything that happened between realizing I had to get ready and now has been working against me.

It started with the shower I tried to take being ice cold. Then my hair straightener sparked mid flat iron, nearly causing a fire, which is why my hair is pulled back into a tight bun. Because I've been gone, my outfit options were limited, so I'm wearing a pantsuit that makes me feel old. And of course, today was the day that I forgot how to put on eyeliner and poked myself in the eye, making me need to dig into the luggage I haven't unpacked to find my glasses. Then of course I realized how late I was running, which is why I'm now hauling ass on I-65 and putting on lipstick while steering with my knee.

This is my punishment for taking my time.

As I signal around to head into the left lane because everyone is going too slow for me today, my Bluetooth rings.

I take what I just said back, *this* is my punishment.

"Hello, Josh."

My ex-husband doesn't call me a lot. Usually things we need to discuss are easily done over text messages. Which, funny enough, is how our relationship used to go. So when I am blessed with a phone call, I know I need to buckle in.

"Don't sound so excited to talk to me."

"I'm on my way to a meeting. What do you need?"

"Why do you assume I need something?"

I let out a sigh. "I don't have time for this today."

"Story of our lives."

I don't know if he said that to get a rise out of me, but even if he didn't, he's not wrong. It was one of the reasons why our marriage barely lasted a calendar year. I was building my business and working a ton. At the time, he was a bartender who barely worked full-time hours.

"I have ten minutes, Josh. Talk fast."

"Fine. I was checking to see if we could adjust the Thanksgiving schedule. I have him for Thanksgiving this year and was wondering if he could just stay with me through the weekend? Then he'd come back Sunday night."

"What? Absolutely not. You have him on Thanksgiving Day. I have him on Friday for my family's dinner. We're having Thanksgiving a day late so he can be included."

"Really? That's it? You're not going to even consider it?"

"Not just based on you asking," I say. "You're bombarding me with this."

"Welcome to my life, when you suddenly need me to take him for another day because of your work and travel schedule."

"That's different."

"How so Maeve?"

"Because mine is work."

"Well, mine is a trip with my son. You know, maybe showing him you can have fun in your life."

That dig stings, and he knows it. Josh has never been a malicious guy, but in the times over our lives we've argued, he's always known what daggers to throw at me.

His go-to? That I used to know how to have fun and have a work-life balance. And if I keep this up, our son will think a good time is hanging curtains.

I didn't used to think that. In fact, part of the reason Josh and I first hit it off is because I worked hard and played harder. I didn't want a commitment, so a friends-with-benefits situation with the hot bartender who wasn't looking to settle down was perfect for me.

Everything changed, though, the day I found out I was pregnant. We had always been safe, but things happen.

At that point, I was thirty and starting to get the itch to settle down. I chalked it up to the universe telling me it was time. And I was ready to be a single mom, because there was nothing in the two years I'd been sleeping with Josh that made me think he was ready to be a dad.

Needless to say I was shocked when he mentioned that we should get married for the baby. I tried to find a reason to say no, but it seemed like the right thing to do. Two people raising a baby together had to be easier than one, right?

Wrong.

I was constantly working because we needed a stable income, and Josh hadn't figured out yet that he didn't have to spend all of his tips the second he earned them. I quickly realized I was going to be the one to support this family, so my entire focus became my business and Jayce.

Goodbye to the Maeve Banks who used to dance on bar tops and pour liquor into guys' mouths. Enter the woman who was designing houses while breastfeeding.

Josh couldn't figure out why I was a different person. I couldn't figure out why he didn't see it. Which is why eleven months and three days after we got married in a courthouse, we signed divorce papers.

Luckily, we didn't have many assets to split. And because Josh wasn't in the financial situation or had any real desire to have more than partial custody, he didn't bat an eye at every other Sunday and Monday. It worked for him. It worked for me. Even now that he's gone from part-time bartender to owner of a very successful bar in downtown Nashville, it's the schedule that has worked for us.

He's never asked for extra days. Hell, any time I ask him to pitch in when I'm out of town is pulling teeth. So the question is, why now?

"Why?"

"What do you mean why?" he answers. "Can't a dad want more time with his son?"

"He can. But you never have. So something's up."

The sigh he lets out means I hit the nail on the head. "Vivian and I want to take him away with us for the weekend."

And there it is. This is Vivian's idea. I should've known.

Vivian is Josh's girlfriend of about a year, which is eleven months longer than I thought it would last. I figured she was just another one of his bar hookups that would fizzle out.

And as a former bar hookup, I felt I had a keen sense of insight on how that plays out. The ones who usually last the longest are the ones like me—can party hard but are also people he could take home to his mom when she wonders why he hasn't settled down and he wants to appease her. But the ones like Vivian? The ones whose jobs are "influencers," even though they couldn't convince a cat to chase a mouse and their real jobs are working part-time at the tanning salons? Those are the ones who fizzle.

Vivian, though, has been the needle in the haystack. I don't know what she does for work these days. She made her name by finishing fifth place in a failed country music reality singing show, but caught some attention on social media because she was the one who caused all of the drama between the contestants. After the show ended, she started getting booked at bars downtown because her name carried a slight bit of weight. This is how she and Josh met. I hoped it wouldn't last long.

I'm still hoping.

I don't know what it is about her, but something rubs me the wrong way. I get the sense that she thinks she should be famous because she's pretty and has a decent voice. She doesn't seem to have a lot of ambition—or know how to spell it—so I'm not sure what her next move is. Though I do have a suspicion she's not rushing to make any kind of decision since Josh has now come into some money because of the success of the bar.

The one good thing—at least until now—is that she never seemed to be around when Josh had Jayce. Jayce never talks about her. He never tells her goodnight during story time. So, if she's just fucking my ex, let her have him. And if he wants to spend money on her, then that's his choice.

"Where is this trip? And why are you just telling me about it and trying to schedule it? You can't just spring this on me."

"It was last minute for us, too, but all the schedules lined up. And we've never taken Jayce anywhere before, just the three of us. Vivian loves Dollywood. We were hoping to take him there and stay in the mountains for the weekend."

Christ…now this woman is going to ruin Dolly for me.

I take a breath and try to think about this rationally. He's right that he's never asked for anything. I don't love the idea of a trip with Vivian, but despite my distaste for her, Josh will be there. He might not be an all-the-time dad, but when it's his turn, he's more than capable. And maybe, just maybe, when I need him in the future for an extra day, I'll remind him of this.

"Okay, compromise," I say. "I'll bring him over Thursday. You have your day and he spends the night. He comes back to me Friday morning for my family's dinner that I scheduled *specifically* because you had him on Thursday. But, I'll bring him back on Friday night so you can either get on the road late or first thing in the morning."

He releases a sigh. "You're the best, Maeve," he says. "Thank you. This trip…it's big for us."

"I'm glad it can happen."

We hang up and I let my head fall back against the seat. I didn't expect any of that to happen today.

I bet it's because I got the breakfast wrap. I girl-bossed too close to the sun.

Josh's unexpected call has me so out of sorts that I nearly miss the turn to my destination. And that's the only reason I almost miss it, because if I was of sound mind, no way I could've failed to notice this place.

For one, it's huge. No doubt the biggest piece of property I've ever seen in my life—and I designed a home that literally had the word "manor" in it in Philadelphia.

I nearly crash into the iron gate as I pull up because I can't stop staring at the structure in the distance.

"Hello, can I help you?"

I nearly jump at the sound of the female voice coming from a call box. "I'm Maeve Banks. I have an appointment with—"

"Come in."

The gates open, and I slowly start driving up the extensive driveway, which has to be a quarter-mile long. Spanish moss hovers over the curved concrete, and I'm in awe of the greened tunnel I'm driving through. Also I clearly don't know enough about horticulture, because I didn't know you could grow

Spanish moss in middle Tennessee, let alone keep it alive in November.

My jaw continues to drop the closer I get to this house. Holy shit, it's huge. I'm guessing it's new construction because my quick search on Google Maps and Earth showed this as just a lot.

It's definitely a lot more than a lot. It's a mansion. No. This is a freaking estate and should have its own zip code.

I pull my SUV in front of the house and flip down the visor mirror. Before any meeting, I like to give myself a pep talk. Make sure I'm in the right headspace. And that's on a normal job for fifteen-hundred-square-foot bachelor pads.

Today is different. Between everything going wrong this morning, Josh's phone call, and looking at a property that could be a career-changing job, I need to make sure I'm focused.

"You can design anything," I whisper to myself. "Be smart. Be confident. Be a fucking badass."

With one last crack of my neck, I grab my tote bag, cell phone, and make my way to the front door. I don't even have to knock before the door is pulled open and I'm greeted by a woman who looks to be around my age.

"Hi, you must be Maeve. Please come in. It's so good to finally meet you."

"Thank you," I say as I step inside. "Are you Katherine Smith?"

"The one and only," she says, showing me in. "Thank you so much for coming today. I'm sorry about all the confusion."

I start to reply with a generic "I'm glad we finally could make it work" or something, but I can't talk. I'm too busy looking at every inch of the house I can see.

"Beautiful, isn't it?" Katherine says.

I don't respond, because I don't have the words. It's that gorgeous. A true blank canvas. High ceilings with more natural light than I thought possible. White walls for me to have a field day with. A staircase with a black iron railing that winds when it gets to the bottom. A marble floor that I'm pretty sure that I can…yup…there's my reflection.

And this is just the entryway. I can't wait to see the rest.

"You can follow me," Katherine says, and as if she has me in a trance, I blindly follow her down the hallway and into a room that I'm guessing is going to be a formal living room.

"He'll just be a few minutes," Katherine says as she gestures to a seat that looks out of place in this massive space. "Can I get you anything to drink? Water? Tea? Coffee? Diet Coke?"

I start to say water when I realize she offered me my favorite beverage. "Diet Coke, please."

She gives me a friendly smile as she turns to leave the room. I put my bag down but don't sit in the offered chair. I can't. This room has me under a spell. All I can do is walk around and imagine everything I could do and design with a space like this.

I slowly walk in a circle, memorizing every detail of the room before closing my eyes, trying to visualize what I want the end result to be. Because I'm likely competing against other design- ers, and this is a newly built home, I'm guessing I'll have to pitch something modern to the point of edgy. A lot of metals. Sneak in pops of color sporadically.

But if I had my way…oh, the things I could do…

The first thing I noticed in this room is the fireplace with the accent wall that seemed to go on forever. Immediately I felt a rustic vibe. I'd want the wall to be brick, with a custom wood mantle that would sit between the high arched windows. I'd want cream furniture to go with the hardwood floors. Normally I'm not a fan of the brown base color palette, but that's what I'm envisioning. It would be finished with a custom-made wood coffee table that would be long enough to cover the length of the two extended couches I'd get. Top it off with the perfect lighting setup to make the room bright without feeling clinical or needing an ornate piece of overhead lighting. Chandeliers have their purpose, but not in this space.

But this isn't my dream world. I keep my eyes closed as I

slowly come back to the present, where I'm Maeve Banks: Designer for the Rich and Douchey.

If I was called, that means there's no wife or girlfriend, which means these beautiful white walls are about to become a dark gray. Maybe I'll get to keep the white crown molding. I might as well make the call to my favorite furniture guy, who can make me a hell of a leather sectional. Oh! And while I'm at it, I should probably start tracking down an original Spud McKenzie portrait. And a pool table. Which I don't have anything against the game of pool, but in a man cave it's so cliché.

But cliché is what keeps the bills paid.

I'm glad my eyes are closed as I feel myself smile at my internal use of that word. Will I ever think of that word the same way again? Maybe one day. But not today. Not when I can still feel his touch. When I could still pick his cologne out of a lineup. And maybe my mind is playing tricks on me, but I swear I can smell it now.

"Beautiful, isn't it, Love?"

9
logan

I GRAPPLED ALL MORNING WITH WHAT MY FIRST WORDS TO MAEVE were going to be. The options were, but not limited to:

"Surprise!"

"Long time, no see!"

Not saying anything, instead just gasping and acting shocked that she's here.

Or, my personal favorite, pulling her into my arms, sending Kat on a senseless errand, and kissing the hell out of her.

I would've preferred that option.

As I was walking into the space that will eventually be my formal living room, I still didn't know how I was going to tell her that I, in fact, was the asshole client that kept canceling.

Shit...she's really going to want to call me an asshole, isn't she?

Honestly, though? I deserve it. Even if I would've told her on the plane who I was, I was still going to be an asshole. Canceling on her as much as I did? I'm a proper prick. It's why I opted not to tell her. Maybe, just maybe, I thought, if she saw me today she'd laugh about it. It was about a two-percent chance of happening, but it was still better odds than admitting my identity to her on the plane. That was a zero percent chance of success.

I knew I had one shot to get this right, which is why I rehearsed lines all morning. What I didn't expect was to walk into the room and have every line I practiced disappear. I stood in the entryway, just watching her. Did she get more beautiful in the twelve hours we were apart? I mean, it's not possible, but somehow she is. Her hair is slicked back in a bun again, showing off the perfect lines of her face and neck. The power suit she's wearing is professional, yet somehow sexy. Probably because of the stilettos she's wearing with it.

Lord, how I love a woman in heels…

She's the whole package, which is why I hate that this is likely going to be the last time I see her. Because in a world where I canceled on her six times, she's embarrassed from our night together, and I lied to her about being the mystery client, I don't see how she agrees to take this job, no matter what kind of money I offer her.

My opening line finally hits her as I watch her slowly come to the realization that I'm in the room with her. It starts with a freeze in her body. It continues with her eyes opening and slowly turning toward the sound of my voice. And it ends just the way I thought it would—fire in her blue eyes and redness on her cheeks.

"You."

Because I can't help but get under her skin, I go along with it. "Me."

I move to sit at one of the temporary chairs in the room. Until this morning we had nothing. Luckily Kat realized it and made a few calls.

The woman is super human, and I don't know how I live my life without her.

I gesture for Maeve to sit, but she doesn't. She even goes a step farther by crossing her arms and popping out a hip, showing me that in no way, shape, or form is she going to have a seat.

And as much as I'd love to poke and prod the bear, I know

there's only one way this ends up with her staying and decorating my home.

I need to grovel.

"Maeve, I'd like to start—"

"What the fuck, Logan!"

Okay, groveling can wait. I have to go right into defense mode.

"I can explain."

"Oh, you're going to explain, all right! You're going to explain a whole hell of a lot."

I don't say anything, as Maeve has started to pace in circles. Call me old fashioned, but I want to look a woman in the eye when I beg for forgiveness.

Because I know that's how this is going to end—me on my knees, begging her to stay. And I'm okay with that. Because that's what you do when you meet the woman you're sure is the one who's going to change your life.

"Are you going to say anything?"

Shit, I must've spaced off. "Sorry, Love. Can you sit, though? You're making me slightly dizzy."

I don't know if it was the use of the word "Love" or my request that currently has her stabbing me with her eyes.

"Don't call me that."

The first one. Got it.

"Apologies, but please, sit. I'll explain everything."

Maeve lets out a huff before doing as asked. "Start talking. Now."

Here goes nothing…

"I didn't know."

Her narrowed eyes clearly don't buy that.

"Not until the airplane!" I clarify. "I promise you, not a second before that, and it even took a few questions for me to be sure."

"Really, Logan? You think I'm that gullible?"

"Not at all, Lo—" I stop myself short before using the pet

name. She's already pissed at me enough. "Maeve, I promise you, everything that happened up until you tossed your mobile in frustration at my canceling again was purely by random chance."

She crosses her arms and narrows her eyes. "So why did you sit down next to me if you didn't know me? Why even talk to me?"

That I can answer.

"Because when you see a beautiful woman at a bar, you buy her a drink. And then you pray she'll look your way."

My direct reply throws Maeve for a second. She uncrosses her arms and sits up a little straighter, but uses the time to harden her stare at me again. I know she's trying to look intimidating, but between the gray power suit, the hard line of her lips, and the slicked back bun, I feel like I'm getting yelled at by a sexy librarian. And as a kid who grew up checking out my maximum limit of books each week, this is unlocking a new fantasy I didn't realize I had.

"Whatever, it doesn't matter," she says. Even though I'd bet today's stock profits it does matter. "You knew on the plane and didn't say anything."

I slowly nod, knowing this is where the real groveling is about to begin. "I know you told me about being a designer the night before, but I never put two and two together. Hell, I didn't even know we were both flying back to Nashville until I stepped on the plane. And if I can be frank, I canceled on these appointments so much I forgot about them."

"Gee, thanks."

Yeah, that stung. But I need to tell the truth from here on out, and I know some of it is going to hurt like bloody hell. "Do you want me to lie?"

"Of course not."

"Well, then, here's the truth. When I walked into the bar that night and I laid eyes on you, I couldn't look away. When I asked you to go back to the hotel, it wasn't to get you into my bed. I just wanted to spend as much time with you as I could because you fascinated me. That night? I thought it was one-and-done, and I know you did too. I was shocked to see you sleeping in the seat next to me on the plane. What were the odds? There I was all morning, trying to figure out how I could see you again, because one night just wasn't enough, and there you were. Hollywood writers couldn't script that."

Maeve's eyes are widening with every word. I don't know if it's a good or bad sign, but she hasn't left yet. That has to be good, right?

"When I figured out who you were, I felt awful. I wrestled with myself for that entire conversation if I should tell you that I was the mystery client. I'm sorry. I'm an asshole."

Her arms go back to cross. "Why am I here today? Why did you finally keep the meeting?"

I lean down and rest my elbows on my legs. Groveling is hard work. "When I realized it was you, it hit me how rude I'd been and how much I hadn't respected your schedule or time. So I told Kat to make it work."

"So this is pity? I'm only here because I slept with you?"

Ouch. That stung.

But she's right. No use in lying about it now.

"If you were a stranger? No, you wouldn't be here."

"Wow," she says, dragging the word out for an extra beat. "Well, thanks for being honest?"

"It's not like that," I say. Though I'm not sure if that's the truth.

"Then please, Logan. Explain."

It's my turn to stand now. I can feel that I'm running out of time before she storms out. "I canceled because I would rather do literally anything other than talk about furniture or decorations. In many ways I'm still that broke nerdy bloke from Birmingham."

"You're a literal billionaire."

I shrug. "I might have ten figures in my bank account, but I am who I am."

"Great. Only I would get a frugal billionaire for a client."

I try not to let my face show that she just called me a client. I doubt she realizes she said that, so I'm going to let it sit and not press my luck.

"Kat's the one insisting I have the house professionally decorated. Something about me fitting in with Nashville elite and hosting fundraisers or meetings or something."

"Or that you're an adult and you can't use milk crates as TV stands anymore."

Oh, that trusty milk crate. It was blue and sturdy and perfect.

"That too. Kat finally convinced me I needed this done, but because I'm a pain, I kept finding reasons for her to cancel it."

"Six times."

I hang my head. "Yes. Six times. And I'm so sorry for that. I admit, I never considered what it was doing to the designer's—I mean, your—schedule. I was selfish. And when I realized yesterday it was you, yes, I had her put the meeting back on. And yes, it had to do with our night together. I'd be a liar if I said it wasn't."

I take a step toward her, hoping she can see the regret on my face.

"But more than that, I had her reschedule because I want to work with you. I want to see you turn this place into something beautiful. When I walked in, and your eyes were closed, you were envisioning the space, weren't you?"

She doesn't say anything, but I take that as a yes.

"Whatever you were envisioning, I want that. If it were up to me, yes, I'd have thrift store furniture, a few couches and a game room. And yes, I'm frugal, but that's because I don't like to spend a lot of money on things I don't think I need. But I trust you, Maeve. I trust Kat telling me that I need to own up to my status. If you tell me I need to spend twenty grand on a couch, then I'll do it. No questions asked."

This seems to get a reaction out of her. "Really? You'd be fine with that?"

"Yeah, I would." I take another step toward her. "In my business, when I don't know something, I find people who do. And that is you, when it comes to this place. This can be what you want it to be, Maeve. That is, if you'll forgive me?"

Well, I might not have gotten on my knees and actually begged, but that was a pretty good grovel if I do say so myself.

I watch Maeve, looking for any signs of which way she might go. I'm trying not to get my hopes up, but the longer she stays, the better I think my odds are.

Just when I'm starting to think I'm in the clear, Maeve shoots up from the chair, grabbing her tote and throwing it over her shoulder.

Dammit!

"That was a nice speech. Mostly believable," she says, our bodies only a few inches apart. "And even if it was true—which I'm sorry, there's just too many coincidental things for it to be—I can't work for someone who lied to me. Or that I slept with. That's just...it would never work. So, it's best that we end this meeting now."

Maeve starts storming out of the room, but luckily I'm quick enough to stop her before she can exit. "Maeve, please..."

A surge of heat passes through us, and judging by her expression, she's feeling it too.

Is she remembering that first kiss? Or the heat and tension that passed through us while sitting at the bar? Or when I had her pressed against the door? Or when my face was buried between her legs?

I study her eyes, and for a second, I see the face of the woman I met the other night. And then just as quick, her eyes refocus, and I realize that this is it.

"Goodbye, Logan."

And with that, she pulls her arm from my hold, marches down the hallway, and out the door.

Game over.

10
logan

"Shocker. I found the video game nerd in his video game cave."

Oh, what would my life be without the snark of my best friend/publicist/temporary assistant?

I don't say anything or turn away from the game I'm playing —a combat game where I can take my frustrations out on some bad guys—as she comes in and sits next to me.

If she was looking for me, this means one of two things: She missed me while I was away or she's coming to scold me about something I did while I was away. It's likely the latter, but I'm going to be hopeful it's the former.

Wild card is she found out about Maeve—that we slept together and that she turned me down earlier today—and I'm going to get yelled at for that.

Honestly, it could be all of the above. Kat knows everything. I don't know how she does it, but the woman has either planted listening devices around my house or she's some sort of time traveler who can put herself into many different places simply by turning clocks.

She always was a big Potter head…

"Do you need something?"

I don't make eye contact with her, which she's used to. She's been my best friend for a little more than a decade at this point, having met at freshman orientation at Stanford.

She stood next to me because she told me that she had a thing for guys in glasses. I snickered at one of her smart-ass comments to the tour guide. We've been inseparable ever since. But not in a romantic way. We got drunk one time and kissed. It lasted two seconds before we both backed away in simultaneous horrified laughter.

Sometimes the friend zone is a bad place to be. For me and Kat? It's the best one.

I take a quick glance at her out of the corner of my eye to assess her mood. She looks stressed. Which isn't new. She doesn't look mad, per se, but she doesn't look happy either.

What has me worried most of all is that she's not talking. She's just sitting still, staring at me, waiting for me to turn off my game and focus on her.

That's when I know this is serious and I'm in trouble.

The question is, for what?

I press pause on the game, set down the controller, and turn to her. Her dark eyes are blank, and her hand is propping her head up as if she's bored.

Oh no, this is about to be a sarcastic verbal spanking. That's when she's the most vicious.

I start to open my mouth to get ahead of whatever she's going to yell at me for, but I'm too late.

"I thought that when I quit the corporate PR world to take you on as my only client, that my life would be easier," she begins. "Only one person to worry about. I know everything about him. And he's a self-proclaimed nerd. A man I once had to do a welfare check on because he was in the middle of a thirty-six-hour video game marathon. What trouble could he get into? He's never been one to stir the pot. Surely I'll be able to sleep more than I did for the first seven years of my professional career."

Lectures like this have happened enough for me to know that I'm not allowed to talk until she tells me to. So I just sit back and brace myself for whatever is coming next.

"But no! Somehow I'm getting calls in the middle of the night from fucking rag news websites wanting to know why Logan Matthews is at a high-society New York party, caught in 4K sitting at the bar, alone, playing a fucking video game on his phone, while his date, Candace Kross, the woman starring in next week's primetime lingerie fashion show, is dancing and all over another man? Care to tell me what was so important that you couldn't even pay attention to her for two hours?"

I shrug. "She said she wanted to dance. I didn't want to."

Kat's eyes go wide. "You didn't want to? Seriously, Logan!"

"I'm sorry, but she was the worst of the dates you've set me up on." I sound defensive because I am. "She told me FarmVille was her favorite video game, and the music at this club was awful. Fucking EDM bullshit. So I sat at the bar and took out my phone. My fingers just happened to navigate to a game. What's the big deal? Better than me being spotted with another woman with her there, right?"

Kat throws her hands up in the air. Apparently that's wrong too. "What the fuck, Logan? I thought we had an agreement. You go on fake dates and have pseudo relationships so your name is out there, you don't look like a video game nerd recluse, and people will still talk about you despite there not being a second game in sight. In return, the models get good press for not dating fuck boys. This is the opposite of that."

I hold up a finger. "In my defense, I didn't want to be out with her. Or any of them. This entire plan is all your doing."

Did I know this comeback was going to anger Kat? Yes. But that doesn't make it less true.

"Oh no, Logan Matthews. You don't get to throw this all on me. Was it my idea? Yes. I'll take that smoke. But you went along with it. There was never one objection. So don't throw all of this on me and act like a victim."

I throw down my controller and hang my head. She's right. The people pleaser in me didn't offer one objection to her plan. In fact, I thought it was brilliant when she first came up with the idea to put me in the public eye.

It was what we had to do at the time to make sure my legacy didn't end as a one-hit wonder.

I was twenty-two when I finished the final design of Space-Craft, but the idea started long before that, back in England. When I needed something for my master's degree project, I knew SpaceCraft was what I wanted to create, and it was the hit I thought it would be. But I wanted more.

What did I know about disseminating a game to the population?

Enter Kat Smith.

We were living together in a small, two-bedroom apartment in Los Angeles after graduation. She got a junior job at a PR firm, and I was slaving away as a coder for some tech company. But I never stopped thinking that SpaceCraft could be more. And one night, as we huddled around our tiny table eating bad Chinese food, bitching about our jobs, she looked at me and said the one thing that would change my life.

"Just fucking do it. Figure it out and quit bitching about it."

I told her she should double as an inspirational speaker. She told me to fuck off.

If that doesn't sum up our relationship, I don't know what does.

After she slapped me with her words of wisdom, I took the challenge she laid out and ran with it. I spent every free second I had further developing the game, and Kat discovered an angel investor, who is the only reason I was able to continue. I was able to bring on a small staff—all five of us—and we worked day and night on development, potential marketing, and distribution. The game went through a year of beta testing before launching, and though it had plenty of great feedback, I was still nervous. What if it was a flop? What if no one played it? What if my one idea was a disaster?

But what happened next, no one predicted.

In the first month of release we sold a million copies. I remember thinking the numbers and stats weren't real. And this was all with a bare-bones marketing effort and relying on word-of-mouth recommendations from gamers.

By the second year of SpaceCraft's existence, I needed a chief financial officer to make sure that everything was on the up and up and more accountants than I thought I'd ever need. We had merch, and expansion packs of the games, and everywhere you looked, SpaceCraft was the top game in the market. There were bloody action figures! My once-small staff of five turned into a staff of five hundred. I was the CEO of a company I originally started for tax purposes. I knew nothing about business or running a private firm. I was just a video game geek who once sought refuge in a digital world and wanted to give kids today the same feeling.

In no time at all the path was clear: it was time to take the company public and hire a board of directors. I figured I could be the CEO by title, and still maintain control of the day-to-day operations, while the board could handle big picture decisions and use their expertise to help guide me and my company.

Which is how we're here today: they want the next SpaceCraft.

One problem with that: I don't have the next SpaceCraft.

Actually, I don't have fuck all.

What I do have is the video game developers' version of writer's block, and I can't snap out of it.

I've tried. I've done everything I possibly can to get me out of this funk. I've tried making it a game to myself, trying to appease the guy who always loves a challenge. Nothing. I did market research to see if anything inspired me. That actually set me back mentally. Hell, I even hired a hypnotist. That was the biggest waste of money I've ever spent. I bloody moved to *Tennessee*, hoping a fresh start could solve my problems.

Then one night I received a not-so-subtle memo from the board, saying that stock prices were dropping and I needed to announce something soon. I was panicking.

But not Kat. She figured out a solution. Even if it was a short-term one.

And the name of the game was distraction.

She pointed out that all the board wanted to see were climbing stock numbers, which means sales. They don't care where they come from, as long as their pockets are getting heavier. So she proposed that while I was thinking of the next big thing, I needed to get out and about. Get my name in the news. Be seen with beautiful women on my arm. If people are talking about me, that means SpaceCraft is going to be mentioned more. The more mentions, the higher sales. Higher sales, better valued stock.

And so began the endless train of galas, parties, and events where I had a different woman on my arm. The press took it as I was dating all of them. Kat never confirmed or denied, because it was working. The stock prices were going up just enough to keep the board happy.

The only problem is that now I'm six months into this charade and I'm no closer to coming up with the next SpaceCraft than I was then. And if I have to go on one more fake date, I'm going to pull my hair out.

Though, if Kat set me up with a beautiful woman who was maybe a few years older than me, had a quick wit about her, with dark hair that I could wrap around my fist, and who lets out the sexiest moans when I drove into her, then I bet I'd be on board for a PR relationship.

Ha! Like Maeve would ever agree to that. And that was before she stormed out of here today, leaving a trail of smoke in her wake.

I don't blame her. I took a gamble, and it backfired. I

should've told her it was me on that airplane. Would it have changed her mind? Who knows. But I know this outcome, so I have to at least wonder what the other would've been.

"I'm sorry," I say to Kat. "You're right. I didn't object. Ever. I agreed to it because I trust you and I needed to buy time. And it worked."

This makes her soften slightly. "I'll never get tired of a man telling me I'm right."

"And I'm sure it's not the last time I'll admit it to you. But I do need to speak up now. I can't do it anymore. I'm tired, Kat. The women…they…"

"Are vapid and you need an intellectual to keep you stimulated and you're so straightforward you can't even fake being interested?"

I tap my nose to Kat's response. "Right once again."

She lets out a sigh. "I know they are. But unfortunately, it's not like I can put an ad out on social media asking for a girlfriend for my rich client. And unless you know someone who would do this voluntarily, or suddenly have the follow-up to SpaceCraft ready to go, we're stuck."

Maeve once again flashes through my mind. And even though I know I could never ask her to do this, I can't help but think how perfect she'd be.

Though I wouldn't want her as fake. I'd want her forever.

Too bad she'll likely never speak to me again. I tried getting her out of my head after she left, but to no avail. I ran on the treadmill so hard I might have snapped the track. When that didn't do it, I tried taking the coldest bloody shower possible, hoping to somehow freeze her out of me. After that I buried myself in my gaming room—also known as the only room in the house that's set up and doesn't need Maeve's expertise.

"I know we are," I say, burying my face in my hands. "I wish I could get out of this funk. Figure out what the next thing is and put my time toward that."

"You know," Kat begins, a hint of "I told you so" in her tone.

"I've read on numerous blogs that a cohesive work space, one that's decorated and decluttered and put together, is good for creative flows."

I narrow my eyes at my best friend. "You're not sneaky."

She shrugs. "Never said I was. But now I need to ask the second reason I came in here today. Why did I see Maeve stomping out of this house and breathing fire like a dragon?"

I refuse to meet her eyes. "You don't want to know."

"Dammit, Logan. I know you weren't keen on spending money on a designer, but I thought she would be perfect for you."

She is perfect. And I fucked it up…

"She's great. But unfortunately, she won't be decorating this house."

This makes Kat pop out of her seat as she starts pacing around the room. "What does that mean? Why the fuck didn't you hire her, if she was perfect? Were you being cheap again? I swear to fucking God, you're the worst billionaire in the world."

"I wasn't cheap. In fact, I told her a budget didn't exist. She turned me down."

This stops Kat in her tracks. She turns narrowed eyes on me. "Logan Matthews…what did you do?"

"Why do you assume I did something?" My tone is pitched so high I sound guilty even to myself. And I mean, I did do something, but she doesn't have to assume that…

"Because I know you. Spill."

I take a deep breath, ready for whatever response is going to come when I tell Kat the whole story. "I slept with her."

"What!" she screams. "What do you mean you fucking slept with her? When? Where? Was there an NDA? Do I need to be on alert?"

I shake my head and bring her slowly down to a seat. "Let me explain."

And that's what I do for the next twenty minutes, and even

after that, Kat is only partially calmed. Probably because she also thinks I'm an idiot for not telling Maeve on the plane.

"Logan James Matthews, I swear to Lady Gaga that I'm going to beat you with your Thor hammer."

Oh shit…she's bringing Gaga into this…she really is mad.

"I'm sorry, Kat! I promise, I didn't know who she was prior to the plane. And if she wouldn't have reacted in that way I probably still wouldn't have known. But please know, you don't need to worry about her going to the press. She didn't even know who I was until I told her. She's not looking for a quick payday, obviously. And I'm beating myself up how I acted, so you don't need to keep doing it for me."

Kat sighs and throws her head back. "I doubt it matters. Either she turns you down, or you would've kept canceling. Either way, this place was still going to be without furniture."

I don't say anything, because she's right.

"Logan, as your friend, I say this with love, but this monstrosity of a house needs decorated," she says, focusing her eyes back to me. "You're twenty-nine years old. Whether you realize it or not, you're kind of a big deal. You need a space that reflects you and the life you've built. You aren't the broke boy who had to pinch pennies for a new video game. You earned this money. Show it off. Decorate a home. Be the man you've become in *all* avenues of your life."

That was the nicest scolding I've ever received.

"Now, the lecture from your publicist," Kat says. "We're throwing a huge Christmas benefit gala in a month. I just finalized everything. If that goes well, stock shares will shoot up before the end of the year. I'll sell pictures to every magazine in America showing that the SpaceCraft creator loves the holidays and is giving back to his new community at Christmas. Buzz will spread and this will give you a break from fake relationships. But I can't throw a fucking party with rented folding chairs and plastic cups. You need this space to look good or it's back to the models who want to know if you can get them an original Sims game."

That was a good joke, but I can't laugh.

Cause I fucked up. Royally.

"I'm sorry, Kat. I really am."

She lets out a heavy breath as she falls back into her seat. "I know you are. We'll figure it out."

I grab her hand and give it a squeeze. "We always do."

guide to love rule #10

You do what you need to do to survive. Sometimes that's selling feet pics. Sometimes that's working for a one-night stand.

11

maeve

Fuck Logan Matthews and the orgasms he rode in on.

My life was so much easier prior to meeting him. Before then, I was a content single mom. I had a tight group of friends, sisters who were my rocks, a family I adored, and a career that kept me more than fulfilled. So on Sunday nights like this, when Jayce spends the night with his dad, I never feel lonely. I usually get some takeout, catch up on work, or watch television that isn't in the form of cartoons or YouTube videos.

But what I'd never do, and I mean never, is think about a man. I wouldn't replay conversations and interactions. I wouldn't go back and forth about whether or not I should swallow my pride and work for him. And I for sure wouldn't pull out my vibrator and take care of myself with him in mind.

Yet, that's what's happening now.

And it's all Logan Matthews's fault.

I close my eyes as I apply the device to my clit, hating that I need to feel a release when all I've been doing is cursing him internally since I walked out of his mansion the other day. How dare he call me things like beautiful and smart. How dare he wear a tight T-shirt that showed off his arms to a business meeting and made me fantasize about him holding me against a wall. And how dare he sound sincere when he said that I'd have free creative rein of the house.

That might have turned me on more than anything else.

And when he grabbed my arm as I was leaving? I know he felt the connection between us too. With one touch, I was transported back to that night. The feel of his mouth on me. How his fingers knew just how to find a spot I didn't know I had. How rough he was, but without being overly forceful. He was the perfect blend of dominant and tender.

I bite my lip and position the bud in the perfect spot as I let my mind wander back, letting myself get lost in the memory of him driving into me, giving me exactly what I needed.

"Now, Love. Come for me now."

"Logan!" I yell as my orgasm hits me. It's not as strong as it was the night in the hotel, but I don't think that will ever be replicated.

Especially since I'm never sleeping with Logan Matthews again.

I take a second to calm myself down, gently put my toy away, and head to the bathroom. Since it's just me tonight, I don't bother changing out of my robe. Why put on clothes when it's just going to be me, Thai takeout, and reruns of *Criminal Minds?*

I splash some water on my face and tug my robe tight as I head out of my bedroom and back to my living room. It's only a little after five o'clock, but because of the time change it's pitch black. I run my hand over the wall to find the light switch, finding it quickly and slowly bringing the lights to life.

"What'cha doing, big sis?"

"Jesus Christ!" I yell, covering my heart because I'm pretty sure it just jumped out of my chest. "What the hell are y'all doing here?"

I tighten my robe as I look into my now-lit living room to see all three of my sisters sitting on the couch. Stella looks curious. Ainsley looks guilty. Quinn looks smug as hell.

Fuck, they heard what I just did.

"We're just checking on you," Stella says.

"Have you ever heard of knocking?"

"We did," Ainsley adds. "But no one answered. We saw your car in the garage and a light on in your room, so we figured we'd come in and wait."

Did they really knock and I didn't hear? How out of it was I?

"Yes, Maeve. We were worried," Quinn says as she walks over to me. "And as good sisters, we came in to check on you. We rushed to your door to make sure everything was okay. We almost came in when we heard heavy breathing."

"I need to say I didn't do any of this," Ainsley says. "I stayed right here."

"Which is a good thing she did," Quinn continues, her tone now mocking me. "We wouldn't have wanted Ainsley to hear the moans."

Was I moaning? "I wasn't moaning."

"Oh but you were," Quinn sits me down on the couch between my sisters. "And now, the question begs to be asked, who is Logan?"

I don't even bother trying to fight the blush that comes across my cheeks. I was able to fend off Stella the other night. Ainsley would never push me if it were just her. But Quinn? With Quinn here, I know my fate—I have to tell them.

I have to tell them everything.

But I need a second first to gather my thoughts.

And a glass of wine wouldn't hurt.

"Why are you even here?" I ask Quinn as I stand up from the couch and head into my kitchen. "Shouldn't you still be in Arizona teaching the youth of tomorrow? I thought you weren't coming in for Thanksgiving until next week?"

Quinn follows me into the kitchen and grabs two bottles from my wine fridge and a bottle of water for Ainsley since she rarely, if ever, drinks. I also throw a bag of popcorn into the microwave, because I need a snack and I have a feeling my sisters aren't leaving anytime soon. "I had PTO and I took it. Now who is this

Logan? Is he in this house? If so, I think we deserve to meet him."

I shake my head as I grab three wine glasses and take them back to my living room. "He's not here."

"Oh! So this was alone time?"

I shoot a look at Ainsley as Quinn and Stella let out deserved snickers. "Ainsley Mae! I expect that kind of comment from Quinn. Not from my good sister."

She just shrugs as she reaches for her water. "Am I wrong?"

"You're not," I say in a sigh. "He's..."

I trail off as I sit across from my sisters in my favorite chair. How do I tell this story? Do I just tell them about the trip? Do I admit that I had a one-night stand? Do I tell them that he was the mystery client? I mean, at some point I'm sure all of this will come out, but am I ready for it to come out in a large heaping of word vomit?

"Oh! Oh my God!" Stella shrieks, making both Quinn and Ainsley jump. "He's the guy! The red cheeks! The trip! Oh my God, Maeve had sex!"

My two other sisters turn to Stella then back to me with looks that are filled with confusion, shock, and maybe a little hopefulness.

I guess that's what I get when I've been five years man free.

"Yes," I say. "But it's a lot more than that."

"Then what are you waiting for!" Quinn says, fixing herself on the couch like she's ready to listen to a fireside story. "All the details. And don't you dare leave a fucking thing out."

"It's a lot more than you think," I admit.

"Great, we'll order a pizza," Stella says. "Now quit stalling. Spill."

I take a breath and start at the beginning. This story is so convoluted, and now has so many moving parts, it feels like the best place.

I tell them about the airport bar, our flights getting canceled, and how I for some reason agreed to go to the hotel with him.

How I knew it probably wasn't my best decision, but I was going to need a room, so I might as well head over. And if another drink happened, then so be it. And that one thing led to another…

"You knew what you were doing," Quinn says. "You wanted to fuck him."

I shake my head, even though I don't know if I believe me on this one. "He was attractive. Yes, but you know me. I wasn't about to just spread my legs just because I thought he was hot."

"Your self-control is both amazing and frustrating," Quinn says.

"And apparently non-existent," I say. "It took only a few martinis, some good conversation, and a hot British guy to make me lose it."

The three let out a gasp.

"You didn't tell us he was British!" Ainsley exclaims.

"Oh, I didn't?" I actually didn't mean to leave that part out. But then I realize that I left out another big detail. Might as well drop it now. "This would probably be a good time for me to tell everyone that his name is Logan Matthews."

It takes two seconds for my sisters to register the name I just dropped.

"Shut the fucking front door!" Stella yells. "You're telling me the man who ended my sister's dry spell is one of the hottest billionaires in the fucking world!"

"Wait!" Quinn yells, taking a little longer to figure it out. "Isn't that the video game tycoon who dates all those models?"

"It is," Ainsley says. "And if I'm remembering correctly, he's Stella's age."

Open mouths and wide eyes turn to me. And yup, here come the red cheeks again.

"Cougar!" Quinn crows, pointing at me.

"He's not *that* young," I defend. Though I did feel like it when I found out. "It doesn't matter. Because it was a one-night thing. And it was great. Memorable even. But then I left in the middle of the night and went to the airport to avoid the awkward talk in the morning."

"I bet it was memorable," Quinn adds with an eyebrow wag.

"I can't believe you slept with Logan Matthews," Stella says. "This might be the best thing to ever happen to one of us."

I roll my eyes. Of course my sister who loves reading her celebrity news would take this stance. "Bask in it now. Because it's never happening again."

"That makes sense," Ainsley says. "You aren't exactly a relationship person. You've gone this long without even dating, let alone having a friends-with-benefits situation. And even if you were up to that, it's not like he lives around here. What are the odds you'd run into him again?"

I try to keep my face under control, but apparently that fails as I feel Quinn's eyes on me. She might live in Arizona now, and I only see her in person a few times a year, but the woman will forever be able to clock my thoughts a mile away. "Where does he live, Maeve?"

I lower my eyes and take a breath. "He just moved to Nashville. He was on my plane."

"What!" The three say in unison.

I let them be in a tizzy for a few minutes as I head into the kitchen to grab my popcorn and doctor it up with extra butter and light salt, and pour myself another glass of wine. When I return to the living room, they are still shocked.

"Did you know he was going to be on your plane?" Ainsley asks.

"I didn't. I hoped to never see him again. I even snuck out of the hotel room in the morning. I was embarrassed and didn't want to have that next-morning talk. So I left without saying goodbye and went to the airport insanely early. Because of that, I was sleeping as soon as I got on the plane. When I woke up, there he was, sitting next to me."

"Holy shit," Quinn says. "What are the odds?"

Oh, if she thinks those odds are slim, just wait until I deliver the final bomb. "It gets crazier."

"It can't," Stella says.

I nod. "Remember the mystery client who kept canceling on me?"

Gasps are the only sound in the room before Ainsley whispers, "No…"

"Yes…the mystery client is Logan Matthews."

Choruses of "holy shit," "no fucking way," and "I can't believe it," fill the space for the next few minutes. While they have their freak outs, I go deal with the pizza delivery that just showed up.

"How did you figure it out?" Ainsley asks.

"When I showed up at his house for the consultation."

"Did he know?"

"Oh he knew," I say, my voice now laced with a touch of anger. "He figured it out on the plane and didn't tell me."

I fill my sisters in with the last bit of details of the story. How the meeting was magically rescheduled. My feelings of shock and anger when I found out it was him.

"So what did you say?" Stella asks. "Please tell me your stubbornness didn't lead you to turn down the job."

"Of course I did," I say. "Stubborn or not, I can't work for him."

"And why not?" Quinn asks, grabbing a slice. "I bet it would be a hell of a payday."

"It would. Likely my highest commission to date, and that's without the up-charge I'd add because he lied and I feel like it."

I don't know why, but my eyes meet Ainsley's, who doesn't look as mad as I'd like my sisters to be right now. "Please tell me you're not taking his side."

Ainsley shakes her head and gently dabs the corner of her mouth. "I'll always be on your side. But maybe you're being too harsh?"

"Too harsh? How? I don't think I'm being harsh enough. Or

did you forget the fact that he lied to me when he knew who I was? And I'm still not convinced he didn't know the whole time."

Okay, that last part is a stretch. But the part of me that is embarrassed and angry needs to believe it.

"For some reason, I don't think he's lying to you about that," she says. "And didn't you say he came clean? I think before you cut all ties, you should maybe weigh that into consideration."

I let out a sigh, hating that she's right. "He did. He kind of begged."

Quinn groans in an overtly sexual way. "Oh God, what I wouldn't do for a man to beg for me. Did he get on his knees? That would be so fucking hot."

"Focus," Stella scolds Quinn. "This is about Maeve and her remembering what sex is and us convincing her to do it again, not a list of Quinn's kinks."

The talk of kinks makes me think back to the elevator…and how I shouldn't have liked that as much as I did.

"It doesn't matter," I say. "I turned down the job. As far as I'm concerned, I'm never going to see Logan Matthews again."

That's the first time I've said those words out loud. I should feel relieved about my declaration. Except I'm not.

No. I'll get over it. I have to. I don't sleep with clients, and I don't work with men I've slept with. It's my two rules.

I just added that last one today.

"Hear me out," Quinn says. "You don't have to sleep with him again. You're a grown woman. Who you choose to—or not to—sleep with, is your decision. But I'm now going to appeal to Maeve the businesswoman. Does she think it's a good idea to turn down a life-changing commission?"

Damn my sister for knowing how to get to me. "She doesn't."

"And think of it like this," Stella says. "You've been saying for months now that you want to transition out of bachelor pads, but you didn't know if you could. Isn't that why you went to that conference? So what if you take this job and use that commission to take time off and rebrand? You'd be able to."

Oh, now that's a thought…

"Oh good one, Stella!" Quinn says, putting down her pizza so she can use her hands to fully get her point across. "Charge him an insane fee. You said he has the money to do it, and I'm guessing if he begged for forgiveness, he won't say no. Use the money as your seed money to start Banks Interiors 2.0. This could be your final bachelor pad before shifting to designing spaces the way you've wanted to for years."

The more they talk about this, the better of an idea it sounds. I *have* been unhappy. I've wanted to change direction, but the pragmatic me couldn't see a good time to do it. How could I turn down commissions just because I was bored? But if I had some padding to get me through a few months, and it was also enough to put together a new portfolio, well, then I'd be willing to see Logan again.

Even if it meant reliving that one night every day.

guide to love rule #60

Sometimes you have to listen to your head and ignore your vagina in decision-making. Being responsible sucks.

12

maeve

"You okay, Mommy?"

Jayce's voice snaps me out of my daze as I sit on the couch, staring off into nowhere. "Yeah, buddy. I'm fine."

He scrunches his nose, clearly not believing me. "Well then, can I?"

Shit, what did he ask for? How out of it was I? How long have I been staring into the abyss as I wrestle with the decision to call Logan and tell him that I'll take the job, even after adamantly telling him no?

"Sure. Go ahead."

I really hope that today is not the day my six-year-old is asking me to do something stupid, or try something he never has before, or wants to show me something his dad taught him because now he wants to be father of the year. Luckily for me, he puts down his video game controller—of course he's playing SpaceCraft—and toddles off to the kitchen. He comes back a minute later with a heaping bowl of Goldfish crackers and an apple juice.

I let out a sigh of relief that I didn't give my kid accidental permission to play with knives as he goes back to his video game.

Nights like this are normal for us. Since my son is in first grade, it's not like he has piles of homework to do, so he's enjoying his hour of video game time that usually turns into two hours. I'm sitting with my sketch book on my lap, trying to come up with concepts for a job I'm starting next week for a recently divorced bank executive. Usually I can come up with ideas at the drop of a hat, but tonight I'm drawing a blank. I can't make myself design another gray-walled, black sofa, all silver and metallic fixture space again. Every time I've closed my eyes to think about the space and envision it, my traitorous mind keeps going back to Logan's mansion and all its possibilities.

"This house can be what you want, Maeve. That is, if you'll forgive me?"

Did he mean that? Did he really mean that I could have creative freedom for his mansion? While I technically have creative freedom with all my designs, I know what the clients are leaning toward, so I always make sure it fits them.

But with Logan? I have a feeling he wouldn't be opposed to the rustic look I thought of the first day I was there. Exposed beams. So much natural light it would be nearly blinding.

Oh my God, I could use shiplap! I miss shiplap so fucking much.

But is the use of textiles I never get to use and a cream-based color palette enough to make me work for a man I've shared my O face with?

I go back and forth with these predicaments no less than ten times when my phone vibrates on the coffee table with a text message.

QUINN

Make your decision?

How did she know I was thinking about this?

MAEVE

Are you psychic now?

I love all my sisters, and my brother Simon, to the ends of the earth. But when it comes to me and Quinn's relationship? It's on another level. She's the sister I'm closest in age to. We went to each other when we had problems with friends or boys. She would call me when she needed picked up from a party she wasn't supposed to go to, and I went to her when I needed blunt advice. We even went to college around the same time, and partying with your sister is a whole other level of bonding you'll never have with anyone.

She's my person. My rock. And the only one right now who can tell me that I'm being a stubborn asshole for refusing to work with Logan.

I could continue texting with her, but I have a feeling I need a verbal smack across the face to get me to make the decision I know is the right one to make.

Even if I don't like it.

"Well, hello, big sister."

"I need blunt Quinn," I admit.

"I figured," she says, and I don't know why, but I have a feeling she's dramatically cracking her knuckles. "Still going back and forth?

"Yeah…I just…"

"Listen," Quinn cuts me off. "If you want blunt Quinn, here it goes. You're mad at yourself that you broke your stupid rule of no dating or sex. You're embarrassed that you wanted it to be a one-night thing and you thought you got away with it by sneaking out of his room. But surprise! Karma is a fickle bitch, and she sat you next to him on the plane. Which wasn't good for you because you wanted to forget about it and never tell anyone, which in your mind meant that you could pretend like it never happened."

Damn she's good…

"But now! Not only do you have to admit that the night of a thousand orgasms happened, now he's holding what could be a new future for you in his big, strong hands."

"How do you know he has big, strong hands?" I ask.

"If you didn't think I stalked every picture of him on the internet after you told me that you had multiples then you don't know me at all."

"I really should've kept that detail to myself."

"Nope. I'm glad you did. Because that's why we're here. If he was a two-pump chump who couldn't find the clit and didn't know how to eat it, we wouldn't be here. We're here because not only did he make you see well-deserved stars, it's because you felt something, and that scares the ever-loving shit out of you."

Damn...I really got what I asked for...

"I'm going to take your silence as evidence that I'm right."

I let out a sigh before getting up from the couch, moving to the kitchen so I didn't have to shield words from Jayce. Though he is so invested in his game I doubt he'd have heard a sonic boom.

"Fine, you're right," I admit. "But I'm not scared the way you think I am. It's...I lose control around him. I do stupid shit. Like drop cups with liquids—"

"And your panties."

"Not funny."

"Kind of funny."

"I'm serious, Quinn. What am I supposed to do? I know what's smart in terms of my business. But I don't know if it's smart for me to be around him."

There. I said it. I admitted out loud what I've been actually feeling. Although it's not as freeing as I thought it would be.

"I don't know if it's smart for you to turn down a once-in-a-lifetime design because you're too scared about keeping your legs closed."

"Excuse me!" I gasp. "That's not it."

Well, not entirely.

"Then what is it? Because the in-control Maeve Banks I know wouldn't even be debating this topic. But apparently now that a new sex-ed up Maeve is here, and she's the one in the driver's seat."

Dammit, she's right. She's so right.

I'm letting one night dictate my future, when it doesn't have to be that way. I'm a grown woman. I can work with a man I've slept with. I can be aware that I need to make sure I keep boundaries with him and do the job he's paying me to do.

I can do that. I can absolutely fucking do that.

"You really know how to get through to me, you know that, right?"

"Of course I do," she says confidently. "Now it's time to suck it up, buttercup. This is the opportunity of a lifetime, and eventually you'll be pissed at yourself for turning it down because you let your vagina make the decisions. So put on the chastity belt, stock up on granny panties, and get a hold of the billionaire. You have a house to decorate."

———

To: Katherine Smith
From: Maeve Banks, Banks Interiors
Subject: Design Opportunity

Hi, Miss Smith. I'm sorry to disturb you after hours, but I wanted to reach back out to see if Mr. Matthews was still interested in having me decorate his Tennessee estate, as I have decided to inquire further about the job after some thought. If he's still interested, I'd be open to having another meeting to discuss particulars.
Thank you for your time. Hope to talk with you soon.

Maeve Banks
Banks Interiors

There, sent. Now I can sleep well, knowing the ball is back in his court and I can move on with my night.

But just as I'm ready to walk back into the living room to tell Jayce he's about an hour extended on his video game time for the day that was already overboard, my phone rings with an unknown number.

Now normally I wouldn't answer something like this. It's likely someone asking me about my car's extended warranty or if I want new windows, but for some reason my senses are tingling that I know who is on the other end of this line.

And I want to know how he got my personal cell number.

"Hello?"

"Hello, Maeve."

My body is immediately on edge. And I don't reflect on the fact that he used my actual name.

"How did you get this number, Logan?"

"In the video game business you pick up some miscellaneous computer skills along the way. Let's leave it at that."

Good to know my maybe-future client has hacking abilities. "I take it that Kat forwarded you my email in record time?"

"She did," he says matter-of-factly.

"And I'm taking it with the immediate phone call that you haven't hired anyone else to perform the job? Or is this your expedited way of saying thanks but no thanks?"

"There was no one else to hire," he says. "It's only you."

Oh fuck me…that hit me straight in the pussy.

No, Maeve. Boundaries! Safe guards! Don't let him flatter you with his accent and praise of your work!

"Okay, then." I swallow the frog in my throat that is suddenly making me sound like a nervous rookie. "If you'd like, I can come over tomorrow and we can discuss everything. Do a walk-through. Price points, vision, likes and dislikes, time table. If you have meetings or—"

"Tomorrow is perfect," he cuts me off. "Say nine? What would you like for breakfast? I can make sure–"

"No, Logan." I know I need to set parameters, and this is the perfect time to tell him that. "No breakfast. No having Kat get me Diet Coke because you happened to notice it's my go-to drink. And while I'm on the subject, no mention of our time spent together. As far as we're concerned, going forward, I'm the hired designer and you're my client. No looks or touches. No inside jokes. And without a doubt, no calling me Love. Are we clear?"

There. I said it. I laid the boundary, and he has to agree to it. And that's how Maeve Banks regains the upper hand.

"Wow. Okay. I was asking about breakfast, because that's about the time I eat and I figured you'd like some. Presumptuous of you to think that I was doing it because of our past."

Thank God he can't see me right now, because my cheeks are overly flushed with embarrassment. I'm really going to need to get a handle on that if I'm going to be seeing him every day.

"I'm only slightly kidding, Maeve. And you're right," he continues. Which actually shocks me. Not that I didn't think he'd agree to it, but I was expecting a little jab, or his knack for knowing how to soften me up. "This is a professional setting. You're here to do a job, and it would be a waste of your time, my time, and my money to distract you with anything other than the furnishing of the house. From this point on, we're just Maeve Banks and Logan Matthews. Designer and client."

"Designer and client," I repeat.

And ignore the pit in my stomach when the words leave my mouth.

13
logan

DESIGNER AND CLIENT, MY ASS.

I've laughed about that statement more than a few times since Maeve and I hung up the call last night. Designer and client only…that's just rich.

If Maeve really thinks I can suddenly turn a switch in my brain that makes me forget about the night we spent together, she doesn't realize how unforgettable she is.

Which I have a feeling she doesn't.

But on the other hand, she's right. This relationship is professional. And I'd be a right prick if I didn't respect that boundary. She's going to be here to do a job. A job that I'm going to be paying a lot of money for. And while normally a price tag like the one she's likely to show me is going to make me itch on the inside, I know it's going to be worth it. I'm going to get to see Maeve in her realm, creating a beautiful space. Kat will get off my back about having a grown-man dorm room for a home. I'll please all the women in my life and get a nice-looking home out of it.

That's what I call a win-win.

"Are you smiling like that because your girlfriend's coming over?"

I give Kat a side-eye as she comes into my office while wheeling what looks like a coffee cart. "She's not my girlfriend. She's my designer. I'm her client. That's it."

Wow. I think that sounded pretty good. I think I can make this professional thing work—even if deep down I'm hoping that us spending time together will allow her to slowly warm up to the possibility of us.

And not the possibility of one more night. I want more than that. I want all her nights.

"Oh, you're fucking down bad," Kat says, taking a seat across from me. "I've never seen you look like this."

"That's not true." It probably is, but I feel like I need to try and at least deny part of it. "What about that girl at university I went to a sorority formal with? The one you set me up with?"

Kat shakes her head in exasperation. "Do you even remember her name? How could you think she was a special person in your past if you can't even say her name when thinking about her?"

Shit, she's right. "I just remember we had a lovely time."

"Of course you did. You had sex in the limo."

"That's right," I say, unable to keep the grin off my face.

"Oh, Logan's manwhore phase. What a memorable time it was."

"I prefer cad."

"I don't care what we call it. I just don't want to ever go through it again. You were exhausting."

I'm sure I was, and poor Kat is the one who had to live through it.

Back in England, I wasn't exactly a catch at secondary school. I was the captain and founder of the inaugural e-Sports team, and the only reason girls talked to me was to do their math homework. Or to see if they could use me to get to my brother, Callum.

But at Stanford I was an unknown. I could shed the reputation I carried back home and could become my own man. A new version of myself. And while the video game geek never went away, I did manage to stumble one day into the gym of the student recreation center.

I was hooked from that day on. I gravitated to the challenge of lifting weights. I loved the feel of the burn when pushing my muscles to the brink. Before I knew it, my body was developing in ways I didn't know it could. And with that, I started getting attention from the girls I had never gotten before.

And like any other nineteen-year-old lad, I let it get to my head.

And my cock.

Yes, I maybe went a little hard, but in my mind, I was making up for lost time.

Oh, if the Logan from back then could meet the Logan now. That guy would've been champing at the bit to date models and celebrities. And laughing hysterically that I'd be willing to spend thousands of dollars just to be around a woman.

"I really do owe you for putting up with me all these years," I tell her.

"Don't worry. I figured that money into my contract nego-tiation."

I laugh. "Of course you did."

A buzzing sound comes through on the intercom system, notifying me that Maeve is at the gate. I mean, it could be someone else, but I'd have to tell them to bugger off.

"Thanks for stopping by, but you can leave now," I say to Kat, wanting a few minutes to compose myself before Maeve enters.

"That's not happening." Kat gets up and starts making herself a drink from the cart she rolled in. From the looks of it, there's hot and iced coffee, tea for me, and a few other options that I couldn't tell you what they are.

"What do you mean?"

She tops off her coffee with some sort of syrup before stirring it with a metal straw. "I told one of the workers to let her in so I can stay right here. We can't take the chance that she walks out again. We didn't think we were getting this second chance. So I'm staying right here to do potential damage control. Plus, if you had it your way, you'd have your bedroom designed in superhero sheets. I need to make sure that doesn't happen. Especially if you want Maeve to ever sleep in them."

"I'd never do that," I say, though I wonder if they make California King sized Batman sheets. "Now a movie room? That could be fun."

She rolls her eyes at me when a knock comes from the door of my office. I try to take a hidden breath from Kat—she already has enough ammunition against me—but it catches in my throat the second Maeve walks in.

How is she even more gorgeous? Her brown hair is down today and in long waves. Her makeup is subtle, making her blue eyes pop. And the outfit she's wearing? Bloody hell, I need to bite my lip to control myself. A fitted blouse that hugs her perfect tits. A pencil skirt that is so tight I don't know how it's not going to rip when she sits down. And the heels? I'd sell every share of every stock I have right now to feel those digging into my ass as I drive into her.

If this is how she's going to come to work every day, maybe making her an offer she couldn't refuse wasn't the smartest move for my sanity.

Or my cock.

"Holy tension, Batman," Kat whispers. "Hey! Jaw up. Remember to blink. And don't fuck this up."

"Shut it." Hopefully Maeve didn't hear my whisper-yell as I take a few steps toward her and extend my hand. "Good morning."

Her eyes rapidly blink a few times when she puts together that I didn't call her Love. And that I'm beginning this in the professional manner she suggested.

Designer and client…just like she asked. Little does she know I'm playing the long game here.

"Thank you again for coming over today. Coffee?"

"Yes, please," she says before noticing the coffee cart, which I'm now noticing has more options than Starbucks. "Wait. What is all this? Logan…"

I hold my hands up in defense. "I know you said nothing extravagant or nothing over the top. You may notice there isn't a breakfast buffet. But with the coffee, it's simply not my morning beverage of choice, and I didn't know what you liked, so we wanted to provide options."

Her face softens just enough to assure me I didn't go too far too quickly. Good thing she doesn't know I set up a recurring order of Diet Coke for her. "Thank you."

We stare at each other for a moment, a rush of electricity passing through us before Kat rudely interrupts us.

"Nice to meet you again. I know we formally met the other day, but please, call me Kat."

Maeve extends her hand. "Thank you for getting back and meeting with me on such short notice."

"Of course," Kat says as the two shake hands. "Thank you for reconsidering. And not punching this guy in the face for canceling six times. As his publicist, I don't know if I could have taken his side when I had to spin that to the tabloids."

This gets a laugh out of Maeve, but properly embarrasses the hell out of me. "It's no trouble at all. I'm glad we're able to finally get this going."

"We were, too," Kat points Maeve to one of the chairs in front of my desk. "And actually, you left the other day before I could see you again. This is for you."

Kat picks up the check we cut the other day for Maeve to make up for the cancellations. I study Maeve closely as she sees what it is. Her eyes nearly bounce out of her head before she trains her gaze on me.

"Really?"

I nod. "It should've been more. Please consider this just a token of an apology from me."

She continues staring at me for a few more beats, waiting to see if I'm going to say, or do, anything else.

But I'm not. She wanted business? Then business is what she's going to get.

"All right then," Kat says with a clap of her hands to break the tension. "Maeve, why don't you start us off."

"Thanks," she says as she grabs her bag and brings out a notebook. "Logan, I know you said I could have free rein. And while that's very nice of you, you're the one living here. I need to make sure every room is decorated with things you're comfortable with."

"I'm really not particular," I say. "I trust your instincts."

"You say that now, but just wait until I start showing you wallpaper samples."

"He's very serious," Kat says. "You should've seen our first apartment together when we were roommates. His room was—"

"Don't you have somewhere to be?" I ask pointedly. For one, I don't need a babysitter. I definitely don't need her wisecracks.

She shakes her head. "Nope. Morning is clear."

I narrow my eyes at her, but thankfully, Maeve continues on with the questions. "Okay, what rooms are we looking to have done?"

Shit, was I supposed to know that answer?

"Everything," Kat chimes in.

"No, not everything," I protest. "My video game studio is done."

"Why am I not surprised?"

Was that a joke from Maeve? It was quiet, like she was trying to keep it under her breath, but I do believe it was. And even if it was at my expense, I'll take it.

"I meant what I said, Maeve, you know more than I do. I'm clueless when it comes to this stuff. I'm sure if you really wanted me to give input on options, I could tell you I like one blue better than another, but if you know one will work, please, go for it. I've checked out your designs. You're brilliant. And I trust you.

Implicitly. I have a hard limit at pink walls, but other than that, this is your project. Wow me."

Our eyes lock, and I think if Kat weren't in the room with us, the tension between us might snap. As I keep looking at her, I have the feeling she's trying to gauge if I'm serious or not.

And I am. Serious as I've been about anything in my life.

I want Maeve's touch all over this house. I want to feel her presence in every room. Because if my plan of the long game doesn't work, and she's out of my life when this project is done, at least I'll know that a part of her is always here.

"Yes, please do whatever you need," Kat butts in again. "And also, I don't know if Logan has mentioned this yet, but we're throwing a big benefit Christmas party right before the holiday."

This takes Maeve's look away from me and turns it into a panicked one to Kat. "That's in like…very fast."

"Yes, I know it's tight," Kat says, her voice turning pleading. "And I know this is a huge ask on top of the already big one, but if you could have this mostly done by then, and decorated for the holidays, you'd literally save us. And I know we don't know each other well, but you seem like the kind of woman who makes the impossible possible."

I don't know if I'm seeing things, but I'd swear on my original copy of Frogger that Maeve just got a twinkle in her eye.

"I mean, it will be tight," she says. "And I don't want to make promises I can't keep—"

"That's all I need to hear!" Kat says with a relieved breath, just as her phone starts to ring. She takes a look at it, only to let out a frustrated sight. "Tight we can work with. Also there's no budget, despite what this guy says. Now, if you could excuse me, I have to take this."

Kat leaves the room before Maeve can say anything else.

"Apologies for her," I say. "She's a lot."

"No need." Maeve makes it a point to look down at her notebook, writing something down. Though I have to wonder if she's just avoiding my glance.

"Do you have any questions for me?"

My question does the trick of getting her eyes slowly meeting mine again. The second I see her beautiful blues I feel my body heating. Fuck me…I know I wanted Kat to leave, but I didn't realize her presence was keeping me from wanting to throw Maeve up on this desk and kiss the hell out of her. If this is how my body is going to react when we're alone together, I have a feeling I have a lot of cold showers ahead of me.

"Was she serious about no budget?" Maeve asks. "Because I can get it done in that time, but I do need to tell you it's not going to be cheap if you're going all out to impress."

"She is," I say, though I don't like it. "I meant what I said—this is all yours, Maeve Banks. Make it your masterpiece."

She looks at me again, a curiosity in her eyes. "You're serious, aren't you? You really don't care what I do?"

I shake my head. "I don't. Though I do have one more request."

"I figured I wasn't that easy. What is it? Gray walls? Black leather couches?"

"Absolutely not," I say, taking a step closer to her. I know I should stay back, but I'm alone with the woman I can't get out of my system, and I might be biding my time, but I also need to steal the moments when I can. "Actually the opposite."

"The opposite?"

"That's right: Nothing cliché. You know I hate being cliché."

And there it is. The smile. The reddened cheeks. The Maeve I know.

"I think I can manage that."

"I know you can. Now dazzle me, Maeve Banks. Show me what you got."

guide to love rule #14

A man who is good with children is instantly hotter.
Those are just the rules.

14

maeve

"I told you Maeve, I don't care about the color of towels. Just pick what you like."

I let out a frustrated groan, because how can I keep having the same conversation with a person over and over? And I say this as a mom of a six-year-old who was once a very inquisitive three-year-old.

"For the hundredth time today, Logan, and like for every other thing we have picked out, it doesn't matter to me. I like both, hence why I picked them. That's why the final decision comes to you. You know, the man who will be using the bathroom every day."

He gives the two samples a quick glance before turning his attention back to his computer, where it looks like he's playing a video game. Because of course he is.

"Black or white? Isn't that a little cliché?"

I shoot him a look. I know what he's doing with that word. But I'm not falling for it.

"There's a difference between cliché and classic. In this case, black and white fall under the classic category. So please, for the love of God, just pick."

"Maeve, I really don't care."

"You have to care."

"Says who?"

Can this man be any more infuriating?

Or any more good looking?

I hate that I still can't get over the second one.

"Me. *I* say you have to. And the quicker you answer my questions, the quicker you can go back to your video games that are clearly more important than this."

He turns his eyes to me, a little softer this time before looking at both samples. "Fine. The black. And I'm not playing a video game, I'm designing one."

"Apologies, I didn't know you were working." And I mean that. Now I feel slightly bad. "And I promise you can get back to it that much faster if you just help me with three more things. Then I'll be out of your hair and I can order all of these before everything's shut down for Thanksgiving."

I know Logan is frustrated, but in my defense, he's not making it easy on himself. I've taken the last few days to narrow down the order of spaces I need to tackle, what I need for these projects, and how many days each of them will take to complete. There's a small list of things that can wait until after—rooms no one will be going in—but the perfectionist in me would love to have it all done before Christmas. Then I can start the new year without the presence of Logan in my life.

But for that to happen, I needed one day of his attention. Hell, I needed two hours. He was prepared for this. I emailed him that I was stopping in this morning and that today was the day he was spending money.

It's also the day I'm seeing if I indeed have an unlimited budget.

I've had clients in the past tell me to spend what I needed to, but in reality, they didn't mean it. They'd either put a stop to a purchase or tell me that I could buy the expensive item, but to watch the budget in other areas.

But not Logan. I told him I was buying a hideous twenty-five-thousand-dollar chandelier. I never would've done such a thing, but this was the ultimate test of whether he trusted my instincts.

He told me to buy it. Said that I must have a vision and to do what I needed to do.

My jaw was on the floor.

He'll find out I didn't buy the chandelier at a later date. But he passed the test, which is good. The favors I'm calling in to distributors, in addition to purchasing on-the-fly, high-end furniture and decor, is costing a pretty penny.

"Only three more items?" Logan asks. "But I'm having so much fun."

I lift an eyebrow. "Sarcasm doesn't hit the same with a British accent."

This makes him laugh. "You're right. It's something in the inflection that doesn't make it as effective. Also, in my defense, I don't think I learned true sarcasm until I met Kat."

"Really?" I ask as I show him two tile samples and he points to the one I liked most. "When did you two meet?"

"University. We met at orientation."

I wasn't expecting that. "Did she go abroad for college?"

He shakes his head. "The opposite. I came here. Stanford specifically."

"Wow." I never would've guessed that. "Can I ask why? I mean, people would kill to have Oxford or Cambridge essentially in their backyards."

His jaw clenches at my question.

"I'm sorry. We don't have to talk about it if you don't want to. Actually, we should move on to carpet samples for the bedrooms."

"It's okay," he says. "Let's just say I wanted out of my situation and wanted to go the farthest I could. California seemed like a good choice."

I can tell he's done with that part of the conversation, but the part of me who wants to know everything in order to fix everything is dying to know the rest at some point. "Well, you picked correctly. You can't argue with the results of your life after college."

His shoulders relax just slightly with the shift of topic. "You're right. And I actually owe it all to Kat. She believed in me. She convinced me to keep developing SpaceCraft. And she helped me in the early days of the company. I wouldn't be here without her."

A sudden, unexpected—and unwanted—twinge of jealousy runs through me. Am I...jealous of Kat? No. Can't be.

I don't think they're together. He said she was his best friend. And he's way too nonchalant about me being around considering our brief history. But were they ever? Does he want to be? Does she?

Wait, why do I care? I'm the designer. He's the client. Who he did, does, or will date is none of my business.

"Everything okay over there Maeve?"

Shit. Am I busted? I try to gauge the temperature of my cheeks, and I don't think they're red. "What? Yes. Fine. Why do you ask?"

Just in case they are, I start to dig through my bag to find carpet samples that I know are on the top. Anything to not make eye contact with him.

"In case you wondered, Kat and I aren't together. We've never been together. Will never be together. She's my best friend and my publicist, and as I get settled in Nashville, my assistant. But she's not my type, and I'm definitely not hers."

"Great," I say, trying to sound disinterested about the words that are internally setting me at ease.

Even though—how could she not be his type? Hell, if she asked me out I might say yes, and I never even went through a college curiosity phase. She's gorgeous, with jet black hair and a perfectly curvy body. She looks like a fifties pin-up girl. Or one of those models I saw him photographed with in my recent Google searches that I made Stella do for me because I couldn't bring myself to do it.

"I must ask, and not that I care, but maybe just curious, how is she *not* your type? Didn't I see an article with you on the arm of a woman who looks nearly identical to her?"

This makes him laugh. "Maeve Banks, I didn't pin you for a gossip rag kind of woman."

"I'm not," I groan, hating that my curiosity is getting the best of me. "But my sister Stella is. She maybe, one time, recently, showed me an article featuring you and your…"

Girlfriends? Hookups? How do you say this tactfully to a man who's your client, who was once your one-nighter, who you can't stop thinking about naked, even though you've specifically instructed your brain to cease and desist?

"Setups," Logan says directly. "Those were setups. Nothing more, nothing less."

I think there is something more, but I don't press. "Okay, then. Anyway, back to carpet samples."

I go to show him two, but Logan puts his hands over the top of mine, covering the two pieces of carpet.

"Maeve." The way he says my name feels different, as if he's pleading with me to hear words he's not saying. "I know I'm in the media a lot. But please, don't believe what you read or see. There's a lot more to the story."

Logan lets go of my hands and sits back in his chair, but I don't think I move.

There's more to his story. I know there is. And I want to know. I want to help. I want to fix whatever he's going through, because it's clearly something.

But because that's what I do. No other reason.

None whatsoever.

―――

"Mommy. This is the biggest house I've ever seen!"

I chuckle at Jayce's reaction as we pull up to Logan's mansion. "I know, buddy. Remember what I said about when we go in?"

"To not wander off because I might get lost."

"Very good. What did you bring to keep yourself busy while Mommy works?"

He holds up his handheld video game controller. "My Space-Craft game."

Of course he did…

"Sounds like fun," I choke out as I put the car in park. There isn't a lot going on here today since it's the day before Thanksgiving, which is also why Jayce is with me. Today began Thanksgiving break, and he doesn't go to his dad's until tomorrow morning. Normally I wouldn't work today, but because of the crazy time table I'm on, I needed to do a walk-through with the painters, carpet installation crew, and the assistants on my team that I'm bringing in to get the job done in time. Hence why today is unofficial Take Your Son to Work Day.

Shit, should I have asked Logan if it was okay for me to bring Jayce? Surely he won't mind, right? It honestly didn't occur to me to ask. I've had to take Jayce to jobs before, but normally clients aren't living in the spaces yet. Then again, Logan designs games for kids, so he can't hate them, right?

Right?

"Mommy, are we going inside?"

"Oh! Yes! Sure! Yup." I ungracefully undo my seatbelt, grab my bag and get out of the car to let Jayce out of his booster seat. With our bags in hand, we walk up to the front door, which is opened by Kat before we can step in.

"Good morning. And oh wow! Who do we have here?"

She steps out of the way so we can come in from the chilly Tennessee almost-winter day. "This is my son, Jayce. Jayce, can you say hi to Miss Kat?"

Jayce buries himself into my leg, being the shy one he is.

"I'm sorry. He's a bit shy at first. But once he gets to know you, be ready for him to talk your ear off."

"No worries," Kat says. "I don't like strangers either. Or most people for that matter."

"Don't let her lie to you. Kat is the friendliest person I've ever met."

My body warms when I hear Logan's voice coming down the hallway. When I get my first glimpse of him, my jaw slightly drops.

Is he wearing a Batman T-shirt? Also known as the one thing in the world—besides anything to do with SpaceCraft—that will instantly make Jayce fall in love with him. Did I tell him I was bringing Jayce and I forgot about it? Or does Logan Matthews really have the oddest use of psychic powers known to man?

"Who do we have here?" Logan says as I shake off the vision of him in a Batman suit. "I'm Logan. What's your name, little man?"

The feeling in my stomach that's currently making me uncomfortable is not just my ovaries exploding, but the sight of Logan kneeling down to talk to Jayce at eye level.

"Jayce." His sweet voice is so quiet it's barely above a whisper.

"Well hello, Jayce. Are you coming to hang out with me, your mum, and Kat today?"

He nods, but doesn't say anything else.

"Well, that's great! But I have a few questions for you."

Jayce looks up at me for reassurance, and I give him the nod. I don't know what Logan is about to ask, but I'm not worried in the slightest. Any worry I had about this man objecting to bringing my son today went out the window when he beelined to Jayce instead of talking to the adults.

"First, do you like cinnamon rolls?"

I have to stifle a laugh. Jayce is simply answering with a vigorous head nod, however, the adult answer would be "Does a bear shit in the woods?"

"Great!" Logan claps. "Now, and this one is a long shot, but do you happen to like SpaceCraft?"

"Yes!" Jayce says with more enthusiasm than he ever has, while also showing him his handheld. "I brought it with me today!"

"Wow! That's awesome. So, how would you like to sneak into the kitchen with me, get a cinnamon roll that we're having for breakfast today, and then we can play SpaceCraft on a massively big screen!"

Jayce's eyes have never been so big. "Mommy? Can I?"

"Of course you can," I say. "But stay with Logan."

"I will!" he yells as he takes off without Logan or me then stops and turns his head expectantly. Kat laughs and follows behind, turning Jayce in the right direction, leaving Logan and I standing alone in the foyer.

I feel the tension between us immediately. It's an instant sensation any time we're alone. Will it ever go away? I know it's only been a few days, but I was hoping to start the desensitizing process by now.

"You didn't have to do that."

He shakes his head. "I know. I wanted to."

Such a simple answer. But sometimes that's all you need.

"Well, thank you. You're going to make his day."

He shrugs, like what he's doing isn't making my son's entire year. "It's my pleasure. Now, you go do your boring work with painters. I'm going to go play video games and eat cinnamon rolls."

The smile on my face is instant. "Thank you, Logan."

"Anytime, Love."

If he catches what he says, he doesn't react to it as he walks toward the kitchen.

And I don't correct him. Because part of me missed him calling me that.

But just part of me. Because he's just a client.

That's all he can be…

guide to love rule #122

Exes ain't shit. That's it. That's the rule.

15

maeve

I've never once regretted divorcing Josh. We weren't right for each other, and frankly, neither of us really wanted to get married; we just did it because we thought it was the right thing to do for Jayce.

That being said, every time I spend a holiday without Jayce, I hate that Josh and I weren't right for each other. Because spending a holiday without your kiddo just fucking sucks.

Over the years, we've done a good job of making sure that neither one of us always gets the short end. We rotate Thanksgiving and Christmas each year, and because my son has an odd fascination with Easter, we decided to give him two of those. We figured it's a different day each year, why not make two and give Jayce his favorite holiday twice.

It's all about the Reese's Eggs for that kid.

But this year is hitting me harder than before. I don't know if there's an exact reason why—if I was held under an interrogation lamp I'd probably say it's a combination of a lot of things—but I do know that with each mile I get closer to Josh's house, the more I hate that I'm about to spend the day without my son.

"Did you pack everything you need?" I ask. I always make sure to take care of any clothes he could need. And Josh has plenty at his house. But when it comes to toys, video games, and any other thing my child is fixating on this week, he's the only one allowed to gather those items.

Except when he forgets them. Then I have to bring them to him.

"Yup!" he exclaims. "I have my blanket. And my video game. And my new action figure that Logan gave me. I can't wait to show Daddy!"

The action figure he speaks of is a new acquisition as of yesterday—fresh from the *extensive* collection of one Logan Matthews. Having shopped for plenty of SpaceCraft toys over the years, it didn't look familiar. That's when I realized that it's not familiar because it's not sold in stores. This is a one-of-a-kind toy. And Logan gave it to my son, who insisted on sleeping with it last night.

Not now, ovaries…chill the fuck out.

I turn into Josh's driveway and notice that there's a new car parked outside the garage. I roll my eyes at the Mini Cooper, which I'm going out on a limb to say is Vivian's.

Also, I didn't realize people still drove those? Especially in mint green…

Trying not to pay attention to it, or do the math of how much that likely cost my ex-husband, I get out of the car and grab Jayce's things while he struggles to get out of his seatbelt because he refuses to let go of his new toy. Eventually he makes it out and we make our way to Josh's front door.

"Happy Thanksgiving!" Josh says as he opens the door. "It's cold, everyone come in."

Really? He wants me to come in? That's not normally how these drop-offs go. Usually it's hey, how are you, bye.

"Daddy! Look!"

Jayce doesn't even have his jacket or boots off yet before making sure he shows Josh his new action figure. "Wow! When did you get that?"

"Yesterday! Isn't it so cool! I thought I had every toy from SpaceCraft, but this is new and I love it so much!"

"It is cool. Where'd you get it?"

"Logan gave it to me!"

Josh's questioning glance turns to me. "Who's Logan?"

Uh....

"Jayce, how about you go put your bag and things in your room?"

"Okay, Mommy!"

Without question, Jayce does as I ask, because bless my son's heart, he's oblivious to everything.

"Logan, huh? I seem to remember you giving me shit about Vivian when we started dating. And now you have a Logan I don't know about? Funny how that comes around."

I shake my head. "I don't *have* a Logan. He's a client. I had to take Jayce with me yesterday to his house that I'm currently decorating and they were playing SpaceCraft together. I didn't even know he gave it to him until we were leaving."

There. The truth. He doesn't need to know exactly who my newest client is.

"Clients are just giving our kid toys now?"

"Why do you care? They hit it off," I defend. "But enough about the toy. Why did you invite me in? I thought we had the weekend figured out?"

As if on cue, Vivian walks into the living room from the kitchen, doing her best impression of the perfect little housewife, apron and all. "Hi, Maeve."

"Vivian," I say evenly as I sit down on one of the chairs. Josh and Vivian sit across from me, and all of a sudden I feel like I'm part of some sort of intervention.

"Maeve," Josh begins. "The reason we wanted to talk—"

"Holy shit!"

I'm not even sorry I interrupted him with my outburst. It couldn't wait. Because on Vivian's hand is an obnoxiously big diamond, and another band underneath it.

And now that I actually look at Josh, I see a gold band on his hand as well.

"That's what we wanted to talk to you about." Josh and Vivian join hands. "We got married."

"You did *what*?" Not that I care. I don't. My outburst isn't because I'm still pining for my ex-husband. But when said ex gets remarried, I think the mother of his child is entitled to know *before* it happens. "When? Why? I'm very confused, because unless this happened yesterday, I feel like I should've been told."

"I know it's sudden," Josh says before looking to his...wife? "But when you know, you know."

No. You don't. Josh and I are case in point. But I'm not getting into that debate right now. "Okay, when? Did you guys elope?"

Vivian nods. "Last week, we were lying in bed, and Josh said that he wished we could do this for the rest of our lives. I said I'd love nothing more. Next thing I knew we were picking out rings and making our way to the courthouse!"

"Congratulations?" I say, mustering up as much excitement as I can. Something feels off about it, but then again, it could just be the shock. "So is this trip..."

"A honeymoon of sorts," Vivian says. "And we couldn't imagine doing it without Jayce."

Interesting. I didn't think she even liked my kid, which is based on the fact that she's rarely around when he's here, according to Jayce.

"This is...well, it's a lot to process," I say. "Does Jayce know?"

They shake their heads. "No. We wanted to tell him today."

"Okay, then..." I don't know what else to say, so I stand up. "Do you need me to bring anything extra for the trip?"

Josh shakes his head as he and Vivian stand up, hand in hand. "We have everything. Thanks, Maeve. This means a lot to us."

"You're welcome."

That's all I can muster to say. I need to get out of here. My head is spinning, and I feel off my axis.

"Jayce! I'm taking off!" I call out. My baby comes running out of his room—action figure in hand—as he crashes into my arms for a hug.

"Bye, Mommy!"

"I love you," I say, hugging him tighter. "If you need anything, or if you want to talk about anything, please call me, okay?"

"Okay," he says, still oblivious to the tension in the air.

I start to walk out before Josh stops me. "He won't need to call you. I can handle this."

"I'm sure you can," I say. "But that's a big change, and kids don't always handle change great."

"I know my kid, Maeve."

"I'm not saying you don't. Just…be gentle."

"I will," he says. "See you tomorrow."

I look over to Jayce one more time, who's sitting in front of Vivian playing with his toy and her not paying one bit of attention to him because she's pecking away at her phone. I straighten my shoulders and walk out the door.

As soon as I get to my car and crank it up I head for home, forcing myself not to peel out of Josh's driveway.

Holy shit…he's married? Like, what the hell? I don't know what to think. I'm baffled and confused and need something to focus on so I don't drive myself crazy.

I look at the clock and see that it's just about one o'clock. My family is doing our formal Thanksgiving dinner tomorrow, but for those of us who didn't have plans, my mom is hosting dinner at six. But I know I can't sit and stew at my house for the next five hours.

Which is how I end up pulling onto the freeway and driving south. Logan might not be the person I want to see today, with my mind going in all different directions, but working on his house might be just the trick.

———

"Maeve? What are you doing here?"

When I got the idea to come and work on Logan's house, it was simply to keep my mind focused on something other than the fact my son now has a stepmother who can't spell stepmother. I never thought I should call and announce myself. I have a gate code now to let myself in, and I have keys.

Except the keys he gave me are at my house, which I haven't returned to. Which is why I needed to knock. And because Kat or one of the other members of the building crew have let me in every time I'm here, I never thought he'd be the one opening the door. Which is why I wasn't prepared to be greeted by a shirtless Logan who's wearing criminally low sweatpants.

Holy fuck that V….

"Hi," I say, though I almost choke on the word. "I was…I thought I could come over and do some work."

"Isn't today a holiday?"

"It is. But I don't have anything going on until this evening. And even that isn't a formal thing. My family is doing Thanksgiving tomorrow, so I thought I could get some things done around here. That is, if it's okay. I'm sorry. I should've called. It's just that I've had a weird day, and I could use the distraction…"

I realize I'm rambling, which is a very not-like-me thing to do. I also notice Logan is smiling, which is never a good thing.

"Can I come in?" I ask. "It's cold, and those curtains aren't going to hang themselves. Unless you're busy and you don't want me around, then I can absolutely leave."

"Come in," he says, stepping out of the way so I can walk past. I try not to breathe in his woodsy body wash when I walk past him, but to no avail. "And you can work, but you need to promise me something first."

I turn back to him as I slip off my jacket. "What's that?"

"That you let me help you hang the curtains. And then after you're done, you let me treat you to lunch."

I shake my head. "You don't need to do either of those things. One, buying me lunch is not in our contract. And I'm perfectly cap—"

He holds his finger to my lip, which not only makes me stop talking, it makes me stop breathing.

"Those are the conditions. Take it or leave it, Love."

There it is again. The name. The name I should scold him for using.

Emphasis on should.

Why can't I? What kind of voodoo power does this man have over me? I'm going to blame my lack of response on the whirlwind of the day.

Yes. That's why.

"Okay. But I'm only letting you hold the ladder and hand me things," I say. "You're my assistant, understand?"

He gives me a mock salute. "Yes, ma'am. At your service."

16
logan

I like to think that I'm a self-aware person.

I've always been quick to realize when something is not for me. It's why I was quick to drop sports as a child and left the athletic endeavors to my brother. It's why I knew after two piano lessons that I was not going to have a future with performance. And it's why within twenty minutes of being Maeve's assistant, I realized I'm no help to her.

It started when she yelled at me for handing her the wrong size drill bit. It continued when I audibly gasped when she climbed an exceptionally tall ladder and I thought she was going to fall. Turns out the gasp scared her more than the height. The last straw was when she busted me staring at her ass instead of handing her the curtain rod. She told me to get out of her way and just let her handle things.

Maeve, mad? Rather scary. And rather sexy.

I could watch her all day. Even now, as I'm standing in the doorway, leaning against the frame, holding our Chinese takeout lunch, I don't want to move. I just want to watch her make magic.

She's so different today. For starters, this is the first day I've seen her in regular clothing. She's always looked like she was ready to jump into a business meeting with her power suits, or even her blazers and nicer blue jeans. Whether it was at the airport, or even this week when she and her crew were starting to work, she was polished and put together. Today's look is casual—a cutoff sweatshirt and leggings that are hugging her perfect ass. Her hair is in a messy knot on the top of her head and she barely has on any makeup.

She's even more beautiful than usual.

Or maybe today's different because her look is paired with her focus on the project at hand. There's a glint in her eye when she gets an idea. I noticed that her nose crinkles when she's concentrating. Every part of her process is fascinating to watch. And I hate that I only have a few weeks of this in my home, because I could watch her forever.

Take now, for instance. Since I left to go meet the delivery driver—to whom I paid an absurd amount of money for delivery on Thanksgiving—she has turned on the music. She's dancing to a hip hop song about shaking your ass that my generation would call old school, but I'm pretty sure if I said that to Maeve she'd pull my insides outside. For a woman who's as tightly wound as she is, I must say, I'm impressed with her moves. Her hips are swaying to the beat as she looks for something in her tool box. And it's taking every part of me to not drop our lunches, walk over, wrap my arms around her hips and start dancing in the middle of the room.

I won't, because I know it will freak her out. I've slipped a few times and called her Love, and she hasn't corrected me. But I know I can't press my luck too much.

So I won't go dance with her. I won't pull her against me so I can feel what I felt that night all over again.

Even if it hurts not to.

Just as the show is getting good, Maeve's moves have her spinning in a circle, and she nearly falls over herself when she spots me in the doorway.

"What the fuck, Logan!" she screams, hand over her heart. "How long have you been there?"

I push away from the door and walk into the room. "Long enough to see that you held back on me that night we danced."

She narrows her eyes, trying intimidate me. Unfortunately, it's not working. "It's rude to stare. And to bring up nights that were previously agreed upon to never be talked about again."

"Apologies, *Maeve.*"

"Thank you," she says as she turns off the music. "What do we have here?"

I hold up the bags. "I promised lunch."

"You ordered for me?"

"I did," I say, putting the bags of Chinese food down on the table as I find a sheet that isn't too dusty and lay it out on the floor. "I didn't know what you liked and didn't want to interrupt, but it's Chinese food, which means the rule is to order some of everything."

"That's the rule?"

"Of course it is," I say as I gesture for her to sit at the makeshift picnic. "Now sit. I might be a shit assistant, but I can be a proper waiter."

She does as I ask while I make a big show of presenting the cartons of noodles, rice, chicken, and dumplings.

"And of course, a Diet Coke to go with it," I say dramatically, bowing as I hand over the can to her.

"What service," she says, a hint of a smile coming out. "But Logan, you really didn't have to do this."

"I did," I say, putting out the last of the containers. "Food is necessary. And you working overtime on a holiday should be compensated in some fashion. Why not with food?"

I see the blush creep over her cheeks. And I realize at this moment I'll never tire of putting that color there.

"Thank you," she says, grabbing a lo mein box. "I haven't had Chinese in forever. Jayce doesn't like it, and somehow I always forget to order it on nights when he's with his dad."

"Neither have I," I say, deciding to start off my meal with steamed dumplings. "It used to be a staple for Kat and I."

"It's amazing you two have developed a friendship that's lasted so long," Maeve said. "I barely talk to my college friends."

"Really? Are they not around?"

She shakes her head as she reaches for the General Tso's. "We all have our lives going on. Marriages. Kids. Divorces. Businesses. We try to get together once a year, those of us that are still relatively local, for dinner. But I think it's been at least three years since that's happened."

"I don't think Kat and I have ever gone three days without speaking to each other," I joke. "Then again, it's just us. We had a group of friends at Stanford. She was in a sorority. I had my gamer buddies. But even with that, it was always the two of us."

"That I can understand," she says. "Then again, I always had my sisters, and they're the best friends I could ask for."

"How many sisters are there?"

Maeve's smiles are few and far between. But I don't know if in our time together I've seen one as genuine as the one she's giving me now. "Three sisters and one brother."

"Let me guess," I say. "Oldest?"

This gets me a laugh. "Oldest daughter. Though I might as well be the oldest of them all. It's my brother Simon, technically, but in terms of who is the family organizer and de facto leader, that's me."

"That must be the dynamic of a large family," I add. "I don't know if my brother or I qualify as the leader of the two."

"You have a brother?"

I nod. "I do. Two years younger."

"Is he in the States too?"

Now it's my turn to laugh. "You really don't pay attention to the gossip column, do you?"

Her eyes grow wide. "Are you telling me your brother is famous too? How many billionaires are in your family?"

"He's not a billionaire, but he does well." I pull out my

phone, bringing up the latest article about Callum Matthews. "Just a professional rugby player."

Maeve's eyes look at the article, then to me, then back to my mobile. "So you're telling me, in one family, came one of the best rugby players in the world and a man who changed video games forever? You must have the proudest parents on the planet."

I know she didn't intend to, but that statement was a stab in the chest.

It's been a long time since someone has mentioned my parents—Kat knows better since we both come from shitty childhoods and never want to talk about it—so I haven't had to hide my face in a while. And judging by Maeve's wide eyes, she realizes she's hit a nerve.

"Oh, Logan. Did I overstep? I'm sorry. I didn't mean—"

I shake my head. "It's not your fault. Most people hear generic questions about their parents without flinching."

"I didn't mean to stir anything up," she says. "And if it was in any article about you or your brother, I promise I didn't read it to know."

"No one knows," I say, putting down my container of food. "Every interview my brother and I give, we always say that we had a normal, average childhood. That seems to satisfy reporters, so they don't dig."

"I'm guessing it was anything but?"

I look up to Maeve, who has also put down whatever entree she was eating. Can I tell her about my parents? I want to. And I know she signed an NDA to work here, but even without that, I feel as if I can trust her. I want her to know about me, including the bad stuff. And there's something about this moment, sitting in the space that will one day be my bedroom, that feels like I can.

Maybe it's because I'm delusional and hope that one day Maeve will share this room with me. Maybe it's because she's the only woman I've ever met who hasn't given two shits about my money. The woman who didn't know me from Adam.

The woman I first met as just Logan.

"We shouldn't have been poor, but we were," I begin. "It's where I get my penny-pinching tendencies from."

"Shouldn't have been?"

"Dad was a drinker. Most nights he'd leave for the pub and not come back for hours. Hell, sometimes he'd be gone for days."

"Oh, Logan…"

"He was what Americans call a blue-collar guy. Worked in a factory. Made a decent living, but we never saw any of that money because it was just going to the pubs. When he was home, he was usually angry at Mum for not being there to cater to him. She then screamed back, because to make up for his habit, she was working two jobs to keep a roof over our heads and food on the table." I feel the anger starting to brew as I think back to that time. "If I close my eyes, I can still hear them now. Fights over money. Over food. But neither would leave the other. The phrase wasn't used then, but they were the definition of a toxic relationship."

I close my eyes as I try to put myself back in that time when I feel a hand on my leg. I slowly open them to see Maeve's manicured fingers resting there, giving me comfort I didn't ask for, but now know I desperately need.

"I'm so sorry you had to grow up like that," Maeve says. "I can't fathom having that for a childhood."

"That's why Callum and I found hobbies that kept us away from the arguing. My brother was always athletic, and putting all of his efforts into rugby kept him out of the house."

"And you found video games?"

"That's my origin story," I say. "I saved up money from odd jobs around the neighborhood to buy my first gaming system, along with a pair of headphones, when I was ten."

"Smart investment."

"It was. I dove into worlds that took me away from the one I lived in. It was my escape."

"The calm amongst the chaos."

A moment passes through us as that phrase hangs in the air. The night I met Maeve wasn't the first time I've used that statement. It started when I was around eight. My parents were having an exceptional fight. Callum and I were both home. Nothing we did could block us from hearing their screams. So we did what any young lads would do—we hid in the closet.

We found calm in the chaos. It was the first time, and it surely wasn't our last.

"Video games were my calm. My only joy. And it turns out, I was pretty good. At the time, some secondary schools in the country were starting e-Sports leagues. I was at the right place at the right time."

I smile instantly while recalling the memory. I think it was the only time in my teenage years I was truly happy. I was doing what I loved. I found friends. I had a place to go outside of my home and away from the fighting.

"That's amazing. I bet your school loves saying that the creator of SpaceCraft once walked the halls."

I laugh, but there's a bitter tone to it. "They're proud. Yes. The donations I send also help."

Maeve senses my change of tone. "Why do I feel like there was a 'but' in there?"

She does know me well. "The school was, and is, proud. My brother is proud and tells everyone he can that I'm the best gamer to ever come out of England. But my parents? They didn't agree on much, but me focusing all of my energy on video games, in their opinion, was a giant waste of time. It didn't matter that I always received top marks in school, or about to be the first champion in school history for anything, all they saw was that I was playing video games and wasting my life."

"Seriously?" Maeve asks. "I mean, okay, back then I can see where they might have a slight trepidation at first because it was new. But even after doing so well, they still didn't get it?"

I shake my head. "Not in the slightest."

"I'm sorry, Logan, but fuck them," Maeve says. "Clearly you made the right choice. But after all these years, now they have to get it. Right? Please tell me that they shout your accomplishments from the rooftops."

I can't keep the humorless laugh inside. "I wouldn't know, but I doubt it."

That throws her. "Wait, is there more?"

I nod, needing a moment to catch myself before I go on. I feel Maeve's hand move, but it's only so she can take mine in hers.

"Take your time, Logan. I'm not going anywhere."

When I look over to her, all I want to do is bring her into my arms. I know she's talking about not going anywhere now, but I don't want her to go anywhere. Ever.

"It just escalated, and it never stopped. Mum started drinking. Dad was drinking more. Callum and I are fairly certain that both were having affairs. It was just a horrible environment to grow up in. And no matter what Callum and I did, no matter the grades we got or the championships we won or the accolades that came from our teachers and coaches, nothing we did could make them stop fighting."

"I hate that for you. And also, please tell me you know now it's not a child's responsibility to fix their parents."

"I do now," I say. "Though Kat often tells me that's why I'm a people pleaser. My therapist concurs."

She shrugs. "My therapist talks to me often about my control issues and my need to want to fix everything. Which, I should have you know, the fact that I can't fly to England right now and smack both of your parents and tell them to get their shit together, is making me very twitchy."

"I appreciate it," I say. "But it's in the past. Callum and I, wanting nothing to do with the family we came from, both changed our names the day he turned eighteen. We wanted to stay a unit, but separate from them."

"I think that's admirable," Maeve says. "And a good way for a new beginning."

"That was our thought," I say. "They made their choices. We made ours."

"Wow," Maeve says. "That's really brave, Logan."

"Thanks. Though I wonder sometimes where that brave guy went. The one who started over. Who started a company from nowhere. Because I haven't seen him in a while."

Where did that come from? The story was over. I could've switched the conversation back to Maeve and whatever she wanted to talk about. But no, apparently me being vulnerable for the first time in years is opening a floodgate.

"What do you mean?"

Luckily, my word vomit doesn't seem to scare her away. "I know you don't read magazines, but I have a feeling from a few conversations we've had that you know about the different women I've been seen with."

Maeve's cheeks blush as she nods. "My sister has shown me."

"It's okay. If we didn't want people to see me with them, I wouldn't have done it."

She wasn't expecting that answer. "What do you mean?"

I let out a sigh. "Every woman you have seen me pictured with, or rumored to be dating, or anything of the sort, over the past six months, is nothing more than a fabrication. They were fake dates and relationships."

Maeve shakes her head, but not in a way that I feel ashamed. In fact, I think she's laughing a bit? "I don't know whether or not I want to tell my sister that she was right. She clocked them as fake immediately."

"She's good, then, because not one person calls us out on it. Which is strange. People had to have known. I was having a horrible time, and no one can fake being happy when you're out with women you have nothing in common with."

"I gave up dating," Maeve says. "And that was part of the reason. I didn't have time, and I'm not about to waste what little time I do have pretending to have fun."

"Exactly," I say. "Now, when you're with someone who intrigues you? That's a smile you can't wipe off your face."

I let the statement hang there for a second before I continue, hoping Maeve gets my meaning. If she does, she doesn't say anything about it before asking her next question.

"Can I ask why? You're a billionaire. You've created a game that's a worldwide sensation. What was the need for it?"

Telling her this might be harder than telling her about my parents.

"In a simple word—distraction. We were actively creating smoke in mirrors."

"I'm now even more confused."

I suck in a breath before telling her about the last six months. The reasons behind the fake dates, about my creative slump, and the pressure from my board of directors. How me being in the news kept the stock prices up.

I cringe with every detail I tell her. Is she going to judge me? Look at me differently? The more I talk, the more I look for some sort of tell on her face that she thinks less of me. Luckily though, Maeve's face doesn't seem judgmental at all. Or appalled. She actually looks intrigued and a bit concerned. I'll take those looks any day over one of pity.

"Wow," she says. "I feel like that's a lot of work just to create a smokescreen."

"It was," I say. "I'm done with it, though. I'm determined to come up with a game, or at minimum the concept of one, by next week. I want to be able to flesh it out and have something big to announce by the Christmas party."

"You can do it," she says. "And as my way of helping, I'll stay away this weekend. I was going to come over and work on some things—Jayce is going out of town with his dad and his new wife—but the last thing you need is me hammering nails into walls."

Whoa, what did she just say? "I didn't realize your ex was getting remarried."

"Neither did I," she says, reaching back over and grabbing a crab rangoon. "They told me this morning when I dropped him off for Thanksgiving. That's why I came here. I didn't know where else to go, and I needed to keep busy. I couldn't just sit around and stew."

"Bloody hell, Maeve," I say. "That's a fucking bomb."

She nods. "I know. But what can I do? I can't control who he dates, or apparently marries, even though I wish I could for Jayce's sake. And I can't control that they did it seemingly on a whim, or that I'm unsure if she's spent more than a few days over the past two years with Jayce. All I can do is sit back and pretend I'm not going crazy on the inside."

"I believe in you," I say. "And consider this your open invitation to come over and work whenever you need to."

"I appreciate that." She pauses for a second, and frankly, I have no idea what she's going to say next. "And Logan? Please know that even if your family doesn't say they're proud of you, know that people are. That...I am."

Her words hit me square in the chest. I've sought validation from many people in my life—starting with my parents—and I'm not sure if that void has ever been filled.

But those words coming from Maeve? My cup runneth over...

I want to kiss her. I want to kiss her so fucking bad. Bring her into my arms. Hold her close.

But this isn't the right time. I don't know when that will be, but I know it isn't after I dump my trauma on her and she vents about her ex to me.

Even though I want to feel her lips on mine more than I want to bloody breathe.

Luckily, I don't have to make that decision as the sound of her mobile ringing across the room breaks our trance.

"I should get that," she whispers.

I lower my head as she stands up and walks across the room.

"I've got to go," she says, not explaining any further.

"Yeah. Of course. It's a holiday for you and all."

I stand up to walk her out but she holds up a hand. "Don't worry about it."

I take a step back, knowing that's probably the best idea.

Even though I fucking hate it.

Maeve grabs her bag and starts to walk out of the bedroom before turning back to me. "Logan?"

"Yeah?"

"I meant what I said. I'm proud of you."

I swallow down the lump in my throat at her words. "Thanks, Love."

guide to love rule #18

Your family knows you better than anyone. Don't try to hide anything from them. Including, but not limited to, details of your sex life.

17

maeve

There are some things I gave up willingly when I became a mom. Dating and sex were the top two. I mean, who has time for likely disappointing outings when you have to raise a human? Another was going out for drinks on a whim. My mindset was that I had plenty of fun in my twenties. Probably too much fun. I took the shots and had the hookups and danced until the sun came up. I filled my quota.

But sometimes you just need the burn of whiskey going down your throat, songs you haven't heard in twenty years, and your siblings surrounding you at your hometown bar on a holiday.

Lucky for me, all of my sisters are in town and the bar in Rolling Hills—our small hometown about forty minutes from Nashville—happens to throw quite the party on Thanksgiving night.

Yes, Porter, the owner of The Joint, knows that typically Thanksgiving Eve is the party night. His theory, however, is that people need a drink even more after spending all day with their families.

Or in my case, having the most weird, confusing, sad, and infuriating day known to man.

"Is no one going to ask the question?"

I look over to Quinn as I finish a sip of my whiskey and Diet Coke, as do Ainsley and Stella. "What question?"

"The one where I ask why you, out of all the sisters, requested we meet at The Joint—a bar you haven't frequented in years, mind you—on Thanksgiving night, arguably it's busiest night of the year?"

"It is a bit suspicious," Ainsley adds, sipping on her club soda.

"What? Can't a girl want to hang out with her sisters?" I protest. "I mean, how often do we all go out like this?"

That part is true. Between Quinn living in Arizona, Ainsley's job, and Stella now happily in love with Emmett, it's a rare occurrence when even three of us can hang out together, let alone all four.

So that's the story we're sticking with. Because I might not want to be alone with my thoughts, but I also don't want to talk about them.

Stella leans forward on her elbows, staring at me so hard I feel like I'm about to be interrogated. "There's something you're not telling us. And…I'm going to go out on a limb and say that it has something to do with a certain sexy billionaire."

I know my cheeks are turning red. I just hope they can't see them in the dark bar. "It's not Logan."

Well, it's not *just* Logan…

"The lady doth protest too much," Quinn replies.

"I said one thing! How is that too much?"

"You could have said nothing," Quinn says. "Now spill. How is it working for one of the world's most eligible bachelors?"

I know Quinn isn't asking about the design and the progress on the house. She might want to know some details about if he's really like who the tabloids and blogs say he is. But all I keep thinking about is today, and the broken boy who is living inside this powerful man.

How can a family treat their children like that? I know that

Jayce will likely need therapy one day—hell, who doesn't?—but even with Josh and Vivian randomly getting married, he still has a pretty normal home life.

And then there's my crew. The Banks family is as traditional as it comes. Five kids. Two parents who are approaching forty years of marriage and still love each other like it's year one. We're loud, chaotic, and there's nothing we wouldn't do for each other.

Then there's Logan, a kid who is now a man, who just wanted for everyone to get along and to love each other. A little boy who thought if he could make his parents proud they'd stop arguing for just a second. A brother who wanted to make sure his sibling was going to be okay. A man who, despite what he says, is probably still trying to make his parents proud, even though they're selfish assholes who don't deserve a second of his accomplishments.

In his own way, he wants to fix things. And I get that more than anyone.

Even with the news that he was in a dozen different PR relationships, his backstory is all I keep thinking about. But I can't tell my sisters any of this. Neither are my stories to tell. And I have a feeling Logan hasn't told many people what he told me today.

So I'll deflect with my sisters and let the whiskey wash away the hurt I'm feeling for Logan. And the urge to go back to his house, give him a hug, and tell him that everything's going to be okay.

"It's good," I say to her question. "He's pretty much given me free rein."

"And he's easy to look at."

"Stella!" I scold. "You're a taken woman."

She smiles and does a little dance in her chair. "I am. I love Emmett and everything about him. But you have to admit, Maeve, he's the kind of man that women add to their hall pass lists and men would put in the category of, 'Yeah, I'd probably try it.'"

"That's ridiculous," I say. "He's not *that* hot."

I mean, he is, but I feel like I have to protest. If I don't, my sisters will be playing matchmaker in a heartbeat. And that's not going to happen. Ever.

Well, ever again…

"He is," Quinn says. "I'll prove it."

She grabs her phone, types in something and stops a woman walking past our table.

"Excuse me. Sorry to interrupt, but can you settle a bet for us?" Quinn holds up her phone. "Scale of one to ten…one being I wouldn't fuck him with someone else's vagina to ten being I'd let him do that thing I said I'd never do?"

She looks at the phone then back to Quinn. "Twelve. That thing I'd never do *and* contemplate leaving my husband."

"Thank you, you've been a huge help."

Ainsley and Stella are in keeled-over laughter while I'm rolling my eyes. "You're ridiculous."

"I'm just proving a point."

At that moment, Porter comes over with a tray of drinks we didn't order.

"What are these?" Ainsley asks.

Porter looks over to Quinn before adjusting his eyes back to Ainsley. "It's not often the fourth Banks sister graces Rolling Hills with her presence. I figured the least I could do was a round on the house."

Stella and Ainsley echo thank-yous to Porter, but I can't help but notice that he looks over to Quinn again. She doesn't realize it as she's reaching over for a bottle of beer, but I can clearly see that this man could be getting robbed right now and wouldn't notice.

What is he doing? Does he even know Quinn? He and I graduated together, and she was a few years younger.

Did they ever—no. She would've told me.

Right?

"Oh Porter!" Quinn says, finally taking notice that he's still here. "Can you settle a bet for us?"

"Didn't we already do this?" I groan.

"On the women's side, yes. But I'd like a male point of view." She shows him the phone. "How many shots would it take?"

He looks at the picture then back to her. "One, just for the nerves. And that's because he's Daredevil level hot."

"Exactly!" she says, fist pumping in the air claiming victory. "Your participation is appreciated."

The two look at each other a little too long for normal before he heads back to the bar. But before I can ask too many other questions, a booming voice comes through the front doors.

"Seriously? What the fuck!" my brother Simon shouts as he stomps over to our table. "Where was my invitation?"

I try not to make eye contact with my big brother, who I intentionally didn't invite. Don't get me wrong, I love him. We've had each other's backs for multiple things over the years. But sometimes, conversations are meant just for your sisters. And since I didn't know how far Logan talk would go tonight—because of them, not me—I decided against inviting the oldest Banks.

"Can't we just have a girls' night?" I ask as he pulls up a chair.

"You can, but it's rude," he says. "I never get to hang out with all of my sisters, and I have FOMO."

"How did you know we were here?" Stella asks. "Did Emmett tattle?"

He taps his nose. "This is what you get for dating one of my best friends, little sister. No secret is safe."

We all chuckle at that one. Oh, if Simon only knew some of the things that Stella and Emmett have done in the office they share with him, I guarantee he wouldn't be saying that sentence.

"Fine, you can stay," I say. "But when we get to conversations you don't like, your choices are to suffer and listen or go to the bar and come back when we're done. Deal?"

He holds up his right hand. "I solemnly swear to not freak out over girl talk."

"We all heard that, right?" The three others nod their heads. "So, where were we?"

As soon as the words are out of my mouth I regret saying them. Because I remember where we were, and I wasn't about to like it. And judging by the Joker-type smile on Quinn's face, I'm right.

"We were rating how hot your client is. I was then going to ask the table to place bets on how big his dick is."

"Whoa!" Simon yells. "This is girl talk?"

"It is," Ainsley says with an eyebrow wag. "Can you handle it?"

Coming from any other person in this town, that sentence would only be mildly funny. But coming from the sister who is the angel of our clan, who I've never seen drunk, and is by far the purest of us all, it's fucking hysterical.

"Oh my God, Ainsley!" Stella says between laughter so hard she might fall out of her seat. "I fucking love you."

The smile that grows on my Ainsley's face is priceless. "He wanted girl talk. So he's getting it."

"Well played." I didn't want to talk about Logan tonight, but something about the topic bothering my brother makes it enjoyable. "And we're not guessing."

"What the hell!" Simon is now downright confused. "What am I missing?"

"Sorry, we'll catch you up," Stella says as she proceeds to fill Simon in on everything. And since I clearly know the story, I take the opportunity to pull Quinn in closer.

"Care to tell me what's going on with you and Porter?"

Quinn takes a pull of her beer and shrugs her shoulders. "What do you mean?"

"Don't play dumb. There were looks, Quinn. Looks you don't

give someone you used to go to high school with and see a few times of the year. So spill."

Here's the problem with Quinn: Her poker face is stellar. She doesn't get my red cheeks. Or Stella's drifty eyes. And she's the opposite of Ainsley, who has never been able to tell a lie. Quinn could look you dead in the face and tell you the sky is green and you'd believe it while looking at blue as far as the eye can see.

"Nothing to spill," she deadpans. "I don't know what you think you saw, but I can assure you it was nothing."

She turns away from me, which is as much of a tell as she'll give.

I don't know what, but something is up. And I don't know when my schedule will allow for me to dig into it, but it needs to be added to the list. Or I'll sic Stella on her. My baby sister has a doctorate in social media stalking.

"Wow," Simon says, indicating he's thoroughly brought to speed. "Look at my sister, banging a billionaire."

"I'm not banging a billionaire." I snap.

"But you want to."

I whip my head to Quinn. "Why do you say that?"

"Because five years ago, when you and Josh got divorced, you sat with us at this very bar and declared to the town with your full chest and both titties that not only were you never getting married again, but you were done with dating and sex was off the table. That you were a mother first, a business woman second, followed by sister and daughter. And that's all you had room for in your life."

"You did," Ainsley says. "You were very adamant about it."

"Thanks for the reminder. But what does this have to do with Logan?"

"I'm just saying, you held on to that mantra for five years and didn't budge an inch. And now you're trying to tell me it only took one hot as fuck guy with an accent and a few martinis to make you throw that out the window? There had to be something more there, even if you don't know it yet."

I stay silent, because I'm pretty sure she's on to something I don't want to admit to myself.

"Plus," Stella continues. "We all know why you took his commission. It was smart for your business. But you have to admit, it's more than a job at this point. Like why were you at his house today?"

I wasn't expecting that callout. "How did you know I was there?"

"We checked your location," Ainsley says. "We were worried about you spending the day alone."

"And I only know one place in that area of town that would've kept you there for hours on end," Stella says. "Did you really need to hang curtains on Thanksgiving?"

I guess now is as good of a time as any to tell them the other breaking news in my life. "I went there because when I dropped Jayce off today, Josh informed me he and Vivian eloped last week. And I didn't want to sit around all day alone, so I went to work."

The table goes quiet until Simon's bark breaks the silence. "He did fucking *what*?"

I wave him off. "Yup. Eloped. And don't ask for more details, because that's all I have."

"Holy shit," Stella mutters. "That's fucking huge."

"It is," Quinn says. "Which then brings us back to the original question—why did this major life thing happen and you went to him, and not to us?"

"I—" Shit...I never even thought of that. In my mind, everyone had things going on today. But in reality, that was just Simon and Stella. I could've called Quinn or Ainsley. But I didn't. On the surface, I wanted to work and keep my hands busy. But in the back of my mind, did I want to see Logan?

"Listen, at the end of the day, and between the teasing, all we're saying is if this man is different, it's okay to change your mind," Quinn says. "At the time of your divorce, you did what you thought was best for you and Jayce. And no one will ever tell you that it wasn't the right decision, because it was the right decision for you."

"But," Stella chimes in. "If Logan's different, if he brings out something in you that you didn't think existed, or had been pushed down so far that you forgot about it, don't run from it. Embrace it."

"And don't close yourself off," Ainsley says. "Maybe he's in front of you at this time because it's the right time. But don't be stubborn and think that you have to die on a hill that you built for survival. Remember that."

Damn. When did I get such smart sisters?

Because they're right. I did and said what I needed to do when I got divorced for my survival and sanity. I was about to be a solo parent, and I went into the only mode I knew—do it all yourself. No distractions. No messiness. Leave the party days behind and focus on the future.

Be in total control.

But they're right; if it only took Logan a few looks, a few drinks, and a few "Loves" to break those walls, even if just a little, doesn't that mean something?

Fuck, now I'm more confused than I was coming in here.

I look over to Simon, who is the only sibling who has yet to say anything. "Got anything to add, big brother?"

"I do," he says, sitting up straight like he's about to make a grand statement. "Is he an *actual* billionaire? Like, what kind of cars is he driving? Does he have a plane? And he's British? Is he James Bond? Or like a British Batman?"

Ladies and gentlemen…my family.

guide to love rule #85

Find things that help you relieve stress. If they also help ensure you don't murder your ex, even better.

18

maeve

Bathrooms scrubbed? Check.

Sheets washed and bed remade? Check.

Baseboards wiped down: Check.

Garage swept and organized: Also check.

There's not another space in my house I could possibly clean. It's sparkling, and you can eat off the damn floors.

But don't, because you'll get crumbs everywhere and I just mopped.

I had heard about stress cleaning, but I didn't think it was a thing. Then again, I'd never been stressed so much that I was pushed to the brink of deep-cleaning my house.

I'd like to blame this on my ex, his new wife, and the man I'm working for. They all have a role in CleanFest.

Usually when I get nervous, or worried, or want to focus on something else, I work. The only problem is that work for me right now is Logan, and after our Thanksgiving together, I thought it was best if we put some space between us.

So that meant I was stuck in my house all weekend. I booked a few jobs for after I'm done with Logan's house, one in a suburb of Florida and one in Raleigh. I double-checked that everything for Logan's that needed to be ordered was in fact placed and en route. I organized my inbox, updated my website, and went through a ton of old photos that were just taking space on my computer.

All of that took six hours.

Hence began the deep clean of my house. And it worked as well as it could've. I've been away from Jayce for extended periods of time, and farther distances. But in those cases, I knew who he was with and the caretaking was under my control. Now my son is with his father, whom I do trust, and his new step-mother, who I don't trust to tie his shoe.

She's the reason my baseboards are spotless.

I check the clock again to see that it's 7:45p.m. Josh promised me they'd be home at eight so Jayce wasn't getting to bed too late, since it is a school night. And because of the long weekend, he was going to forfeit his Monday, which was a nice move on his part.

As I'm looking for one more thing to organize or tidy up to get through the next fifteen minutes, my angel of a sister calls me.

A phone call with Quinn is the perfect distraction.

"You make it home?" I ask when I pick up, knowing Quinn's flight back to Arizona should've landed about an hour ago.

"Just sat down," she said. "They back yet?"

I check the driveway again to see if they magically pulled in over the last fifteen seconds. "No. Any minute now."

After sliding in the tidbit of information on Thanksgiving night that Josh and Vivian got married, I gave my family the debrief at our Thanksgiving dinner, away from Jayce of course. Jaws were on the floor. Foul language was used. Theories were drawn up as to why this marriage was suddenly happening. Those ranged from they actually loved each other to one of them needed to get married in order to accept an inheritance.

And I swear, if Josh has a secret inheritance I didn't know about, and I paid him alimony for the first three years of our divorce, we're going to have words. And a court date.

"I still don't get it," Quinn says. "From the little you've told me about Vivian, and the Instagram stalking that Stella did, she doesn't seem like the kind of woman who wants to elope because she just loves Josh so much. This woman screams "I want a big, showy wedding!"

"I was shocked too," I say. "But hey, maybe they're just two soulmates and couldn't bear to spend another day without being legally bonded together for life?"

It only takes a second for the two of us to bust up in a fit of laughter.

"Oh, that was good," Quinn says. "Your humor doesn't get enough credit in the family."

"I'll take that as a compliment."

"You should. Especially since I've always been the funny sister."

I know why she says that, and I know why she thinks it, but I wish Quinn knew that she was so much more than just the funny Banks sibling. Then again, she's the true middle child of the five of us, so using humor, and sometimes pushing that humor over the line, is on brand.

"So when do we get to see you again?" I ask.

Since Quinn moved to Arizona after college, she's made it a habit to only come back a few times a year. Mostly for holidays. A few unexpected trips. And we understand. It's a long flight, it's not cheap, and she has a life out there that she's made for herself. And when it comes to the holidays, if she's home for Thanksgiving, then she's not making it in for Christmas, or vice versa. Which means it could be another year until I see my sister.

"Little over three weeks, silly," she says. "I'll be home for Christmas."

"Really? You're coming home again?"

"Yeah? Why not?"

"Because you never have."

"Oh," she says, and am I catching Quinn Banks actually

searching for an answer? This is new territory. "I just thought it would be nice. You know, Lainey's first Christmas and all."

Really? Using Simon's six-month-old as an excuse? She's lucky we aren't FaceTiming so she can't see the look I'm shooting her right now that screams "I don't believe a fucking thing you're saying."

"Really, Quinn? That's what you're going with? Be real."

"I am," she says. "And aren't you the one always begging me to move back? More visits should please you."

She's right about that. I miss my sister like crazy. But that's not the point here. "I *am* happy. It's just suspicious."

At that moment, I see headlights turning into the driveway. And I let out a deep breath of relief.

"They're home. We're pausing this conversation for a future time."

"Oh no. I'm so sad," she deadpans. "But please call me back later if there's new information about the marriage. I'm now leaning toward her being pregnant."

Oh God, I never even thought of that. "Quinn! Why would you say that?"

"Shit. Sorry. Call me back!"

My sister hangs up the phone as now my brain rushes into a whole different direction.

Jayce with a half sibling? I never even considered that.

But my brain can't fixate on that for too long as I hear the rattle of the front door handle being jiggled open by Jayce.

"Mommy!" he yells as he drops his backpack at the doorway and sprints to me. He doesn't even take his boots off and is tracking water all through my clean house, but I don't care. My boy is home.

"Hey, buddy," I say, wrapping him in maybe the biggest hug I've ever given him. "Did you have fun?"

"I did!"

Jayce begins a rapid-fire rundown of all the rides he rode, and the shows they saw. He's about to start going into detail of every meal he ate when I see Josh staring at us from just inside the doorway.

Josh and I have only ever had two good communication styles in our life—in the bedroom, and silently with our eyes. Which is probably another reason why our marriage didn't work.

The silent conversation is going something like this:

Me: "Why are you standing there?"

Him with a stare and a head nod: "We need to talk."

Him shifting his eyes to Jayce then a head nod toward his room: "Alone."

And frankly, Josh and I talking alone isn't the worst idea right now. Vivian isn't here, and I don't hear his car running, so I'm guessing he didn't leave her in there.

If Quinn were in the room, she'd be making a crack about him leaving the window open for her. But as the oldest sister, I'll take the high road and just think it to myself.

"Jayce, I want to hear all about the trip. But we also have school tomorrow. So how about you go upstairs, put all your dirty clothes in the hamper, get in your pajamas, then come back and tell me everything else."

His excitement still at a high, he doesn't say anything as he sprints out of the living room. God, I love having an agreeable, and sometimes oblivious, son.

"Did the trip go well?"

I don't invite him to, but Josh takes it upon himself to sit on the chair across from me on the couch. "Really well. Thanks for letting us do this."

I don't know if letting is the right word. More like court ordered, but that's neither here nor there.

"I'm glad you guys had fun. But I don't think you're sitting down here so you can recap your trip to the Smoky Mountains."

He nods and takes a second to look down at his clasped hands, elbows resting on his legs. His position is giving me pause. The last time he looked like this is when we sat down and decided it was best that we got a divorce.

"I know you think the marriage to Vivian was quick, but I want you to know it wasn't," he begins. "I've wanted to ask her for months. We just sped up some parts."

I'm glad he's addressing the elephant in the room. "I'll admit, I do think it was fast. But as long as you're happy, then I'm happy for you."

I don't know what else to say. Does he want my approval or something?

"And she really loves Jayce," he adds. "You should've seen them together this weekend. She wanted to go on every ride with him and take pictures of everything."

"Great," I grit out. "Why are you telling me this?"

He lets out a sigh, but it's the seriousness in his gaze right now that's making my stomach flip in the worst kind of way. "Vivian and I want primary custody."

At first I'm sure I'm not hearing him right. I couldn't have. He didn't say that. This is a man who just opened a savings account two years ago. I've had to beg him to take an extra day here and there to help me out.

I'm waiting for him to start laughing. To tell me that he's playing an April Fool's Day joke on me in November. To say that *Punk'd* is coming back, and I'm the first victim.

Except he doesn't. His face is as serious as I've ever seen it.

"What do you mean you want primary custody?"

"I know it seems out of the blue, but it's not."

"The fuck it isn't!" I scream and stand up, but quickly remember that Jayce is upstairs and I need to keep my voice down. "Where is this coming from Josh? Never once have you asked for more time, let alone a change in the custody arrangement."

"Things change," he says. "I want Jayce in my life."

"He is!" I yell. I know I need to keep my voice down but it's pretty hard right now. "And why the fuck are we just skipping past the fifty-fifty compromise of co-parenting and going straight to you having him a majority of the time?"

None of this makes sense. And I want answers, but I can feel myself spiraling.

"Let's think about it, Maeve," he begins. "You've been traveling a lot with work lately. How long was that last trip? Ten, eleven days?"

"Yes. Eleven with a weather delay. And I asked you to keep him for five. You couldn't even do that."

"Because it was last minute," he defends. "If Jayce is with us primarily, we'd get into a routine. And think about it, Maeve. Then you can travel as much as you need for work. This is really to help you."

It takes every ounce of strength in me not to throat punch him. I won't because I'm an adult, my son is upstairs, and I don't want to get vomit on my freshly cleaned carpet.

But holy fuck do I want to.

"Josh, this doesn't make sense," I try to say rationally. "You spent one weekend together as a happy little family and suddenly you've got the itch to do this all the time?"

"Give me more credit than that, Maeve. Vivian and I have been discuss—"

And there it is. The reason my Spidey senses have been going off. "Oh! I see. This is Vivian's idea."

"No. It's not," he says, though maybe a little too defensively. "Yes, she has mentioned that she thinks we should have Jayce more. But I make my own decisions."

I can't keep in my laughter. "*Sure* you do. I'm sure getting married on a whim was your idea too. How about her new car? Just think of that out of the blue?"

My sarcasm isn't appreciated, based on his glare. Good thing I'm impervious to the moods of men. "Listen, Maeve. I don't want this to get ugly."

"Ha! Fucking rich coming from the man who's trying to take my son out of the life he's used to."

"But that's where you're wrong. Yes, he's used to being with you and just visiting with me. But is it good for him? What do you think it's like for him when you travel and he has to bounce around houses? Or has to go to work with you because he's off school or sick and you refuse to ask me for help?"

He is really saying all of this with the confidence only a mediocre man can possess, and I am not having it. "I've asked. More than a few times. You've never been able to. And also never volunteered. Your rewriting of history is impressive right now but since I'm not senile, please don't gaslight me."

Apparently I'm right, because he doesn't try to defend those things. Instead he just skips to his finale. "Vivian and I are married now. Jayce should grow up primarily with parents who can back each other up when something happens to the other. A true family."

I'm seeing red right now. How dare he think Jayce is suffering because I'm not married!

And where is this coming from? It has to be from her. Josh has never even hinted at anything like this. It's blindsiding, in so many ways.

"He does have a family. He has a father and a mother who love him, and aunts and uncles and grandparents. Maybe it's not a traditional one, but that boy has never wanted for love or support." I stand up, because my mind is racing and my need to do *something* is overpowering.

"For years, our system has worked. You've *never* asked for anything more. I never knew you even *wanted* more. Now you're just going to pop up to my house and say that you want to take my child from his home and his mother because you and the trophy want to play house? Got a little taste of it and now you think you're Dad of the Year? Tell me, Josh. Because none of this makes any goddamn sense."

He doesn't answer any of my questions. He just stands up and looks me square in the eye. "This was just a courtesy conversation, Maeve. But we're doing this. I'm filing papers with the court next week. Be ready."

With that he exits my house, leaving me standing there terrified and panicked.

And feeling more out of control than I've ever been in my life.

I don't know how long I'm standing there, but the only thing that breaks me from my mental spiral is Jayce sprinting back in the living room, an armful of souvenirs in hand, talking a mile a minute about his trip.

I try to listen. I really do. But I don't hear one thing he says. All I can think about is that my entire life has just been turned upside down. This could be gone. All of it. All it would take is one judge to buy Josh's stories, and Jayce could be nothing more than a visitor in my home.

And I can't let that happen. No. I have to do whatever it takes to make sure my son stays with me.

Except I have no clue how to fix this.

19
logan

"Dammit!"

I realize it's not my keyboard's fault for not being able to come up with any sort of idea, but that doesn't stop me from heaving it across the room. I hear a crack when it hits the hardwood floors, but I don't give a shit right now.

I've sat here for four days trying to come up with an idea. A concept. The concept of an idea.

And I've got nothing. Zero. Diddily fucking squat. It's like every time I think I'm onto something, I realize this is just a slightly tweaked SpaceCraft, which I don't even think we could repackage into a spinoff, or an idea that has already been done by a competitor.

"Face the music, Matthews," I whisper to myself. "You're a one-hit wonder."

"Whoa! What the hell?"

I don't even look over to Kat as she lets herself into my office. She's walking into a room with a broken keyboard on the floor, takeout containers covering my desk, and my hair more disheveled than usual. I somehow remembered to shower a few times, but that's as much care as I've done for myself.

"I take four days off for Thanksgiving, and this is what happens? We revert back to dorm room Logan?"

I just shrug as I turn my chair to face her. I should feel bad that she immediately goes into cleanup mode, grabbing all of the empty food containers I've racked up since Thursday night.

"I lost track of time," I say, which is partially true.

Kat eyes me, trying to detect how much I'm leaving out of that statement. The answer is a lot. "No. I've seen you go on no-sleep benders before, including the week-long marathon before SpaceCraft launched. This is different. Spill."

I rub my eyes, trying to figure out how I want to put this to her. Luckily, I have time because she's still cleaning up my mess.

"I'm sorry," I say, and I truly am. "I meant to have all of this tidied up before you got here this morning."

And Maeve, but I don't want to say that one out loud.

"It's fine. You're clearly going through something, and I obviously can't ever take that much time off again."

"Absolutely not," I say. "You should take more time off, if anything."

She eyes the desk, the keyboard, and then me. "Really? That's the argument you're going to try and make right now?"

"Touché."

"Let's move off the mess. What's going on with you, and why does it look like you haven't slept since the last time I saw you?"

I shrug and let out a well-timed yawn. "Because I haven't."

"Oh shit," she says, all humor and sarcasm that's normally in her voice is now gone. "Okay. What's going on?"

I look back to my monitor, which has up a bunch of screens with a lot of nothing on them. "I don't know."

"Talk to me, Logan," she says. "Whatever it is, let's figure this out."

I tell Kat that I spent all weekend trying to come up with any semblance of a game. Since no one was here, it was the perfect opportunity to buckle down and finally come up with the idea that would put my life back in order.

I leave out the real motivation of doing so.

When Maeve left on Thanksgiving, I suddenly felt inspired. Because when the woman you're infatuated with says that she's proud of you, you want nothing more than to earn that sentiment.

And so I sat down. I went back to my roots, from when I really started developing SpaceCraft. When I did that, I was just a kid in my dorm room with a notebook, a sketch book, and my computer. Surely I could use just those things, tap into the idea I'd had for years, and come up with a game that would blow away the board and everyone who works for my company.

That was four days ago, and all I have to show for it is a bunch of crumpled papers, a lot of empty takeout containers, a broken keyboard, and not an idea to be found.

"Damn," she said. "I hate that you're going through this. I figured you were just in a bit of a brain block. I never thought it would go on this long."

"You and me both." I sit back and stare up at the ceiling. "What's the matter with me, Kat?"

"Because you're going through it, and haven't slept, I'm not going to make a smart-ass remark."

"Appreciate it."

"But in all honesty? I don't know. We've tried everything. Hell, we moved you across the country, in hopes that a new environment would spark something. But here we are, just as lost as we were six months ago."

Silence falls over the room, because neither of us really have anything to say. What is there to say besides the eventual inevitable conclusion: SpaceCraft is my one and only good idea. I'm tapped out at twenty-nine.

"What time is it?" I figure it's Monday since Kat's back, though that was my only clue. "I figured Maeve would've been here by now and I'd hear hammering from somewhere in the house."

Kat shrugs. "She's not here."

That wakes me up more than any energy drink could ever. "What do you mean she's not here?"

"Not sure. One of the painters said that she called them and said she wouldn't be in today. They were just to finish projects they had going and she'd be back tomorrow to give them next steps."

I jump up from my desk and look around for…I don't know what. Keys? My glasses? My sanity? "Something's wrong."

"You need to settle down. She's fine. Maybe Jayce is sick? I'm sure it's nothing to be worried about."

I find my phone and bring it to life. No texts or emails. Maeve is nothing but professional, maybe overly so because of our history. Every official day she's worked I've had detailed itineraries of what her plans were for that day. If she was sick, she'd have let me know. I know that in my bones.

"No, something's wrong," I say. "And don't ask me how I know, I just do."

"Well then call her," Kat says. "Double check before you go all crazy about it."

I bring up Maeve's number before the words are even out of Kat's mouth. I hit send, only for it to go right to voicemail.

"Fuck," I said. "Where does she live?"

"What?" Kat replies. "Logan, chill out. You don't have to go—"

"Where. Does. She. Live?"

Kat and I stare at each other for a few seconds as I silently beg her to understand what I'm feeling now. She's never seen me like this, so I can understand her confusion. But that also means she should realize if I'm acting like this, it's for a reason.

"She's in Brentwood," Kat says. "Head to the highway. I'll text you the address."

I give her a kiss on her cheek before sprinting out of my office.

————

Twenty minutes later I'm pounding on Maeve's door, yelling for her to open up. I can't see if her SUV is in the garage, but there are enough lights on to tell me she's home.

So why isn't she answering?

"Maeve!" I yell again, my fist pounding into the wood of her door. "Open up!"

Seconds later and mid pound, I feel the door start to open. I catch my hand and pull it back as Maeve slowly opens it, peeking out around the opening just enough that I can see that she's crying.

"Logan? What are you doing here?"

I slowly push the door open, needing to get inside. Luckily, Maeve doesn't fight me, and I quickly shut the door behind me.

"What happened? Who did this to you?"

I don't see any physical markings on her, but it's clear she's has been crying for hours. Her eyes are bloodshot and puffy, her face is pale and tear-streaked, and her hair is a wreck, part of it sticking to her face.

"It's not like that."

"Then what's it like?" I ask as I cup her face in my hands. "I need to know who's making you cry like this so I know who to end."

Maeve's eyes go wide when she realizes I'm bloody serious.

"Who, Maeve? What's happening? Please, Love. I'm worried…"

She starts to say something—I think she says Jayce's name—before she breaks down again, collapsing into my body.

"Hey, I got you," I say, picking her up and walking her over to the sofa. I sit down with her on my lap, and I know Maeve has to be distraught, because instead of fighting me like I half expected, she does the opposite—she clings to me like she needs me to breathe.

"Shh…I'm here. Do what you need to do. Find the calm."

Maeve's tears continue for minutes on end. I don't hear anything else in the house, so that means Jayce isn't here. But I swear she tried to say his name before this wave of tears came out. Is he okay? I'd have to guess he is or she'd be wherever he is. Is he with his dad? At school?

Fuck, I want to help her. I want to fix this. But I don't know what to do. So I do the only thing I can think of—I just hold her. I stroke her hair, hold her tight, and let her use my shirt as a handkerchief, anything possible to give her any sort of comfort until she's able to tell me what's wrong.

"He wants to take Jayce."

"What?" I wasn't expecting words from Maeve yet, let alone those ones. "Who?"

She settles her breathing and slowly sits up from me. "Josh. My ex."

I don't push her as she fights like hell to block the tears from starting again. Instead I just take her hand and hold it, so she knows I'm here.

That I'm not going anywhere.

"He told me that he and his new wife think that Jayce would be better if he had a 'real family.' They want to be his primary household."

"Bloody hell!"

"Exactly. He said that I'm traveling too much, even though it's work. And that it's not right that I have to take him with me to work sometimes. And that Jayce would be better off with them since they're now a united family."

I can't believe what I'm hearing. As someone who grew up with shit parents, I can speak firsthand as to how good of a mum Maeve is to Jayce.

"Forgive me if I'm missing something, but didn't they just get married *last week*?"

This makes her laugh just a little. "You didn't miss anything. They did."

"And suddenly they're qualified to be a family?"

Maeve just shrugs. "I don't know what the end game is. Something isn't right. I had a weird feeling when Josh told me they got married. And now? Something still isn't adding up. But I don't have time to figure that out. I need to figure out how to stop them."

"No, Love. How *we* stop them."

She shakes her head. "I couldn't ask you to do that, Logan. You have enough on your plate."

"I know you didn't ask, Maeve. I offered. I'm helping."

We stare at each other for a beat before she's the first to break eye contact. "I don't know, Logan. I don't even know what we *could* do. That's what I've been trying to do all morning. Because no matter how much I think this is a travesty and that I'm missing a piece of the puzzle as to why they want this, Josh is right—in the eyes of the great state of Tennessee, they are a family. They're married. And I do work a lot. I travel more than I'd like, but that's what I need to do to take care of my business and Jayce. What if a judge looks at that and says, 'Sorry, Mom. I know you did the hard stuff. Dad's going to take it from here.' I don't know if they would, but it's a possibility, and I can't stop freaking out about that. Just the *possibility* is driving me insane. I feel out of control. And I can't stop it."

I can see the panic in Maeve's eyes. I don't blame her. She feels like her world is crumbling, and for a woman who likes to control everything, this has to feel like an avalanche.

I want to help her. I *need* to help her.

And that's when it hits me.

"Is that all they have over you? That they're married?"

Maeve's eyebrows shoot up her forehead. "As far as I know."

"Well, then, that settles it."

"Settles what, Logan?"

I smile and take Maeve's hand back in mine. "How we're going to fix this."

I move her off my lap but just so I can go to the floor in front of her couch. Her eyes are nearly popping out of her head by the time I'm down and on one knee.

"Maeve Banks?"

"Logan, what the fuck are you doing?"

"Marry me."

guide to love rule #50

Love isn't always convenient. Sometimes marriage is.

20

maeve

"What did you just say?"

He didn't say that. He couldn't have. In my fear and grief, I'm now hearing things.

"Marry me, Maeve Banks."

I'm frozen as I wait for him to give me the good ol' "Bazinga!" How many times can I be on *Punk'd* in a week?

But he doesn't move. Not an inch. If anything, his devilish smile that I clearly remember from that first night together is coming out in full force.

"You're fucking serious, aren't you?"

"Never more serious about anything in my life."

Holy shit…he's for real.

And he's out of his goddamn mind.

"Marry you! Marry you? Logan, and I say this respectfully, you're fucking crazy."

I jump up from my spot on the couch and immediately start pacing back and forth in my living room. "How can you even suggest that? In what world is that the thing to do?"

I'm starting to make myself dizzy from the circles I'm walking in, but somehow the notion of getting married again is sending me further off my axis.

"Love, how about you sit down and let's talk about this?"

That stops me mid step. "Don't call me Love. And there's nothing to talk about, because it's not happening."

Logan doesn't reply, but I can feel his eyes on me as I walk back and forth.

"What are you looking at?"

"Just waiting for you to get out your initial feelings. Or are you going to be stubborn for a little while longer?"

Sometimes I forget how much audacity this man has. Why am I surrounded by men who think they fucking know everything?

"We can talk, but that's not going to change my answer," I say as I sit down. But not because he asked me to—because I'm lightheaded.

"Can I at least explain my reasoning?"

"Fine," I groan as I lean back on the couch. "But just so you can talk this out and we can agree that this idea is ridiculous."

"Challenge accepted."

I snap my head to him. "That wasn't a challenge."

"We'll see." Logan sits on the couch so he's facing me. I don't return the look, but that's because I'm scared that in my vulnerable state I'll either kiss him, punch him, or worse, agree to marry him.

"Logan, I appreciate this. I really do. But getting married does not fix the problem."

"You sure?" he says. "You said it yourself; he thinks he has the upper hand because he's now married. So, if we get married, he doesn't have that card to play anymore. Anything he can do, we can do better."

I purse my lips and cross my arms over my chest. Point one goes to Logan, because while it's a juvenile response, it's true.

"Second: I'm not sure what Vivian brings to the marriage, but I'm pretty sure she's not Logan Matthews."

Okay, now he's saying things I can dispute. "You're right.

She's not. However, doesn't it scream that something is off when *the* Logan Matthews is suddenly married? And not just that, but to a woman no one in the world knows? That you go from dating actresses and models and pop stars to a cougar single mom who's decorating your house? The alarm bells are flashing, Logan."

"Counterpoint." He pauses for an instant, and I swear in that time his eyes go from focused to laser beams. "Logan Matthews jumps from relationship to relationship so fast because that's just who he is. But when he sees the woman he wants to spend the rest of his life with, he doesn't hesitate to make her his."

Oh no, vagina! You stay still! Do not—I repeat, do not—clench at his words!

But my pussy is a traitor and apparently remembers the night that it came out of retirement.

Oh, does it remember…

"Okay, fine, let's play devil's advocate." I begin. "Let's say, and this is just for the hypothetical, we get married."

His grin is unsettling. "Of course, hypothetically speaking…"

"So we're married. Everyone thinks we're just this happy, lovely couple. How would it work?"

"What do you mean?"

"I mean, am I moving Jayce to your home? Who are we telling the truth that this is a marriage of convenience? That also means that I have to play the dutiful wife to Logan Matthews, which means parties and appearances and what not. This is more than just you doing me a favor, Logan; this is a train that could just keep rolling and become more and more out of control."

He nods, and for the first time since he brought up this ridiculous idea, I feel like he's stopping to think. "Yes, there are logistical things to figure out, and we would. I wouldn't do this without you and I sitting down and having a very long and detailed conversation."

"Well that's a start."

"But I can answer a few of your questions." Without asking, or hesitation, Logan takes my hand in his. And without thinking, or hesitating, I give it to him.

Because I'm clearly insane.

"Yes, I'm guessing we would have to move in together. And frankly, I realize that moving Jayce is difficult, especially with his schooling. So I'll move here."

Excuse me, what? Live with a boy? No, thank you.

"You'll move in here?"

He shrugs. "Sure! Why not? Your home is lovely. My home is a wreck right now, with the decorating and parts still under construction. Plus, that house is too large for just one person. Maybe I'll just sell it."

My eyes pop out of my head. "You are *not* selling that house. Not after what I'm about to do to it."

"Okay, then," he says with a smirk. "But for now, I'll live here."

"Logan, be serious, you'd move out of an *actual* mansion to move in here?"

He doesn't hesitate. "Maeve, I'd live anywhere with you."

His gaze doesn't budge. His hand tightens around mine.

And I know I've said this to myself roughly twenty times in the past ten minutes, but holy shit...he really wants to fucking do this.

"Why are you really doing this, Logan? Why would you help me?"

He lets out a big breath. "Because I care for you Maeve. Even if this marriage is a sham, and after this is over we go back to client and designer, I'll always care for you. And when you have the means to help someone you care about do something so important, you move heaven and earth to do it. Or in our case, get married and move to the suburbs. Plus, a marriage for me means a few months of distraction to keep my board from realizing I'm a one-hit wonder. Kat will be delighted."

I shake my head. This can't be happening. I can't be actually considering this, can I?

"Logan, I can't ask you to do this. Yes, sure, being married would even the playing field. Yes, it might help me in the courts with custody, but…"

He shakes his head. "No buts, Love. And you didn't ask. I offered. Because as someone who grew up with a shitty mother and a shittier father, I'm going to make damn sure that the good mums keep their kids."

And that's it. That's what's going to break me.

I *am* a good mom. I do what I have to do for my kiddo. And yes, sometimes that means bouncing him around houses so I can make a living. And sometimes it means him staying up a little late because I want to see him before he goes to bed and I'm working late.

And now, apparently, marrying a billionaire I once slept with.

"I do."

It takes a second for Logan to register my words.

"You do?"

I nod. "For Jayce. I'll do what I need to do for my son."

"Exactly," he says. "We're going to make sure he stays exactly where he belongs."

Yes. He's right. This is for Jayce. No other reason.

Not one other single reason…

"So how is this actually going to work?" I ask. "There's…I don't even know where to begin."

Logan just shrugs. "Neither do I. But I know someone who might…"

———

"Holy shit, this is amazing! My guy graduated from PR dating to PR marriage!"

On the drive over here I had a sliver of hope that Kat would be the rational adult in the room. That she'd talk me and Logan out of this ridiculous idea.

Not so much.

In fact, after hearing our story, she might be the most into it out of anyone present.

"Really?" I ask, hoping to break her from her excitement. "You don't see any massive red flags or warning bells about this?"

"Oh, they're glaring, blaring, and as red as the bottom of my favorite shoes, but that doesn't make it any less amazing. For both of you."

Good Lord, what am I getting into...

"Okay, I can see you're freaking out," Kat says, leading me to one of the chairs in front of Logan's desk. "Let's talk this out."

"Please," I say, suddenly feeling a migraine coming on. "First of all, before we go any further, do we think this will *actually* work?"

"I'll be honest, I don't know," Kat says. "I'm not a lawyer and certainly know nothing about divorces and custody agreements. But, I do agree that if Josh's biggest advantage over you is that he's married and can provide a stable home—which is horseshit, but here we are—then marrying Logan evens that out."

"He also said I travel too much and have to arrange rotating childcare because of that. And that essentially Vivian will be staying home to help raise him while he's at work. I don't have anything to counter that..."

"Easy," Logan jumps in. "We're at work when he's at school. When you have to travel, I make sure that I'm home. And vice versa. Also, when you run the company, you control most of your travel. Plus, and remember, I'm obscenely wealthy. Paying for a nanny, or supplemental child care, is nothing."

I shake my head. "I'm not going to have you spend your money on us."

"If we're married, what's mine is yours."

"No! Absolutely not!" I exclaim. "First of all, we'll be signing some sort of contract, or prenup, or whatever it may be. This isn't real, Logan. We'll be married *on paper*. We're not combining finances. We're not splitting bills. And I have money too. Not as much as you, but I do well for myself. If we need a nanny, I'll pay for a fucking nanny!"

There. I said it. The biggest hill for me to die on.

I might need his help in this way, but I don't need his money. I don't need his name. I just need to prove to a likely super-conservative family court judge that I'm married and stable so I can keep primary care of my son.

That's it.

"She's right," Kat says. "I mean, you two can figure out the money thing. But contracts do need to be signed. NDAs need to be arranged. I need to know who we're telling, how we're spinning this, and what the story is for the press. Because Logan Matthews suddenly getting married is going to make news."

I look over to Logan, who already has his eyes on me. "Are you okay with that, Maeve? You'll be in the papers. On the blogs. People will look at you. Paparazzi will follow you. They'll think you're just another in my long string of women."

I think about it for a second. "I don't love the idea of being followed, watched, and written about, but if that's the price to pay to keep Jayce, I'll do it."

"I understand it's a lot. And if you are adamantly against it, we'll find another way. I don't want you to lose Jayce. But, this helps us both. I become a family man and keep the distraction train rolling. You get a husband, a family unit, and can fight fire with fire against your ex."

I let that sink in. He's right. And as much as I've tried to think of ways over the past how-ever-many hours of making sure Jayce stays with me, I hadn't been able to think of a thing that wasn't quitting my job.

Which I refuse to do. It was never a problem until now. Which also tells me something else is up.

But I don't know what that is, and I don't have time to go

chasing theories. What I do know is that Josh is married. And he does have a traditional family now. So as much as I hate this, and wish there was any other way, this is what I have to do.

I have to become Mrs. Logan Matthews.

guide to love rule #46

When marrying a man for convenience and you have to kiss
your now husband, don't use tongue.

21

maeve

Things I've learned today: You can get a marriage license and have a judge marry you all on the same day. Who knew?

When Josh and I got married in this very same courthouse, we didn't do it on the same day. We applied for the license and took a few days to make sure our families could be there for it. That was as romantic as it got.

Then there's today's elopement. It's just going to be me and Logan, with Kat as our witness. I didn't tell my family, which is killing me. I don't think Logan has told his brother or anyone else. I haven't even told Jayce what I'm doing yet.

Partially because I don't know how I'm going to tell anyone. And partially because I still can't believe this is happening.

Logan gave me twenty-four hours to change my mind, which I appreciated. What I didn't appreciate was waking up today—after a dream I'd rather not talk about featuring a naked Logan Matthews—and not having a single other idea that is better than tying the knot.

I have a problem. I need to fix it. This is how I'm fixing it. Nothing more. Nothing less.

So here I am, driving to the courthouse in a cream dress and nude heels, for the second courthouse wedding of my life.

Funny…I never saw myself as a marriage girl. And here I am doing it again.

I guess you can never say never…

At that moment, an image of my siblings flashes through my mind and what their reactions are going to be when they find out.

Simon will be pissed he wasn't invited.

Ainsley might cry in happiness.

Stella will be shocked then want every detail of what's really going on.

Quinn will see right through me *and* the wedding.

Which is why they won't be there today. And more so, why I'm not telling them the truth.

At least for now. It's what's best. I don't want to lie to them, but even more, I don't want them to have to lie *for* me. It's not their job to protect my secret, so I'm telling them what Logan and I agreed last night was going to be our story. And most of it is actually the truth.

Or a version of.

Simply, we met months ago on a business trip. We ran into each other again just recently—after the photo was taken with him and Candace, since that was the last woman he was rumored to be with—and we've been inseparable since. And, because we are so in love, we decided why wait? We're just two crazy kids who couldn't wait another day to be Mr. and Mrs.

That's our story, and we're sticking to it.

I've been panicking that something will mess this up. But Logan? He's been nothing but amazing, easing my fears while also giving me a sharp dose of reality when I need to hear it. And yes, I know he's getting something out of this too, but something in my gut is telling me that even if he didn't need me, he'd still be doing this.

Now I just hope this will work.

As I navigate the streets of downtown Nashville, part of me still can't believe this is happening. When I officially agreed to this yesterday, I didn't realize we were going to do it in twenty-four hours. But it makes sense. Jayce is with his dad tonight—since Josh wants to be father of the year, he asked for another night and I agreed without a fight, mostly to keep him unaware that I have a counter to his master plan.

We're not sure when Josh is going to file the paperwork, so we wanted to make sure this was done before I was served. And since I was going to be downtown anyway today for a consultation, I told Logan we could just meet at noon and get it over with.

Because "get it over with" is how every bride should describe their wedding day.

A few minutes later, I'm pulling into the Davidson County Courthouse. Like I'm getting ready for a new job, I do what I always do and close my eyes, take a breath—only this time, the mantra is a little different:

"You can do this. Be confident. Know you're doing this for a greater good. Don't fall in love with your husband."

There. That seems like the right things to say as I get out of my SUV. Logan sent me a message that he was already here, so I make my way through the metal detector and head to the chambers of the judge who had a gap in his schedule and could proceed over the wedding on short notice.

I let myself take a few deep breaths as I head to the third floor. When the doors open, I'm shocked to be staring at Logan, who's holding a beautiful bouquet of flowers and looking way too good in a black suit.

"What are you doing?"

He just sends me a dazzling smile as I walk out of the elevator. "I know roses are cliché. But I was also once told that there's a difference between classic and cliché."

For the first time in three days, I feel myself smiling. "She sounds like a smart woman."

"And beautiful." Logan gives me his arm, offering to escort

me down the hall. "Even in a wedding like this, every bride should have a bouquet."

An unexpected tear threatens to burst through, but I push it back. I know he doesn't know, and no way could, that when I married Josh, I didn't have a bouquet. I forgot all about it, and so I walked down the aisle with a single flower we picked from the park across the street from the courthouse.

"Come with me," Logan says as he guides me down the hall. As we turn the corner, I see Kat sitting on a bench, typing something furiously on her phone.

"You look beautiful, Maeve," Kat says as she stands up. "Fair warning, Logan: A crime reporter from *The Nashville Banner* saw you coming in. Questions are being asked. We might need to put on our game faces quicker than we expected."

I nod and take a deep breath.

You're doing this for Jayce. For your family. This is how you fix the problem.

"Okay," I say as I look up at Logan. "Should we go in?"

He shakes his head. "I know we need to get a move on, but I have something for you first."

I'm speechless as Logan takes a ring box out of his pocket. "I know the tradition is to do something old, something new, something borrowed, and something blue, but since I didn't have much time, I had to combine a few of them."

When Logan opens the box, my jaw nearly hits the floor when I see the gorgeous aquamarine ring. "We'll consider this something new and something blue. I hope it's okay. It reminded me of your eyes."

I nod furiously, trying my best not to cry, though that's proving futile.

"I thought you could borrow this for the day," Kat says, handing me a beautiful vintage handkerchief. "I don't cry much, but on days like today, it's good to have one just in case."

I nod and hug Kat, who I'm quickly realizing is just as great as Logan said she is. "It's like you can read my mind."

When I back away and lightly dab my eyes with the something borrowed, I turn back to Logan.

"I don't have a lot of old, for obvious reasons," he begins as he takes his wallet out of his back pocket. "But I guess for us, we'll consider this old."

I look down as Logan opens his wallet and takes out what looks like a key card.

Is that…

"Yes, I kept it," he says, handing it to me. "I wanted something to remember that night by."

Now I'm not a crier. My sisters joke that at some point over the years, Mama Maeve's heart turned black. And I don't disagree with them.

But this? What Logan's doing right now? And not just the gifts, but agreeing to marry me, to help me when he didn't have to? Let's just say I'm glad Kat lent me the handkerchief.

"Thank you," I say, doing my best to keep every emotion at bay. "But you didn't have to do this. Any of this."

Logan takes my hand and brings it to his lips. "Oh, Love… one of these days you're going to realize I know I don't have to. But I want to."

"Matthews-Banks wedding? We're ready for you."

Our names being called breaks the spell Logan cast over me. I dab my eyes one more time, slip the key in the purse, and turn back to Logan.

"You ready?"

He nods and takes my hand, bringing it to his lips. "Let's go get married."

———

"Have either of you prepared vows and would like to speak them at this time?"

Shit…vows? Was I supposed to do vows?

To be fair, I didn't even know we were in this part of the ceremony. After I walked down the makeshift aisle, handed Kat my bouquet, and gave my hands to Logan, I kind of blacked out.

I'm still getting over the gifts and the whole "getting married" thing.

"I...I didn't prepare any," I admit.

"That's fine, dear," the judge says. "Logan? Would you like to say anything?"

"I would," Logan says before leaning into me. "Don't worry, you don't have to say anything back."

Easy for him to say. When this judge is asked one day to testify if we were a loving couple, he'll be able to say, "The groom? Great. The bride? Not so much."

"Maeve," Logan begins. "From the moment we met, I knew there was something different about you. To this day, I still don't know what it was, but I knew you were going to change my life. And even if that night would've ended there, you still changed it. You're brilliant and beautiful. Smart and kind. You amaze me with your talent, and you're the best mum to Jayce. I'm just glad that I can be a part of your life, no matter where that road takes us."

I swallow the lump in my throat. Is this how he really feels? I mean, I knew from comments he's made and the looks he's given, that he wouldn't say no if I said "let's give this a try." But this? This is much more than I expected.

"Thank you, Logan," the judge says. "And now—"

"Excuse me," I interrupt. "Can I still say a few words?"

The judge smiles and slowly nods his head. "Of course."

I suck in the biggest breath I've ever taken and close my eyes for a second. When I open them, I'm looking right into Logan's, who are nothing but warm and filled with...love?

No. That's not what that is.

"Logan," I begin, refusing to let my brain go down that rabbit hole. "Thank you. For everything."

I pause for a second, wondering if I should really say things I haven't rehearsed.

Fuck it. We'll do it live.

"You've stepped up in my life when others haven't. You've seen things in me that I didn't know I had in myself. And your faith in me is…well, I don't know what I did to deserve it, but thank you for believing in me. Thank you for going on this journey with me. Just…thank you."

A wink from Logan allows me to breathe.

"And now, may I have the rings?"

My eyes go wide as I realize we didn't get rings. What the hell? I'm the shittiest bride ever.

However, and I should've known, magically out of Logan's pocket comes two wedding bands.

"Do you, Logan Matthews, take Maeve Banks to be your lawful wedded wife?"

Logan sends me a perfect smile. "I do."

I take the ring from the judge and slip the ring onto Logan's finger, pushing it gently past his knuckle.

"Excuse me, Maeve?"

I look over to the judge, wondering why he's stopping the ceremony. "Yes?"

He eyes the ring. "You put it on the wrong finger."

"Oh! Shit!" The snickers from Logan and Kat aren't helping as I hurriedly pull it off his hand and put it on the other. "Don't you dare laugh, Logan Matthews. You could've given me a high sign or something."

"Apologies. I was too in the moment."

I finish putting the ring on his correct finger and let the wave of embarrassment pass through me. This is how I know I'm not supposed to be a married woman; I can't even get the rings correct.

"Sorry again," I say. "We can continue now."

The judge gives me a warm smile. "All right then. Do you, Maeve Banks, take Logan Matthews to be your lawful wedded husband?"

This is it. Last chance.

Yet, I don't hesitate. And I'm not willing to take questions on that topic at this point in time.

"I do."

Logan slides the ringer on the correct finger, giving it a squeeze as he finishes.

"By the power invested in me by the state of Tennessee, I now pronounce you husband and wife. Logan? You may kiss your bride."

Oh shit-fuck-damn! The kiss! How in the world did I forget about the kiss!

My eyes have to be pure panic as I look at Logan. And this mother fucker—also known as my husband—just has the audacity to smirk at me.

Smirk!

I suck in a breath as he steps to me, bringing me into his arms, and I think covering my reaction from the judge.

"Don't worry, Love. I've got you."

And he does. Logan brings me in for what some might call the perfect kiss. Not me. But some.

No tongue, but not a peck. He cups my face in his hands and expertly uses his lips to kiss me the exact way he wants to. It's sensual without being sexual. Intimate but somehow still acceptable for public.

And I hate that I want more.

guide to love rule #101

If you want complete, brutal honesty about anything, ask a child. Even if it regards your love life.

22

maeve

STELLA

Maeve Marie Banks what in the world am I seeing!

AINSLEY

What happened?

STELLA

According to every celebrity news outlet in the world, our sister got married yesterday.

QUINN

What!? No fucking way!

QUINN

Also could you hear me screaming from Arizona?

AINSLEY

Yes. And I almost cursed I'm so shocked.

STELLA

See, Maeve! Quinn is freaking out and Ainsley's swearing. Care to tell us what's going on?

SIMON

Whoa! Wait! Just catching up. What the fuck happened?

STELLA

According to multiple news reports, Maeve Banks is now Maeve Matthews, because our oldest sister got married yesterday to the billionaire.

AINSLEY

Without telling us.

QUINN

Or inviting us.

SIMON

I never get invited to anything!

Twenty-four hours.

That's how long it took before the headlines across the internet read something like this:

SpaceCraft creator Logan Matthews ties the knot in courthouse wedding. You won't believe who he married.

SpaceCraft's Logan Matthews is entering his Husband Era.

Who is Maeve Banks? Meet the new Mrs. Logan Matthews.

Once I saw the first one pop up, I knew it wouldn't be long until the Banks group chat would fire up. I wanted to get ahead of it, but I also wanted to tell Jayce first, which means I have to wait until he gets home from school. I'm just glad Stella was smart enough to use the sibling chat and not the one with my parents. I'm going to tell them, but I don't want them finding out in a text thread.

> Yes. It's true. I'm married. I'll fill you all in at a later time.

No one responds, which I don't think has ever happened in the history of the Banks family.

Actually, their pause is helpful. I don't have time to tell them everything right now, because I need to finish packing bags and suitcases for me and Jayce.

Because in a change of plans, we now have to move in with my husband.

God that's still weird to even think about…

Kat was right yesterday when she thought that a *Nashville Banner* reporter spotted Logan. When we left the courthouse, a group of photographers were not so subtly waiting for us. Thankfully, Kat is two steps ahead at all times and reminded us to make sure we were holding hands and smiling as we exited. She then directed me to go home with Logan and leave my car at the courthouse.

Now that I'm thinking of it, is my car still there? Shit, with the craziness of the day I didn't even think about it.

Seconds after I saw the first article, I was on the phone with Logan, who was adamant about us coming to his home. And even though my stubborn ass wanted to argue, he was right. Between the articles that have come out already, and the photographers who aren't being sneaky about hiding down my road, it's safer for us to be at Logan's with gates and cameras and an actual security system that isn't just my Ring camera.

Now we just have to tell Jayce.

My phone vibrates again, and I audibly groan, thinking that it's one of my siblings. Or another message from Josh asking me if what he and Vivian were seeing online was true. It's neither. Just my husband.

Still so fucking weird to say…

LOGAN

I'm pulling in the driveway. Come meet me at
the door so I can help with the bags.

MAEVE

I can get them, Logan. You don't have to.

LOGAN

Maeve…let me into the house so I can help
with bags. Please.

Why am I so fucking stubborn and independent on everything? Yes, I need help with bags. But even when he's offering,
I'm too damn head strong to accept it.

MAEVE

Fine. But only so we can do this in one trip.

LOGAN

Whatever you need to tell yourself.

I slide my phone into my pocket as I quickly check my closet
and Jayce's to make sure I have everything I could need. I don't
know how long we'll be there, but I have to assume a long
period of time. And yes, I can come back if I need something, but
I'd rather not if I don't have to.

With the final check done, I head downstairs and open my
door to see a waiting Logan.

"Hi," I say, quickly turning so I don't accidentally stare. He's
casual today in a gray sweatsuit and his glasses. Now, I'm not
one to gawk at men. But Quinn has sent me enough videos to
know that gray sweatpants can be quite…revealing. And the last
thing I need today when I'm uprooting myself and my son is to
stare at my husband in hopes of seeing…anything.

"Is everything ready?"

I nod and look at the huge suitcases I've packed. "This is all
my clothes and Jayce's for the time being. Our toiletries. And I

hope you don't mind, but I packed his video games and console."

Logan sends me a confused look. "Why would I be mad about that? You remember who I am, right?"

As if I could forget.

"Yes, but I also know that you probably own, or developed, all the ones that he's attached to. And I didn't know if it was rude or weird to bring them, but if they aren't with him, he will have a not-so-minor freak out."

Logan just gives me a warm smile. "Sounds like my kind of kid."

I turn away again, needing to hide my reaction to how he already talks about Jayce so affectionately. One of the reasons I was adamant about not dating is because I didn't want Jayce to have to develop a relationship with someone I was dating, only for it to end badly. And yes, part of me is worried Jayce will get attached to Logan. Hell, in their one interaction already, I could see how much they bonded. When we have to leave his house, Jayce will be devastated.

"Logan?"

I turn back to him as he's picking up one of my duffle bags. "Yeah, Love?"

"Before we do this, I need a promise from you."

He puts the bags down, hearing the seriousness in my tone. "Anything."

I take in a breath before beginning. "You and I know this is only temporary. But Jayce has stars in his eyes every time your name comes up."

"Does that mean you talk about me?"

I roll my eyes at his comment and his fucking smirk. "Focus, Matthews. This is serious. My kid idolizes you, and when we tell him that we're now living with you, he's going to become attached in three seconds flat. So I need you to promise me, no matter what happens with us when this is over, that you won't let my kid down. That you'll stay in his life however he wants you to. I just…I need that promise."

Logan puts his grin away and walks toward me, taking my hands in his. I also notice that he immediately starts rubbing his thumb over the engagement ring and wedding band I've worn since yesterday.

"When I first met Jayce, I swore I was looking at a picture of myself as a kid. I was shy. Used to hide behind my mum's leg when we were in public. And talking to him that day? He's a great, bright, funny kid, Maeve. Believe me, I don't give my only-one-ever-made action figures to just anyone."

Shit, I'm going to cry…

"I know this is scary and has been a whirlwind. And it's not going to be easy on Jayce either. I hate that we can't stay here, but it's safer to be at my place right now. So no matter what you tell him about us, no matter how long we stay married, no matter anything, as long as he wants me in his life, I'll be there. No questions asked."

Okay, now I'm crying.

I've cried more this week than I have in the past God knows how many years. I didn't even cry when Josh and I divorced.

I start to say thank you to Logan when my phone starts vibrating like crazy in my pocket. When I pull it out, the Banks family group chat has suddenly come back to life.

SIMON

You really got fucking married? What do we really know about this guy?

STELLA

I'm on it!

SIMON

When can I meet him? I think he and I need to have a talk.

AINSLEY

Simon, she's not your daughter.

SIMON

I know, but as the oldest, this is part of my duties.

QUINN

Forget that, who had Maeve getting remarried on their Bingo card this year?

SIMON

No one. But I do believe that Ainsley was the only one to place her money on Maeve dating again before Jayce was in middle school, so she wins the pot.

AINSLEY

Woohoo!

QUINN

I knew taking the over on freshman year was a bad move.

STELLA

Y'all I'm going to send you all the articles coming out. Simon, you're even mentioned in a few.

SIMON

Fuck yeah! Send that shit over.

AINSLEY

This is so romantic. I swear, this is what romance novels are made of.

QUINN

Ainsley, you don't even know their story.

AINSLEY

The single mom and the billionaire? Come on, Quinn. That's a cliché.

I can only laugh at the antics of my siblings, and especially at the last text from Ainsley.

"What's so funny?"

I smile at him and grab my purse and Jayce's suitcase. "My sister called us cliché."

"Oh, Love," Logan says with a laugh. "We're anything but."

———

Another day that ends in the letter "y" and another day that I'm a horrible mom.

Which, you know, is great timing since my ex-husband wants to tell a judge I am one.

The last forty-eight hours have been a whirlwind. I haven't had a lot of time to figure much out. And one thing that I let fall through the cracks is what, and how, I'm telling Jayce. How did I realize I forgot about this very important thing?

Yup. Mom of the Year right here.

"Mommy? Where are we going?"

I swallow a giant lump in my throat as I turn toward our final destination. "Logan's."

What to say…what to say…what to say?

In my defense, I did have a plan when Logan was moving in with us. That Logan was new in town so didn't know a lot of people, that his house was being worked on, and as friends, we were going to let him stay with us, because that's what friends do.

Nice life lesson to teach your son about kindness? Yes. A lie? Also yes. But a justified one to protect my child from disappointment when this ended? Hard yes.

But now that we're going to Logan's, I don't know if that same kind of fib is going to work. Do I tell him that we have bugs and our house needs fumigated, and Logan was nice enough to let us stay? Sure, great for the short term. Horrible for when we get back home and Jayce decides to look in every nook and cranny for non-existent bugs and can't sleep in his own room for fear they will crawl up his nose and into his brain.

"Yes! Can I play SpaceCraft with him?"

I nod, trying to keep my face even as I turn into Logan's driveway. "Maybe. You'll have to ask him and make sure he's not busy."

"Yes! This is going to be the best day!"

Sure, best day for him. He's moving into his idol's mansion. I'm moving in with my husband.

Same actions, two very different responses.

"Actually, buddy. When we get there, and before you ask Logan to play, we're going to need to talk to you about some things."

"What kind of things?"

"Um...well..."

"Is it that you and Logan are married?"

What in the fucking world did my child just say?

"Jayce? Can you repeat that, please?"

"Are you talking to me because you married Logan? Like Daddy married Vivian?"

Well, now I am.

Fuck, how did this happen? And how did I not wreck my car when those words came out of his mouth?

Without blinking, and maybe without breathing, I pull the SUV to a stop. I hear Jayce unbuckle his seatbelt and let himself out. I hear the engine rumbling beneath me as I stay seated in silence. Well, not silence, my ears are ringing and my head is pounding because what the actual fuck just happened?

I'm only knocked out of my daze by a light tapping on my window. I look over and see a concerned Logan, standing next to a confused Jayce.

"You okay?" Logan asks, opening my door.

"I told her I heard you two were married and then she quit talking," Jayce says. "Can we go play SpaceCraft now?"

"Oh." Logan blinks so much at Jayce's words he might fly away. "Um...how about you go inside and get the game ready while I help your mum?"

I hear Jayce's little victorious "Yes!" as he runs back inside.

I, on the other hand, might just live in my car for the rest of my life.

———

Apparently I can't live in a car in my new husband's driveway.

Though I think I could've. I'm a resourceful woman.

But I knew I needed to come inside, breathe, take a few shots of whiskey, and figure out how the hell my six-year-old found out about my shotgun, not really real marriage.

Turns out the first-grade gossip line is stronger than the Banks' family group chat. From what I could follow—because holy hell, it was a winding road with a first-grade narrator—Corban heard his mom talking about it, and then told Maddox. Maddox told Addison, who's Rosie's best friend. She said she'd know because Jayce is her boyfriend and that Addison was a liar. Rosie asked Jayce, and all Jayce said was that Logan was his best friend and he's been to his house, which apparently is confirmation for six-year-olds that people are married.

In all the ways I thought about telling my son, that for sure wasn't it. It also reminded me that I need to send his teacher a large bottle of wine. And I need to find Corban's mom and tell her to keep her mouth shut.

But now, with the elephant out of the room and I've had a chance to think, it's time for me to sit down with Jayce. And what better time than right before bed?

"Teeth brushed?" I ask him as I hear the faucet running from his bathroom. He had his own at our house, but this one is connected to his room, and he thinks that's the absolutely coolest thing. Well, that and the SpaceCraft posters Logan at some point put up today for him. To make things less confusing for him, I'm sleeping across the hall. And far away from Logan's bedroom.

"Yup!" He comes bopping out, footy pajamas on, as he hops into the bed, making sure his trusty blanket is tucked under his arm. "Is it story time?"

I shake my head. "Not yet. I thought we could talk about you, me, and Logan."

He climbs into bed and under his covers. "I like him."

That makes me smile. "I know you do."

"He's nice. And funny. And he plays games with me."

"That's awesome, buddy, but—"

"I like staying here better than being at Daddy's."

Well that makes my heart stop. "Really? Why do you say that?"

He shrugs. "Daddy and I always have fun. But I don't like Mommy Viv. She doesn't like my games."

"Mommy Viv?"

"She told me to call her that. But she's not my mommy."

Damn fucking right she's not.

"Does she do anything with you? Or say anything?"

He shakes his head. "She doesn't do *anything*. She just plays on her phone. She needs a screen time limit."

I hold in a snicker. "Is that it?"

He thinks about it for a second before giving me a nod. "Mommy? Are we living here now? Because you're married?"

Here we go, the conversation of the night.

"For now," I say honestly. "But, we're not getting rid of our house, just in case we need to go back for something. But for a while, we're living with Logan. Because you're right, we are married. Is that okay with you?"

Like he's going to protest, now that he's living in SpaceCraft central. "Yeah. But does Logan have my cereal? What am I eating for breakfast?"

I laugh and grab his book. "If he doesn't, I'll go out and get some tonight."

This seems to satisfy him as we go into our nightly routine of the goodnight book. We read our pages, and do our lines, and then it gets to our favorite part.

"Goodnight Mommy, Goodnight Daddy," he says. I'm not proud at how pleased I am that Mommy Viv hasn't made it in yet, but serves her right. "Goodnight Aunt A-Mae and Tella and Quinn. Goodnight Emmett and Winnie the dog. Goodnight Uncle Simon, Aunt Charlie, and baby Lainey. Goodnight Didi and Pappy. Goodnight Rosie. And goodnight Logan."

That last one takes me by surprise. "Really? Goodnight Logan?"

He nods, his eyes growing heavy. "Yup. We live here now, and he's awesome, and you're smiling."

"What was that?"

Did I smile today? I barely remember today as it was nothing but a whirlwind.

"You've been smiling today, and I like it when you smile."

Before I can say anything else, Jayce starts nodding off, leaving me stumped and wondering what my six-year-old is seeing that I'm not.

Smiling? No…that doesn't sound like me.

23
logan

I never thought of myself as a family man. And why would I? Because I have an idyllic view of what family life should be? Nothing in my past should make me say the words, "Yes. One of those, please."

But the past week with Maeve and Jayce has made my outlook on family life a bit different. I know it's only been a few days and that our situation is temporary, but I can't help but feel that this is actually how a family is supposed to be.

Maeve and I work during the day while Jayce is at school. When he gets home, the three of us have taken to meeting in the kitchen, grabbing a snack, and talking to him about his day before he and I exit for some much-deserved SpaceCraft time. One hour exactly, because Maeve sets the rules and I dare not defy them. But that hour? It's the best part of my day.

It's been years since I've played the game through the eyes of a player and not as the creator looking to see what I could make better or tweak. Seeing the excitement on Jayce's face fills my heart and makes me excited again. Especially since video games have brought me nothing but strife the past six months.

"Are you beating him, Jayce?"

I hit pause on the game as I hear Kat come into the gaming

room, coincidentally when the one-hour timer goes off. What I don't expect is for Maeve to be with her.

"Not yet, but he's close," I say.

"I bet I can beat you by Christmas!"

He probably can. The kid has skill. "We'll just have to keep playing."

He nods and puts down his controller and exits the room, but not before doing our just-invented secret handshake, giving Kat a fist bump, and his mom a hug before taking off.

"He's a good kid," Kat says. "Not enough to make me want children. But in a general sense."

"Thanks," Maeve says as she takes a seat next to me. "But can I ask why you needed me in here? I feel like I'm being called to the principal's office."

"No trouble at all," Kat says as she takes a seat in front of us. "In fact, the newest modern family is loved by the press. Who knew family man Logan Matthews would make my job so easy? I should've married you off months ago."

I cringe at the thought of marrying any of the women that Kat set me up with. They were all nice enough—well, everyone except the last one—but I can't imagine spending any more than our few nights together.

"Really? It's working?" Maeve asks. "The headlines I've seen have been mixed."

Kat shrugs. "You're always going to have some bad. And that's because you're an unknown, Maeve, and gossip columns want scandal. And unfortunately, they can only call you a cougar so many times before it gets old. What they're doing now is trying to create things out of thin air. Luckily for you, there aren't any skeletons in the closet. Wait…are there?"

Maeve shakes her head. "No scandals. Never even had a speeding ticket."

"Love to hear that," Kat says. "Now, be warned: They might try and create some drama, which is probably why they were on your tail those first few days. They need to stir the pot."

I tense up at the mention of that. "They're not following Maeve and Jayce to school anymore, right?"

Kat shakes her head. "No. I shut that shit down real quick. I told them to come after you all they want. But the second that they start involving Jayce, Auntie Kat is going to make their lives fucking miserable."

We only noticed cameras the first day of Maeve and Jayce living here, but that was one day too long. He's a kid, and more than that, him being followed by paparazzi is something Josh could use against Maeve, which would defeat the purpose of all of this.

"Thank you so much for that," Maeve says. "I really owe you."

"You don't owe me anything," Kat says. "Though now I have to come in with the next bit of news."

Maeve and I share a glance. "What news?"

"The news that you two need to make next week."

Maeve and I share a confused look. "What are you talking about?"

"Next week is your trip back to Los Angeles," Kat says to me. "And the newlyweds should be there together."

"No," Maeve says immediately. "Josh's biggest strike against me is how much I travel. I can't be jet setting off to LA with my new husband and leaving my child days after he filed."

Yesterday was the day that Josh officially served Maeve papers, saying that he wants to renegotiate Jayce's custody. Luckily, Jayce was at school so Maeve could say every curse word in twenty different languages about it.

"She's right," I say. "She shouldn't go."

Even though I'd love her to…

I've always dreaded red carpets when I was with whatever woman I was set up with. But Maeve? I'd be honored to have her on my arm.

I bet she'd look bloody stunning in a formal gown.

"She doesn't need to be there the entire time," Kat says. "You have meetings Wednesday through Friday. Friday night is nothing. Saturday is the big night. It's the Tech for Tots gala that would be the place to be seen together."

She's right. On my side of this, having Maeve on my arm would do wonders. A now family man showing up with his wife for a gala benefiting educational toys for underprivileged children? The good headlines write themselves.

But in my opinion, the bad outweighs the good, which means Maeve needs to stay here.

"If you can't make it, I understand," I say. "If anyone asks me, I'll tell them that you're at home with your son, make it all about you and Jayce, and that maybe next time we can make a family trip together."

Maeve shakes her head. "If it's Saturday, then I can make it. Maybe Friday, too—I haven't firmed with Josh what the plan is for the weekend. With the holidays, our normal schedule with Jayce is all over the place. If it works that he's taking him all weekend, I wouldn't have to worry about neglecting my child."

I hear the sarcastic bite in that last part.

"Are you sure? Don't do anything for me that would jeopardize you and give that man ammunition."

She shakes her head. "I won't. I promise. Let me make sure everything lines up."

Kat nods, and Maeve and I share a look. I mouth a "thank you" to her, giving her hand a squeeze for good measure.

"One more thing," Kat says. "Our charity party that we're hosting is in the final stages. Maeve, since you're here, I figured we'd get a status update on the setup and everything else you've been doing."

And just like that, Maeve is sitting up straight, her shoulders back, and clearly in her element as she talks about what stage of progress the house is in. Every day she amazes me with how much gets transformed and seeing her vision come to life has been beautiful to watch.

She's magnificent.

Brilliant.

And I'm damn proud of her.

"I think that's it," Kat says. "I'll see everyone tomorrow?"

We all say our goodbyes and exit the gaming room. I should go back to my office and try to get some work done. Maybe actually invent a video game.

But I want nothing to do with video games. Well, at least in that way.

"Are you done with work today?" I ask Maeve.

"Mostly," she says. "Why do you ask?"

The more I think about this idea that just came to me, the more I want to do it.

"Have you started cooking dinner yet?"

Not that I care or demand Maeve does it, but she's insisted. I keep telling her that she doesn't need to cook for me. That I'm a grown man and can properly order carryout since I'm a shit cook. Her response was she was already cooking, so what's one more plate?

"No. Actually was just going to start getting it going. Why?"

I check the time, and if we leave now, we can have plenty of fun while also getting Jayce back in time for bed.

"How about our first family outing?"

———

"Yeah! Take that! You better watch out!"

I try to duck and weave my character as best as possible, but Maeve's character—and Maeve—are machines right now.

And before I know it, my wife has knocked me out in *Mike Tyson's Punch-Out*.

"Yes!" She shouts, doing a little celebratory dance. "Take that, Matthews!"

"Did you win, Mommy?"

"Darn right I did!" Maeve says, giving Jayce a high five. "And we thought Logan was the video game guru?"

I shake my head, wondering how I didn't know that the woman that I'm married to, who I'm also quite infatuated with, was somehow a video game savant. "Where did you learn to do that?"

She shrugs as she helps Jayce onto a stool so he can play a game featuring everyone's favorite video game turtles. "I grew up with an older brother. There were some years in there before I had sisters to hang out with. That game just happened to be the one I was very, very good at."

I laugh, now realizing why she suggested we play that specific one out of all the ones available to us.

"I was hustled," I say as I stand next to her as we watch Jayce in action.

When I got the idea to come to this vintage video game hall—that also makes a pretty good pizza—what I'd wanted to do is rent it out. Pay them whatever amount of money they asked so that Maeve, Jayce, and I could have it all to ourselves.

But apparently even when you're a billionaire you can't make a call out of the blue and shut down a video game shop within an hour. Even when you're Logan Matthews.

Now I know I need to give them a day's notice.

And I will next time. Because that's what you spend your money on when you have it to spend—on the people you love. The people you care about. You spend it to watch their smiles.

And the one on Jayce's face right now? It's a look I'll never forget.

"Thanks," I whisper to Maeve. "I needed out of the house."

She playfully bumps me with her shoulder. "So did I. And this is perfect."

"Take that!" Jayce yells as he starts to figure out the mechanics of the game.

"I remember when this first came out," Maeve said. "I don't think my brother played anything else for months."

"Did you play it when you were little, Logan?"

"A bit..." I don't want to admit that it wasn't as popular

when I started playing games because of how long before it had come out. Luckily for me, my wife makes the crack instead.

"He was too young," Maeve said, giving me a wink.

"Really?" Jayce says without taking his eyes off the game. "How old are you?"

"I'm twenty-nine," I say while simultaneously wondering how good Jayce is at math and figuring out that his mum has a few years on me.

"You're younger than Mom," he says immediately. "But you're older than Vivian. She's twenty-four. I asked when we were on our trip, but I think she was lying. She looks old."

Both Maeve and I do everything in our power not to snort laugh.

"What do you think old is?" I ask, now needing to know more of what's going on in this kid's head.

"Hmmm," he thinks about it for a second, but doesn't stop playing the game. "Thirty."

"Jayce!" Maeve gasps. "You know I'm thirty-six, right?"

"Yeah," he says. "But all moms are old so it doesn't count."

I laugh as Maeve just shakes her head.

"Thanks, I guess," she says. "Hey! Watch out for the bad guys!"

"Let me help you out," I say, moving to stand behind him as I put my hands over his, making sure to show him what I'm going to do. "Keep pushing this button. Faster! Now…power up! Yes! Brilliant!"

Before I know it, I've moved on to another set of controls, Jayce and I playing in tandem with one of the most classic arcade games ever made.

God, what I would've done for this as a kid. I mean, an arcade would've been great, but there were none around me. And no money, even so. But just to have a friend to play games with, it would've been the best escape. Not just sitting in my room alone, trying to drown out the noise with headphones, pretending that I was anywhere but there.

"Logan! We did it! We won!"

Holy shit, we did. "Heck yeah, buddy!"

I was barely prepared as Jayce somehow jumps into my hold, his tiny arms squeezing my neck. I hug him back, and that's when I see Maeve. She's standing next to the game, leaning against it, biting her lower lip, and if I wasn't mistaken, her eyes are maybe a bit watery. Is she crying?

"Are you okay?" I whisper.

She nods. "Thank you."

I don't know what exactly she's thanking me for, but I want to thank her too. Because I want another day like this.

I want a hundred days like this.

With them.

The family that's able to find the calm in the chaos.

guide to love rule #90

Flowers are nice. Jewelry is fine. But a man who sends you
dinner? He's a keeper.

24

maeve

"Sister, you've held out on me long enough. It's time I formally introduce myself to my billionaire brother-in-law. Put him on the phone."

I roll my eyes at Quinn's terrifying request. "Sorry if this is the only reason you FaceTimed me. Logan's on a business trip. Left for Los Angeles today."

"Sounds fancy," she says. "I still can't get over the fact that you're married. How in the ever-loving shit did that happen?"

Oh, what I wish I could tell her. "Things just happen."

I know it sounds lame. And she knows it's lame. But yet, we're just going about our conversation like nothing is weirder than it needs to be.

"I can't wait for the day you can actually tell me what's going on," she says. "The story is going to be epic. Maybe even worth a surprise trip home."

I laugh at that. "So this is what would get you home when it isn't a holiday? The story of how I got married?"

"Absolutely," she says. "I would even pay for it and not use my frequent flyer miles."

"I'm honored," I say as I take a seat on the couch in what has become the TV living room. At least, that's what Jayce has coined it.

"So you're living with him?" she asks.

"Yes. We're all moved in."

"Are you two…sleeping together?"

I'm silent, because I never thought of how I should answer this. Obviously, we're not. This isn't a real marriage. But no one knows that. Well, except Quinn, who doesn't know but also does know.

"I'll take your silence as no, but you want to."

I let out a sigh and make sure Jayce is still oblivious to our conversation. "It's complicated."

And it is. I'm married. I technically broke my holdout of men and sex with him long before we said "I do." In theory, I should have no qualms about exploring a sexual relationship with Logan.

In reality I'm a stubborn woman who refuses to budge, because I dug in my heels and I don't want to dig them out.

Even if he's been wonderful.

Even if he's been nothing but sweet and amazing with Jayce.

Even if he's so hard to resist I have to use my toy at night to make sure I don't do something like go climb into bed with him.

I thought I was going to crack and kiss him that day at the arcade. I mean, no one with a pulse would've blamed me. You try and resist a man who's playing a game with your son, purely enjoying the moment, and not falling a little bit for him.

Then I remember that my husband is seven years younger than me, wasn't born when the Ninja Turtles were at their peak, and that I'm nothing but a dirty cougar using a man for marriage.

"Sounds like it doesn't need to be," she says. "You're married. So whatever reason this happened, and don't argue with me because I know there's a reason, why not use it? Scratch that itch, girl. You have to be itching. I'd be itching, that's for damn sure…"

I think about it for a second, but only a second. "I'm not sleeping with my husband."

Maybe if I say it out loud, I'll believe I really don't want to.

"Your loss...I sure as shit wouldn't be that strong." she says as the doorbell rings. "Now I know you live in a mansion. No real doorbell sounds like that."

I laugh a little as I get up. "It's the gate."

"You have a gate! Now I really need to get home. Oh! Can I come over for Christmas? I want to stay just one night. I have this scene from a movie I saw once that I want to reenact, but I've never had a mansion to do it in."

"Absolutely not," I say as I see that it's some sort of delivery driver at the gate and buzz him in.

"Who is it?"

"Delivery I think," I say. "But I didn't order anything."

"Oh, now I'm intrigued."

I ignore my sister and head to the front door. When I open it, I find a food delivery person, carrying multiple bags from who knows where.

"Hello? Can I help you?"

"Delivery for Maeve Banks."

"That's me."

"Here," he says, handing me the bags before turning to walk away.

"Wait. Who ordered this? Do I owe you anything?"

"No, ma'am. All taken care of. Have a good night."

I step back inside and set the bags down.

"What is it?" Quinn yells from wherever I put down my phone. "I want to see."

I can tell from the smell that it's Chinese food. And upon further investigation, I can see that the boxes are strangely famil-iar. It's from the place Logan and I ordered from on Thanksgiving. And there's a typed note stapled to one of the bags:

Maeve,

Is sending food cliché? I'm not sure. But even if it is, I don't care.

Can't wait to see you in a few days. Enjoy the food.
Yours, Logan
P.S. I know Jayce doesn't like Chinese, so there should be an order of
chicken fingers in this.

"I gotta go," I quickly say to Quinn.

Her smile turns devilish. "Yeah, you do. Go call your man."

My cheeks flush instantly. "I'm not doing that."

And I'm not.

I'm *texting* him.

"Whatever you say, big sis. Whatever you say."

I hang up the phone and quickly send a message to Logan.

MAEVE

Thank you. You didn't have to do that.

I somehow balance my phone and the bags as I take them all
into the kitchen, calling Jayce to follow me so we can eat.

Also, I don't know how Logan knew that I had no desire to
cook tonight, but I'm glad he did.

LOGAN

Not too cliché? I really worried about that.

MAEVE

Food is never cliché.

LOGAN

Good to know. You know, for the future.

MAEVE

Future? Logan, you sent so much food it will be
years before we need more.

LOGAN

Maeve, in case you didn't know, I'm kind of
rich. So I can send you food every day if I so
choose.

MAEVE

Yeah, but I'm going to guess you scrunched
your nose when you saw the price tag.

LOGAN

I did no such thing.

MAEVE

Liar.

LOGAN

Never.

MAEVE

Prove it.

Logan proceeds to text me not only a copy of the receipt from what he ordered tonight, but receipts of food he's sending me over the next two days he's away.

MAEVE

Logan…

LOGAN

Yes?

MAEVE

You didn't have to do that.

LOGAN

I know.

MAEVE

So why did you?

LOGAN

Because no matter the reason, you're my wife. And I want to take care of you. Even if I'm miles away and that means sending food so you don't have to cook.

I don't think I could wipe the smile off my face if I tried.
Am I blushing?
From words from a guy?
To whom I'm married?
Who the hell am I, and what did I do with Maeve Banks?

"Mommy?"

Oh shit. My kid. "Yeah, buddy?"

"Why are you smiling like that?"'

Was I smiling differently? I felt it on my face but it didn't seen weird. "What do you mean?"

Jayce gives a little shrug. "It was a really big smile. Not your normal one. And your cheeks were really red. You looked really happy and really pretty."

Fuck…that was an unexpected punch in the gut. A good one, but holy shit…

"I'm just thanking Logan for sending us dinner," I say, starting to dig for his chicken tenders.

"I like Logan," he says as he climbs onto his stool at the island.

"I know you do," I say. "I mean, he's your best friend."

"He is. But you smile when you're with him. That means I like him more."

My jaw drops as I watch my son grab for the box of tenders, not having a care in the world of what he just said.

Out of the mouths of babes…

———

MAEVE

Question for you.

I swear Logan either keeps his phone always attached to him or has a special alert for when I text, because I never need to wait more than a minute.

LOGAN

The answer is yes.

MAEVE

You don't know the question.

LOGAN

Doesn't matter. If it's about the house, yes. Or whatever you think is best. Whichever one fits this situation. If it's about any other thing, the answer is also yes.

MAEVE

That's not how this works.

LOGAN

Fine. What's the question, so I can show you, in fact, that IS how this works.

MAEVE

First question that neither of those answers will do: What thread count of sheet do you prefer?

LOGAN

See? I'm sorry, but you're wrong. The correct answer is whatever you think is best, because I couldn't tell you the first thing about thread counts.

MAEVE

You're impossible, you know that? I never thought I'd say that about a client who agrees with everything.

LOGAN

I prefer amiable.

MAEVE

Whatever it is, do you want the sheets and accent pillows in a certain color?

LOGAN

Whatever you want.

MAEVE

Logan, you have to make this decision. This is your bedroom.

LOGAN

It is. But I'm hoping one day it will be our bedroom as well. So this is me saving an expense and letting you pick out your future bedroom set.

He did not just say that…

MAEVE

Logan…

LOGAN

I know. Too far, right?

I mean, it was. But it wasn't. Oh, if he knew how confused I was these days.

MAEVE

Just what color do you want?

LOGAN

I'm breaking down your walls with food, aren't I?

MAEVE

No comment.

LOGAN

I'll take that as a yes…

———

"Hello?"

My voice is groggy as I get my bearings, considering this phone call woke me up from a full-on sleep. What time is it? Where am I? Who's called at this ungodly hour? Am I late for school? What year is it?

"Maeve? Did I wake you?"

Well, that wakes me up. "Logan? What time is it?"

"About nine-thirty out here, so eleven-thirty for you?"

I pat around my bed to find my glasses, only to realize that I fell asleep with them on my face. I adjust them slightly and pray they aren't too bent as I look over to my bedside table. Yup. It's only eleven-thirty at night. I was sleeping so hard I would've thought it was the middle of the night.

Or next Tuesday.

"Is everything okay?"

Maybe it's the mom instinct in me to ask that question first, but even in my dazed-from-sleep mind, I want to know. Why else would he be calling me this late?

"Everything is fine. I just wanted to talk to you."

Now that wakes me up.

I roll over onto papers that I fell asleep around and push myself up to sit against my headboard. He's just calling to talk to me? About my day?

Is this what married couples do? If so, Josh definitely missed that memo.

"Oh. Okay then." I'm trying to get my bearings, but between his unexpected call, and being woken up so suddenly that I felt like I was late for the bus, I'm pretty scattered. "How was your day?"

It was the first thing I thought to ask, but somehow I think it was the wrong thing.

"Long. Boring. Frustrating."

"I'm sorry. Want to talk about it?"

He doesn't say anything for a second, but I can only guess by the slow breaths he's taking that he's trying to figure out where to start. Or maybe what to say. And I don't know what compels me to do this, especially because I know my bed-head is probably pretty epic right now, but I switch the call to FaceTime. Luckily, and before I can overthink that decision, he answers.

"Hello, Love."

My body heats as those two little words run through me. Also doesn't hurt that he's also in bed. Shirtless.

Maybe I should've stuck with the phone call.

My mind suddenly flashes back to the first night we met and the very inappropriate thoughts I had about him in bed. It's also funny that he has to go two time zones away for me to see him in his sleep attire.

But I only stare a second, because it doesn't take long for me to realize that I was right to think something was wrong. There's pain on his face that isn't as bad as the day he told me about his horrible family, but it's there.

And I want to fix it.

"I felt like you might've needed a friendly face to go along the voice?"

He nods. "You know me so well."

Do I? I was just going on gut reaction and years of wanting to fix problems for my siblings. Or, maybe I'm getting to know Logan better than I realize. "Talk to me. Anything specific happen or just a whole lot of shit?"

He nods. "Both. I hate meetings. They're long, boring, and most of the time can be done over an email."

"I remember you canceling many on me, so that tracks."

My playful dig hits the mark as I see a slight blush creep across his cheeks. Good. About time someone else's face gave them away.

"Touché. But today's meetings were utterly horrible. What do I care what shade of blue the packaging for the new toys is? It's space. Make it midnight blue and be done with it."

"Oh the problems of a CEO," I tease, but this time, my joke doesn't land.

"It wasn't just that," he continues. "The board wants the new game. They're tired of waiting."

"Oh shit, Logan." I know this has been bugging him for weeks now, and even months before we met. "Still nothing?"

"I had a small idea," he admits. "But today I started fiddling with it, and it...I don't think it's there."

"Okay, then," I say, sitting up. This I can help with. "Let's talk it out."

"Talk it out?"

"Yes," I say confidently. "When I can't see something, but I know it's there, I call one of my sisters and just ramble."

"And they help?"

"Oh, absolutely not. They don't know the first thing about design besides basic color coordination. And even Quinn doesn't know that. But me getting the words out there sometimes helps unscramble my brain. So, let's unscramble."

"Maeve, you don't have to…"

"Logan," I say sternly. "I know. I want to."

There's a silence for a second before he just starts spewing ideas. Admittedly, I don't know much about games besides the few I played as a kid, but I'm happy to listen. I ask questions when I think he needs me to, and I throw in counterpoints when needed. But mostly I'm just here. Because that's what I can do. In this moment, this is how I can fix the problem.

I don't know how long Logan and I talk, but I feel my yawn hit me and I slump a little down into my pillow. I bring the phone with me, and I don't know if my eyes are playing tricks on me, but I watch as Logan shifts in the bed, putting one of his hands behind his head, perfectly showing off his sculpted arms. I don't know who came up with the stereotype that video game guys were scrawny nerds, but I'd like to tell them they are damn wrong.

"Love? Are you staring at me?"

"What!" I screech a little too loudly. "No."

His devilish smile clearly says that he's not believing me at all. "It's fine. I like it when you do."

I swallow a lump in my throat. "I do? You do?"

He laughs under his breath. "Every once in a while I catch you. And it's fine. Believe me, a man loves it when he sees his wife looking at him."

I must be tired, because I swear when he just called me "his wife" something happened downstairs that is making me think I need a date with my battery-operated best friend tonight. He's said it before. I've heard the phrase with my own ears, so I don't know why it's hitting different this time.

"You're tired," Logan says.

"I'm fine," I say through a massive yawn.

"Go to sleep, Maeve," he instructs.

"Okay."

"Thank you, though. This…this really helped."

"Good," I say, though I don't know how much I actually contributed. "Are you feeling better?"

If I wasn't already laying down, his smile would knock me over. "Better than I have in ages."

25

logan

"Logan Matthews. We need to talk."

I lean back against my rental car, which is parked outside the small executive airport in Los Angeles as Maeve walks toward me, fresh off her trip from Nashville on the private plane I'm renting.

And probably buying.

"What's that, Love?"

She shakes her head. "Don't you 'Love' me. A private plane? What happened to my frugal billionaire?"

I lean in and give her a kiss on the cheek before taking her suitcase to stow in the car. "Still frugal. But I'm not frugal when it comes to your safety."

"Safety? Logan, the press has realized I'm boring. We haven't seen a camera in days. I'm pretty sure I would've been fine with commercial."

"Didn't want to risk it," I say as I come around to open her car door. "But you've got to admit, it was nice, wasn't it?"

She tries to fight the smile, but it's a losing battle. "It was really nice. I had a full desk to work, and I wasn't battling for tray space with my laptop and my drink. I could stretch my legs, and I slept for a half hour and didn't have to worry about snoring. Oh, and I'm pretty sure you did this, but having Diet Coke and popcorn on it for me was a nice touch."

"Glad to hear you enjoyed it," I say as I get back into the car to start making our way to the hotel.

"Can I ask you something?"

I look over to Maeve, who looks less stressed than she has in days. Maybe this little getaway will be good for her. "Anything."

"I know how you grew up, which is horrible, and that's not what this is directly about. But I've heard of so many people who didn't have money, got a few bucks, and blew through it in a few months. But not you? Didn't you suddenly want to spend all this money you never had?"

"Wanted to? Of course I did," I say, remembering back to the first time that I had multiple commas in my bank account. "In fact, when I received my first large earnings, I went out and bought a brand-new car."

"As you should have," Maeve says. "You earned it."

"That's what Kat said when I came home and immediately felt guilty. I beat myself up for days about it. It was a nice car. Expensive for me, but not exorbitant. I just felt so selfish."

"Not selfish. Not when you've earned it."

"In my head, I know that. It was just hard to turn that switch in my brain," I say. "Kat had to sit me down and say that it was okay to spend some money. And if I was going to feel guilty on splurges, then to make sure I had reasons behind them. And if I didn't have good reasons, then don't do it."

"And you never had a good reason for a plane?"

I shake my head. "It felt wasteful. It was just me and Kat who would've been using it. Maybe an occasional board member, if they asked nicely."

"But now?"

I look over to my wife and shoot her a wink as we start to approach the hotel. "Now I have a reason."

As we pull into the hotel, I want to pull right out. It's a beautiful California day, and I want nothing more than to rent a convertible, put the top down, and drive down the Pacific Coast Highway with my wife. I want to put my hand on her thigh and let our problems fly in the wind. Maybe stop and sit at the ocean, Maeve in my arms as we just sink into the peacefulness of the waves. Skip the gala tonight. Forget about my work problems. Forget about the custody case.

Forget that this is fake.

The rope I'm walking with Maeve is thin right now. Not in terms of how we're getting along—that's been splendid. There's a pull between us that's always been there, but was easier to keep at bay when we were just designer and client.

But since she moved in? Since I see her every day and we've now shared things that are vulnerable and real? The pull is so strong I don't know how much longer I can stay away.

I want her. I want her more than ever.

I want her to be my wife, in every sense of the word.

We don't say much else as we get to the hotel and step into the elevator for the penthouse. This is the first time we've been in a lift together since that first night, and I can't help but notice that Maeve is conveniently standing on the other side of the car from me.

"Why are you over there?" I tease.

"No reason." Those might be her words, but she said it while staring down at her phone, refusing to make eye contact with me. I could tease her about it, but it's probably safer if I let that one go.

Especially because she's not going to be happy when she walks into the *one-bedroom* suite.

———

"Logan?"

"Yes?"

"Care to tell me where the other bed is?"

Here we go…

"There isn't one."

Maeve's face morphs from confusion to anger in less than a second. "Excuse me? Don't penthouses have multiple bedrooms?"

"Some do. Some are one bedroom," I say, guiding her to sit down. "I should've warned you, but it slipped my mind until just now, and I apologize for that. But Kat didn't want anyone taking anything out of context if the paparazzi did some non-ethical digging, and they could make a headline out of something like 'Logan Matthews and new wife already need separate bedrooms.'"

"That's a shitty headline."

"I know," I say. "But we're just being cautious. I promise, Love. This has nothing to do with anything except keeping up appearances."

Her shoulders relax a bit as my words sink in. "You're probably right. And we're adults. Right? We can share a bed and have nothing happen."

I raise an eyebrow. Really? She can just sleep next to me and not be affected whatsoever? Am I the only one who feels this? I know I've always been ahead of her when it comes to us, but I thought, or maybe foolishly hoped, that she was coming around. But the way her face is leveled and her tone is even, it's like we're back to designer and client.

Which is not where I'm at. Not one bloody bit.

"Maeve, respectfully, I'm going to be sleeping on the sofa."

"Really? Come on, Logan. We can be—"

I put my finger to her lips. "Maeve, if I'm in bed with you, I can't promise that I'll be a gentleman. Knowing my wife is next to me? The woman I can still feel if I close my eyes and think hard enough? Being in a bed with you and not be able to touch you, or hold you, or kiss you, would be pure torture. I know you're not ready. I don't know if you'll ever be. And that's fine. But for my sanity, and to respect your boundaries, I'll be on the sofa. Because I'm just a weak man who wants his wife more than he wants air to breathe."

I lean in to Maeve and place a soft kiss on her cheek before stepping back. "I'm going to get in the shower so you can have the bathroom for as long as you need to get ready for tonight."

She nods, her eyes averted from me as I make my way to the shower. Do I regret what I said? No. I needed to vocalize it. But, the wishful thinker in me was hoping for a different reaction.

I flip on the shower and wait until I can see the steam before getting undressed and stepping inside. I let the hot water run down my back as I hang my head underneath the shower head, wondering how the hell I got here. And how Maeve and I went from strangers in an airport to bedmates to husband and wife? Thinking back on every tiny moment and event that led us to here almost feels like a dream.

Except it's not. This is real. My feelings for her are real. And I can only hope that maybe one day she might feel the same way.

I think about picking my head up and beginning to actually bathe myself when I feel a rush of cold air hit my back. When I turn around I'm shocked to see Maeve—completely naked—stepping into the shower with me.

"Maeve? Are you all right?"

She doesn't say a word as she steps toward me, cupping my face and bringing me down for the most unexpected kiss of my life.

My wife is kissing me…

The second our lips touch, my arms are around her, bringing her into my chest. I feel the hot water running around us, sluicing off as our lips sync in perfect harmony.

It's hungry and needy, yet passionate and wanting. Not too hard, and definitely not too soft.

Bloody perfect.

I let my hands move up her body, holding onto her wrists as we slowly pull away, our foreheads still touching.

"I don't want to be scared anymore," she says. "I don't want to be stubborn. I don't want to miss out on things because I dug my heels so far into the ground that they're stuck forever."

"You don't have to."

"I know," she says as I push back a piece of wet hair from her face. "But then I feel out of control, which usually freaks me out so bad I reverse it and dig in even harder. I see that now. You've made me see that."

I use my thumbs to push away the water from her eyes, knowing that she's not done. Which is fine. I'll stand in here with her all day.

"You've made me see a lot, Logan. You've made me realize my life doesn't begin and end with my career. Or with Jayce. That if I lean on someone, that's not admitting weakness. It's allowing for help, which lets you experience more. I knew that in the back of my head, but I could never come to the realization of how much I was missing out on because of my control issues."

"Glad I could be of service."

She laughs softly but balls her fists together as she rests them on my chest. "I don't know how to do this. And even as I'm saying that I want to, I know I need to take this slow. I've never conventionally dated. My first marriage was nothing to write home about. And now my second only happened because of circumstances. I've never gone into a situation more blind than I am right now. My head is wondering what the hell I'm doing. But for the first time in my life, my heart is winning the battle, and I now realize I'd be the most stubborn woman on the planet if I didn't listen to the winning team. Me and you."

I know I should say something. Anything to reassure her that the last thing I want to do is hurt her. But all I want to do is kiss her.

And so I do. I kiss her with every ounce of affection, emotion, and dare I say love, that I have for her. I kiss her to let her know I'll take care of her. Her heart. Jayce. Anything else that life throws at us.

"If it makes you feel better, I don't know what I'm doing

either," I say. "I never thought I wanted a family. Christ, until a few years ago, every ounce of my energy was on SpaceCraft and nothing else. We're not that different, you and me."

"Oh we're very different," she says lightly. "Which is another reason my head is still way behind the heart on this one."

"Well then, let me convince it."

I bring her to me and turn her toward the water, letting the warmth hit her as I'm sure she has to be freezing. While her body is warming, I let my hands graze over her perfect curves.

"Yes, our ages are different. Our backgrounds are different," I begin, not being able to help myself as my hands graze over her perfect breasts. I fight down my cock, because it's not the time and place. "Right there should be enough for us to realize this might not work."

Maeve's eyes close and her head falls back, resting on my shoulders. I let my hands continue to run over her body, hoping to guide her to the relaxation she probably desperately needs right now.

"But what's more important is that, besides our differences, we understand each other. I know that you like to be in control, but there are times you need things off your plate, even if you refuse to ask."

"And I probably never will," she cracks, eyes still closed.

"I've come to learn that. But that's okay. I know you, Love. And I'm going to keep learning about you. Just like you're going to learn that I will lock myself away for days when I feel stuck, thinking that I need total isolation for a breakthrough."

"When all you really need is someone to talk you through it…"

My eyes close as I pull her in tighter, remembering how much she helped me the other night when I was going through that exact feeling. "Precisely. So yes, we might be different. But we're both driven individuals. We want to be the best. We love a challenge. But most importantly, we want to make sure everyone around us is happy, even at the expense of our own happiness."

"Especially at our expense," Maeve adds.

"Because as long as everyone else is happy..."

"Then so are we."

Holy shit, that's it. Suddenly, everything in my life is clear as day. I wanted to make my parents happy, and I thought good grades and being the best would do it. I even developed a video game in hopes of earning their praise, believing my mind would be the glue to bring them peace. I dated women for months because I couldn't fathom my board and my company being disappointed in me for not having the next big thing—even though I was miserable the entire time.

And Maeve? She married Josh because she thought it would be best for Jayce. She prides herself on being in charge of her family, even if it means bending over backwards. She only has a few members on her staff, and those are only for jobs that are painstaking and expansive. I've heard her say the words "I'll take care of that," more than I'd like during the decorating process.

Two opposites on the outside. But inside? More alike than even we knew.

Maeve and I don't say anything else as we let the hot water rush over us. I pump some of the hotel shampoo into my hand, lathering it together before running it through her brown locks. I massage her head, which I'm guessing she likes as she keeps leaning into my touch every time I apply pressure, before turning her to rinse it out. She returns the favor for me, though she decides to fill her hands with body wash, running her hands over every inch of my body.

"Fuck, Love," I say as she strokes my cock. I turn into the water, wanting the suds off me as Maeve's hand keeps working me.

"Logan?"

"Yes. Like I've said before, whatever you want, the answer is yes."

Her giggle is infectious, and I truly don't know if I've ever heard that sweet sound before. "The event we're supposed to go to tonight…how important is it?"

"To Kat, it's a huge deal. To me it's just another fundraiser; they want my money more than me."

Her smile gets a little bigger. "So how much trouble would we get in if I suggested that we skip it and spend the night here, just the two of us?"

My wife is a damn genius. "I'll double my donation. And it'll be money well spent."

Her giggle turns into full-on laughter as I pick her up in my arms and pin her against the wall of the shower. Her legs wrap around me, as do her arms, as water rains down both of our faces.

I still have soap on me. She probably has some in her hair. Neither of us care. Our lips find each other, and suddenly, despite everything going on in our lives, we're able to find a different kind of calm in the chaos.

guide to love rule #73

Private planes are a good signifier of wealth. They're also great when you want to fool around with your husband at 40,000 feet.

26

maeve

"Good morning, Love."

I slowly start to wake up as I feel Logan's lips on my shoulder. His soft kisses are the best alarm clock as I realize there's light coming through the curtains of the hotel room.

"What time is it?" I ask groggily.

"Eight-thirty," he says, his kisses now traveling down my bare arm. "I hate to wake you, but if we want to eat breakfast before we fly out, we should get up."

Did he just say eight-thirty? I don't remember the last time I slept until eight-thirty. And what time did we go to bed? I remember looking at the clock around midnight when Logan and I yawned simultaneously. We were both exhausted from the night, though not in the way that most people would be if they had a penthouse suite to themselves and actually never got dressed from their showers.

Last night was…I don't know if I have words. After we exited the shower, Logan called Kat to let her know we'd be skipping the function. He told her to make up an excuse that one of us was sick. She yelled that this was supposed to be our first public appearance and to go. He told her he'd send two million to the charity for an apology, and that he was going to spend the night in the hotel with his wife and nothing she could say could change his mind.

I might have felt a rush of warmth when I heard him say that.

The rest of the day and night were relaxing and perfect. After the shower, we wrapped ourselves in the fluffiest robes I've ever felt and ordered room service. We talked, we laughed, and we were vulnerable. He talked more about his childhood and the loneliness he first felt when he came to Stanford, and I talked about my family and how I started in interior design.

We kissed. We cuddled. Our hands got a little handsy. At some point, the robes came off. But that was it. Yet, I don't think either of us really wanted more. I mean, I did. But I also didn't. Yesterday was so perfect just the way it was, I didn't want to add more. Plus, I meant it when I said I wanted to take it slow. And Logan understood that perfectly as we talked and kissed until we both fell asleep in each other's arms.

"I'm starving," I say, which is probably because my body thinks I should've eaten hours ago.

Logan's smile is infectious as he looks down at me, his hand gently brushing the hair off my face. "I already ordered room service. Should be here within thirty minutes."

I take his hand as it gently slides down my face, pressing a kiss into his palm. "You know you're too good to me."

He shakes his head. "Oh, Love, we're just getting started."

With one more kiss Logan pops out of bed, letting me take in his exquisite body that is now donning a tight pair of boxer briefs. I didn't get to do this the last time we shared a hotel. Then again, I was more concerned about getting the hell out of Dodge than thinking about watching Logan get dressed in the morning.

How did I not know this was hot? Also, why is it hot? I can't put my finger on it, but I'm transfixed as I watch Logan slide his arms through his white dress shirt, leaving it open as he looks for his pants.

"Are you staring again?"

I smile as he calls back our conversation from the other night. "I thought you liked it when your wife stared at you?"

Logan turns around, giving me an amazing view of his perfectly sculpted chest. His eyes are on fire as he stalks back toward the bed. "When do we need to pick up Jayce?"

My breathing is heavy as Logan takes off the shirt he just put on and tosses it to the side. "He's with Josh until after school on Monday."

I expect Logan to descend on me, and I'm ready. Excited even. So consider me confused when he walks away to grab his cell phone.

I mean, talk about a buzzkill. Just when you think you're going to fool around with your husband, he stops to what? Phone a friend?

"Who are you calling?"

Logan signals for me to be quiet before the call connects. "Hello, this is Logan Matthews. I had a flight scheduled to take off at eleven-thirty this morning?"

He looks back at me, sending me a wink that hits just right. "Yes, I was wondering if we could push that back until later this afternoon? Something has come up that I need to attend to."

He nods and says a few other things, never taking his eyes off me, before he hangs up and tosses the phone aside.

"You're really getting used to this private plane life."

"I've come to see there are advantages," he says as he walks to the foot of the bed. "Especially when I want to enjoy the morning with my wife."

My laughter fills the room as he grabs my ankles and pulls me down to him.

"Room service is taking way too long," he says, licking his lips. "I think I'm going to need an appetizer."

I watch as Logan kneels down at the end of the bed, pushing the silk nightgown I'm wearing up past my hips. I pull it off the rest of the way, my body suddenly overheating as Logan begins pressing kisses on the inside of my thighs.

I try to prop myself up on my elbows, wanting to watch him, but with the first swipe of his tongue over my center, I lose any strength needed to hold me up.

The night we spent together plays on a loop in my mind often. Maybe more than I'll ever admit. But part of me also wondered if I was blowing it out of proportion. Because between the martinis, and the moment, and the excitement of the night, there was a real possibility I could've created this memory that was better than what it actually was.

I'm now realizing I was mistaken.

This is better.

Maybe it's being sober, or being in the light of day. Maybe it's because I know Logan so much more than I did that night. But the way he's worshipping me now? How his tongue is licking and exploring, while his fingers are working in tandem to find the spot that's going to send me over the edge? This is better than any fantasy.

"Logan," I moan grabbing at his hair as his tongue starts doing a fluttering motion that is making my hips and body have a mind of their own.

He doesn't say anything, instead doubling down on every single thing he's just done that my body has reacted to. It's like he memorized every buck my hips did, or every time I pulled his hair just a little harder. The man can read me like a book, and while in some ways that's terrifying, in this moment it's anything but.

"So close." I grab onto the sheets, needing something to brace me for whatever Logan is about to do. And just as I think I'm ready, that I feel the orgasm coming from deep within me, Logan takes one of his hands and tweaks a nipple, sending just enough pain to balance the pressure.

And the perfect combination is my undoing.

My scream is as loud as my orgasm is intense. Thank God we're on a private floor of the hotel.

"Jesus Christ," I pant as my orgasms finally subsides. "That was..."

"Beautiful," Logan finishes for me. He leaves kisses on the inside of my thighs and on my stomach as he climbs onto the bed. I realize where his mouth has just been, and the trail he likely left on my body, yet I can't help but want to kiss him and taste myself on his lips.

As soon as he's within reach, I wrap my hands around his neck and pull him down on me, kissing him exactly how I want. And I'm right, I do taste myself. What I wasn't expecting was it to be slightly intoxicating. Knowing what we just shared? Knowing how my body reacted to him? It's quite the unexpected high.

Just as I'm about to reach down, wanting nothing more than to feel his length in my hands, a knocking on the door breaks the bubble of the moment.

"Don't answer," I protest. Though as soon as I say that, my stomach loudly announces how hungry it is.

"You need food," he says, dropping one more kiss on my lips before popping out of bed. I groan as he answers the door—and I sure hope he put on a robe, because no server needs to see what was just pressing against my body.

"Breakfast in bed?" I ask as I bring the sheet over my breasts and sit myself up against the headboard.

"Bacon, eggs, toast, and juice," he says—now wearing a robe. "If you don't like that, there's more on the cart and you can take whatever you'd like."

"Aren't you eating?"

He shakes his head. "I will after my shower. You eat first."

I throw out a pouty lip. "Maybe I wanted to shower with you?"

He shakes his head. "If you get in that shower with me, I'm going to fuck you. I don't know if I'd be able to help myself."

"Is that a bad thing?"

"Normally it wouldn't be. But the next time I feel you wrapped around my cock, I want it to be in *our* bed."

My still-throbbing pussy clenches at his words, and I'm left speechless.

His wife? Our bed? If he keeps using words like that—and my body keeps reacting—I'm going to want to stay in this marriage forever.

———

A few hours—and one lonely shower—later, Logan and I are on a private plane back to Nashville.

A plane I have a feeling he's about to purchase.

Normally when it comes to flying, I have my routine down. I either use it to sleep or work. I don't watch an in-flight movie. I don't read a book. To me, plane time is precious time to either catch a nap because I'm likely exhausted from traveling, or use the time to check off work that doesn't take effort, but time.

But today, I have none of that to do. And both are Logan's fault.

"Quit fidgeting," he says, though I don't know how he can tell since he's typing something on his laptop.

"I'm trying not to," I say. "But I don't have anything to do."

That makes him push the screen down. "How do you mean?"

"I slept like a baby last night, so I don't want to nap. And my only work for another week and a half is your home. And even that I have nothing to order or design. At this point it's all installation, or waiting on pieces to come in. Therefore I have nothing to do on this plane that took off..." I check my watch. "Twenty minutes ago."

Logan chuckles. "And here I thought that I'd get to hear Maeve's airplane snores again."

I narrow my eyes and hate that the seatbelt signs are still on so I can't reach over and smack him.

"I wasn't snoring."

I probably was.

"Stubborn to your core," he says, sending me a playful wink.

I slump down into the comfortable leather seat. I didn't know seats like this could exist on airplanes, but apparently they do when it comes to private jets. I actually wish I was tired; this seat would be great for napping.

Allowing myself to get comfortable, and shockingly not feeling guilty, I pull out my phone and bring up a social media app. I don't scroll often—who has the time?—but apparently I'm a new woman in many ways right now, so might as well indulge a little.

Even though I haven't been on here in weeks, there's nothing new. Photos of families getting ready for Christmas. Posts in community groups asking about what the weird sounds and booms are. People vaguely asking for prayers for their children, making it sound like they're having major surgery when it's really just a routine dental cleaning.

Same ol', same ol'.

I'm just about ready to exit the app when a news story catches my eye.

CASTING CALL: Are you a wife and mother in Nashville? Then we want you for our new reality show.

"Oh you've got to be kidding me," I say, laughing hysterically as I open the story.

"What's that?" Logan asks.

"Apparently they're starting some sort of Wish.com version of Real Housewives, but only in Nashville." Nashville is a special kind of city. It's not big like LA or New York, but it has the star power of it. Between the country music scene, the pro athletes, and now the tech boom we're seeing, it's become a destination. Oh, the houses I could've decorated if I wasn't stuck in Man Cave Central. "Honestly though, kind of surprised it took them this long."

"You should audition."

Oh, my husband's got jokes...

"You're hilarious. I've said it to my sisters before, I'd be the worst reality star in the history of reality stars. I'm too mean and honest."

"I beg to differ. Those are the best ones."

I tilt my head. "Am I learning that the man I'm married to is a reality junkie?"

He playfully shrugs as he puts his laptop to the side. "I wouldn't say junkie. More like, sporadic observer who has a definitive order of Bravo shows. And before you ask, it's all Kat's fault. Though, if you had a show, I'd be much more than a casual fan."

This man...I swear. We're married. I've said that I'm open to actually being a couple. Yet, he's still flirting with me.

And I didn't expect to like it as much as I do.

"Well, if the time ever comes for a design show, I do, unwillingly, have a concept."

"Do tell."

"Stella came up with it. It's men who want me to decorate their homes, I tell them that they're douchebags for wanting stereotypical items or designs, and then I give them the home that will actually show off their money and impress women, not their expensive bachelor pads."

Logan's eyes light up. "You should absolutely do that."

I can only laugh at his hilarious joke. "You're ridiculous."

"I'm being serious. That would be a hit. And I can even invent the game that would go along with it. People can design their houses in the game and then you can come in and rate them. Tell them they did a good job or tell them they're shit."

"I'm sure everyone is dying to play a game with me as the main character," I say.

"I'd play with you all day."

"Okay, that one was bad," I say. And it was. But also something about it gave me a shiver up my spine.

"Was it? Or are you just realizing that you married a video game tycoon on the outside, but inside is still a nerd who loves a bad pun or two?"

"I'm realizing a lot of things about you."

"Care to share?"

At that moment, the seatbelt light goes off, and I don't hesitate to unbuckle the latch and take the few steps I need to climb onto Logan's lap. His arms wrap around my back as I straddle him, and I can't help but notice the little twinkle in his eye as I put my weight on him.

I lean in for a soft kiss that quickly deepens. I didn't mean for it to happen—I really just wanted time to accurately put together the words I wanted to say. But like hell I'm going to stop it. I'm on a private plane, with my husband, who gave me an orgasm just a few hours ago that I can still feel. I'm with a man who in just a short amount of time has come to know me better than most people. Who has stepped up for me in ways that I never thought I could trust anyone to do.

I know this marriage was for convenience. That we've still not talked about what we're going to do when the end arrives. But I know one thing right now.

I'm going to enjoy these moments with my husband.

Especially ones on a private plane.

I gradually pull back the kisses as I slide off Logan's lap onto the floor. His eyes go wide as I start undoing his belt.

"Love? What are you doing?"

I lick my lips as I bring down his zipper.

"I'd rather show you."

27

logan

"YOU DIDN'T HAVE TO COME WITH ME."

I give Maeve a side eye, making sure not to take my eyes off the road. "You're going to pick up Jayce from his father's, who is the same man who wants to take him away from you. Who, judging by messages he's sent, isn't thrilled about our marriage. Sorry, but me not tagging along wasn't an option."

"He's not holding him hostage," she says. "I've done this hundreds of times without you, Logan."

Luckily I have to bring the car to a stop, so I can turn and look at her. "That was the past. This is the present. And in the present, I'm your husband. Which means that when you go and see your ex, I come with you. Deal?"

Her sigh signals that she realizes this is a losing battle. "Fine."

"That's my girl."

I give her thigh a squeeze as I pull through the stop sign. Did she really think when she told me that she was leaving to go pick up Jayce that I wouldn't come? And she said it so nonchalant, like she was running to the store for some milk. Then again, she's been doing things by herself for so long it probably never occurred to her that I'd *want* to come. I'm probably lucky she told me.

"Now, when we get there, please don't go all Logan Matthews on him."

I give her a quick look before turning onto Josh's road. "What's that supposed to mean?"

"It means that you like to play the rich billionaire card when it suits. And I can see a situation where you're standing in front of my ex and need to one-up him, so you're going to drop that you just bought a plane. Or remind him that you invented the video game that he and his son love to play."

I shrug. She's right. It's always my ace in the hole. "No promises."

She mumbles something about an "infuriating man," but I just smile as we approach Josh's home.

Yes, we're about to have a likely drag-out with her ex. But something about this whole interaction feels so normal, which is not a word I use often.

I'll be the first to admit I've never had a life that anyone would consider mundane. Between my upbringing, being a Brit in an American college who wasn't on a study abroad program, and then gaining fortune quite early in my career, I couldn't tell you the first thing about a normal life. But this? Going with Maeve to get Jayce, then heading to dinner at a chain restaurant because Jayce will likely want chicken tenders and neither of us want to cook, then going home as a family, feels pretty normal to me.

I mean, how we got here wasn't. But I must say, I don't mind the outcome. Not one bit.

"Okay, then here's the plan," she says as I turn into the driveway. "We're going to go in. We're going to address the elephant in the room immediately. You and Josh are going to shake hands. We're going to be civil. We're going to talk about that the date has been filed for February, but maybe try again to see if we can come to an agreement outside of court. What we're not going to do is give him any ammo for the custody case. Deal?"

I put the car in park before holding my hands up in defense. "You have nothing to worry about from me. I'm British. I'm polite by nature."

She raises an eyebrow with that side eye that she loves to give me. "Promise?"

I make an "X" over my heart. "I promise."

I exit the car and come around to open hers for her. I offer her my hand, which she takes, as we exit her SUV, and I don't drop it as we approach the house. And I'm glad I don't since we have greeters at the door.

"Oh, look, it's the welcome wagon," Maeve drawls, a touch of snark coming from her voice as Josh and Vivian stand on the front porch.

So much for being nice…

I take a second to try and get a read on them. Vivian is standing like a dutiful wife, arm wrapped through Josh's and striking a pose like she's waiting for a photographer to take her picture. He's staring at us—more so me—as we approach, like he's trying to figure out how to beat me in a fight.

Won't happen.

Maeve still thinks something is fishy about everything, and now that I'm seeing the two of them, I'd have to agree.

Josh takes a step forward, and while he might be talking about me, he's talking *to* Maeve. "Just wanted to be the first to introduce myself to your new husband."

Their eyes lock and I can tell they are having some sort of silent conversation.

Maeve's nostrils flare.

Josh's eyes narrow.

Vivian is looking at a bird that just flew past.

Yup. Polite is out the door.

"Why don't we go inside?" I ask. "It's a little chilly, and I think we should talk where neighbors won't be able to hear us."

No one says anything, but Josh does turn and open the door as we follow inside. The door is barely shut before Jayce comes scampering down the hall.

"Mommy! Logan!" he yells as he barrels into my leg. "Logan! I made it another level. It was my first time doing it. I just did it! Want to come see?"

I lean down and give him a hug that is more like a pat on the back before I ruffle his hair. "I'd love to. But me and your mum need to talk to your dad and Vivian. How about you see how far you can get, and then start packing up your things."

"Okay," he says, running back to what I'm assuming is his bedroom.

"Look at you, Bonus Dad of the Year."

I promised Maeve I'd be polite. And I don't want to start anything. As she said, I refuse to give this man something to use against me.

But what's the expression though—ask for forgiveness and not permission?

"Just trying to be the best person I can be for Jayce," I reply. "You understand that, though, right? As a dad. Wanting the absolute best for your son."

We have our own stare down before Maeve's words break it up.

"Okay, how about we sit and try to be adults."

And we do—Maeve and I take one couch as Josh and Vivian take the other. I immediately go for Maeve's hand, which she gives me. Josh sees that, tries to do the same, but Vivian is using both of her hands to type on her phone.

"I thought we should all meet," Maeve begins. "It's been a crazy few months."

"Yes," Josh says with a bite. "It would've been nice to meet the man who apparently my son is now living with, you know, before my ex-wife married him."

"That's understandable, and I apologize," Maeve says diplomatically. "But maybe we can wipe that slate clean since you also gave me no warning that you two got married. And, correct me if I'm wrong, but I seem to remember you not telling me that you two were dating for months before we met."

By the look in Josh's eyes, I'm guessing that point goes to Maeve.

"Fine," he huffs. "But that doesn't change anything. I'm still filing for primary custody."

Interestingly enough, that's what gets Vivian to start paying attention. I don't like to judge books by covers—or judge women simply by their clothing and makeup choices—but she doesn't strike me as a woman who has deep-seated motherly desires.

Take last night, for example. Maeve and I FaceTimed Jayce when we got back from Los Angeles. She does it every night, and I asked if I could join. The three of us were laughing, talking and catching up. And I don't think he meant to tattle, but Jayce did make mention that he and Josh went to the movies, but Vivian was too busy to go. And when they got home, she wasn't there either. And while all of that wouldn't strike anyone as strange, if Josh's whole argument is that he and Vivian are a family, maybe she should do family things.

But what do I know? I've been a stepdad for two weeks and was raised by parents who shouldn't have had kids.

"Josh, I need to ask you again, why are you doing this?" Maeve asks, a slight bit of desperation in her tone. "Is this what you *really* want? There's still time for us to figure something out where we don't have to get lawyers and the courts involved. I'd be willing to maybe talk fifty-fifty, or more days a week?"

"It is what we want," Vivian interrupts, suddenly very present in the conversation. "We're a family."

"Oh, you're here," Maeve says. Yup. Polite has gone up the spout. "Glad you finally decided to join us."

Vivian doesn't respond, I'm assuming because she doesn't pick up on Maeve's sarcasm.

"Jayce is happy here," Josh begins. "He's stable. He's not

being shipped around. My job is here. So is Vivian's. You have to get that Maeve."

"The fact that you insinuate he's not happy with me is absurd," Maeve says, her voice growing louder. "Does he stay with my parents or with Ainsley or Stella sometimes? Yes. They're family. It's not like I'm asking strangers daily to watch my son. And now I have Logan. You know, because we're a family too."

Maeve makes sure to direct that last comment straight to Vivian. I understood the full meaning of what she said without saying it—that we can get married quickly too—but I don't think Vivian did.

As they say in my new region of the country, bless her heart.

"Twenty-three."

"Twenty-three what?" Maeve asks Josh. I'm confused as well.

"Twenty-three weeks last year you were gone for at least two days. That's more than half of the weeks in the year, Maeve."

"It wasn't that many," Maeve defends.

"It was. I checked. That's a lot of days you were away. A lot of time figuring out what to do with Jayce."

I glance over to Maeve, who looks like she just got slapped in the face. I hate not being able to do anything right now, but I've been in enough board room negotiations to know when it's not your fight, you stay out of it.

And this isn't my fight, as much as I want it to be.

"Let's say it was twenty-three," Maeve says. "Let's hypothetically say—Vivian, that means let's pretend—that you get primary custody because of my absences. That our lives switch up. Do you not think you'll be taken away for work? You're going all around Nashville telling anyone who listens that you're the guy who opened the honky-tonk with Walker Boone. What if you decide to open another location? You might still be in Nashville, but you wouldn't have the normal, cushy hours that you've built for yourself now with one location."

Maeve turns to Vivian, now looking like she's trying to be

nice. I know that's a lie. I don't think Vivian does by the way she perks up in her seat. "And Vivian. I know you have aspirations of fame. What happens when the night comes? You know the one…the one that every singer in Nashville hopes for. The one where you're singing at the bar and the producer comes in and notices you? Remembers you from your reality days and offers you the contract of a lifetime? You'd be traveling. You'd be constantly on the move. What then?"

The way that Maeve is playing this woman like a fiddle makes me want to bring her into the next board meeting when my directors are being daft.

"That's behind me now," Vivian says. "I'm just ready to be home and be a mom to Jayce-y."

I don't have to look at Maeve to know that her eyes just rolled in the back of her head. Which is how Josh is able to reenter the conversation.

"Maeve, you can spew all of the scenarios you want. We're married. We're a family. And whatever this is between you two? It's a sham. Everyone knows it is. And a judge is going to see right through that."

And that's enough. I know Maeve asked me to not be Logan Matthews, but I'm not going to sit idle and let him bulldoze her.

Plus, what good is it to be a billionaire and not let assholes know about it?

"I'm sorry Josh, it just occurred to me that our introduction got cut short outside," I stand up and extend my hand to him, which he doesn't return immediately. "I'm Logan Matthews, CEO of GameTech and the developer of SpaceCraft. I hear you're a fan. Thank you so much for playing."

"Oh!" Vivian squeals. "You used to date Candace Kross! She and I are mutuals on Insta. And you're like…super rich."

All three of us look over to Vivian, who really thinks she just contributed to the conversation. I also don't miss the way she just eyed me up and down.

"As I was saying," I continue. "You're correct that yes, Maeve and I did just get married. But so did you both, so I feel that point is null and void. But what isn't to be ignored is that if you choose to take this to court—and you're choosing to disrupt Jayce's life because you feel that my wife is somehow a bad mother for doing her job that used to support *you* before you stumbled into fortune by kissing the right ass—I'll be there every day next to her. As will her lawyers. I'm sorry. *Our* lawyers. They'll bury you in paperwork. We'll drag this out until you have to sell your precious bar just to pay your lawyers for the senseless paperwork our lawyers are making them do. I might be new here, but I happen to have a lot of disposable income and have discovered I really enjoy spending it on the people I love. And Maeve and Jayce? They're my people. We're a family. So if a fight is what you want, then a fight is what you're going to get."

I look down at Maeve, who's eyes are huge as I hold out my hand for her. "Let's go home."

Josh and Vivian are speechless as we call for Jayce and leave their home without another word. It's not until we're a few minutes down the road when I realize Maeve still hasn't said anything.

"You okay?"

I feel her eyes on me, and when I glance quickly to her, they're big, and blue, and wide and maybe in shock.

"What is it?"

"You just said you loved us."

Did I? I think back to my monologue—eat your heart out Shakespeare!—and…oh wow, I did. And by the looks of it, I just scared the piss out of my wife.

"Maeve…I…"

She shakes her head. "Don't take it back. I…I don't know if I'm there yet, but I know you had a head start. So, if you truly feel like it, don't take it back. Just…wait for me to get there?"

I nod and grab her hand, bringing it up to my lips. "I'm not going anywhere."

"You're not going anywhere?" Jayce says, apparently having

overheard our conversation. "I thought we were going to Applebee's! I want tenders!"

Maeve and I can't keep in our laughter as I turn toward the restaurant. "You're right, mate. We are going somewhere. And that place is Applebee's."

"Yes!" he exclaims from the backseat as I pull in. The car is barely in park before Jayce has his seatbelt off and is opening the door. Maeve hurriedly gets out, trying to make sure Jayce doesn't run into traffic in his excitement.

But me? I sit back and take a second to watch. On the outside, this scene is probably hilarious: the billionaire and his successful business owner wife dining at Applebee's, because the six-year-old truly runs the house.

But in reality? It's perfect. And exactly where I'm supposed to be.

And like hell I'm going to let Josh, or anyone else for that matter, take this away.

28
logan

"Well, don't you look dapper?" Kat exclaims as she walks into my bedroom.

I chuckle as I finish putting on my watch, the last accessory needed to complete my outfit for tonight's Christmas party. "And here I thought you didn't want me wearing my green tuxedo jacket."

I make a show of showing off my ensemble to Kat, making as if I'm some sort of runway model.

"Save it for America's Next Top Billionaire. We have things to go over. Where's Maeve?"

"I'm here, I'm here," Maeve says as she walks into my bedroom, trying, but failing, to put on the diamond necklace I left in her room.

And looking so bloody gorgeous I can't breathe.

"Here, let me help." I walk up to her, taking the necklace from her as she turns around to stand in front of me.

"Jewelry is very cliché, Mr. Matthews."

I smile as I take the tiny clasp in my hand and gently drape the diamonds around her neck. "Some say cliché. I think it's classic. And most important? It looks beautiful on you, Mrs. Matthews."

I kiss the top of her shoulder, and if I'm going to be honest, I don't know how I'm not going to just do that all night. The strapless, red, floor-length gown she's wearing is stunning. It fits her like a glove and somehow makes her seem taller than she is. Her brown hair is down and over one shoulder in soft waves. She's a breathtaking vision of beauty.

And she's mine.

"Get a room, you two," Kat groans.

"I have one. You're in it."

Maeve giggles as I place one more kiss on her shoulder, not wanting to ruin her makeup.

Yet smudging that red lipstick does sound fun…

"Okay, love birds, we have some things to go over tonight since this is actually your first appearance as husband and wife since you two decided to play hooky last time."

Maeve and I sit on my bed, feeling like scolded schoolchildren.

"The floor is yours, Katherine," I say. "Give us the instructions."

Kat's look goes from stressed to murderous. "Why did you just call me Katherine? Are you teasing me? Do I look like I'm in the mood to be teased?"

"Apologies," I say. "Just trying to lighten the mood."

"There's no light mood tonight. Tonight we have specific things to accomplish, and since I can't be with you both at all times, I need to tell you who to talk to, what to say, and most importantly, what not to say."

Maeve and I listen intently as Kat goes through the guest list and the order of events. She goes over talking points, topics to avoid, and the pictures we need to make sure to take.

"This doesn't sound like a party," I protest. "It sounds like work."

"Because it is," Kat says with a heavy sigh. "But before I tell you to try to have fun despite the work, I have one more thing."

"What's that?" Maeve asks.

"Your ex is coming."

Maeve's eyes are wide and my blood pressure just spiked.

"My ex? As in Josh Tucker?"

"How the fuck did he get invited?" I ask.

"Walker Boone's record label bought tickets," Kat explains. "I'm guessing Josh schmoozed his way from there."

"Lovely," Maeve mutters. "He's going to have a field day that —God forbid—Jayce is spending the night at my parents."

"We'll worry about that later," Kat says. "Also, Logan, Candace Kross will be here—also known as Farmville model, if you don't remember from your string of horrible dates. I don't think she'll be a problem, but I just didn't want you shocked."

"Who the hell is she here with?"

"She was just listed as a date for someone who knew someone. I don't ask questions I don't want answers to."

Okay. That's fine. We went on one date, and I barely talked to her. "Anything else?"

Kat looks at her iPad and shakes her head. "I think that's it. Just remember, you two are married. You're happy. You hold hands and smile and kiss if you want. Which, I'm guessing by events of the last week, won't be hard."

I sneak a look at Maeve, whose cheeks are as red as her dress.

"Maeve, if Josh or the wannabe mom from the *Parent Trap* say anything to you, nod and move on. If they try to cause a scene, call me, and they'll be out of here faster than she was out of that shitty reality show."

Maeve stands up and goes over to hug Kat. "Thank you. For everything."

"Yeah, yeah," she says, patting Maeve on the back. "Now I'm going to go and get ready and say a thousand prayers to nonexistent gods and Lady Gaga for a smooth night."

"Relax, Kat," I say, shooing her away so I can steal one more minute with Maeve. "It's just a party. What could go wrong?"

———

"Bloody hell...is this the same place?"

I've had a front-row seat for the past month to watch Maeve turn my once empty, all-white house into a home. But looking at it tonight? With every inch decorated to perfection? It's like I'm seeing it for the first time.

Greens, whites, and golds, with subtle touches of reds, are sparkling through the foyer and down the hallways. There isn't an inch of the staircase that isn't covered in lit garland, accented with white and gold poinsettias. The tree that's in the corner is at least twenty-feet tall, and I don't know who Maeve hired to decorate it, or what kind of ladder she used if she did it herself, but it could be featured in a magazine spread.

In fact, this whole house could be.

Oh...I should make a phone call.

I wanted to make an entrance with Maeve, but she insisted on going downstairs before me, wanting to make sure every piece of decor was perfect before guests started arriving. Which is why I find her at the bottom of the steps, toying with a ribbon on one of the numerous trees in the foyer.

"Gorgeous," I whisper, slowly putting my hands on her hips. She jumps slightly, then quickly relaxes into my touch. "And the tree is lovely too."

She slowly turns toward me, and the only reason my knees don't give out is the hold I have on her. I know I saw her just moments ago, but that doesn't mean she's any less stunning. Maeve wears makeup daily, but something about tonight makes her look even more beautiful than she already is. She's wearing a red lip that is sending a straight shot to my cock. Her eyes have some sort of smoky look to them. And her cheeks are sparkling and rosy, and not from the blush that gives her away.

She's magnificent in every sense of the word.

Her hands travel up my chest as she lazily, and unnecessarily, fixes the lapels of my deep green tuxedo jacket. "So this is it, huh?"

I smile and take her wrists into mine. "The official debut of Mr. and Mrs. Logan Matthews."

We both look to the entryway as a host of people start entering. The sound of Christmas music from the quartet Kat hired starts playing from a nearby room, and servers are bustling around, offering guests hors d'oeuvres and champagne.

"We can do this," she says, and I don't know if that's to herself or me, but we could probably both use the reminder.

"We're just going to be ourselves," I say. "Talk to people. Mingle. And if people ask why we got married seemingly overnight?"

"We say 'when it's right, it's right.'"

"And then if it becomes too much?"

"We find each other. And go find the calm in the chaos."

I smile and press my lips to her forehead. "That we do."

I take Maeve's hand and lead her toward the door, stopping to say hello to people as they come in. Of course, I introduce Maeve to everyone, making sure they know that not only is she my beautiful wife, but also the ultra-talented designer who's responsible for my new Nashville residence.

As I figured she would be, Maeve is a pro. She's talking with everyone she meets, doing a good mix of small talk while also getting to know people. She's even networking a bit. I think I overheard her talking to one of my board member's wives about redecorating their vacation home in the Hamptons.

At some point we got pulled apart, but now that's giving me a chance to watch her work the room. She's a vision in that dress. And the way she's talking with everyone, despite me not being next to her, is something not every person can do. But Maeve? It's as if she's holding court, and these are all her subjects.

"She's got a way about her, doesn't she?"

I didn't see Josh come up next to me, and I do my best not to have a visible reaction to Maeve's ex-husband being in my vicinity.

"That she does."

The two of us don't say anything for a minute, both watching a woman who has a meaningful place in our lives talk to a group of women, and I don't know what she just said but they are all holding their stomachs in laughter.

"When we first met, I was a dumbass bartender," he says. "Thought it was a great job. Good tips. My pick of women. A bachelor's dream."

I don't say anything, wondering where he's going with this.

"Women came into my bar every night. But that first night I saw Maeve, it's like I couldn't see anyone else. She has that way about her, you know?"

"Oh I do," I say, thinking back to that first night I saw her at the airport bar. "Why are you telling me this?"

"I don't know," he says. "All this fighting we've been doing, I forgot until right now about the girl at the bar I first fell in love with."

I snap my gaze to him, but he's immediately shaking his head. "It's not like that, man. Did I love her? Yes. But we weren't right for each other. We tried to force it for Jayce's sake. But she's the mother of my kid, you know? And I think I've lost sight of that…"

I don't say anything, not wanting to push this too far, but also at the same time wondering where his new wife is.

"Thanks for attending," I say. "Now if you'll excuse me."

Josh tips his head, and I make my way toward Maeve.

"Ladies, can I be so rude as to steal my wife?"

Maeve waves goodbye as I place my hand on her back, leading her toward what I'm calling the dance floor in the main room where guests have gathered.

"What are you doing?" she asks as I pull her in tight to me.

"I think it's about time we find a little calm."

As if I gave them some sort of cue, the string quartet changes from a Christmas song into a popular ballad. Maeve leans into me, resting her head on my chest as we move to the melody of the song. I close my eyes, not wanting to catch the eye of anyone else here, only wanting to focus on the woman in my arms.

"I remember the last time we danced," I whisper. "I thought that at any moment this was going to end. That you were going to be a snapshot in time, never to be seen again."

"Am I a horrible person for saying that I hoped to never see you again?"

"You're not," I say with a laugh. "And if I didn't know it when you snuck out of the room, I would've figured it out on the plane."

"You mean the most embarrassing hour of my life?"

"You were cute," I say. "All flustered and covered in drool."

She narrows her eyes at me in a mock glare. "Watch it, Matthews. I know where you sleep."

I twirl Maeve out, before bringing her back in. "And I know how to make you scream."

Before she can respond, I press my lips to hers, deepening the kiss as I dip her low. Is the kiss a little much for a room full of CEOs, celebrities, my board, and a handful of media? Probably. I feel the cameras flashing. I know what they're doing.

And I couldn't care less.

Because I'm kissing the woman of my dreams.

The woman I married for convenience.

And the woman I want to spend the rest of my life with.

guide to love rule #32

You'll never be prepared to realize that you're in love with
your husband.

29

maeve

"Do you think you'd be able to design something like that?"

I have to blink a few times, because I'm not sure this is real life. Because how is it that Hunter McAvoy, the head coach of the Nashville Fury—a football team I've watched my entire life because of my father and brother—is wanting to hire me to decorate and help design a new surprise office and wing of the house he's building for his wife.

"Think? I know I can. And I'd be honored to do so."

We shake hands quickly since his wife Sadie is walking back toward us, putting her phone back in her purse.

"I hope he didn't bore you," she says. "If he was talking too much football, blink twice and I'll pull him away."

Oh, I like her. "I grew up in a football household. Graduate of UT and family are season ticket holders."

Sadie's smile immediately grows as I hear Hunter let out a groan. "I knew I liked you."

We talk for a few more minutes, since apparently I'm in company with a fellow Tennessee grad, before I feel a hand on the small of my back.

"There you are," Logan says. "Just wanted to check on you."

I smile up at the man who has done a wonderful job tonight

of introducing me to those he wants to, while also letting me forge out on my own. "Everything's great."

"Good," he says, formally introducing himself to Hunter and Sadie. The two excuse themselves, but not before Hunter gives me a look that says he'll be calling me.

"Another commission?"

I couldn't keep the smile off my face if I tried. "Hunter was asking me if I'd be interested in decorating a surprise office he's building for his wife."

"That's amazing," Logan responds, bringing me in for a kiss that I feel through my body. "I think by the end of tonight you're going to be booked for the next two years."

I might be. And none of them, not one, was a man cave for a post-divorce bachelor pad.

I think I might cry.

"Thank you," I say, pulling him in by his lapels for a kiss. "This is all happening because of you. I don't know if I could ever say thank you enough."

"No thanks needed, Love. You did this yourself. Your talent did this. I might have put a spotlight on you, but your brilliance has always shined on its own."

Logan has called me beautiful. He's called me smart. He's called me sexy. When he calls me his wife I'm embarrassed how my body shivers. But when he compliments my work? Calls my talent brilliant? That's my definition of talking dirty…

And while I'm overwhelmed by the response I've gotten tonight, I've also never been prouder of how a project turned out. Just this grand room alone is something that I'll be putting in my portfolio for years to come. We gave it a rustic feel that will look good in June, but in December with trees and holiday decorations spread throughout? It looks like a cabin at a ski lodge in Colorado. The whites and creams against the browns of the wood are the perfect backdrop to the Christmas lights and trees I've put around. It's a huge room, but somehow we were able to give it a cozy, intimate feel.

Most important? I enjoyed designing it. I found my love for creating spaces again, and I owe it all to Logan for letting me go forward with my vision.

In what feels like a blink of an eye, Logan Matthews has gone from one-night-stand, to client, to the man who helped me find my love again for my job, to husband. He helped me in a time he didn't have to. He's brought Jayce and me into his home, and we've created this unpredictable little family. And maybe the biggest thing of all, he's made me feel again.

It's a Christmas miracle.

"Thank you," I say, taking his hand in mine. "For so much."

His smile hits me just as hard as his words just did. "As much as I'd like to suggest we sneak away so you can thank me properly, I have to make a speech."

At that moment, I feel my cell phone vibrating in my clutch purse. Having an estimated idea of what time it is, I figure it's Jayce for his nightly call.

"You're fine. I'm going to step outside and talk to Jayce."

Logan leans in to kiss my cheek as we go separate ways. I hurry and take out the phone, and luckily my mom has prepared him for an abbreviated goodnight phone call, knowing I wouldn't be able to talk long.

I step outside onto the terrace as Jayce starts reading from the book. I let the cool air hit me, but love the slight bite against my skin. Sometimes you get a winter like this in Tennessee, when it's not too cold, but just cool enough to do the trick.

After we say our goodnights, and he tells me to tell Logan goodnight specifically, I put my phone away and start making my way back inside. But just as I'm about to open the door, I smell the distinct smell of cigarettes, and a whisper from the other side of the terrace.

"I can't believe he married her!"

"Right? She's...ugh."

Now, I'm a proper Southern woman. I'm not one to spread gossip.

But I sure as shit am going to listen to it.

I do my best to inch closer to the whispering voices, but I can only get so far as a row of shrubbery is separating me from them. Though the mask of green plants is allowing me to sit and listen in, I have a distinct feeling they're talking about me.

And I have a feeling I know who *they* are.

"It can't be real. I mean, he was doing PR relationships well before her. That's what I was. She has to be another one of those."

Yup. That would be Candace. And the other voice sounds like the distinct shrill of Vivian.

"But marriage? Like they full-on got married. Like at the courthouse. They were pictured leaving and everything."

Good to know Vivian keeps up on the news of the day.

"I didn't even know he was dating anyone," Candace says. "I hadn't heard about him seeing anyone since me. And let's be real, he fumbled me. I know we were set up by our publicists, but I was ready to sleep with him. And he just wanted to play his stupid game."

Oh, I'm so glad that didn't happen…

"I just don't get it," Vivian says. "She's, like, okay looking for a mom. And that's what I thought when Josh introduced us. But like, with Logan? She's so…blah."

Blah! I'll show her fucking blah…

"Clearly he's done with models and is now slumming it," Vivian continues. "Just look at her. She's old. I mean, what is she, like forty? I didn't know he was into grandmas."

I let out a gasp and quickly cover my mouth. How dare she? I'm thirty-six, and I think look damn good for it! Especially since I pushed out a kid. So—and I'd say this to her face if I wasn't hiding in the bushes—in all disrespect, fuck right the fuck off, Vivian.

Though she does have a point…I am a cougar. I'm lusting over a younger man.

Oh, who am I kidding? I'm in love with him…

"Though, I will say, her dress is pretty?" Candace says, though with the question mark at the end I don't know if that's a compliment.

"It's off the rack," Vivian says. "And I bet she made him wear that ugly green tuxedo."

It takes all I have in me to not let out a gasp. How dare she!

My dress is, in fact, designer, though it might be rented because I'll never wear it again. And I want to chime in that it was his idea to coordinate green and red. And I think he looks *very* handsome.

"I don't know. I think Logan looks fucking hot," Candace says. "I don't care that he's married. If he said the word I'd fuck him."

"We all would. He's Logan Matthews. Which is why it's a travesty he's with *her*."

I take a deep but silent breath, as I rein in the urge to take off my earrings, jump this fence, and swing both Vivian and Candace around by their extensions.

I won't, because I'm a fucking adult. But if my sisters were here? Or maybe if this was college-age Maeve? It would be game fucking on.

"Do you know how they met?" Candace asks.

"I mean, isn't it obvious? He's now shopping on a clearance rack for fake relationships."

Okay, that's not a bad joke, even if it's at my expense. And frankly, I didn't know ol' Vivian had it in her.

"But it's obvious why they got married," she continues. "And it's because of me."

Vivian's voice is suddenly very cocky. And I hate that she's not wrong about that.

"What do you mean?"

"So, when I finally convinced Josh to marry—"

I lean into the bushes, nearly falling through them to hear what Vivian's about to say. I even grab my phone to start recording it. But someone—and when I find out who I'm going to steal all their spoons—opens the door on the other side of the terrace, effectively ending their conversation. I stay in my seat for a second to make sure they don't start again, but it starts getting too cold and I have to force myself inside.

When I walk back into the ballroom, I can't see either of them. And as much as I want to go on a hunt to track them down and figure out what the last part of that conversation would've been, I know I need to find Logan and return to my role as the dutiful wife.

"There you are," Logan says, coming behind me, rubbing my arms to warm me up. "That took longer than you thought?"

"Yeah, I'm sorry I missed your speech," I say. "But I heard—"

Before I can tell Logan what I started to overhear, and that I think Vivian was about to spill her secrets, someone grabs his attention.

And that person is Candace's date. With Candace on his arm.

I have no idea who he is, and frankly, I don't care. All I can do is stare at the woman who I just overheard talk openly that she'd fuck my husband and not care that I was in the picture.

I'm shooting daggers at her, and I don't know if she's just ignoring me, or oblivious, but she doesn't even look my way. Which is fine. I'm patient. I can wait for her to realize that no one talks about fucking my husband other than me.

Holy shit…I just referred to him as my husband.

I knew Logan was different. I always knew, but I could never put a finger on it. Between him making me feel relaxed enough to break my vow of no men on the first night we met, to convincing me that marriage was a good idea, I knew this was not any normal man. Or any normal relationship.

And I was coming around to the feelings that I had pushed down for so long and refused to feel for anyone. Things like want, and passion, and just enjoying another person…they are finally coming out of retirement.

But these? These are new. Loathing. A little jealousy. And a brand-new one—possessiveness.

This man is mine. Candace and any other woman can look. But they can't fucking touch.

Finally Candace realizes that I've been staring at her for going on three minutes while the men blabber on about whatever. She tries to give me a smile—it's fake—and I return one—also fake.

I might not talk about it, but I was in a southern sorority. I can be fake with the best of them.

"You must be Maeve," Candace says, daintily holding out a hand. "I'm Candace."

"Hello. And yes, I'm Maeve Banks-Matthews. Or Mrs. Logan Matthews. I haven't decided which one I like best yet."

I mean, I'm keeping my name. But Blondie McBimbo over here doesn't need to know that.

Our eyes narrow at each other, both of us realizing what we're doing. But before I can start a cat fight, I feel Logan's hand back on the small of my back.

"We should be going," he says. "Good seeing you both."

I wave goodbye as Logan quickly leads me out of the main room. He looks around the hall a second before pushing me toward his office, quickly shutting the door behind him.

"What—" My question is cut off by the force of his kiss on me. He has me pressed against the door. The room is pitch dark, and all I can feel is the wood against my back, Logan's lips taking what they want, and his dick pressing into me.

"Were you jealous, Love?" Logan's mouth is just far enough away that our lips aren't touching.

"Yes." The word is nearly a whisper as it comes out of my mouth.

"Why? You know we never were really together."

"I know. But I heard her talking outside…and she said she wanted you."

Logan lets out a groan at my admission. "And how did that make you feel?"

I take in a breath. "Jealous. Possessive."

"Is that so?"

I bite my lip as I grab the lapels of his jacket. "I wanted to tell her that you're mine."

"Fuck..." Logan smashes his lips into mine again, taking whatever he wants, before he suddenly pulls back. "Say it again."

His eyes are on fire. I feel his cock twitching against me. My breathing is heavy, and my body is heating.

And I don't even hesitate.

"You're mine, Logan Matthews."

guide to love rule #148

Sometimes you want to be the dirty talker. Sometimes you want to be the dirty talkee. It's called balance.

30

maeve

I've been in Logan's bedroom more than a dozen times over the past month. I know every inch of it, from the feel of the carpet to how many steps it takes to get from the bed to the dresser. I know without looking that the far-left switch is the one that turns on the main lights and that the room is lit perfectly with just the LED headboard that's currently giving off a soft white light.

And yes, I know the thread count of his sheets and reluctantly picked the color since he wouldn't tell me what he wanted.

Yet as I walk into his room and hear the click of the door behind me, it's like I'm walking in here for the very first time.

"Finally," Logan sighs as he starts to kiss the slope of my neck. After we left the office, we tried as hard as we could to sneak upstairs and perform a proper Irish goodbye. But that was easier said than done.

Hence why, two hours later, we're finally here.

But the word "finally" is now hitting me with its double meaning. Finally Logan and I are going to be together. No more waiting. No more taking it slow. And yes, I know we've been together before, but this is different. Then we were two strangers who were going to have one night of fun.

Tonight is not that. Tonight is the first night of what is likely many to come. Tonight has meaning. Tonight is the beginning of a new chapter.

And while I'm a little nervous—what woman wouldn't be?—I'm also excited. Energized. I feel like the woman I used to be, but in a new and improved way.

And I must say, I like this version of me. I like her a lot.

"Breathe," Logan whispers, his hands on my shoulders. "You're in control, Maeve. What do *you* want?"

My pussy clenches at those four little words.

What do you want?

What do I want? I want him. I want to feel his hands and lips on me. I want him to make me come so hard that the remaining party stragglers hear what we're doing.

Those are just the few things off the top of my head. But then it hits me: Have I ever been asked that question before? I don't think I have.

It's so simple, yet somehow so complex at the same time. I've had to be in control with men more times than I can count. And it's not because the person I was with was giving me that control. No, I had to take it. Because if I didn't, no one else was going to, and then I was going to be left with a sore jaw, a dry pussy, and a best actress award for Best Faking of an Orgasm in a Comedy.

But here's Logan, a man who I know could take control in five seconds if he wanted to. He did that first night we were together. But no. Instead he's giving it to me. Letting me take the lead because he knows that's what I want. What I'm craving.

And I don't know if he could do anything sexier…

"Take off my dress," I ask, turning to the side to give him access to my zipper. Could I do it myself? Yes. But I'm not about to turn down the opportunity to feel Logan's fingers running down my side, sending goosebumps through me with every inch of skin he touches.

"Gladly."

He steps to me, kissing my shoulder as he finds the zipper. His lips continue tasting every bit of exposed skin as his fingers do exactly what I hoped they do as my dress slowly releases from my body.

"Beautiful," he says as I stand before him in nothing but a strapless bra, my three-inch heels, and a barely-there G-string.

All in black, of course.

"You've been wearing this all night?" His words come out in a near growl. "Jesus fucking Christ, Maeve…"

My body heats as his kisses become harder. I let my hand search for his cock, wanting to feel what I'm really doing to him.

I purr as I start to stroke him through his tuxedo pants. "You're so fucking hard, Logan."

"For you, Love. Only for you."

My head falls back as Logan starts kissing around my neck, making sure not an inch hasn't been neglected by his lips. He feels so good I don't want him to stop. But there's something else I want more.

I step away from Logan's mouth, which I miss instantly. He's slightly confused, and maybe even more so as I take his hand and walk him to his bed.

And yes, it has on the sheets, blanket, and comforter I picked out.

I sit down on the edge, crossing my legs as he stands before me.

"I'm in control?"

I know I am, but the verification would be nice, especially since I'm asking him to do some things maybe not every man would be into.

"Completely."

Our eyes lock and a fire passes between them. "Strip."

My command is simple and to the point, and I pray in this

moment that I'm not freaking Logan out. Not all men would be willing to do this for the women they're with, no matter what stage of a relationship—or hookup—they'd be in.

But only seconds after the word leaves my mouth, a twinkle hits Logan's eye.

"You want a show?"

I relax back a little on the bed, my hands behind me so I can lean back but still get a full view. "I want to look at what's mine."

Fire. That's the only word I can think of to describe the look Logan gives me as those words come out of my mouth.

The weirdest part? I'm not even fazed by it. If tonight has proven anything to me, it's that I'm in this. My brain and my emotions might be playing a little bit of catch up, but this man is here and real and the feelings I'm feeling are real, too.

And when you find them, you don't let them go.

No. You claim them as yours.

Logan doesn't say anything else as he slowly unbuttons his jacket, taking his time as he slips it off his broad shoulders. He tosses it to the side and makes quick work of his bow tie. I bite my lip as I watch in awe as he somehow unbuckles his cufflinks while never taking his eyes off me. With every second that passes, my body heats just that much more for him. My pussy is throbbing as I watch the show I asked for. But as much as I want him to relieve that pressure, I also don't want to miss a minute of this performance.

"Do it," Logan says as he takes a few steps toward me.

"Do what?"

He slowly starts unbuttoning his perfectly fitted white shirt, stopping right before the bed. "Touch yourself. You know you want to."

How did he know? Is he a mind reader? He has to be. Either that or my sexual poker face is just as shit as my real-life one.

I didn't even think to do it, having never done anything like this before, but between Logan's words, my sudden boost of confidence, and thirsting for the man who's stripping in front of me, there's nothing more I want right now.

Well, other than Logan's dick. But that will come.

And maybe first I will…

"Take them off for me."

My request is received with nothing but a lusty groan from Logan. He does as asked, hooking two fingers through each side of my G-string and slowly pulling my panties off my legs. My legs slowly spread open, and yes, I could feel it before, but I can feel even more now.

"Jesus Love. Your pussy is soaked. Is that all for me?"

I nod as my hand trails down, rubbing myself, feeling my wetness and coating some on my fingers, while letting out a soft moan. I lift them up, not wanting to force it on Logan, but he doesn't turn down my offering. He takes my fingers in his, grabs onto them and slowly sucks off every drop.

And that is, without a doubt, officially the hottest thing that's ever happened in my life.

"You taste so good," he whispers. "Keep going. Find your pleasure. Let me watch you come."

I don't know what I'm more transfixed by—Logan's strip-tease that has just resumed, or his words. Both are sexy as hell in their own way.

There's his body, which I assume is what sculptors' dreams are made of. His shoulders are broad and built. His arms are big without being so bulky that they bust through a jacket. And his abs? I can't help but lick my lips when I take them in.

He's perfect. A god on earth.

My husband.

It might have started off as convenient, but it's more now. So much more.

With his shirt off, he starts unbuckling his belt, and I start working the spot I know will send me into oblivion. I keep rubbing small circles at my clit as he snaps his belt off in one motion. He goes right in on unbuttoning his pants, and just as I think he's going to slide them down, he stops.

"What are you doing?"

The smile on his face is wicked as he leans over me. "I know you're in control. But that pussy looks so pretty."

Shit, I think I just came from those words alone. "Do you want a taste?"

He nods and licks his lips. "Please."

"Since you asked so nicely," I say as I lay back. I want to tease a little more, but the words are taken right out of my mouth the second Logan's tongue is on me.

I fall back on the bed, physically unable to hold myself up as Logan begins feasting on me. With my new position, he takes it upon himself to spread my legs wide and hook them with his arms, bringing me to his face so I have nowhere to go.

Like I'd want to go anywhere.

I cling to the comforter that I once thought would be a good accent piece for Logan but now realize I should've tested out its durability. Because this piece of fabric is the only thing that's keeping my body on this earth right now.

My body starts to tighten up, my orgasm not far away. I don't know how I even held out this long with what Logan's magical tongue is doing to me.

"Logan…"

His name on my lips is all he needs to hear. His tongue continues rapidly flicking at my clit as I feel him push two fingers inside me. With one small hook I'm orbiting somewhere between here and Pluto. My back arches, I think I yell out words that aren't English, and my orgasm rips through me, leaving my body visibly shaking.

"So fucking perfect," Logan mutters as he brings me down. "And mine."

That's never happened to be before. Never in my life have I

actually shook while having an orgasm. And one would now think that I'll need three to five business days to recover. But no. I feel energized. Wanton. A woman possessed.

A woman who knows what she wants.

And I want my husband.

"Pants off. Now," I demand, though Logan is already three steps ahead of me. I use the energy I have left to back up on the bed as I watch Logan's cock spring free from his boxer briefs.

"Fuck…" I mumble. I've felt it since that night against me. Hell, I've had it in my mouth on the jet. But somehow I forgot how big he is.

"What do you want, Love?" he asks as he stalks to the bed, condom in hand.

"I want you to throw that condom aside and fuck your wife how you want to."

His eyes are wide. "Are you sure?"

I nod. "Nothing between us."

Logan drops the condom on the floor next to him before climbing into bed with me. He wraps me in his arms, kissing me as hard as he can as he rolls over so I'm on top of him.

"Ride me," he says. "Take what you want. I'm yours."

Those words hit me square in the chest, maybe more than anything he's said. Harder than the first time he called me Love. The day we said "I do." The day that he told me he'd never let anything happen to me or Jayce.

No, right here, right now, in the throes of passion, Logan Matthews telling me that he's mine is what does me in.

I do as he says, gripping his cock in my hand and stroking it a few times before lining it up to my begging center. I start to feel full instantly as I let each inch of him slide into me.

"Fuck," he moans, taking my hips in his hands and guiding me as I start to slowly ride him. "So tight. So perfect."

My hands grip onto Logan's chest as I begin moving up and down on him, doing my best to stay present in the moment and enjoy every second. The man has made it his mission to give me everything I've asked for—in and out of the bedroom. I don't want this moment to go by and not memorize everything I can.

Our eyes are fixed on each other, each watching the other with such intent that it fills my heart. The sensation only makes me fuck him harder, wanting to bring both of us to the release we both want so much.

"Fuck me from behind," I beg. "Just like that first night. Fuck me until I scream."

I see the dilation in his eyes with each of my words. He doesn't say anything, instead just does as I ask and rolls me over as I position myself on all fours.

Now, I know every inch of this room. I'm the reason each piece of furniture is where it is. But never did it occur to me that I so artfully placed a mirror in the perfect position so that one day I could watch Logan lining himself up to fuck me doggy style.

Wait. Should I add sex room to my resumé?

"Look at you, Love. So wet and desperate," he says, realizing that he can look me in my eye as he's fucking me. "Are you going to watch me make you scream?"

"Yes," I pant. "Fuck me, Logan."

"It would be my honor."

And he does. This man who is a gentleman in every other facet of life fucks me like our lives depend on it. I feel his hand on my ass and the sound of the crack fills the room. The slight twinge of pain is perfect. And watching it through the mirror? Possibly the hottest thing I've ever seen.

Logan's hands begin to squeeze at my hips, driving into me harder and harder.

"I need you to let go, Maeve. Come with me."

His words are a direct line to my orgasm that was slowly building but right now balances at the precipice. With just a few more thrusts I'm over the ledge, screaming for Logan as the orgasm rips through me. He joins in, a deep groan of pleasure leaving his lungs before he collapses on top of me.

I don't know what time it is. I don't know if anyone is still in the house. Frankly, I don't care.

Because I'm Mrs. Logan Matthews. And I want everyone to know it.

31
logan

The first board meeting I ever attended was the most nerve-racking day of my life. There I was, a twenty-something video game geek who had barely any idea what he was doing when it came to running a corporation, sitting in front of titans of industry. I think I sweated through my suit that day.

Those nerves are nothing compared to the ones I'm feeling now as I pull into Maeve's childhood home on Christmas Day.

"Relax," she whispers. "They're going to love you."

"I've never met parents before," I say. "Let alone siblings."

Maeve takes my hand in hers as I put the SUV in park. "My Dad is the most relaxed man on the planet. He'll just want to talk stocks. My mother will smother you because she's just happy I'm not going to die alone. The sisters won't let you breathe, they'll be asking you so many questions."

"What about your brother?"

"He's the wild card. On paper, you two should get along swimmingly. But I can also see him trying to assert some sort of fake dominance. Just roll with it. He doesn't mean anything by it. And as a last resort, start talking to him about your plane. He seemed oddly fascinated by that."

"Good to know."

Today has been…surreal. It's been years since I've had a proper Christmas. Growing up, it was a day with a few presents under the tree and everyone waiting on pins and needles for my parents to start fighting. In college, I never left for holiday, choosing to stay in the dorms they kept open for students who couldn't travel. As adults, I've occasionally gone with Kat to visit her family, but always felt like an odd man out.

But this morning? This morning felt like a dream. Jayce ran into our bedroom—yes, my wish came true and my bedroom is now the one I share with Maeve—to announce that it's Christmas and that Santa came. I felt like we had just gone to sleep, and in reality, I wasn't wrong, considering it was six-thirty in the morning and Maeve and I didn't finish wrapping and setting up until after one.

Maeve, though, being the thoughtful, yet exhausted, mother she is, came up with an idea so she could get five more minutes of sleep. She sent Jayce back downstairs with the directions of grabbing all of our stockings. He was to get them, bring them to our room, and we were going to open the presents in our stockings from bed. Jayce's eyes lit up at the idea, and the kid went sprinting out of the room. Maeve went back to sleep for five minutes. I figured my energy was best used to make Maeve coffee, grab juice for Jayce and tea for me, and to make sure Jayce was able to carry everything.

We then spent the morning cuddled in bed, unwrapping the small presents in our stockings before going down and watching Jayce rip through the larger items under the tree.

Seeing Christmas through the eyes of a child is truly a thing of wonder. The excitement he got with every gift. How he wanted to inspect every single toy and begin playing with it right away, Maeve having to remind him that he had others to open. Watching him jump up and down for the new bicycle and wanting to ride it in the living room.

But the biggest highlight for me, and I realize I'm biased, was his reaction to the newest, one-of-a-kind, SpaceCraft action figure I had developed specifically for him—of course with help from my lead designer. It's of a character we've never made a doll or action figure of, and it's one of Jayce's favorites. Seeing his eyes light up is a memory I'm never going to forget. Nor is the hug that I received after he jumped onto my lap to thank me.

It's been a Christmas morning like no other. And I have a feeling that trend is going to continue on as I meet Maeve's family.

"Let's go!" Jayce yells. "It's Christmas!"

We laugh as Jayce expertly lets himself out of his seatbelt and opens the door, sprinting to Maeve's parents' front door and letting himself right in. I know we need to follow, but I have one more question that I didn't want to ask in front of Jayce that Maeve and I haven't talked about.

"What are we telling them?"

After the Christmas party, there wasn't a magazine or gossip column in the world that wasn't putting together some sort of story with the headline, "The new Mr. and Mrs. Matthews hard launch relationship with charity party." None of them said anything bad, or accusatory of our speedy marriage, but you can't walk through a grocery line, according to Kat and Maeve, and not see our faces plastered on the cover of a magazine.

Her family knows, and thankfully, they haven't pushed her too hard for details. However, I have a feeling that's not going to happen now that everyone is in the same room.

Maeve takes in and lets out a deep and thoughtful breath. "I hate lying to my family. And frankly, they know something is up. They aren't dumb, and they know me. They know I wouldn't do something like get married without a reason. Quinn has clocked us since the first day. Stella sniffed out your PR relationships before we met. So, if it's okay with you, and only if the conversation comes up, I'd like to tell them. We can trust them. They won't blab. If it's one thing the Banks family does well, it's having each other's backs. But only if it's okay with you."

I lean in and kiss Maeve, just a small one, before pulling back and letting our foreheads rest against each other. "I'll follow your lead. If you're comfortable with it, then so am I. But Love? I need you to know something."

"Yeah?"

"I'm in this. I know we said that this would last until we didn't need it anymore. Until you figured out the custody and I had my situation under control. But I love you. I love you and Jayce and this family we created in a blink of an eye. I want more Christmases like this morning. I want birthdays and vacations and lazy Sundays. I want it all."

"Logan—"

"Let me finish," I say, wanting to make sure I get everything out that I need to. "I love you. When we walk inside that house, I want your family to know that I love you and that I'm your husband in every sense of the word, not just on paper. That I'll be—"

Maeve cuts off my speech in the best way possible—her lips on mine.

"What I was going to say is that I love you, too. That I know we still have a lot to figure out, and we did this completely backward. Have we even gone out on a real date? Anyway, that's beside the point. I'm starting to catch up. And...I love you too, Logan Matthews."

My heart grows three sizes with her words as I bring her in for one more kiss. I probably let it deepen a little too much when we're interrupted by a pounding on the door.

And window.

And the windshield.

"Come on lovebirds!" a sister, who I'm going to guess is Quinn, yells. "Quit making out in the driveway."

Maeve and I laugh as the harassment subsides and we get out of the car.

"You know, one of you could have come and got us," Maeve says as we unload the presents. "Did we really need the cavalry?"

"They made me do it," another sister says. That must be Ainsley.

"Like she didn't know that." Quinn makes her way over to me, hand extended.

"I take it you're Logan."

I switch the present in my hand to shake hers. "And you must be Quinn."

"You're the sudden husband who was her slump buster?"

Oh, I like her. "And you're the sister I call when she's being stubborn."

The two of us give each other one knowing look before shaking hands.

"He passes! Now let's open some presents!"

The three sisters talk and giggle as they head back into the house. When I turn to Maeve, her face is completely red, and I don't think it's from the bite in the cold air.

"I'm going to kill her," Maeve groans.

"She wasn't so bad."

Maeve shakes her head. "That was her warm-up. You've been warned."

———

"Is it true you're worth six billion? Or is it eight? I've seen both." Quinn asks before Stella chimes in.

"Were any of the relationships real?"

"Oh! Yes!" Ainsley chimes in. "Didn't you date Sabrina Rome? Because she's my favorite singer of all time, and I need to know everything about her."

"Can you all stop," Maeve says. "It's Christmas. Not an interrogation."

"I'm sorry, we can't help it," Stella says. "And actually, this is your fault for keeping him hidden for so long. If we would've met sooner, all of these questions would have been out of the way."

"She's right," I say, giving her a quick kiss on her temple.

"I know you're trying to score brownie points with them, but remember who you have to go home with."

I know she's trying to act tough. But I also know exactly what I could do to her in five seconds that would make her forget that at any point today she was annoyed by me. "Whatever you say, wife."

"Did he just call you wife?" Ainsley asks. "Oh my God, Maeve. You have a real-life book boyfriend."

"Book *husband*," I say confidently. "And thank you. I appreciate that."

"Whoa!" Simon shouts. "He's a book boyfriend? I'm one! Aren't I?"

He looks over to his wife, Charlie, who's holding their daughter while she waves around a piece of wrapping paper. "Of course you are, dear. Just the best."

This gets a laugh from everyone in the room but Simon. "Really? You're going to side with them? I have money. I look good in suits. I know people. And might I remind you, my lovely future wife and mother of my child, that I bought you a whole-ass restaurant."

"Well..." This comes from Emmett, who I've learned is Stella's boyfriend, and Simon's business partner. "Did you really buy it *for* her?"

All eyes turn to Simon, including Charlie's. "Let's not play the semantics game, Mr. I Started Dating My Business Partner's Sister and Hid It From Him."

Emmett rolls his eyes. "Yep, best book boyfriend-slash-husband ever. Logan and I can't even compare, so we should stop trying."

"Damn straight," Simon says.

Emmett looks over to me and stage whispers, "It's just easier to agree with him. You'll learn."

I return Emmett's fist bump as the laughter continues in the room.

"Enough already!" Quinn yells. "Stella stumbled into a bar and met her true love. Apparently my brother is super. That's just great. Let's get back to the skinny on Logan."

"Quinn, quit badgering the poor man," Maeve's mom, Demetria scolds as she brings me a glass of eggnog. "You keep this up and he's never going to want to come back here again."

"Thank you, Mrs. Banks, but I'm fine," I say. "I'm just glad that I could finally meet everyone."

"Logan, please. Call me Demetria. Or Mom. Whatever you'd like."

"Jesus Christ," Maeve groans. "Mom, you've known him *four hours*. He can call you Mom?"

She shrugs. "He's your husband, Maeve. Therefore he's family."

"You never let the first husband call you Mom," Quinn notes with a raised brow. "Just stating facts."

"Oh? Didn't I?" Demetria holds up a finger like she just got an idea. "You'll have to excuse me. I hear the timer going off in the kitchen."

Everyone in the room snickers as Demetria not so slyly avoids Quinn's statement.

"Should we do our gift exchange?" Ainsley asks. "I feel like that would be best."

Everyone agrees—I don't weigh in because I'm the new guy and I don't feel like I have enough time in to vote on anything—and the gifts start being passed around. Maeve explained to me that for the past few years, the siblings and significant others decided to start doing Secret Santas instead of everyone buying for everyone. And even though I came into the picture pretty late, they were able to include me, which I appreciated.

Especially because of who I got.

"All right, oldest to youngest," Quinn announces.

"Damn straight," Simon says as he starts tearing open his gift.

"We did oldest first so he didn't get fussy," Maeve says. "Again, it was easier."

I sit back and smile, my arm around Maeve as Simon starts tearing into his present.

"Who had me?" he asks.

"You know you're not allowed to ask that," Ainsley says. "Will you ever follow the rules?"

"You should know that answer by now, little sister." Simon continues working the tape and ribbon that Maeve expertly wrapped for me and finally gets to the non-discreet box. He's still mumbling something, but stops when he opens the actual present.

"Are you kidding me?" Everyone's eyes are on Simon as he takes out an original Nintendo gaming system, along with add-ons for up to four players.

"It's the original," I chime in. "Not the new ones that claim to be. I took a pass through it, and it should run as good as new. And there are extra controllers in there so four people can play. I threw in a few games, too."

Simon has a look on his face like Jayce did this morning when he unwrapped his SpaceCraft toy. "Oh my God! It's the fucking *Turtles*!"

Everyone laughs as Simon shows Charlie, then Emmett, then each of his sisters the present. He even starts explaining it to his baby daughter, Lainey, who tries to get one end of a controller in her mouth before Simon gasps and snatches it away.

Simon walks over to me and extends his hand. When I reciprocate, he pulls me up and brings me into a hug. "Welcome to the family, Logan."

Family. That one word from Simon hits me in the heart.

I sit back down and watch as the rest of the group open gifts. I look over to Jayce, who's playing with one of his many toys on the floor by the fireplace. I glance at Maeve, who's laughing and smiling and looking as free as maybe I've ever seen her. Demetria is sitting next to her husband, who I'll only call Mr. Banks despite him wanting me to use his first name, and they're looking on at their children, enjoying them all in one space.

This room right now is filled with love and warmth.

This is family.

This is what I always wanted.

And all because of one night, and then one decision, I have it.

And like hell am I going to let Josh, or anyone else, take this away.

———

"Hello? Logan?"

"Hey Callum. Happy Christmas"

I don't know why I was nervous to call Callum today. It's not like we haven't spoken in years. We have, but not frequently. We both have our lives going on—me here in the states with Game-Tech and him back in England playing professional rugby. Between time zones, careers, and personal lives, we don't talk nearly as much as we should—or maybe better said —as much as we promised to when we struck out on our own.

Spending today with Maeve's family reminded me how important family is. And what better day than Christmas to let your loved ones know that you're thinking of them.

"Happy Christmas to you," he says. "And, might I say, congratulations."

I laugh and have a seat on the stairs, away from the commotion of Maeve's family. "Thanks. I'm sorry I didn't call and tell you about it. It's been a crazy few months."

"I understand," he says. "From what I read, it seemed like it was quite sudden."

"You can say that again."

For the next few minutes I fill Callum in on Maeve and brush over the important parts of our relationship. I know Maeve wanted to tell her family the truth about us, and I support that, but I'm not sure if telling my brother I married a woman for convenient reasons is the wise choice after not talking for the better part of the last six months.

"Enough about me," I say. "What's going on with you? How's the season treating you?"

Callum pauses for a second before answering. Which isn't unusual. He's done it since we were lads. It started then because he was careful about what to say, not wanting to feel the wrath from our father. It continued into adulthood to make sure he didn't give away more than he wanted.

"We're in season now. Off a few days for the holiday."

"Did you spend today anywhere?"

"Didn't leave my flat," he says. "I was invited to one of my teammate's family dinners, but I politely declined."

He doesn't need to say anything else. If I wasn't with Maeve, I'd have done the same thing. Holidays were always a sore spot with our family. They started off full of hope, but usually by the end of the day mum and dad were at each other's throats again.

"Is the season going well? I apologize that I don't check the scores as much as I should."

"Big brother…are you telling me you don't live stream every one of my matches?"

I hesitate for a second before Callum starts laughing. "I know you don't. And it's fine. I wouldn't be streaming a video game league if you were playing in it."

"Good to know," I say with a smile. "But please, fill me in. How are things with you?"

"Nothing much to report," he says. "Season is going well. I haven't got injured yet, which is always a good thing."

"Is there anything besides rugby going on?" I ask.

"Is my suddenly-married big brother asking me if I have a personal life?"

"I am," I say. "I know how hard you worked for this. And I'm bloody proud of you. But burnout is real. And you chose a career that has a younger retirement age than most fields of work. I just don't want your career to come to a close and then suddenly you don't have anyone around you."

This is the most I've ever vocalized to Callum about the fear I've always had for him. Rugby is an insanely physical sport. Every match he puts himself at risk for injury. But this has been his dream since I can remember, so there was never a backup plan. He never even considered going to university as he knew he'd go to an amateur team, then pro as soon as he could. We both knew it was his path.

I'm just worried what his path will be once the game is up.

"Don't worry about me, big brother. I'm fine. Trust me."

"I do. I just…"

I trail off as I see Maeve peek her head around the corner, signaling that it's time for dinner.

"Callum, I hate to cut this short."

"No apologies needed. I'm glad you called."

"I am too," I say as I stand up. "Talk soon?"

"I'd like that."

We say our goodbyes as I walk into the dining room where a feast is laid out on the table. I feel Maeve's arm around my waist and I lean into her touch.

"Everything okay?" she asks.

I lean down and kiss the top of her head. "Everything is perfect."

guide to love rule #25

When having relations with your husband in your childhood bedroom, remember the trick to locking your door.

32

maeve

"Maeve, I know you weren't looking for a husband, or even a boyfriend, but you sure did hit the jackpot with that one."

I smile at Stella's statement as I look back toward the living room, where Logan, Jayce, Simon, and Emmett are all huddled around the TV, playing one of the video games Logan got Simon for Christmas.

But what I really can't take my eyes off is Logan cuddling my niece Laney on his lap. She has taken quite a liking to the newest member of the Banks extended clan.

"Okay, now that's an ovary buster," Quinn says. "God, your children are going to be freaking beautiful."

"Whoa! Slow down," I say as I walk back into the kitchen, because she's right, that sight was way too fucking cute. "I'm just getting the hang of being married. And being pregnant again? We haven't even gone remotely there yet."

"Did I hear the word pregnant?" That ridiculously hopeful voice comes from Mom, who, not shockingly, could have twenty grandchildren and still want more.

"Not yet," I say. "Much to everyone's surprise, this time I did *not* get married because I was pregnant."

"Damnit," Quinn says. "I owe everyone ten."

"Excuse me?" I look around to the numerous guilty faces of my sisters, sister-in-law, and mother. "Did y'all have bets as to why we got married?"

"What were we supposed to do?" Stella asks. "Just *not* take guesses and try to make money off it?"

"Really, Maeve," Quinn says as she shakes her head. "It's like you don't know us at all."

I shouldn't be shocked or surprised. If this was happening to any of my siblings, I'd not only be in on the bet, I'd be the one collecting the money.

"So are you ever going to tell us?"

Ainsley slaps Quinn's arm, though not hard because she's the nice one. "We said we weren't going to ask."

"She brought it up!" Quinn points to me, and I know we're talking about my marriage, but I have a flashback to the old days of Quinn trying to pin something on me that she actually did.

"Still. She'll tell us when she's ready."

Quinn looks back to me. "Maeve, it'll just be easier if you tell us. Get it out in the open. Take that weight off your shoulders."

Maybe it's time. I mean, by this point, I think telling them might help things. If I keep lying they'll come up with crazier scenarios. Or make more money off me.

Then again, my mother's here, and I'm not sure Demetria Banks is going to appreciate certain aspects of this story.

Like she knew I was thinking about her, she weighs in. "I'm just here, not saying a word, just listening to my daughters talk. What I hear or not hear, I will take in and process the information however you would like me to."

I look back to the living room, where the men are gathered, completely unconcerned about what we're doing. My father is napping in his recliner—you know, because he's had such a hard day holding the garbage bag for the wrapping paper to go into.

"Fine. I'm only telling this story one time, so everyone better buckle in."

"We need wine," Stella says.

"And snacks," Ainsley adds.

"Wait for me!" That comes from my soon-to-be sister-in-law, Charlie. "I am *not* missing out on this story."

Minutes later, all of the women are huddled around the dining table, drinks and snacks in hand, like I'm about to tell them the best story they've ever heard.

"Spill," Quinn says. "And don't leave a thing out."

Even though my sisters know how Logan and I met, to make sure everyone is up to speed, I start at the beginning—though it's an abbreviated version. Charlie has probably heard it already, between Simon and seeing my sister Stella every day. And my mom, well, she doesn't need to hear about my one-night slutty escapades.

What I do focus on is the situation with Josh, and repeat, or fill in gaps, of everything he's done and asked for over the past month. His sudden marriage. Him asking for primary custody. Being unwilling to even talk out of court about going fifty-fifty, or extending his time if he really thinks I'm a horrible mother.

"I still don't get it," Quinn says. "Nothing about that seems like something he'd do."

"I know," I say. "But he's not budging."

"Would the courts really give him primary custody?" Ainsley asks. "You're Jayce's mother!"

My shoulders slump at the question. "I'm not sure. I don't think they would, but could I take that chance? I couldn't, so I did what I had to do. And luckily, Logan needed some help from me as well."

A second of silence is interrupted by a loud gasp and Stella pointing at me. "Oh my God, you're a PR wife and he's helping you keep custody!"

"Bingo," I say. "I'm taking it that was your guess?"

She does a little shimmy in her seat as everyone around the table, including my mother, groans. "We're going to put these winnings to some new boots I was eyeing the other day."

"Fuck your boots. Back to the story," Quinn says.

"Quinn Elizabeth! Language!"

"Sorry, Mom."

She might be in her thirties. She might live in another time zone. But my mother will never not scold Quinn and her perpetual potty mouth.

"In basic terms, yes, I was a PR move for Logan. And he was a husband in a pinch for me. Your classic marriage of convenience."

Without telling too much about why Logan needed me, as it's not my story to tell, I fill in my family with the rest of the details —most importantly, that Josh is still fighting me for custody, even though now I've evened the playing field in terms of a traditional family, and that our court date is set for February.

"I can't believe my sister is in the category of relationships for Logan Matthews as Candace Kross and Sabrina Rome," Stella says. "This is a big day for me."

"Glad I could be of service."

Little chit-chat fills the table, and as I look around for people's reactions—especially my mom's—I see Quinn staring at me.

"What?"

"It isn't really PR is it?"

"What's that supposed to mean?"

I mean, I know, but I didn't realize I was that easy to read.

"You love him, don't you?"

Yup. Busted.

"I do."

Wow, I said it out loud for real.

And judging by everyone's faces, they're just as shocked as I am about that.

"I wasn't expecting it. I didn't see it coming," I continue. "And God knows if you would've told me a year ago that I'd be married to a twenty-nine-year-old billionaire, I would have laughed in your face, let alone being in love with him."

"But you are," Ainsley says, a loving look in her eyes like she just finished reading a fairy tale. "Your smile says it all. You're happy."

"I am." I can't help but realize that now Ainsley is the second person I love who has commented that I'm smiling again. "He was unexpected, I admit. But I'm happy."

Every woman's face around the table softens, including the head of our family.

"Mom? Anything to add?"

She takes a second to gather her words, and when her eyes meet mine, I know that she's one-hundred percent Team Maeve and Logan.

"I hate to rehash the past," Mom begins. "You would've never married Josh if it wasn't for getting pregnant with Jayce. And while he was a surprise, I know none of us can imagine life without him. But what I also can't imagine is you still being married to Josh. Y'all did it for the baby, and I respected it. But you weren't happy. Neither was he. No one ever thought it was going to work out. And *that's* why I never told him to call me Mom."

She pauses for a second and glances back out into the living room where Logan is still in video game heaven with the boys. They're loud, and screaming, and my dad is the most unbothered man on the planet.

"That man out there, though you might've married him for reasons that weren't originally for love, I could tell from the second that he walked in my front door that he was somebody different. The pictures I saw of you two the other night online, I've never seen you look happier or glowing in my life. I saw my daughter in love. And that's all we ever want for our children. That's all I ever wanted for you."

I stand up and walk over, embracing my mom in a hug as the tears start leaking from my eyes. "Thank you."

Before I know it, a group hug has engulfed me, with all my sisters wrapping their arms around me. The sentiment is wonderful. The love that I have for these women is unmatched. But I also can't breathe, so I need this to stop.

"All right, air is necessary." My message gets across as everyone walks away while laughing and dabbing tears from their eyes. "I do, though, want to apologize to all of you. I hated having to keep the reasons quiet and not be completely honest."

Quinn shakes her head. "You did what you had to do."

Stella follows. "Like you always do."

Just when I think we're done, Mom clears her throat. "Yes, you did. You're a fighter, and you do what you need to do to protect your family."

"I feel a but coming on…"

"You're right." Demetria Banks is nothing if predictable. "But if this is going to be something that's going to last, I would love to see my daughter get a proper ceremony. It doesn't have to be big or fancy, and your father and I will pay for everything."

"Mom, she's married to an actual billionaire. I don't think they need you to help with flowers for their redo."

"Shush, Quinn."

"I understand," I say, not knowing how to gently temper my mother's wishes. "But can I have some time? Contrary to what people are seeing today, I just realized within the last week that I love my husband. I'd like to go on an actual date with him before our second ceremony."

"Fine," Mom groans, but then sets her sights on my eventual sister-in-law. "Now, Charlie! When is that son of mine going to get his head out of his ass and put a ring on your finger?"

With the interrogation lamp off me, I walk back toward the guys, who are still in their video game glory.

Actually, I'm just looking at Logan. Between the baby on his lap, the words I just said, and well, him, how could I not?

"I know that look." Stella says as she slides up next to me.

"What look?"

"Like you want to fuck your man but your family is around so you can't."

"Stella!" I whisper yell. "I do not."

"Liar." She leans a little closer. "I'll cover for you. Do what you need to do."

"I don't need to do anything," I say. Though now that she's put it in my head, I can't get it out.

"Go. I got you. But be quick. I can only distract for so long."

I smile and bump her shoulder. "I got you next time."

"I know," she says with a smile. "Now go! You're on the clock."

The guys are celebrating something. Well, everyone except Simon, whom I'm guessing just lost, and I take that opportunity to grab Logan's hand.

"Hey," I whisper and tilt my head. "Follow me."

Without asking where we're going, Logan places the controller on the coffee table, and hands Simon's daughter back to him, as I do my best to discreetly sneak away with my husband.

"Is this the grand tour?" he asks.

"Something like that." I look around for a second, making sure no one followed me, as I grab his hand and pull him upstairs.

I try to be as quiet as possible, which, luckily for me, doesn't need to be too quiet since every member of my family is here, as I lead Logan into my old bedroom.

"Is this what I think it is?" Logan asks as his eyes move around the walls that look like I left the house last week, not twelve years ago.

"It is," I say as I shut the door, lock it, and for extra measure, jam it shut by putting a desk chair under the knob.

"Love, I've been up front and honest that you married a certified nerd," he says as he takes down my spelling bee trophy. "What I didn't know is that I married one as well."

"I wouldn't say I was a nerd," I say as I take the trophy from his hand and place it back on the shelf next to my valedictorian cords. "I just wanted to be the best. And since I clearly wasn't going to do that on an athletic field, the classroom was the logical place."

"Sure," he pretends to agree, but also points out my district champion debate plaque. "And what about this?"

As much as I love when Logan compliments me on my brain or my work, right now I just need my husband to fuck me. So I do the only thing I can think of at the moment to make him focus on the task at hand—I take off my shirt.

"Oh...Oh!" he says, and I shush him immediately as I hurriedly shove down my leggings and panties.

"We don't have long, Matthews. So quit looking at my trophies and take off your pants."

He does as I ask, his switch flipping from surprised to aroused in a second. I take a moment to look around to figure out exactly where I want this to happen. The bed would get too crumpled and we'd have to remake it. The floor means someone could hear us if they walked below as we're on the second floor. And against the door, while a good option for tidiness, is more of a sound problem than the floor.

But before I can make a decision, a shirtless Logan is behind me. His hard cock is pressing against my ass as his arms come around me, one hand around my waist while the other is gently placed at the base of my neck.

"I'm assuming we have to be quick?"

"Yes," I say as a breath.

"And quiet?"

This time I can't say anything as Logan's fingers start tracing lines down to my breasts. "Then you better not scream when I fuck this pretty pussy."

Logan spins me around and captures my mouth in his before I can say anything else. Our hands are all over each other, knowing we're on the clock, but also wanting—no, needing—to bring each other to pleasure.

Logan begins backing me up while simultaneously trailing his fingers down my body. As soon as my legs hit the back of the bed and I fall back, Logan's fingers are inside me, working me quickly, efficiently, and most important, perfectly.

This man wasn't lying that first night when he said his fingers were his superpower. I swear to the Goddess of Orgasms, this man could make me come with just his fingers in two seconds flat and no warm up. He knows just the spot, and his fingers do some sort of acrobatic moves to get the job done.

I swallow a groan as Logan picks up the speed and pressure, and just as I'm about to let out a sound that would probably be a half scream/moan, Logan's mouth is on mine, swallowing any reaction as my orgasm hits me fast and hard.

"Just like that, Love," he says as he starts to bring me down. "Come on my fingers. Soak them."

Oh this man and his dirty mouth…

And while I'd love to just lay back and bask in this afterglow, I came up here with a reason—and that was to fuck my husband.

"Your turn," I say, pushing him down so I can straddle him. "I want to ride you."

Logan gives me a devilish grin. "Happy Christmas to me."

I quickly line him up to my center and easily slide down on his cock. I throw my head back as I let him fill me, always needing a second to get used to him before I can chase what I want.

"That's it," he says as he grabs my hips. "Take all of me."

His hands run up my stomach and take down the cups of my bra, letting him squeeze and tease both breasts as I begin to ride him. My hands find his muscular chest, needing his built pecs to hold onto as my speed picks up more, especially when he tweaks my nipples like he's doing now.

"Logan…" I moan, and probably a little too loud, but both of us are too in the moment to care. "You feel so good."

"Yes…" Logan replies, his hips starting to buck into mine. "So perfect."

I throw my hands back behind me, letting my back arch slightly as the new angle is hitting just the spot I needed to scratch. And judging by the low groan from Logan, he likes it too.

"Right there," I say. "It's right there."

"Keep going," he says. "Take it. Take me. Take whatever you want."

With his words of encouragement and Logan's fingers flipping the switch on my clit, I'm coming harder than I ever have in my life. Logan's not far behind, grabbing onto me and holding me against his chest as I we both do our best to ride out, then recover, from orgasms that seemed to pulse through our entire bodies.

"Maeve! I know you're in there!"

My bubble of bliss is popped when I hear Quinn outside my door.

"Don't say anything," I whisper to Logan, who nods in agreement.

"I can hear you whispering, and frankly, I'm just glad I didn't hear other things. Stella's trying to distract, but Mom is starting to ask where you two are. You have five minutes, tops, before she goes on the hunt."

"You're my favorite sister!" Logan yells, which earns him a playful slap on his chest.

"Damn straight."

"Hurry!" I instruct, responsible Maeve coming back to her senses. I slowly pull myself off him, but realizing in the process that I'm a mess, both of us need to be cleaned off, and this comforter needs probably more than a tumble through the wash cycle.

"This isn't good," I say. "What are we going to do?"

Logan chuckles as he grabs his pants and pulls them back on. "Offer to decorate this room for your mother? Maybe she'd like to make it her sewing room."

"Oh! Good idea!" I say. "Then I can just burn the comforter."

Logan kisses my head, then gently slaps me on the ass. "You think of ideas for that. I'm going to go back downstairs and distract her with my accent and compliment her on her cooking."

"Kiss-up."

He just shrugs and leans in to kiss me on the nose. "Correction. People pleaser."

I wrap my arms around him, but as soon as I do, I hear footsteps coming from outside the door. "I love you."

He rests his forehead against mine. "Not nearly as much as I love you."

33

logan

I DID IT.

I fucking did it.

I have an idea.

And not just any game idea. *The* game idea. One I know is going to be successful, marketable, and profitable. And not just that, I'm going to enjoy the hell out of developing this.

And it's all thanks to Maeve and Jayce.

"Whoa!" Kat says as she walks into my office. "Why am I having déjà vu?"

I don't look up from my computer as she comes walking over to my desk. "Probably because I haven't slept and I've lost track of times you've found me in one of these situations."

"Yeah. It's called a month ago," she says. "But this is different. You look…happy?"

"Not just happy. Bloody thrilled," I say, my fingers flying across the keyboard. "I fucking did it."

"Did what?" It takes Kat a second of silence to realize what "it" is. "Holy shit! You figured out a game!"

"Not only did I figure it out, but I have basic specs, the story, and a few character mockups."

"Fuck yes!" Kat celebrates, running around my desk to give me a hug. "I'm so proud of you. I knew you could do it."

"Thanks," I say, returning her gesture. "I was starting to get worried."

"Honestly? Same." We share a laugh as she steps away. "So? Are you going to tell me what it is?"

"Tell you what what is?"

Good, Maeve's now in here so I can tell my two favorite women together. "The game I came up with."

Maeve's eyes quit blinking for a second before she lets out a screech of excitement. "Oh my God! You did it!"

Maeve runs over to me and nearly tackles me in my desk chair. Wow, I didn't know she could get this excited.

Well, this kind of excited.

"Is this why you got up in the middle of the night and I hadn't seen you since?"

"Yeah, sorry about that," I say as she takes a seat next to Kat in my newly furnished, and might I say, quite posh, office. "But I woke up in the middle of the night, and for some reason, that was the time my brain turned on. I didn't want to take the risk it would be gone by morning."

I didn't just wake up in the middle of the night; I shot up from a dead slumber. I don't know if it came to me in a dream or what, but one second I'm holding Maeve's naked body against mine, and the next I've come up with the idea that will no doubt be the next big thing in video games.

"Well, quit making us wait," Kat says. "Especially me, because no offense to the missus, but I've been here a lot longer and have had a lot more headaches."

"None taken."

I turn my computer screen, showing them the mockup I've started. "Ladies, may I introduce to you SpaceCraft Eras, name subject to change."

Maeve and Kat look at each other, slightly confused, which I don't blame them. The name makes no sense without explanation.

"Okay, follow me," I say, unable to keep the excitement out of my voice. "I kept thinking of how much fun we had on Christmas with the old video games," I explain. "And not just the old guys who were reliving their youth, but Jayce, who was seeing these classic games for the first time."

"It was a hit," Maeve says. "But, and I hate to be the Debbie Downer, I'm pretty sure those games are spoken for. Or at the least, the characters are."

"Correct, which was where I was getting stumped," I say. "Then last night it hit me. Bring in the old with the new."

I bring up the screen that has the SpaceCraft characters on it. "People know GameTech for SpaceCraft, and even if the sales have evened out, it's still one of the most popular games in the world. So why not bring in the characters everyone knows and loves, and put them in situations that resemble the games of the past."

"Because scenarios and scenes aren't copyrighted," Kat adds with an excited nod. "It's the best of both worlds."

"Exactly," I say. "We can have scenes where they fight each other in a boxing ring. We can have them shooting at launched stars. Or maybe fighting in underground sewers while eating tacos instead of pizza. Whatever we want. As long as, at the end of the day, it gives the feeling of those old, vintage video games that we love but in the modern gaming world."

"Bringing the new generation and the older generation together."

I smile at Maeve. "Exactly."

"Fuck yeah!" Kat yells, clapping for extra measure. "This is perfect, Logan. The board is going to go nuts."

"Right? I have so much to do. I need to get development on it. Give a presentation to the marketing team to make sure we nail the name and the concept of the packaging. Oh! And the board. Those crotchety old men need something to get excited about."

"Well, then, it's your lucky day," Kat says. "I came in here to remind you about a call with the board and the department heads today. Might as well let the good news out."

Maeve stands up and leans over my desk. "I'm so proud of you."

She gives me a kiss, and for the first time maybe ever, I feel like I'm proud of me too. I was when I came up with SpaceCraft, but I always felt like I couldn't take time to feel good about my accomplishment because I felt like I had something to prove.

Somebody to prove something to.

But now? Knowing what I've come up with is, what I feel, going to be a hit, and getting to share that success with the people who mean the most to me? Who I know are proud of me even without the words being spoken? That's a special feeling.

That's love.

———

Today might have been the only day in my entire career that I was excited for a virtual conference call meeting.

That excitement lasted ten minutes.

Just like I thought, they loved the idea of mixing SpaceCraft with vintage games of days gone by. One member even suggested one of his favorites that I'd totally forgotten about.

SpaceCraft characters on a race track? Hell, yeah!

But now that the excitement has died down, and I'm sitting here pretending to be an engaged CEO, I'm remembering why I dread these calls.

I don't hear much of what my CFO starts talking about—I'm going to take a stab that it's about finances or budgets—as out of the corner of my eye I see Maeve come into the office. She's dressed in a robe, which is odd since it's after lunch, but I don't have time to think anything of it as I luckily hear the conversation be tossed back to me.

"Sounds good." Did it? Not sure. If there are bad things to report, I'm usually notified ahead of time so I'm going to assume everything is going well. "Let's keep everything on track. We want to have a strong Q1..."

I don't mean to trail off. I was actually doing well in sounding like I had any idea what was going on.

Then again, I wasn't expecting my wife to flash me in the middle of my conference call.

I swallow the massive frog in my throat and try not to squirm in my seat due to my suddenly hard cock, as Maeve stands just off to the side of my vision, gloriously naked, while I'm trying to be a proper CEO.

"Mr. Matthews? Are you okay?"

"Yeah...Yes," I say, blinking a few times as I try to resist not looking at Maeve's beautiful body. "As I was staying. Q1. Let's do good."

Let's do good? I sound like a bumbling idiot. Though, they're lucky I'm speaking at all right now as Maeve isn't moving, just continuing to stand just out of my reach, and plenty out of sight of the camera, teasing me like the vixen she is.

"You heard the man, let's do good." I don't know who said that, but I'm thankful as it naturally segues to the head of accounting taking the floor.

"I'm on camera," I mumble, making sure the microphone is off. I don't turn off the camera, though, because the last time I did that, I fell asleep, and Kat had to come in and slap me awake.

"I know."

My eyes glance to her, then back to whoever is talking, then back to Maeve. She's inching closer to me, and I'm now doing anything I can to hold myself back.

I want to touch her. I want to feel her. I want to suck on those perfect tits while she straddles my lap. I want her to ride me here on this chair. I want to bend her over this desk and make her scream.

And I will, I'll do all of that. Once I unmute and get off this godforsaken bloody meeting.

"Great," I groan out as Maeve starts walking around the desk. My eyes can't help but follow her, and I know everyone on this meeting has to think I'm insane. They would be too if they had a goddess in front of them like I do. "What else do we have on the agenda?"

I shut off my microphone quickly as I realize Maeve has done an expert job of perching herself on my desk, perfectly out of camera view, but now so close to me I have to physically sit on my hands to keep from touching her.

I start scribbling gibberish on a piece of paper, anything to try to focus on the speaker, when all I want to do is bury my face between Maeve's legs.

"Great. Fine. Let's do it." I say, and judging by the expressions on their faces, that takes everyone off guard.

"Mr. Matthews...you want to give everyone every Friday off?"

Oh shit...do I? That's what they were talking about? Fuck it, might as well. If it means getting off this call quicker, and stop Maeve from snickering in the background, we can work three-day weeks for all I care.

"Yeah! Sure. Why not? Four-day work weeks should be a thing. Let's try it through the end of the quarter and see how productivity goes and then make a permanent decision."

Everyone starts talking among themselves on the call, apparently thrown by my decision. I take the opportunity as a perfect time to wrap this up.

"Let's leave this here," I say. "Happy New Year to you all. We'll chat again next month."

I hit end on the call and turn my chair, putting me at eye level with Maeve's perfect, pink pussy. "Quite a show you just put on..."

She shrugs, as if Maeve Banks-Matthews has ever been coy a day in her life. "Just wanted to see how your meeting was going."

"Really?" I say, leaning back in my chair so I can fully take her in. "That's it?"

"That's it." Though as the words leave her lips, she slides off the desk. "I thought maybe you could use something to keep you awake. I know you tend to find them boring."

I've seen a lot of versions of Maeve since we met. Flirty and seductive Maeve is a new persona.

She might be my favorite.

"Come here," I say, motioning with my finger to do the same. She doesn't hesitate as she comes to me, leaning down so I can finally taste her lips on mine. I just have to move my hands slightly to squeeze her tits that have been beautifully on display. I start to bring her on my lap when the godforsaken sound of a Teams call rings through.

"Bloody hell!" I yell, looking to see that it's the head of human resources. Probably wanting to make sure I wasn't crazy for declaring four-day work weeks.

"Answer it," Maeve says as she slides down from my lap. "And don't mind me."

Jesus fucking Christ is she about to…

Holy shit, she is. I hear the telltale sound of my zipper coming down, and I lift up for just a second before realizing I still need to answer the phone.

"What, Tom!"

Was that aggressive? Yes. Does Tom look frightened? A little. But I don't care—my wife is sucking my dick during a work call.

"Apologies, Mr. Matthews," Tom says. "I just wanted to go over the statement you made during today's meeting, if you had the time?"

"Sure. Yup. Great." Those are the only words I trust myself to say, otherwise I stay quiet as Tom starts giving me the facts and figures of what making a four-day week happen looks like. I nod and do my best to pay attention to him, because he's just doing his job. It's not his fault he chose the literal worst time for me to remember a thing he says. The way Maeve's hand is working in tandem with her mouth, I can barely remember my name.

"Mmhmm," I gasp, gripping onto my desk chair for dear life as Maeve takes me to the back of her throat. Luckily this coincides with Tom saying something that warranted a response. Hopefully "mmhmm" is appropriate.

Just when I think Tom's done, he keeps going. How much more can he talk about? More importantly, how long can Maeve suck my cock without taking a breath? I swear the woman hasn't relented. Between her strokes, and her tongue, and the way her hot mouth forms around me to provide just enough suction, I'm about to come in her throat and hope that Tom doesn't realize it.

"Tom, I have another call coming in."

And by call I mean come in my wife's mouth.

"No problem, boss. I'll just send you over—"

I end the call before Tom can finish his statement. Which I feel bad about for two seconds before I feel Maeve's mouth against my pelvis, deep throating me and taking every inch.

"Fuck!" I groan, gathering her hair in my hand. "You take my cock so fucking good."

My words seem to spur her on, working me from root to tip in a way where I never know what's next. I feel my balls start to tighten, and I can't help but start thrusting my hips into her, wanting her to take every inch of me.

"Are you going to swallow my cum like a good wife?"

She doesn't answer with her words; no, she just doubles down, sucking harder, and faster, and working me so hard that I'm...

Holy....fuck...

I pull her hair and grip my seat, needing something to keep me centered as an orgasm like I've never had pulses through me. I have to actively try and calm my breath, because I might pass out.

"So, was it a good meeting?"

I pick her up and bring her to my lap, her sweet laugh filling the air. "Best meeting ever."

guide to love rule #42

Marriage vows say in good times and in bad. Make sure your partner really means it in case your past comes back to bite you in the ass.

34

maeve

Normal weeknights when it was just me and Jayce included dinner, bath time, and then him either playing a game or watching television while I worked on designs from the couch.

These days it's the same—only now I have Logan next to me working on his computer. And after Jayce goes to bed, we usually have sex.

That's definitely a change from the old days.

It's been more than a month since Jayce and I moved in, and while I was wondering how my son would handle the move, it's been the easiest transition I could've asked for. Yes, there is the added pain of driving him to school each day since we're now out of district. But the school knows about the custody situation, and has said as long as we can get him to school, he can finish out the year, and by then we'd know what Jayce's home life would look like.

And it better look like this, because right now is pretty perfect. Especially now that Logan's put his computer away for the night and has started rubbing my feet.

"Mommy? Can I have a snack?"

I check the time and see that it's just after seven. "A small bowl of Goldfish."

Logan looks over to me. "Can I have a snack too?"

I don't know whose puppy dog lip is more ridiculous, Jayce or Logan's. Though, a little snack does sound good. "Popcorn?"

"Extra butter, light on the salt," he says, finishing my thought. "Be right back."

He leans down to kiss my forehead as he and Jayce head off to the kitchen.

What is this? Is this domestic bliss? I mean, I know it's not going to be this way forever, but even if some of our nights are like this, I'd say that I'm one lucky woman.

I don't bother wiping the smile off my face as I feel my cell phone vibrate next to me.

STELLA

Maeve, I'm going to preface this text thread under the category of "Don't Hate Me."

AINSLEY

Stella…what did you do?

STELLA

Nothing bad.

QUINN

But probably nothing good.

I look at which thread this is, and realize it's the sisters-only chat. Usually this thread is reserved for girl talk or to bitch about Simon. But if she's giving me a warning and no one else, I have to wonder what she's up to.

MAEVE

Just tell us, Stella. I guarantee we won't hate you.

STELLA

I know you won't, but you'll probably tell me to stay out of your business.

MAEVE

Stella Leigh...

STELLA

I might've gone on a very deep internet stalking mission to dig more into Vivian.

AINSLEY

Stella...

QUINN

Good. I've never met her, but I hate her on principle.

MAEVE

Stella, while I appreciate your efforts, my lawyers are on it.

At least, I hope they are.

STELLA

Hear me out. After you told us about Josh wanting custody and that it seemed to pop up around the time that he and Vivian suddenly got married, I had a weird feeling about it.

AINSLEY

We all did.

STELLA

Exactly. So I started stalking her social media, which, there wasn't anything on the outside that was glaring. But! I searched her saved stories—and this woman saves everything— and noticed she's discreetly posting about auditioning for something and also hinting that it's back in the reality world.

QUINN

She was fifth out of ten in a singing reality show. Literally the definition of mid. And she wants to do it again?

STELLA

No, see, that's what's interesting. It doesn't seem like she's doing another competition. She's been posting a lot about lifestyles, and daily vlogs, and things that seem more like she's going more for influencer rather than country singer.

AINSLEY

Who would want to take lifestyle advice from her? She's not a good person.

QUINN

A lot of people are trash, so I'm guessing other trash people?

MAEVE

Focus! Stella, what does any of this have to do with the custody case?

AINSLEY

Wait! Isn't there a new reality show about to start casting in Nashville?

STELLA

Correct, dear sister. Real Lives of Nashville Wives.

I think about it for a second and then I remember I read something about that when Logan and I were coming back from Los Angeles.

MAEVE

Wait, are you telling me that you think Vivian is auditioning for this show, and that's why she suddenly married Josh?

QUINN

And more dastardly, are you saying that she wants Josh to have primary custody of Jayce so she can act as if she's bonus mom of the year?

That's…that's absurd.

Right?

I mean, who would go and put together a family just to get on a likely-to-get-canceled-after-one-season reality show?

STELLA

> I'm not saying anything. I'm just saying that I'd bet my new boots and my Chanel bag that this woman has had at least an audition. And that the timing is suspicious.

"Who are you texting, Mommy?"

I look up from my phone to see Jayce and Logan coming back into the living room, snacks and drinks in hand. And yes, I didn't ask, but my husband knew to bring me a Diet Coke.

"Your aunts," I say. I want to see if he wants to FaceTime them, but the second everyone gets settled, we hear an alert that the gate is opening.

"Who's bothering us at this hour?" Logan says as he checks the cameras. "What on earth is Kat doing back here?"

Logan heads to the door to greet her, but I'm sitting up straight in my seat. Kat has been enjoying life these days now that we're married—and it's not just for show—and that Logan is full steam ahead on his new idea. She even told me she might take a vacation this year.

So her coming back to the house, and driving like she's running from the cops, at seven in the evening is something to be concerned about.

A few minutes later, Kat and Logan walk into the room, both looking pale and frantic.

"Jayce, buddy, how about you go to your room and start getting ready for bed."

"I get it," Jayce says with a sigh as he picks up his bowl of crackers. "Adult time."

My son made a really good joke, and I can't even enjoy it

because Kat and Logan look like they're about to drop a bomb on me.

"What is it?" I ask once I knew Jayce was out of earshot.

"Now, I want to start this off with saying that I just don't work for Logan, but I work for you too. So however we decide to handle this, I have your back one-hundred percent."

I feel my stomach starting to drop. "What is it?"

Kat pulls up her phone and shows me a picture that looks like it was taken on a digital camera in the 2000s.

And in the midst of that group of girls is me.

Topless.

"What the hell?" I say, zooming into make sure that it is me. Which I know it is. It's from Spring Break 2008. I was twenty. In college. And was living my best life in Cancun, where I didn't need an ID to drink. Or to enter a wet T-shirt contest where none of the shirts ended up staying on after they were soaked.

"It's not just that."

What? I have to blink a few times as Kat takes the phone from me and starts scrolling through more photos. It's a whole gallery of compromising pictures from that Cancun spring break, to other college escapades, and from my party girl years in Nashville before Maeve Banks made a name for herself in the design field. But what makes me gasp is the final picture, which is of Logan and I the first night we met at the hotel bar.

Our first kiss.

But it doesn't look like just a kiss. Somehow the picture has been manipulated to look like he's groping me on the dance floor. I know I was drunk that night, but I don't remember that happening.

"What the fuck?" I scream, grabbing her phone and looking through them again. "How the hell did someone get all these?"

"I'm not sure," Kat says. "All I know is that somehow they were leaked to a non-friendly Logan Matthews gossip blog and so now this gallery is live with the headline 'See the other side of the new Mrs. Logan Matthews.'"

"Jesus fucking Christ," I say, collapsing to the couch. My head is pounding. I feel like I can't breathe.

"Who did this?" Logan barks. My eyes are just open enough to see him pacing back and forth across the living room. "Whoever it is, they're fucking done. I'll ruin them."

"I don't know," Kat says. "Usually if it's a blog or creator I'm friendly with, they won't tell me who sent in what, but they'll give me enough hints to figure it out for myself. But either they know that this site hates me or they just got lucky, because if I try to make a phone call, they'll run a headline that I'm trying to pay them off. They're that petty."

"Fucking wonderful," I say, trying to control my breathing. "Logan, I'm so—"

"No. Don't you dare apologize," he says. "We all have pictures from our youth that we'd rather not have in the public."

"Logan, I know you're trying to make me feel better, but your pictures are you looking dorky in eighth grade. Mine are of my tits on a Tuesday when I won a wet T-shirt contest to a song about a lollipop that wasn't a lollipop. We aren't talking about the same things."

"You won?" Kat asks. "Nice."

"Thanks, but not the point, Kat. What the fuck? This is… this is so fucking bad." It's at that moment that the actual gravity hits me. "Jayce…the custody case."

The mood in the room drops even more than it was.

These pictures are out there now. I mean, they existed somewhere before this, but now they are available for the world to see, and because of who I married, this is going to circulate like wildfire. Which means that this is going to be brought up at the custody hearing. Now Josh and Vivian can say that I work too hard, I'm never there, and apparently when I'm not there, I'm entering topless contests, always drunk, and making out with men in public.

"Oh God," I say, starting to hyperventilate. I'm out of control. I'm spiraling. My head is spinning, and I can't breathe.

"Love. Come here." I hear Logan's words and I feel his arms around me, but that's it. "Shh…find the calm. We're going to figure out who did this."

"How?" I say between gasped breaths. "How do you find something like this? How do we stop this wildfire? Does it even matter who?"

"Don't worry. I'll take care of this."

I don't know if I believe Logan. I don't know anything anymore.

Because all I can think is this is it. This is the end of my road.

35
logan

I've pulled many all-nighters in my life. Kat has been there to witness nearly all of them. But in all those years, and through all those cans of Red Bull, I don't think we've ever worked side by side—or with more purpose.

Because we're finding out where these pictures came from if it's the last thing we do.

"I don't care if it's three in the morning. If you valued sleep you wouldn't be in the business of fabricating celebrity news. So get your scrawny ass out of bed now!"

Ah, she finally reached the editor of the blog that posted the pictures.

"Now you listen here, you pencil dick weasel. You're going to take those pictures down right now. You're going to say that upon further review, you couldn't verify them, and that you publicly apologize to Mrs. Banks-Matthews for the massive invasion of privacy."

I can't hear anything on the other end of the phone call, but my finger is ready to tap on the button of my mouse in a second when Kat gives me the signal.

Because yes, I'm about to shut down their website if they don't agree to her demands.

Why? Because they fucked with my wife.

And I can.

"Oh, you're not? That's cute. So now…how about you get on your website? Why? Oh, just because I want you to see something."

Kat gives me the nod, and with one click I've hacked into their servers, blaring an error message on the page that says their site is shut down. Also featured on it is the most unflattering picture we could find of him. It felt poetic.

"Oh…now you want to play ball? I figured you might."

Kat continues to talk to the editor as I switch out my screen and try to figure out where these pictures came from. I ran every reverse image search I had—the legal and not legal ones—only to come up empty. Well, not completely empty. The photo of Maeve and I dancing the first night we met apparently had been circulating on the internet for a while, but somehow it never came up on Kat's radar. Though that picture was innocent. The one that's attached to the other pictures has clearly been doctored.

But who? Who would do this to Maeve? Or are they doing it to me?

That's the other part of this—we don't know why this is happening. On the surface, it looks like Maeve. But did they do it out of vindictiveness to her, or was it a way to get to me through her?

"I'm glad we've come to an understanding," Kat says as she hangs up. "Pictures are down from there."

I go to restore the page before Kat stops me. "Not yet. Make him sweat. He's a prick."

"Did you learn anything?"

She shakes her head. "He wouldn't give up a source. And frankly, I don't know if my threat of his website being shut down is enough to keep the pictures down forever. And even if those stay down, this is becoming a game of whack-a-mole. I can't keep up with them. Any luck with you?"

"I know I'm not a world class hacker, but I thought I'd be able to find something. But all I've found is the email that sent the pictures originally to the editor. It came from a burner account from an IP address that's a coffee shop."

"Do you know when? Are there cameras? Hack away, computer boy!"

I laugh. "Hacking into cameras at some random coffee shop is beyond my skill set. And before you tell me to make a call, I already did. My friend told me he'd find the camera footage and send it to me within the hour."

"God love hackers for having the worst sleep hygiene on the planet," Kat says. "Really comes in handy in times like these."

Both of us fall back into our chairs, exhaustion starting to hit us.

"Is it against me or her?" I ask, needing to know the answer that's plagued my mind.

"Her." Kat says flatly. "This was a direct attack against Maeve."

I clench my fists, and my blood starts to boil. "I'll kill them, Kat. I won't think twice about it."

"I know you're pissed, Logan, and so am I, but a premeditated murder charge doesn't help here."

"Then what fucking will? How can I fix this for her?"

And that's what I want most of all—to be the one to fix this for Maeve. For her entire life, she's been the fixer. The controller. When there's a problem, Maeve's the one to solve it.

But here we are, a problem she can't fix—and one that can ruin her career and take her son away in one swoop—and I can't fix it, either. Even though between my smarts, skills, and bank account, I should be able to.

I can't fail her. I won't fail her. I don't care if I have to stay up all night and call in favors from everyone I know including the fucking King of England, I'm going to do this for her.

"Who would do this?" Kat asks. "I mean, they have to be

semi-smart to remember to send from a fake account, but dumb enough to do it in the first place."

"It's Vivian."

Kat and I both pop up from our seats to see an exhausted, swollen-faced Maeve standing in the doorway of my office.

"Maeve? What are you doing up?"

"I couldn't sleep."

I hurry over to her, bringing her in my arms and all but carry her to the couch. Once the initial shock of the events swept through her, she said she needed to go upstairs with Jayce. That pictures or not, she had a child, and she needed to do bath time and make sure he went to bed for school in the morning. I went up to check on her after a few hours to find her asleep in his bed, holding him tight.

"Maeve, I know it's been a long night for all of us, but did you say this is Vivian's doing? As in your ex-husband's new wife?"

Maeve nods. "I don't know if it's the lack of sleep, the headache, or pure delusion, but something is telling me it's her."

Kat and I look at each other and share a shrug. It's not like we have any other leads to go on.

"Why do you say that?" I ask. "I mean, all because of the custody case?"

"I think so," Maeve begins. "Earlier tonight I was talking to my sisters, and Stella mentioned that she was doing some social media stalking and thinks that Vivian is auditioning for that *Real Lives of Nashville Wives* reality show. And the insane theory that came from the sisters' collective is that Vivian got married and is trying to get custody so she can be this bonus mom of the year and help her chances on the show."

"That's..." Kat pauses for a second. "Not as insane as some other things that have happened in entertainment."

"There's more," Maeve says. "Back at the Christmas gala, I heard her and Candace talking. Before they were interrupted, she was about to say something to Candace about the reason that

Logan and I got married was because of her marrying Josh. Which is true. What if she was about to tell her that she married Josh for the show too, and the chain of events ended with Logan and I getting married?"

"I mean…" I trail off for a second, because again, this sounds bananas. Or does it? I don't have a second to ponder that because at that moment an email notification pings from my computer.

"Is it the footage?" Kat asks as I walk to go check it.

"What footage?" Maeve asks as she follows me.

I fill her in on the email we found with the pictures, and that a friend of mine was pulling security footage for me.

"I know that place," Maeve says as we start to watch the tape. "It's not far from Josh's house. I used to go there occasionally if I was running early to pick up Jayce."

The three of us are all on high alert as we watch the time lapsed footage. We know the email was sent around six o'clock, but since not all chairs are visible in the footage, we have to watch every second to see when customers come in.

"I think I'm going cross-eyed," Kat says. "For the love of God, Vivian, just show your overfilled face so we can get on with this!"

As if she willed it into existence, in the next minute the three of us watch Vivian walk into the coffee shop, laptop bag in hand.

To her credit, she tried to disguise herself with a ball cap and oversized clothing. Too bad we were all on a mission to spot her.

"There! We got it!" Maeve announces. "Let's go fucking get her."

"Not yet," I say, starting to bring up programs that will help me get into Vivian's computer and email. "We need more."

"More? We've proved she was there! She fucking sent the email!"

"He's right," Kat says, doing her best to calm Maeve down. "Right now we have a hunch and circumstance. What we need is evidence."

I take Maeve's hand in mine. "Let me find the proof. Because if I do, and it's in fact her, this ends forever. Names cleared. Custody case dropped. It will all be behind us, and we'll go back to the calm. It's going to take a few days, but I promise, it'll be worth it to put all of this behind us."

Maeve nods, and when she closes her eyes, I think she might fall asleep standing up. "Please, Logan."

"I got this," I say, kissing her forehead. "I'm going to fix this for you. I promise."

guide to love rule #117

Never sleep on the computer geeks. They have a specific set of skills that will at some point come in handy.

36

maeve

I'VE NEVER FELT MORE OUT OF CONTROL OF MY LIFE THAN I HAVE over the past five days. I felt like I was out of my body, and watching my life explode in front of me. All I could see was that with one set of leaked photos, and a dumb decision I made when I was twenty, I was going to lose my child, my business, and my husband.

I couldn't see straight. Thank God I had Logan beside me, who even though I was bringing down his name with mine, didn't seem to care. No, all he cared about was getting to the bottom of it and doing anything he could, or calling in any favor, to make that happen.

Which is how we're standing here on my ex's doorstep, ready to confront them with proof Logan assures me will end all of this.

And I mean, he has a point. When he showed me everything he found, it was like a treasure chest that kept on giving.

"You ready?" Logan asks, holding my hand as we step up to Josh's front door.

"Yes. Let's end this once and for all."

I knock on the door, though Josh knows we're coming. In just a few seconds, he's opened the door, but no Vivian to be seen.

"Maeve. Logan. Come in."

Neither Logan nor I respond verbally, just nodding our heads as we try and assess Josh's demeanor. Logan thinks he's also responsible, or at the minimum in the know, but I don't think so. When I messaged him earlier asking to talk, his answers were normal. He didn't freak out about me asking for Vivian to be there as well, nor did he make mention of the photos. My guess is that he's living under a rock, doesn't know my boobs are on display for the internet to see, or has no idea what we're about to drop on him. Possibly all of the above.

"Thanks for seeing us on short notice," I say, sitting on one of his couches, Logan sitting right next to me. I keep my purse tight to my body as it has the folder that contains all of our findings, which also makes me feel like I have a bomb on my lap.

"It sounded urgent."

"It is," I say as Vivian walks in. Her hair is big and blonde, and I don't know if she's trying to prove a point by coming out here in a workout set that shows off how much bigger her boobs are than mine, but the point is made.

Too bad that's the only point she's winning today. Because I'm about to end this bitch. "Vivian. Glad you could join us."

"It's no problem, Maeve. I can't *imagine* what you've been going through," Vivian says with mock sincerity. "Just a shame."

The two of us have a mini stare down and it's at this moment that if I didn't know she did it, I would now.

But my ex? He's clearly clueless.

"What happened? Is everything okay?"

"It is now," I assure Josh. "Some unflattering pictures of me leaked onto the internet. Caused quite a stir. Took days to sort out. I'm surprised Vivian didn't show you or tell you about it?"

"Well...I knew you had to be embarrassed," Vivian says.

"See, I want to believe you," I say as I take the envelope out of my purse. "But I don't."

"Why would you say that? I'm a good person, despite what you think about me."

Neither Logan nor I can contain our laughter. "Oh, Vivian. You're a proper fool."

She gasps at Logan's statement. "How dare you say that!"

"Watch it, Matthews," Josh says, taking Vivian's hand. "That's my wife you're talking to."

"Exactly, and it's *my wife* that was fucked with. And I don't stand for things like this." I hand Josh the first set of pictures. "These are just some of the pictures that were leaked to the media."

Josh protests at first, but eventually takes them. I should be embarrassed that half of them are of me, half naked, dancing on the bar that Josh used to work at because I thought I was in *Coyote Ugly*. Some are from that drunken Cancun trip. It took me days of looking at them to figure out where they came from. How did these surface after years? They were never on social media. It didn't make sense.

Until one night it hit me—they were on my old laptop.

A laptop I gave Josh.

One I'm betting he still has and Vivian found.

"These are from the old bar," he says, flipping through the printouts. "I haven't seen these photos in years."

"I honestly forgot they existed," I say. "But when we were going through the photos that were leaked, we couldn't help but notice that a majority of them were ones I remember taking from the old days."

"Wow…" Josh says like he's longingly looking through good memories. "I don't even know where these came from…"

"I do."

My voice is confident as Josh looks at me, confused—and Vivian looks anywhere but at me.

"Where?"

"My old laptop. The one I gave you. Do you by chance still have it?"

It takes Josh a second to register what I'm saying. "Yeah. I think? It's buried in my closet somewhere."

I turn my eyes to Vivian. "Where is it, Vivian?"

She lets out a scoff. "How would I know?"

I figured she was going to play dumb. "We can make this easy, or we can make this hard. Either way, you're going to leave this conversation exposed for the shit you did. You just get to choose how we get there."

She rolls her eyes at me. Cool. Hard way. Awesome. That's more fun.

"This first part is me guessing, so please feel free to tell me what I'm wrong about." I start laying out more of the photos. "You were auditioning for that trash reality show about Nashville housewives, but the producers said that you'd be a more attractive candidate if you were a mom as well as a wife. They were very adamant in their casting calls about having mothers on the show. So you quickly married Josh and stuffed ideas in his head about taking custody of Jayce. And everything was going to plan until I married Logan."

I stop for a breath and stare at Vivian, who's sitting with her arms crossed, trying to pretend I'm not spouting the gospel truth.

"After I got married, you got desperate. So you go digging. Somehow, and somewhere, there had to be *something* that could help you. And like magic, you stumble onto the laptop I gave Josh years ago."

Josh looks to Vivian, begging her with his eyes to say I'm wrong. I then watch his face fall as she continues to say silent.

"Nothing yet? Cool. I'll go on." I lay out the final photos. "From there, you hired someone to manipulate the picture of Logan and I to make it look like I'm giving Logan a hand job in the middle of a hotel bar."

"I don't even know anyone who could do that," she defends.

"Oh, Vivian, don't you realize that I'm fairly good with computers?" Logan says. "And I'm rather rich. Put those together, and it's very easy to find and trace bank records once you know the road to look down. And sometimes, you find things you don't even know you're looking for."

For the first time since we started this conversation, Vivian looks scared.

And Josh looks pissed.

"Vivian…what did you do?"

"Josh…baby…"

"Don't fucking baby me."

"They're lying to you. Don't believe them."

"Oh! We're not done yet," I say. "There's more for Josh to not believe. Logan? Care to explain?"

"I'd love to," he says, putting down a copy of the email he retrieved. "This is the email that was sent out with Maeve's photos to the gossip blog. And while Vivian did an admirable job on the surface of sending it anonymously, nothing is ever truly anonymous. Because we were able to trace the email to a coffee shop down the road. And, lucky as we may be, there's security footage of Vivian there at the exact time the email was sent."

"That's just a coincidence," Vivian defends. "That doesn't prove anything."

"You're right," Logan says. "It doesn't. But I'm also then wondering why right after the time stamp of that email went out, another anonymous email went to your custody lawyer. And then after that, an email from your personal account went to a producer at *Real Lives of Nashville Wives* saying that you're about to get custody of your stepson and asking if you should film it for them as they reconsider offering you a spot?"

Josh whips his head to Vivian as Logan hands him printouts of everything he just explained. "What the hell is he talking about?"

Oh shit…I mean, I thought all of those emails were pretty damning, but Josh's reaction has me wondering if Vivian's been keeping him in the dark about more than my viral topless photos.

"Josh. They're lying."

"We had an understanding—you weren't going to audition for that show."

"I didn't think you were serious," Vivian protests.

"What part was I not clear and serious about? I said that I wasn't crazy about having our lives on camera. And even if I was, Maeve would never agree—"

Josh stops mid-sentence. At that moment, it hits all of us what's going on. It was right there all along.

Jayce is a minor. I'm his primary guardian. For him to be on that show, I would've had to sign off on him being on camera. Which I *never* would've done.

But if Josh was primary, and Vivian could eventually convince Josh to do the show, they could bypass me without asking for permission for Jayce to be on it.

"You—God I'm an idiot." Josh gets up from the couch and starts pacing around the room. "I thought the wedding was quick, but we had talked about it a few times, so I went with it. But the custody thing…now that I'm thinking back…that was all you, Vivian. All you."

"Should we leave?" Logan whispers to me.

"Absolutely not," I say. "I'm not missing a second of this."

I just wish we had popcorn. Extra butter. Light salt.

"It wasn't all me," she says, standing up to try to meet his gaze. "You said you wish we had Jayce more."

"Of course I did! Like, maybe another day a week. But you… you couldn't stop talking about how much Maeve traveled. After what? Because we picked up a few extra weekends? You… God, how was I brainwashed by my own wife?"

"I didn't brainwash you!"

Josh stops on a dime and turns to her, now saying this directly to her face. "You were the one who counted how many days she'd been traveling. You encouraged me to file for primary custody. And for what? A crappy reality show?"

"It's not going to be crappy. It would've made my career!"

"Maybe you can still get on," I interrupt. My voice seems to startle Josh. I think he forgot we're still here. "If Josh won't film with you, maybe you can convince one of your other boyfriends?"

She can't hide her face as it goes ghost white. "Again, I don't know what you're talking about."

"Let me explain, since clearly you're having a moment or you're still thinking you can save face," Logan says, taking the last of the photos from the envelope from me and dropping them on the table. "See, I had a suspicion about you, once we found out that you were the one who leaked the pictures of Maeve. Because, you stayed at the café a while. You didn't leave after the emails were sent. So I watched a little longer, and I happened to notice you got a visitor. At first I thought he might be your father, as he was much older than you, but then I realized no one kisses their father like that."

I feel the smile grow on my face as I sit back, arms crossed, and watch this bitch's life fall apart. Couldn't happen to a better person.

"So I have a friend who likes to do some private investigating on the side, and turns out, you're a busy little bee when Josh is at the bar."

That private investigator was Stella. And boy was she elated when her and Emmett's new nighttime hobby was to follow Vivian around Nashville.

"The count we have is four," I say as Logan spreads out the photos with each of the men. "Four different men, not counting Josh, that think you're in a relationship with them. Hmm...I wonder if reality television has a spot for a cheating bitch who tries to ruin families for her own gain?"

I stand up, ready to be out of this house. "I'll be filing restraining order paperwork tomorrow. You are never to be around my son again. If you try to go through with this custody case, every single one of these photos will be used, and I'll find more. Because no one, and I mean no one, fucks with me and my family."

I turn to Josh, hating that he's going through this, but until he makes a move, I can't trust him. "Jayce won't be here with her around until the courts step in. And just fair warning, I'll be asking to amend the custody agreement that she can't be here when you have him."

"That won't be a problem," Josh turns his eyes to Vivian. "Our divorce will be filed as soon as I can get the paperwork done."

She gasps…the bitch *actually* gasps like she's surprised.

"Don't act shocked," I say. "You fucked around. Now you're finding out."

And with that I grab my purse, turn on my heel, and hope Logan is following me out for my grand exit.

I don't look back; I just march to the SUV and don't even take a breath until I'm inside. I throw my head back against the seat and close my eyes. I hear Logan's side of the car door open and close, and before I know it, we're pulling out and driving back home.

"It's over, Love," Logan says as he takes my hand in his. "The chaos is over."

37

logan

~~ One Month Later ~~

"AND THAT'S THE IDEA. I'D LOVE TO HEAR YOUR THOUGHTS?"

I look over to Maeve, who I don't think has blinked during the entire presentation we've just sat through, let alone have thoughts to verbalize.

One for a reality television show, starring none other than my wife.

"Maeve?" I ask, more to make sure she hasn't gone into a catatonic state. "Do you have anything you want to add? Questions to ask?"

She shows signs of life when she starts blinking, but they're rapid and she might've blacked out for a second. "I'm sorry. I think I misheard you. Can you say again, one more time, and very slowly so you don't have to say it three times, what you want me to do?"

I chuckle under my breath at Maeve's request to Christopher, the producer. In Maeve's defense, I kind of sprung this meeting on her. Not because I didn't want her to be ready for it, but if she knew she'd have made me cancel. She would've been against it from the jump, but not because of what it is, because of her stubbornness.

And she can still say no. There's no gun to her head. But I

wanted her to actually consider it, because I think it could be a smashing success.

"I'd be happy to," Christopher says, clicking back to a recap slide he's presenting to us. "The idea is for you to be unapologetically yourself. Just from this conversation, your realness and bluntness are tools that will set you apart from other home makeover stars. What we want you to do is be honest, and sometimes that comes off as gruff. Which is what we want. We want you to take the most stubborn clients—preferably ones with horrible taste—and convince them to let you help them decorate the home of their dreams."

"Okay, that's what I thought you said." Maeve shakes her head a little, but more I think to try and gather her thoughts. "This is all very overwhelming."

"I understand," Christopher says as he puts away his tablet. "Please though, give this some thought. When you have ideas and have wrestled with this one, I'd love to talk to you about it more. Get your ideas. This was just a starting off point. I'm open for suggestions."

Maeve nods and the two of them shake hands. "Thank you. We'll be in touch."

I walk Christopher out to the front door, tell him thanks again for meeting on short notice, before heading back into my office.

"What was that?"

And that is why I walked Christopher out. "Okay, Love, hear me out."

"Oh no, don't you 'Love' me," she says as she points her finger into my chest. "Did you really set up a meeting with a reality show producer and not tell me?"

"I did. But I have good reasons."

"Oh there better be," she says, perching herself onto my desk. "Start talking, husband."

I know she's miffed at me. But that doesn't stop the tingle I feel when she reminds me of our marital status.

"It happened to come up in conversation," I begin.

"Really? You just happened to be talking to a reality producer and you just happened to bring up an idea that I joked about months ago that I was never actually serious about?"

I think about it for a second, but there's no other way to say it. "Yeah. I did. But if you *really* want someone to blame if you're angry, I suggest being pissed at Vivian."

"Vivian? What does she have to do with it?"

"Because if it wasn't for her, I wouldn't have been on the phone with a reality producer."

"Are you…"

"I am. Christopher is one of the producers of *Real Lives of Nashville Wives*. And now a personal friend if I do say so myself."

If I had any hopes of our lives calming down after we exposed Vivian for what she did to Maeve, those were quickly shot out of the window.

The next day we were delivered notice that Josh was dropping his petition for custody. It also came with a text message from Josh saying that he needed some time to figure things out. He explained that he was divorcing Vivian and needed some time to reevaluate things in life. Maeve understood and told him to take the time he needed. That they'd talk everything through when he was ready.

That talk came this week. Josh profusely apologized to both Maeve and myself—because yes, I went with her—and asked if things could go back to how they were. He admitted she was right, that he wasn't ready to have Jayce full-time, but was interested in adding one night per week. Maeve agreed, and after he promised that Vivian was permanently out of his life, they agreed that each Tuesday night, Jayce spent the night with Josh.

It was the best outcome we could've hoped for when it came to our family. And really for Josh. But for Vivian? She's…well… as Stella has said bluntly, "She's going through it."

It started with Josh serving her divorce papers. It continued with *Real Lives of Nashville Wives* announcing their casting without her on their list. Did that have anything to do with me contacting the producer—who just happened to be the one sitting in my office today—with all of the information we found? Actually no. Christopher said all that did was solidify their suspicion that she would've been too much drama.

For a reality show.

Featuring catty rich women.

Of course, Vivian blamed everything on us and tried to take to social media with her claims that Maeve and I ruined her life. Little did she know that we had a woman named Kat Smith waiting in the wings to drag her through the mud.

And drag her she did.

There wasn't a media outlet that wasn't told the story about how a would-be reality wannabe was willing to ruin the lives of an innocent woman and her child just for fame. Pictures were leaked of all of her affairs. Hashtags and social movements began to not only cancel Vivian, but to support Maeve. It was a whirlwind few weeks, but when it was all said and done, we came out of the other side stronger than ever.

Which is why we're sneaking away this weekend with Jayce to a beach house at an undisclosed location. Just the three of us, sand between our toes, and quiet all around us.

The perfect calm after all of the chaos.

"Is it bad that I want to take this reality show just on spite?" Maeve asks. "The final fuck you to the woman who put me through hell?"

I laugh and shake my head. "Maybe not have that be the entire reason why you take it? But sure, it can be a cherry on top."

"You're right," Maeve groans. "You know, for being a young billionaire, you're annoyingly responsible."

I laugh and walk up to her, setting my hands on either side of her on my desk. "When you say annoyingly, do you really mean sexy?"

Her eye roll is playful and signals that she's not truly mad about the impromptu meeting. "More like infuriating."

"Sure, Love…" I break down her last wall with a smile as I lean into kiss her.

Am I ever going to get tired of this? I can't imagine a time when. I damn well know it's not now.

My life has only gotten better since the moment I met Maeve in that airport bar. Has it been a rollercoaster? Almost immediately. But I wouldn't trade it for anything.

Because in these small moments, between the meetings and the work, the media and the headlines, the play dates and family outings, are the moments of calm.

And those are bloody perfect.

"Mom! Logan!"

We slowly back away as Jayce comes barreling into Logan's office.

"Hey, buddy," Maeve says as I stand away from her and adjust myself. "How was school?"

"Logan? Can I ask a question?"

Something I've come to learn from Jayce is that he's inquisitive beyond belief. If there's something he wants to know an answer to, he doesn't hesitate to ask. And then return with the approximate two-hundred follow-ups he'll likely have.

Seeing that he has a very serious look to him, I sit him down on one of my chairs and kneel so we can be eye level. "Anything, mate."

"Can you come to my school and tell my friends that you made SpaceCraft? They don't believe me."

Amid the craziness of our lives the past months, one night we were sitting around watching the telly when Jayce asked what my job was. It started as curiosity that my office was at home, when Maeve and Josh's jobs weren't. It then dawned on Maeve that in only telling him what he needed to know at the time for an arrangement we thought was temporary, she never *actually* told him what I did for a living. The stars in his eyes were a memory I won't soon forget.

It has also led to approximately two-hundred questions about why certain things were designed the way they were, a definitive ranking of who my favorite characters are, and questions about the game I never even thought of, let alone had an answer to.

"Let me guess," I say. "You told all your classmates at school that your mum's husband invented SpaceCraft."

"I did. Rosie believes me, but Corban and Maddox said I was a liar."

I don't know who these Corban and Maddox tikes are, but they're about to get embarrassed in front of all their classmates. I wonder if I can hack their gaming systems and make it have an unexpected bug?

"Of course I'll come in," I say. "I'd be happy to. Maybe I can see if Kat can dig up some gifts for your classmates."

"Yes!" Jayce yells. "You're the best, Logan!"

Jayce leaps into my arms for the biggest and best hug. I know that I'll never be his actual father, and that's okay. He has a father who, despite going off path for a minute, loves him and is very much part of his life. And as a lad who had a father who couldn't be bothered, I'm glad that I can be part of someone's life who has *two* father figures who love him endlessly.

And if I'm able to give him cool points with his friends at school? Then that's the role I'll take on.

"I'll be there too."

I look to Maeve, who has a look in her eye that looks familiar. "And why would you be doing that? I talk to titans of industry on a regular basis. I think I can handle a group of first graders."

She shakes her head. "Absolutely not. Once word gets out that you're coming, every class mother will be chomping at the bit to volunteer that day."

I love it when my wife gets possessive…

I give her a wink, because we're going to be saving this

conversation for later. When we're alone. "Jayce, I'll email your teacher and set something up."

"Thanks, Logan!" Jayce makes his way out of my office, forgetting about his backpack, which he left in the middle of the room. And his shoes.

"I think he's comfortable here," I joke.

"Are you kidding me? He was comfortable from the first cinnamon roll you gave him."

I put the shoes near his backpack and make my way back over to Maeve.

"Was that my wife being possessive?" I ask, resuming my position that I was in before Jayce stormed in. "Don't want the PTA moms trying to swoop in?"

She shakes her head, though I see the devilish look in her eye. "I wouldn't call it possessive."

"Oh really?" I ask as I lean in to start kissing up and down her neck. "What would you call it?"

She pulls me in by my shirt and wraps her legs around me. "Just me wanting them to know that you're mine."

I don't know if the day will ever happen that I get tired of Maeve saying that. I can't imagine so. Because in a short amount of time, this woman changed my life.

She was a stranger at an airport bar.

She was one night I was never going to forget.

She was my reluctant designer.

She became my friend.

And now she's my wife.

I get a chance to have a life I never believed possible. I get to be a bonus dad to the best kid. I get to have a family that's full of love and not toxicity.

And it's all because I bought a beautiful woman a drink at the bar.

guide to love rule #130

Never say never.

epilogue

Maeve

"Guys! We need to get going! I don't want to be late!"

I finish putting in my earrings as I'm speed walking to the gaming room, where I'm hoping my son and husband are ready to go and just killing time for me to finish before we head to my parent's anniversary dinner.

Forty-one years. What an accomplishment. Also a weird year to have a big dinner to celebrate, but who am I to judge? When you've been married that long I think every year should come with a fancy dinner.

But as soon as I walk in, I realize that was just wishful thinking. Because there they are, looking like twins in Batman T-shirts and gray lounge pants, hair a mess, as they play a beta version of Logan's new game.

Don't get me wrong. I'm annoyed. They should be ready. I've told them to be ready. But it does melt my heart a little every time I see them playing games together.

"Seriously?"

My snark bounces off them both. Neither turn off, or even pause, the game.

"We're almost done, Mom," Jayce says as he starts moving

his body along with the controller. Because, you know, that helps.

"I need you both to be done now."

Hearing a little edge to my voice, Logan stops the game, though it's accompanied by sighs.

"I know, I'm the worst," I say. "Now go get dressed. Brush your teeth. Both of you be back down here in fifteen minutes."

The two let out one more groan for good measure before turning off the game and heading to their respected rooms. Well, Jayce does. Logan decides to walk up to me before heading to our bedroom.

"Is it bad that I like it when you're a little mean? You know, I've always thought you had a sexy librarian vibe. Especially when you wear your hair in a bun like that."

I know what he's doing. He's trying to get me worked up. Too bad it's not working. After nearly three months of marriage, I'm on to his tricks.

"I'm about to be more than a little mean if you don't get going. Oh, and can you please fix Jayce's hair for me? Just so it looks like he didn't just roll out of bed?"

I've apparently lost my touch, because my gruffness only makes Logan lean in for a kiss. "I love it when you talk dirty. And yes, I'll fix his hair."

"Thank you. Now go!" I say, pushing him away, which only makes him laugh. "Ten minutes now, and if you're not back, no sex for a week."

He looks at me to see if I'm bluffing. I am, but I really need my cheeks to not give me away right now. Thankfully they don't, and he shoots up the staircase toward our bedroom.

Men. So predictable and easily manipulated.

I take the time I have while the guys are getting ready to check my purse and make sure I have everything. Wallet. Keys. Compact. Lipstick. Phone. Bag of Goldfish crackers in case Jayce is not a fan of the food.

Even in a nice evening bag, it's always going to be a mom bag.

As I toss in the last of my things I hear the buzzer for the gate. Which is odd. We're not expecting anyone. It's a Saturday night, so no meetings are scheduled. Kat is taking a well-deserved vacation somewhere unknown and tropical. So when I ask who is buzzing, color me shocked when I hear a familiar voice.

"Bitch! Let me in!"

What in the world is Quinn doing here?

"Quinn?"

"I hope so. If anyone else is calling you bitch besides me and the failed reality star then you have more enemies than I realized. Now let me in!"

I hurry and open the gate, racking my brain as to why Quinn's here. And not just in my house, but in Tennessee.

Yes, it's my parents' anniversary dinner, and of course they wanted her here. We all did. But all of us realize it's smack dab in the middle of the school year. It's March, so there were no federal holidays giving her a long weekend. And she was just home not long ago for Christmas. My parents insisted that she not pay for a plane ticket for a dinner.

Now, could they pay for one for her? Absolutely. They'd love to. Hell, they'd buy her a house if that meant she moved back to Rolling Hills. But my sister—the very middle of the Banks children birth order—is the most independent and stubborn woman I know, myself included. She's never wanted a handout. Always made sure to pay her own way. So whether it's plane tickets home, a house, or five dollars for a coffee, Quinn Banks refuses any and all help. And I know she's joked before about using fly miles to come home, but eventually those run out, and you have to fly and pay to earn them, so where else is she going?

As I open the front door, I see Quinn exiting a car, I'm guessing a Lyft, and grabbing a book bag as well as her carryon suitcase. I'm speechless as I watch her pull the suitcase up the steps, but am too stunned to help her.

"Start talking. Now," I say as she walks in.

"That's the greeting? No hug? No 'Oh my goodness I'm so surprised!'"

I shake my head. "No. Talk. Now."

Quinn shakes her head. "You can ask me all the questions you want, but can I change and go to the bathroom first? We have to leave pretty soon, right?"

How dare she use my love for punctuality against me. "Fine. But we're not done."

Without another word, Quinn heads into the first-floor bathroom, bags in hand, leaving me stunned in my foyer.

"Are you talking to someone?" Logan asks as he and Jayce come down the stairs.

And holy shit, there go my ovaries.

I don't know if he planned it, or if this is all very happenstance, but the two are coordinated in the best way. Both are wearing navy blue dress pants and a white collared shirt. Logan has paired his with a jacket, but no tie. But Jayce? He went for a vest and looks so handsome. They're both wearing brown shoes, and I've never asked Logan to fix his hair before, but how he did it makes him look like such a little man.

My guys. The two men in my life I don't know what I'd do without. One made me a mom. One made me a wife.

Both made me complete.

"Look at you guys!" I say as I greet them at the bottom of the staircase. I kneel down to get a better look at Jayce and give his vest a tug to make sure it's laying right. "Where did you get this?"

He looks up to Logan with the biggest smile. "Logan and I went shopping. Do you like it?"

I nod and smile from ear to ear. "I love it."

I stand back up and pretend to fix the lapels on Logan's jacket. "When did you do this?"

He just gives me a mischievous smile. "Last weekend. When Maeve's away, the boys will play. And buy new clothing."

I've tried to limit my travel since everything with Josh went down, even if it came out that his reasons for wanting custody were bullshit, the numbers he threw at me weren't wrong. I've made it a point to cut back on my travel, but unfortunately I'm not able to get rid of it all together. And sometimes those trips don't always coordinate to weekends when Jayce is with Josh. Like last weekend, when I had to head to Dallas for three days. Luckily I now have a husband who is more than capable of handling a weekend of solo parenting.

And I must say…not having to figure out which one of my family members was keeping Jayce was rather convenient.

"You both look so handsome," I say, giving Logan a small kiss before hugging Jayce. "Now, as soon as our guest is ready, we'll go."

"Guest?"

I can't answer Logan's question as Quinn pops out of the bathroom. "Surprise!"

"Aunt Quinn!" Jayce sprints toward the bathroom, barreling into her. "Where did you come from?"

We all laugh at Jayce as I grab Jayce's jacket. "Your mom would like to know that as well."

"Well, I came from Arizona on an airplane," Quinn says. I don't appreciate her sarcasm, but technically she answered Jayce's question so I'm not going to say anything. "I just wanted to be part of tonight so much!"

I raise an eyebrow as she slips on a pair of knee-high boots. "Really? That's what you're going with?"

She looks at me like I'm nuts. "What do you mean really? It's my parent's forty-first anniversary party. Of course I'm going to come home for it."

Something is up, but because Quinn wouldn't feel bad lying to a nun, I can't tell what it is. "You've been home three times in four months. And that's on top of the few times you came home last year that were unusual. Is something going on?"

Quinn nonchalantly shakes her head. "Nothing going on. Just didn't want to miss out. But can we continue this interrogation in the car? If we don't leave soon we'll be late, and what would the people say?"

"I don't appreciate your sarcasm."

Quinn gives me a side hug. "But I do appreciate you being my taxi. Now let's go!"

———

There aren't many fancy restaurants in Rolling Hills. And when I say many, I mean none. Which is why when you want something nicer, you come to Franklin, which coincidentally is where Logan and I live.

Convenient on a night when we're running late and no one seems to care but me.

"Move it!" I yell, quickly unbuttoning my seatbelt. "Everyone out!"

"Maeve. Chill," Quinn says from the backseat. "It's just dinner with our family. Literally no one will care that we're five minutes late."

I snap my head back to her. "First of all, have you met me? I thought we were close. Second, when they do ask, I'm throwing you under the bus. So can you please get out of my car so we can go in?"

"Sheesh. Touchy tonight," Quinn says, acting like she's not the reason we're late. Because she is. Besides her unexpected arrival, the second we were buckled she informed us that she left her phone inside. She wasn't in that many places, so I don't know why it took her ten minutes to find it.

"Mommy! I have to pee!"

I groan from Jayce's words. "Okay. We'll go inside."

"I gotta go now!"

I look back and his eyes are big and oh shit—is my son about to have his first accident since he was four?

"Got him!" Quinn yells, quickly jumping out of the car and pulling out Jayce behind her as they sprint inside the Italian steakhouse that is a big hit with Simon Banks.

Just as I'm about to unlatch my seatbelt and get out of the car, I feel Logan's hand on mine.

"What?"

"Breathe," he instructs.

"I'm fine."

"Maeve. Please. Just take a second and breathe."

I'm annoyed for a second before I do what he says. And he's right. I do need to calm down. It's not that big of a deal that we're ten minutes late, right?

Right?

"Why am I like this?" I ask as I bring my heart rate back to normal.

"It's who you are. And why I love you."

We lean in and share a quick kiss before I pull away. "If I keep that up, we're going to be even later."

"Is that a bad thing?"

My raised eyebrow is all the signal Logan needs to know that I'm serious.

Which sucks, because I haven't had a good car make-out session in years.

As the two of us walk inside, I'm surprised not to see Jayce and Quinn waiting for us.

"Banks party?"

The hostess nods. "Right this way."

Logan takes my hand as we follow the hostess. I've been here a few times, and the food is delicious. I start making my way to the dining room, which is to the left. So consider my surprise when Logan pulls me to the right.

"Where are we going?"

He sends me a wink. "You'll see."

I narrow my eyes, because why is he being weird? I go between looking at him, and making sure I don't run into a wall, as we're guided back to a private dining room.

Still not having any idea what's going on, it takes me a second to even realize it once the doors are open.

In the room is all of my family. Friends from high school and college. Kat. They're all applauding and cheering and I'm so confused, especially when I see a table in the front of the room covered by an ornate flower arrangement.

"Logan? What is this?"

He leans in close so I can hear him over the applause and hollers.

"Happy wedding reception."

My jaw drops to the floor as Logan leads me into the room. My parents are the first to greet us, hugging us both as we continue saying hi to everyone. It's overwhelming. It's amazing. It's shocking.

And it has Logan Matthews written all over it.

When we get to the front of the room, I notice there's a micro-phone waiting. No one better be waiting for me to give a speech, because that's not going to happen. Luckily, Logan picks it up as everyone's applause quiets down and they take their seats.

"Thank you everyone for coming out tonight for this surprise wedding reception." Cheers begin again, though not as long this time. "Please enjoy the bar as its open all night. Please order whatever you'd like off the special menu myself and my sister-in-law Charlie came up with. I have more to say later, but I feel my wife's eyes staring into me, so I'm going to excuse myself as I think I have some explaining to do."

The joke—which is also the truth—lands with every family and friend in the room as Logan walks me out through a door and into a back hallway.

"Before we go any farther, I need to know…did my mother put you up to this?"

He smiles and takes each of my hands. "She didn't. But when

I told her my idea, she was more than happy to take over the majority of the planning."

"I'm sure she was."

Even though she promised me some time to get used to the idea of being married, my dear mother still makes comments from time to time about us doing a ceremony. Oh! Maybe this will satisfy her for a little while.

"I know why we had to get married in the haste we did," Logan says. "But now that I've seen how the Banks family works, I hate that you didn't at least get to celebrate with a dinner after. I wanted you—us—to have that."

Oh damn. I didn't wear the appropriate eye liner if he's going to be saying sweet things like that.

"Thank you," I say as something hits me. "Wait! Is this why you weren't ready tonight?"

He smiles and nods. "Our timeline was based on Quinn's arrival. Luckily she texted me right before you came to get us that she was on her way."

I knew something was fishy with her. But damn, she's a good liar. And speaking of liars…

"Did you have Jayce in on this?"

Logan can't hold in his laugh. "The lad was more than ready to play the part. The bathroom thing, though, in the car? All him. Bloody brilliant."

I throw my head back, realizing that there's a very good chance that my son has more of his uncle and aunts in his genes than I realized.

"I hope this was okay," Logan says. "I just wanted to show you—"

I press my lips to his, not only wanting him to stop talking, but to show him just how okay this is.

Honestly, a surprise party is a fitting thing for us, considering he was the surprise I never saw coming. And every day he surprises me even more. Whether it be the support he gives that somehow tops the day before, or how well Jayce and I have molded into his life, every day is new and exciting. A surprise behind every corner.

And I can't wait for a lifetime of them.

"This is more than okay," I say as I slowly pull away. "I love you, Logan Matthews."

"Not as much as I love you."

Thank you for reading Single Mom's Guide to Love!
Are you wanting more from Maeve and Logan? I know I wasn't ready
to say goodbye. Click here for an extended epilogue of their "actual"
wedding ceremony. And maybe, there might be a surprise for one Mr.
Logan Matthews.

acknowledgments

This is now the third series I've written in my author career, and it's a proven fact that one book along the way tries to kill you.

Welcome to Single Mom's Guide to Love.

Don't get me wrong, I love these two. Like where can I get a Logan? He jumped to the top of my hero pyramid (I never understood the "my wife" thing until this book) and there is so much of me in Maeve. But their story? I couldn't get it. I knew what I wanted. I knew it in the back of my head, but I couldn't seem to find it.

Until one day it hit me. Literally out of nowhere I had the biggest lightbulb moment of my career (hint: it was while writing the sexy scene after the Christmas party). And that's when this book made sense.

But man…getting there? It was a journey. But it's one I'm glad I went on because I love these two, and this family, so dang much.

Thank you for going on the journey with me. I hope you loved it as much as I do.

Now, to the thank yous…

First and foremost, my parents. As always, you're my biggest cheerleaders even if you still have no idea what I'm doing. Mom, thanks for telling everyone at Boscov's what I do and for my Dad who was pimping my books to his nurse's during his last hospital say.

Amanda, who would have thought when we met ten years ago that one day we'd be here together? Thank you for keeping my life in order. Thank you for reminding me to drink water. And thank you for being my best friend. I promise I won't fire you this week.

Kelly, you've been with me on this book journey since day one. Not only are you an amazing alpha reader, but you are an amazing friend. One day I'll write your country star.

Valentine, thank you for everything you, your mom, and the VPR team have done for me. Thanks for talking me off the ledge more times than I can count.

Julia, Georgia, Bella, Mae, and Claire: How did I write a book before I met you ladies? All I know is I don't ever want to write one without y'all again.

Kiezha, thank you for correcting my bad grammar habits and being an amazing editor. I'm sorry I wrote canceled/cancelled/cancellation so much. Michele, thank you for dotting the Is and crossing the Ts. Jamie, thanks for jumping in with a helpful eye and a good eye for the catnip.

Corinne, I'm here because of you. If you wouldn't have given me a chance I wouldn't have started writing. You forever changed my life.

Last but not least: Readers. I love you all. Whether this was your first book by me, or you've been here since Reformation, I'm truly thankful for all of you. There are so many amazing authors you could be reading. I'm humbled that you chose me.

about the author

Known for her witty sense of humor, Chelle Sloan is a former sports editor who after years in the newspaper business, decided to become a romance author. You know, because that's the normal path to writing happily ever afters.

An Ohio native, she's fiercely loyal to Cleveland sports, is the owner of way too many tumblers and will be a New Kids on the Block fan until the day she dies. She does her best writing at Panera, or anywhere that's not her office.

When she's not writing, you can find her in the kitchen attempting to become a baker, fixing up her condo (badly and by watching YouTube videos), or falling in love with a book.

As for her own happily ever after? Maybe one day...

Stay up to date with all things Chelle & join the VIP Squad!

also by chelle sloan

THE NASHVILLE FURY, PRO FOOTBALL SERIES

Off the Record: A secret office romance

Off Track: A surprise pregnancy romance

Off Season: A second chance romance

Off Limits: A sibling's best friend romance

LOVE ONLINE SERIES

Thirst Trap: A social media romance

Match Maker: A fake dating romance

Run Run Rudolph: A celebrity, holiday romance

ROLLING HILLS

The One I Want: A single dad / nanny romance

The One I Need: An accidental marriage romance

The One I Love: A friends to lovers romance

The One I Hate: An enemies to lovers romance

GUIDE TO LOVE SERIES

Runaway Bride's Guide to Love: A brother's best friend, age gap
romance

Single Mom's Guide to Love: A billionaire, marriage of convenience
romance

Roommate's Guide to Love: A small town, single dad, romance

Good Girl's Guide to Love: A fake dating, pro football romance

GUIDE TO LOVE WORLD

Vixen's Guide to Christmas: A rivals to lovers, holiday romance

NASHVILLE PLAYERS SERIES

Unplanned Play: A pro football, reverse age gap, romance (Coming March 2026)